Aftershock

Also by Liz McSkeane

Fiction

What to Put in a Suitcase – short stories
Canticle – novel

Poetry

Learning to Tango
So Long, Calypso
Snow at the Opera House
In Flight

Aftershock

Liz McSkeane

First published 2025
Turas Press
6 – 9 Trinity Street
Dublin D02 EY47
Ireland
info@turaspress.ie
https://turaspress.ie

Copyright © 2025 Liz McSkeane

The author asserts her moral rights in accordance with the provisions of the Copyright and Related Acts, 2000.

All rights reserved. The contents of this publication are protected by copyright law, except as may be permitted by law, no part of the material may be reproduced (including by storage in a retrieval system) or transmitted in any form or by any means; adapted; rented or lent without the written permission of the copyright owner.

British Library Cataloguing Data A CIP catalogue record for this book is available from the British library.

ISBN (PB):978-1-913598-59-4
ISBN (EPUB):978-1-913598-60-0
ISBN (KPF): 978-1-913598-61-7

Cover image by Liz McSkeane

Cover design by Angie Crowe

Typesetting by Printwell Design, Dun Laoghaire
printwell@mac.com

Printed in Ireland by Sprintbooks

Contents

Cast of Characters	7
The First Shock: All Soul's Day, November 1ˢᵗ, 1755	11
Part One: 1754	**19**
1. A Quarrel and a Dance	21
2. A Sleepless Night and Good Counsel	39
3. A Musical Interlude and the Perils of Eavesdropping	51
4. A Carriage Ride and a Brief Encounter	67
5. An Unexpected Guest and a Resolution	81
Part Two: 1755	**99**
6. Living the Shock	101
7. An Audience at Court and an Unexpected Encounter	115
8. Unwelcome News and a Request Rebuffed	129
9. First Impressions and an Uneasy Alliance	141
10. A Testy Encounter and a Glass of Port Wine	155
11. A Missed Appointment and an Unwelcome Visitor	169
12. Two Troubling Interludes and One Alarming Order	181

Part Three: 1758 - 1759   **191**

13. A Carriage Ride and a Heinous Event   193

14. A Worrying Conversation and a Job Well Done   205

15. A Challenging Day and a Pleasant Dinner   221

16. A Troubling Encounter   237

17. Exciting Insights and a Fruitless Endeavour   251

18. The First Reckoning   267

Part Four: 1775 - 1782   **281**

19. A Birthday Celebration and an Important Book   283

20. The Second Reckoning   293

21. A Final Return   305

22. The Past Revisited   315

23. The Road Back   325

24. In the Gathering Dusk   337

Acknowledgements   **345**

About the Author   **347**

Cast of Characters

This is a work of fiction, based on historical events. Most of the characters in *Aftershock* are historical figures who played a part in the events of the time which corresponds to their role in the events depicted in the novel. A few, whose names are shown in ***bold italics***, refer to characters who are either wholly invented for dramatic purposes, or are an amalgam created from two or more real-life people. Names shown in *light italics* denote people who were deceased at the time of the action.

The Carvalho e Melo Family

Dom Sebastião José Carvalho e Melo, government minister, diplomat and statesman; Minister of War and Foreign Affairs, Prime Minister, Count of Oeiras, Marquis of Pombal.

Dona Eleanor Ernestina Von Daun, Dom Sebastião's second wife, an Austrian noblewoman and mother of his children.

Henrique, Eva, Maria, Francisco, **Amália** living children of Dom Sebastião and Dona Eleanor.

Elvira, maid to the household of Dom Sebastião.

Leo, trusted servant to the household of Dom Sebastião.

Dona Teresa de Mendonça first wife of Dom Sebastião.

The Royal Family of Portugal

Dom José I, King of Portugal.

Dona Mariana Vitória (Victoria), wife of Dom José, Queen Consort of Portugal, Infanta of Spain, sister of King Ferdinand VI of Spain.

Dona Maria, oldest daughter of Dom José and Dona Mariana Vitória, Princess of Brazil and heir to the throne of Portugal, later Queen Maria.

Dom Pedro, full brother of Dom José.

Dom José
Grand Inquisitor of Portugal

Dom Gaspar
Archbishop of Braga

Dom António
Doctor of Theology

The Palhavã Princes: illegitimate half-brothers of Dom José, sons of his father, Dom João, from different mothers. The three Palhavã Princes, thus called because they were brought up in the Palhavã Palace on the outskirts of Lisbon, were publicly recognised as Dom João's sons after his death, in accordance with his wishes.

Dom João V, King of Portugal, father of Dom José.

Dona Maria Ana of Austria, Queen consort and wife of Dom João; mother of Dom José and Dom Pedro; Archduchess of Austria and aunt of the Empress Maria Teresa of Austria.

Dona Bárbara, princess of Portugal; sister of Dom José and Dom Pedro, later Queen consort of Spain on her marriage to Prince Fernando, later King Fernando VI of Spain.

Aristocrats and Courtiers

Dom José Mascarenhas, Duke of Aveiro, a brother-in-law and rival of the Távora family.

Dom Francisco of Assis, Marquis of Távora, brother of Dona Teresa of Távora, father of Luís Bernardo and José Maria.

Dona Leonora, Marchioness of Távora, wife of Dom Francisco; mother of Luís Bernardo and José Maria; matriarch of the Távora dynasty.

Dom Luís Bernardo, oldest son of Dom Francisco and Dona Leonora, heir to Távora title, often known as 'the young marquis'; husband and nephew of Dona Teresa of Távora.

Dona Teresa of Távora, sister of Dom Francisco; wife and aunt of Dom Luís Bernardo, often known as 'the young marchioness'.

José Maria, younger son of Dona Leonora and Dom Francisco; brother of Luís Bernardo.

Count of Lourenço, a courtier and trusted confidant of the king.

Count of Atouguia, brother-in-law of Dom Francisco of Távora.

Countess of Atouguia, his wife, sister of Dom Francisco and intimate of the queen.

Duke of Alentejo, an aristocrat attached to the court of Dom José.

Marquis of Angeja, trusted ally of Maria, Princess of Brazil, later Queen Maria.

Dom José de Séabra da Silva, courtier and ally of Dom Sebastião, fallen into disfavour.

The Clergy

Father Gabriel Malagrida, an Italian Jesuit; missionary and confessor to the royal family and members of the aristocracy; beloved of the common people.

The Patriarch of Lisbon, Cardinal and bishop of the Archdiocese of Lisbon, enjoying privileges similar to those of the pope.

Father Luís da Souza, a Franciscan priest who works in the city to succour the poor.

The Diplomats

Mr Edmund Stanton, an English diplomat attached to the British Embassy in Lisbon.

Sir Abraham Castres, British Ambassador to Portugal

M François Martin, a French Diplomat attached to the French Embassy in Lisbon.

The Professionals

Pedro Teixeira, valet and general factotum to His Majesty Dom José.

Custódio da Costa, coachman to His Majesty Dom José

Dom António Soares Branolão, Royal Surgeon to His Majesty Dom José.

Doctor Gonçalvo Cardoso, medical doctor commissioned to oversee interrogations of prisoners.

General da Cunha, a high-ranking military man commissioned to oversee interrogation of prisoners.

Judge Cordeira Pereira, expert in law commissioned to oversee interrogation of prisoners.

Doctor Eusébio Tavares de Sequeira, a lawyer and Public Defender.

Doctor João Marquis Bacalhau, a Judge of the Tribunal.

Soldiers and Sailors

Captain Fernando da Oliveira, soldier and assistant to Dom Sebastião.

A ship's pilot, an unnamed sailor who observes the changing tides of the river Tagus.

Captain Silva, Captain of the *Nossa Senhora de Adjuda,* a ship that sails to the Azores Isles.

Witnesses and Suspects

Manuel Alvares Ferreira, a servant of the Duke of Aveiro.

Bras José Rameiro, footman of Marquis of Távora.

João Miguel, footman of Marquis of Távora.

Ceveira, a glove-maker and acquaintance of Ferreira.

The First Shock

All Souls' Day, November 1st, 1755
Bairro Alto, Lisbon

At last, the earth is still. The ground underfoot is stable and, to all appearances, calm. But for how long? And who can know what new disasters will befall this wretched city before day's end?

A solitary figure contemplates a vista that is no more. This outcrop on the prettiest of Lisbon's seven hills commands a panorama of the city, the mighty river Tagus and the shimmering sea beyond that never fails – failed – to warm his heart and soothe his unquiet mind. Now he stands rigid, immobile. The church spires, the patchwork of roofs, houses and shops that straggle down from the Bairro Alto, past the convent of Carmo towards the grand square of the Rossio below have all vanished, swallowed in a dense cloud of dust. A thick fog covers the sky, blots out the sun.

After a time, the cloud dissipates, dispersed by a north-east wind gusting in from the river. A faint outline of the city appears. Broken spires; heaps of stones piled high as the tallest building; masonry that an hour before was the stuff of palaces and convents and churches where the faithful had gathered to celebrate one of the holiest days of the year. There must be people crushed to death, buried beneath those rocks. Survivors, too, how many? And how many dead?

At last, he moves. A sharp-eyed observer – were there a single soul left with attention to spare – would see him reach beneath his cloak, draw out his silver timepiece (a valued gift from a well-disposed minister when he was assigned to the embassy in London) and a fine linen handkerchief, which he uses to wipe the watch face clean of dust.

A few minutes past ten o'clock. So, the third tremor ceased about a quarter-hour before. The last of three massive convulsions of the earth, a minute apart, each lasting about sixty seconds, perhaps a little more.

As the dust floats off on the wind, Dom Sebastião José Carvalho e Melo, His Majesty's Minister of War and Foreign Affairs, beholds a vision from Hell, a spectacle that recalls those terrifying paintings created with the singular intention to display images of horror: severed limbs, half-naked victims of disaster or war trampling over corpses, women and men alike kneeling, arms raised to the heavens, intoning *Aves* and *Acts of Contrition* to a merciless God indifferent to their sufferings. The Day of Judgement. The Apocalypse.

But this is no work of art fashioned to adorn cathedral or palace. This is his city. Streets swallowed entire, ancient buildings reduced to rubble or tumbled into fissures rent in the earth, women and children buried under fallen pillars, crushed by collapsed roofs and walls, the ghastly images accompanied by the screams of survivors, prayers, exhortations to God to deliver them from this terror.

His oldest girl, Eva, had been the first to notice. In a house with four young children, preparing for a holy day was always a noisy, chaotic affair and a rare pleasure, for the mornings were seldom his own. But earlier, as the king and queen and their four daughters had packed up the royal carriage on a whim and made off to their summer palace in Belém, he was free to spend the day with Eleonor and the children. Maria and her baby brother José would remain at home with Elvira. Henrique, who was almost of an age to take confession, and ten-year-old Eva donned their good shoes and their best clothes, excited in anticipation of joining the crowds of the faithful spilling out on to the streets and crowding into their parish churches.

So it must have been a half-hour past nine o'clock when Eva, seated at the breakfast table while her mother finished braiding her hair, pointed to her cup and said that the water was dancing. Eleonor's deft fingers flew, smoothing and plaiting her daughter's fine, flaxen curls, while explaining their plans for the morning. This would be a special one, for Papa was so rarely home on feast days. There would be Mass in the church of Mercês at the end of the street, followed by a stroll around the grand square of the Rossio, then back to the rua Formosa for a special meal that was already simmering on the stove.

The rattle of glass, a scratching of wood and a picture slides down the wall, landing on the tiled floor, its frame shattered. Eva and Henrique look up at their mother, puzzled, not yet afraid.

Until a roar erupts from outside, as though a team of horses were thundering past the door. The king's carriage? He has the habit of driving very fast through the city. But not in these parts, for the steep lanes and winding alleys and hilly terrain make most of the streets close to the Bairro Alto impassable by coach. But when the breakfast table bounces and a lighted taper falls from the mantle and the external wall sways inwards, he understands, though Eleonor does not, for earthquakes are uncommon in Austria. By a lucky chance the taper has landed on the tiled grate and is easily extinguished by his boot. The children are weeping. He bids them all lie on the floor, Eleonor too.

'Is there a fire set in the kitchen?'

Elvira had started to roast something or other. He makes his way towards the door, struggling to keep balance on the tilted floor.

'Stay down.' Eva starts to sob, as much shocked by sharp words from her Papa as by the trembling walls and floor.

The kitchen fire remains contained within the chimney breast, but another tremor could easily scatter hot ash. If it spills out over the wooden floor and beams, the place will be an inferno.

'No!' He stays Elvira's hand as she reaches for the bucket. 'Not water. Sand?' He hoists the barrel kept for such eventualities – not these eventualities, exactly, but in the kitchen, there is always the danger of a blaze – and heaves the lot on to the flames, which splutter and go out.

The third tremor strikes as he and the maid are staggering into the dining room. The children are trembling, the little ones whimpering, except for Henrique, who is rigid and silent.

By a quarter-hour before ten o'clock, when they should all have been settled into their pew to hear Mass, the tremors had ceased. For a few minutes, the room eerily silent, they all remained on the floor face down, Eleonor crouched over the baby, Maria clutching Henrique's hand. One by one they uncurled and huddled together in a corner. Except for the broken picture-frame, there was no damage. It would be too much to hope that the rest of the city had escaped.

'Must you go out?'

Eleonor fetched his cloak while he buckled on his sword.

'I cannot attend the king and say, Your Majesty, I have been hiding in my cellar or taking shelter in my garden while others…'

She must be wondering, as he was himself, where he might safely lodge his family whilst they awaited his return. In the cellar they would be safe from flying rocks and toppling walls and wooden beams, should the quakes resume; or they might all be trapped, the cellar become a tomb for the whole family. The attic threatened the opposite danger, that they would be cast from a height and dashed to the ground. The garden? Yes, perhaps they should set up camp in the garden, safe out in the open, as far from walls and pillars and roofs as they could find. Yet open ground could be just as dangerous as indoors, perhaps more so. No doubt many of the poor souls who must be lying wounded, dying, dead, had been crushed by falling masonry whilst going about their daily business in the open air.

'Go upstairs to the nursery.' It was a large, bright room on the first floor where they were less likely to be trapped or buried than in either the cellar or the attic. But in truth, it was impossible to know whence the greatest danger might come and therefore, where, and how, to shelter from it. So random was the peril, that there was no course sure of keeping them safe, even for the next hour. Logic and reason counted for nothing. All that remained was judgement and blind trust in Divine Providence. But why should the Almighty spare Dom Sebastião José Carvalho e Melo and his young family, before any others? Was the king's Minister of War and Foreign Affairs more deserving of mercy than any of the wretches who had this day perished?

'Lie on the floor. Make it a game. I will be back as soon as I can.'

In normal times, a brisk walk of less than five minutes would bring him from the house on rua Formosa to his cherished viewing spot. Today, as he clambered over piles of rubble, having tried and failed to free a young man pinned beneath a fallen beam, it had taken almost twenty. He must now return home, settle the children and somehow make his way to Belém.

Moving away from the edge of the outcrop, he surveyed the buildings in the immediate vicinity. About a quarter of them were down. In the western area of the Bairro Alto, things might be worse. The rua Formosa had survived almost intact and although it was too soon to know for certain, structures on higher ground had most likely suffered less devastation than those in the low-lying centre, where all the buildings around the Rossio and as far as the river looked to be destroyed.

Was the Royal Palace gone? The Opera House? The Hospital of All Saints, which he himself helped to restore after that terrible fire, years ago? A thorough inspection of the entire city would be needed. This very day, if possible. Or tomorrow, perhaps, when the threat of more tremors subsided. If it subsided. Moreover, there was yet no telling the scale and extent of the devastation, or the turmoil it had provoked amongst the people.

This was intelligence that the king and his government would need in the coming days. Also: the exact time and duration of the tremors, their direction, the behaviour of the tides...

A piteous wailing emerged from the ruins of a fine stone house. He hesitated, but as there was nothing to be done, he clambered on. The handful of terrified souls he had earlier bullied into helping him to raise that fallen beam from the young man's torso had melted back into the ruins. As soon as they understood that movement of any part of the structure would destabilise an adjacent wall, their instinct for self-preservation triumphed over habitual obedience to the power of his office.

Under happier circumstances, the sharp-eyed observer might wonder at the appearance of this strange fellow, uncommonly tall, not young, who has just passed the last few minutes planted like a statue on the edge of a famous viewing spot, peering out on a cloud of black dust. Some might mock him as he trips on a loose bit of paving – his wig only slightly askew but covered with dust, his voluminous cloak in the way, though offering some protection from the wind just got up from the Tagus. And is that a *sword*! Of what use is a sword, here, now, when there are no streets left to speak of? But this must be a person of quality, if he is indeed wearing the sword by right.

And those elegant leather boots. Riding boots. Where does this fellow think he is going? Of what use are riding boots on a day such as this? Someone should tell him, he is going nowhere, not today, nor for some time. On All Souls' Day, November 1st, 1755, the jaws of the earth opened and swallowed a city whole while the faithful made their way to Mass, altars ablaze with celebratory candles, at the very moment they were preparing their souls to take communion. Most of them would not be coming home, unless wrapped in a shroud or carried on a door. They would certainly not be on horseback, for the roads are impassable, choked by a desperate procession of ragged survivors jostling their way out of the city to the fields beyond, before that north-east wind does for them.

And yet. Any person who mocked him would do well to be discreet. For this man's stillness deceives. It is a stillness that absorbs everything, understands everything, forgets nothing.

A horse would never pass through this chaos. In the absence of a clear route, the only recourse might be to walk to Belém. If it came to that, he could borrow a horse from the king's stable for the return journey.

As he pauses for breath, a pinprick stings his forehead. A mosquito? In November? He inspects his finger. Ash. Hot ash, floating up from Rossio Square. Those faint glimmers flickering through the dust, born of church candles and hearth fires, are gathering strength, making their way skywards, fanned by that spiteful north-east wind. The earth is not the only element to attack the city today.

Perhaps Eleonor and the children would be safer in Belém. They would be welcomed. She had been the old queen's lady-in-waiting, after all. But there was no knowing if things were better or worse in Belém. And the journey would be dangerous. A well-to-do group, a family with four small children, one a babe in arms, albeit escorted by the king's minister, would be easy pickings for brigands and ruffians, or even ordinary, desperate people turned feral in terror.

The king must be convinced to implement measures to re-establish law and order. Save the people from their baser selves.

Eleanor and the children would be safer at home.

If the streets to the west, then south, were in better condition than here, the mare might be led downhill, towards the coast road. Thence the ride to Belém was not above half an hour at a trot. He had done it in twenty minutes at a canter, many times, when the roads were dry and there was no wind.

There was no time to lose. The king must hear all, all there was to know of the catastrophe. For there was no telling what other disasters might yet be visited upon the ruined city.

Part 1

1754

1

A Quarrel and a Dance

November 1st, 1754, Riverside Palace, Lisbon

For the first time since she had arrived in the country five years before, Eleonor Ernestina Carvalho e Melo von Daun allowed herself to wonder whether her marriage had been a mistake. Might her mother have been right after all, that the obligation of a wife to follow her husband wherever his duty dictated was no small thing? And now here she was, homesick for her native Austria, trying to make her way in the royal court in Lisbon where, this last conversation proved, she would forever be an outsider.

The late autumn day was unseasonably balmy. Pleading the need for air, she rose from her seat and escaped to the balcony, leaving the gaggle of ladies-in-waiting in silent consternation, all feigning interest in their embroidery. Relieved to escape the over-heated room, she breathed in the faint tinge of salt wafting in from the sea, its sparkling strip of blue just visible from Queen Mariana Vitória's apartments in the Riverside Palace, her mood assuaged by the screaming of gulls and the murmur of river waves lapping against the palace walls.

She had not at first believed Sebastião when he assured her that this enormous expanse of water where ships moored close to the quays, whose tides undulated or churned in fury according to season and weather was not the sea, but the mighty river Tagus which rose in the far-off mountains of eastern Spain to wind its way across the entire peninsula, here and there a meek trickle but ever gathering heft and strength, so that by the time its waters reached the city, ships of all sizes could drop anchor in the bay and visitors would mistake it for the edge of the sea.

Until one summer's morning just after dawn, when only a few fishermen were awake, he led his family to a little secret cove between Belém and Oeiras, she and the two small children she had borne in Austria. When they finally dared to immerse themselves, the little ones squealing with delight, sure enough the water was fresh, not salty. If ever they swam at a place closer to the estuary, he said, they would taste a hint of the salt where the ocean waters mingle with the river.

Her beating heart steadied, she half-listened to the voices of the queen and her ladies-in-waiting as their words blended into an amorphous hum emptied of meaning. After five years in this country and almost ten married to Sebastião José, her understanding of the Portuguese tongue was good, provided she could see the person speaking. But sometimes, in a large gathering, when voices chimed together, when words and whole phrases were swallowed, lulled by the beauty of the cadences and the music of the language she realised that the rapid twists and turns of conversation had eluded her. As a result, even though she could express herself well, if with some hesitation, many seemed disposed to believe that she understood less than she did and probably imagined her a simpleton. I am a foreigner, she wanted to say, not a fool. I would like to see you at the Austrian court, making your way in my native tongue. Of course, she never did, but smiled and repeated that useful phrase, perfectly enunciated thanks to Sebastião's tutoring: *Desculpe, não falo muito bem, mais se quer falar um poco mais devagar, chego a perceber.*

'Dona Eleonor!'

When she stepped back into the room, the Countess of Atouguia addressed her with exaggerated animation.

'Her Majesty has had word from Spain. What do you think of this?'

The countess held out a letter, her eyes flickering with unease, no doubt unsure whether her earlier behaviour had been forgiven. Judging by the glare on Queen Mariana Vitória's already stern visage, the missive contained unwelcome news. Not yet quite composed, Dona Eleonor returned to her seat and adopted her interested expression in readiness to listen to the queen's litany of complaints.

'My sister-in-law, Bárbara, declares that Farinelli cannot be spared from her court,' said Queen Mariana Vitória. 'Apparently my brother Ferdinand will fall into a melancholy unless he hears him sing daily; and an absence of even a few weeks to allow him to perform here for Christmas is impossible. Also, Farinelli is an old man now, she says, almost fifty, his voice much weakened since his youth.' She took the letter from the countess's hand and held it aloft. 'I do not believe a word of it.'

Mariana Vitória was always tetchy when Bárbara was mentioned, stung from once having heard a courtier remark that in the long-ago exchange of the princesses, her brother Ferdinand, and Spain, had got the better bargain. Then there was the good fortune, or cunning, of the Portuguese Princess Bárbara, much beloved sister of Dom José and now Queen of Spain, to have ensnared two of the greatest musicians of the day. Scarlatti, her harpsichord teacher, she spirited away to Spain when she married; and she had persuaded Farinelli to remain at the Spanish court when his patroness – Mariana Vitória's own mother, the redoubtable Elisabeth Farnese – had finally been banished from the court to live out her days at her palace in Aranjuez. It was said that Bárbara and the renowned Italian castrato sang duets most nights. Of course they did.

They were all looking at her, Queen Mariana Vitória and her ladies-in-waiting. It seemed that she was expected to reassure them she bore no ill will arising from the unpleasant turn the earlier conversation had taken.

'I think,' she enunciated, with a smile, 'that for a man of much energy and accomplishment, fifty is not so old.' Then, with a straight face, 'I should know.'

Tension broken, three of the four ladies and the queen burst out laughing, though her daughter, the young Princess of Brazil, remained quiet.

'Indeed not,' said the countess, who was now making a special effort to be agreeable. She had not been the instigator, true, but she had followed the lead of the princess and had by far the sharpest tongue of them all. Even now, there she was, opening her mouth to deliver yet another barbed comment, perhaps to point out that Sebastião was closer to sixty than fifty, but appeared to think better of it.

In common with many of the minor disagreements that she had observed since she had been permitted to join their little group, this morning's unpleasantness had been sparked by a small matter that was of no practical importance to any of them. This time it concerned swords. It seemed that her husband had undermined the security of the state and caused the fabric of society to unravel by his proposal to introduce legislation that would permit certain men not of noble birth to wear the sword in public, on performance of specified services to the nation. Many of these were of a commercial nature. Thus, the new sword-bearers would be mere merchants – merchants! – devoid of lineage, who would now share this privilege with nobles whose families were a thousand years old.

The marquises, counts and dukes had responded with outrage. The Duke of Aveiro, the highest-ranking noble in the land and President of the Supreme Court, made special representations to the king on the dangers of extending to commoners one of the birthrights reserved for the aristocracy. The king had told him he would think on it and give his answer through his minister, Dom Sebastião José Carvalho e Melo. Who explained that this was but a symbolic gesture, designed to generate commercial activity and investment. In private, his tone was less courteous. 'If I have two men awaiting an appointment in my anteroom, one a man of commerce and one a duke,' he declared over dinner one evening, 'it is the duke I will keep waiting, for the businessman's time is more productive.'

That the ladies had today taken up the argument, was already a veiled criticism of her husband. And, thanks to the troubling intervention of the young Princess of Brazil, it had escalated to an outright attack on Sebastião, and therefore, on herself.

Now returned to the circle, acquiescing in the pretence that all harsh words were forgotten, Dona Eleonor managed to force a tight smile, whose restraint the queen chose to misinterpret.

'Are you quite well, my dear?' Queen Mariana Vitória placed a hand on her own belly.

The other ladies looked up from their sewing. Only the queen and probably the Countess of Atouguia had known. Always slender, her body yet gave no sign; it would be some weeks before her condition became obvious. Now, of course, they all knew. Murmurs of congratulation were tinged with surprise and uncertainty. Was this really a cause for joy? Was another pregnancy wise, so soon, when in the last few years, Dom Sebastião's wife had already borne three and buried two babes?

A question she had asked herself many times in the last weeks. One she would no longer discuss in the present company, for the former intimacy that would have permitted such confidences had vanished in the new chill that had descended on the queen's apartments.

What had changed?

'Maria, please fetch me the score of Mr Handel's latest oratorio.' The queen glared at her daughter. 'Jephtha. It has just arrived from London. You will find it in the library.'

Princess Maria remained seated. Really, for a young woman of twenty years, Princess of Brazil and heir to the throne, her demeanour too often displayed a troubling agitation. After a moment's hesitation, the princess rose to her feet, head bowed. It was a relief to see her go. Notwithstanding their own barbed comments, even the ladies-in-waiting had blushed at her remarks. That the wife of a government minister, even a foreigner, should hear such an outburst from the princess, however attributable to her nervous disposition, was not proper.

'She is at a difficult age,' Mariana Vitória said, 'and ever concerned about her future. Her marriage. Finding the right match for her. It is not easy for a young girl in her position.'

Indeed. But she was not so very young, nor so lacking in experience that she did not know how to conduct herself in the company of her mother's intimate circle.

'It is said that he intends to end the trade in slaves on the Portuguese mainland. Also, to change utterly the studies programme in the universities over the heads of our clergy. That he will constrain the duties of the Jesuits, our confessors. There is even talk of him removing Father Malagrida to Setúbal! What other hellish measures, pray, does your husband plan for us?'

There was a shocked silence. Of course, the princess was only repeating what others had said and what many believed. But to chide the minister's wife with rumours concerning her husband's intentions was unthinkable. Especially as her status as heir to the throne shielded her from retort. But a foreigner, an interloper from the Austrian court – whose own family lineage, by the way, reached back more than a thousand years – might be excused on the grounds of ignorance of the etiquette of this court.

'My husband has done none of these things, Your Highness.' Her tone was benign, the observation mild, far milder than the princess deserved. She would not give the present company the satisfaction of an open display of discomposure. 'Any measures introduced in the five years since Dom Sebastião took up his ministerial duties have been enacted by decree of the king. Dom José. Your illustrious father.'

The princess flushed.

'So you say, Dona Eleonor. But ever since my father ascended the throne, everyone knows...'

Mariana Vitória placed her hand on her daughter's arm.

'We ladies are fortunate that we do not have to meddle in the affairs of the state.'

'But the sword is a symbol...'

'Of loyalty and devotion, Princess.' Queen's intervention or no, they would hear her. And she could not resist a barb of her own. 'I know my husband values achievements arising from talent and hard work at least as much as privilege arising from an accident of birth. As indeed, notwithstanding my own illustrious lineage, I do myself.'

It was an outrageous impertinence. And an enormous pleasure.

The astonished silence of the countess, of those two inane marchionesses but especially of the young princess, who made no answer, was an even greater pleasure. One which Sebastião might not share. But then, he was not present.

Meeting the princess's eye, her resolve wavered. She is only a girl, almost fifteen years younger than I, a young woman of nervous temperament. I should be above this, who knows what damage I may have done. If the old queen were here, she would be shocked at both of us.

Her benefactor. Dom José's mother, Queen Maria Anna, fellow Austrian and dear aunt of her own Empress Maria Teresa, dead for less than three months. Her great protector, to whom she owed her position at this court. Her husband's greatest patron, to whom they owed their very marriage. And with her death, their greatest champion was gone.

Since the old queen's obsequies at the end of the summer,

there had been a gradual cooling of relations with Mariana Vitória and the other ladies. Might Dom José have conceived a fancy for her? The queen was known to take against women who caught the eye of the king. But no. The reflection gazing back from her mirror was no more beautiful than it had ever been. She was still plain, there was no burgeoning beauty that might arouse the jealousy of the queen, any more than beauty had brought Sebastião into her life.

That she was plain, she did not mind too much, for she had many other qualities to recommend her. There was that thousand-year lineage, her sweet temper and the favour of the empress, who credited members of the von Daun family with saving her throne. Which was more than enough, even without a fortune, to secure a brilliant marriage into another distinguished family, to a young man with a large fortune of his own or who would soon inherit one. It would not be a love match, but one day, duty might blossom to friendship, she would bear the children that would continue their bloodline and, if her husband took lovers, she would endure.

It was a little more than a decade earlier, at a ball. He was at the far side of the dance floor in the company of a group of admirers, not a few of them ladies, all no doubt congratulating him on his diplomatic success. The Empress Maria Teresa was in attendance, her presence lending gravity to a celebration of the achievements of this obscure Portuguese diplomat who had been seconded from his position as ambassador in London to mediate between the empress and the Pope in a dispute which had resisted all attempts at resolution.

The vast ballroom with its high white ceilings, mirrored walls, silver and white drapes and pale marble floor was an anteroom to heaven, even if marble was not her favourite surface for dancing. Which did not matter, for she was a mediocre dancer and in any case preferred to watch, her habitual serenity rising to a crescendo of quiet joy as her senses thrilled to behold the glimmer of chandeliers, heavy with hundreds of candles that cast their soft glow upon the circling bodies, flickering flames dappling the ladies' velvet and satin gowns in light and shadow, firing their jewels with little rainbow sparks, pale drapes billowing in a light breeze in from the Danube, her friends and relatives all around, little knots of ladies and gentlemen, some of the men in military uniform. A frisson of anticipation pulsed through the room, for the tempo of the music had changed from a sedate quadrille to a Länder. Was this daring new dance permissible in the presence of the empress?

Apparently it was, or perhaps she had left, for couples were forming, men and women coming together in a tentative embrace, open of course so that at first only arms and shoulders touched but soon the man's arm encircled his partner's waist, her arm lying along his shoulder, the two connected with an intimacy alien to the demure quadrilles and minuets where the only touch was a fleeting brush of fingertips as the dancers moved around the figure to their next partner. But in this Länder a man and a woman held each other, face to face, bound together in that embrace for the whole dance. Little wonder, as the orchestra got up a rapid tune in three-four time, that only the most daring couples took to the floor.

They had not been introduced. Moreover, the Länder was not a dance to risk with an unknown partner. Too many possibilities of missteps. Too many opportunities for liberties. A hand positioned a little lower than was correct. A finger lightly caressing a palm... However decorous their posture, once a man and a woman entered this embrace, this circle that isolated them from the rest of the room, from the rest of the world, a frame whence all movement was propelled, there were endless ways in which communication could be understood. And misunderstood. No one outside that embrace could know what was happening within, the couple is turning in three-four time, slowly, or birling rapidly to keep pace with the ever-increasing tempo. All appearance. But within that magic circle dwelt a mystery only two people could know and understand.

Mesmerised by the hypnotic motion of the swirling dancers, she had not observed him approach and became aware of his presence only when he stood before her, a few paces distant, bowing slightly from the waist so that he did not tower over her, for he was very tall. Only a slight tremor in his voice betrayed a hint of anxiety, perhaps conscious of the many breaches of protocol his approach constituted when he asked, in excellent French, if she would do him the honour of accepting him for this dance.

Since the Länder had become a favourite, if somewhat risqué, dance at court balls, she was convinced that a turn around the dance floor could tell her all she needed to know about a man. It was true that dancing was not her forte. But this deficiency allowed those young men who had spent many months perfecting steps and technique to reveal their response to her relative absence of skill. From the moment he reached out his hand, to the instant she stepped into his embrace, she knew whether this partner was a man she could like or even endure.

So far, most had been at best bearable. Some gripped her hand tight, as though in fear that she would flee. Some, with unwarranted authority, would draw her a little too close. Others, whose timid embrace and uncertain movements hinted at chronic indecision, dangerous on a lively dance floor, made her fearful that they would crash into other couples, and indeed this did happen once. Then there were the sturdy young men, handsome and confident in their skill, who whirled her around at speed, delighting in missing other couples by a whisker. Most irritating of all were those who advised her on her footwork and exhorted her to be calm whenever the turns and tempo were too fast for her to follow. They were right, of course. Often conscious of her missteps and overwhelmed by a fast-paced figure, her anxiety sometimes created yet more missteps, which those well-meaning young men did not hesitate to explain. In her mind, she scolded them in return.

'Sir, exhorting an individual to be calm is the surest way to produce the opposite effect!'

She did not care for any of them.

Her mother despaired.

'You do not like him because of how he dances?'

But her mother had grown up in the age of quadrilles and minuets, where each person was individual master and mistress of their own movements, elegant or clumsy, empowered to approach, retreat, move around their partner with grace, unencumbered by the touch of another, always showing their best side. But the Länder... Well, once the dance began, there was nowhere to hide, they could not but reveal their very essence on the floor, she as much as her eager young partners, if only they knew how to look.

He was not a young man.

They had not been introduced.

A family friend, the heir to a great fortune to whom she had promised a dance, was even now threading his way through the crowd to claim her.

The tall stranger reached out to her.

She placed her hand in his.

His grip, though fast, was tentative at first, his arm encircling her waist just firmly enough to guide her steps with confidence but light enough for her to withdraw a fraction, should she wish. Yet within a very few bars, her arm upon his shoulder moved of its own accord closer towards his neck, her right hand relaxed, secure in the comfortable clasp of his hand until, unencumbered by thought, she, they, were moving around the floor, weaving between other couples with grace, gliding, turning without effort. She began to breathe again and for a moment closed her eyes. When she opened them, he was smiling at her.

A few other couples were whirling and laughing, those careless antics threatened collision, yes, they would have crashed had he not at the last moment pulled her close to him and spun them both out of danger. At the sudden jolt, they regarded each other in surprise, both laughed, and he released her from the close grip. On they danced, he surveying the floor for other unruly couples, she, eyes unfocused, having yielded to his lead, trusting in his skill to navigate a crowded place fraught with sudden movement and unknown dangers, oblivious of the stares of her friends and family who were even now remarking on the sober young Eleanor von Daun dancing a waltz, and a very fast waltz, with the handsome Portuguese emissary, moving in perfect harmony with the rhythm, with the melody and each other, immersed in the moment. All was music, the scent of his skin, her body disappearing and at the centre of it all was a great stillness.

When the music ended, she found herself transported back to her own corner of the dance floor. He hesitated a moment before leading her to her chair.

'Thank you, my lady. It has been a rare pleasure. You dance very well.'

Before she could temper her words, a true answer escaped her.

'Not habitually. But I have danced well with you.'

He did not look shocked. Forgetting to keep the careful distance he had maintained earlier, he took a step towards her.

'I am glad of it. I felt we were in harmony. I have wondered,' he continued, 'what it is that constitutes harmony between dance partners. Do you know?'

'I have observed that even a mediocre dancer such as I' – she dismissed his protestations – 'in the arms of the right partner, is capable of dancing far beyond her own ability.'

'And what, my lady, are the qualities of the right partner?' He was in a playful mood now. 'I would welcome instruction.' His warm smile teased her a little.

'Skill, of course. But not only skill. Just as important – perhaps more important – is the ability – no, the predisposition – to wish to understand their partner. To perceive what gives her comfort and its opposite; to recognise what she can do and what she cannot. And, having understood the strengths and weaknesses in her dance, to accept them. To refrain from insisting on figures beyond her capabilities. Or inclinations. And most of all, to be kind.' She looked away and blushed. 'You know all my secret longings. For the perfect dance partner.'

Now she really was embarrassed. I did not know that I thought all those things until I began to speak to him of them. But he must not have been too shocked, for here he was, reaching for her hand again, then thinking better of it.

'There is great profundity in what you say, madam. You have just described the perfect leader.'

Before he could explain what profundity her meandering thoughts on good dance partners and bad ones might possess, she spied her mother making her way through the crowd towards them.

'I fear my mother requires my company.' Before the old lady was in earshot she added, 'we were not introduced. I am Eleonor von Daun.'

'I know who you are.' He bowed again. 'Sebastião José Carvalho e Melo, at your service.' And as he turned to go, 'I hope we will dance again soon.'

'I, too.' As he disappeared into the crowd and her mother bore down upon her, she had understood that yes, it was possible to fall in love in the course of a single dance

It had not been easy. Enquiries were necessary. A minor politician in his own country, or so it appeared, until the ambassadorship in London. How did that come about? Recommended by a relative. Possibly even by the Queen of Portugal herself, Maria Anna, beloved aunt to our own dear Empress Maria Teresa. She seems to have taken a fancy to him. But he acquitted himself well in London, well enough to be entrusted with that delicate mission at the Austrian court. Yes, he is of noble rank in the Portuguese aristocracy, but only by marriage, his first wife, some years deceased, belonging to an ancient family with a significant fortune. Mendonça was her family name. His own people mere *hidalgo* class, minor nobility, country squires at best. Though there were a few influential people in the extended family. A canon or some such who had recommended him for political office.

A marriage into the family von Daun would raise him to the highest echelons of European nobility, without question. Of course, this branch of the von Dauns has no money. But it seems that his first wife may have left him comfortable.

The recommendation of the Portuguese queen cannot be overlooked. He has greatly impressed her, both his abilities and his person. She approves him unreservedly for this marriage. And any measure approved by Queen Maria Anna of Portugal will be well regarded by her beloved niece, the Empress Maria Teresa of Austria.

'But why did the family of his first wife object to the marriage?' her mother asked.

There were reasons. The woman – Teresa, her name was, the woman he had loved before her, though it pained her to hear the words from his lips, he would not lie, yes, he had loved before – had been much older than him, by more than a decade. And in poor health. She was very beautiful and had the sweetest temperament. Her parents had wanted to protect their daughter from a young man whom they saw as an adventurer. His low birth, his having no fortune to speak of, only his work and his person to recommend him, had not satisfied them.

So they had eloped.

Eloped! The word leaped out at her. The daring, the romance. He had not taken no for an answer. Though others had decided he did not deserve this woman, he would not accept it. And he had achieved his heart's desire.

'He is twice your age.' Eleanor's mother was not convinced. 'More. And what manner of man leaves his sick wife in their country home to take up position as ambassador in a far-off land?'

'A man who is disposed to do his duty for his country and his king.'

In the end, her mother had relented, perhaps persuaded by the eager suitor's paying a large debt incurred during Eleanor's coming-out year which they had never managed to clear.

'And if his king should recall him to his country after you are wed?'

'Then I will follow him.'

The wedding took place less than a year after their first meeting. During those five years in Austria they had three babes. One, little Leonor, had died, not quite five years old. When the summons came to return to the court at Lisbon, she had packed up their household and their two living babes and they had made their way back to his strange land, where Dom José soon ascended the throne upon his father's demise. She had borne three more babes, two of them now with God, their deaths still a burden on her soul and on his. And another child to be delivered in a few months, God willing. For almost a decade, she had done her duty as a wife, without regret.

Until now.

Elvira had put the children to bed.

'My dear, you are troubled.'

Dinner was over, the events of the day weighed heavy upon her, as she wondered how much to reveal to him of the gossip amongst the ladies and especially, the troubling words from the young Princess of Brazil.

'Eleanor – will you not speak to me?'

What would be gained by burdening him with knowledge of the spiteful words uttered that afternoon? He already knew that the husbands and fathers and brothers of the ladies who had spoken such harsh words were opposed to him. And not only to the proposed measures of which he was, in truth, the architect; but to his person, consumed by a visceral disgust that a man born of a lowly family should influence great events.

'Eleanor?'

She drew her chair closer to him.

'If you were ever to take a lover –' The look of horror on his face was almost comical. 'Could I count on your discretion?'

'I never would! I never will!'

'But it is the way of this world, Sebastião. And not only this world. Of many men.'

His face flushed, he rose from his chair and knelt on the floor beside her.

'It is not our way,' he said. 'I am not many men. You are not many women.'

He took her face in his hands. 'Do you no longer trust me? Is this what troubles you?'

She shook her head.

'Eva.'

'What of her?'

'I am wondering, what kind of a match can we make for her? Considering –'

He burst out laughing.

'She is ten years old!'

'Even so, in noble families, these matters are resolved in a timely –'

'Hang the nobility. Their ways are not our ways.' He released her and rose to his feet, rubbing his knees. 'When the time comes, she will make a brilliant match. I will see to it. Now,' he grasped the single candelabra they had left casting its soft light across the dining table, and made for the door, 'let us take a peep at our little ones.'

It was a nightly ritual, at least when he was home at bedtime, and their favourite part of the day.

'Take care,' he warned, as he preceded her on the staircase, holding the candelabra aloft to light their way. 'There is a loose board on the tenth step.'

He extended his free hand and together they mounted the stairs, each step illuminated by the flickering candlelight. Yes, he would see to it, he would see to everything, she would continue to follow him and all would be well.

2

A Sleepless Night and Good Counsel

November 4th, 1754, Riverside Palace, Lisbon

Another sleepless night. Past three, and there was no sign that he had returned from his meeting with the minister. If there had been such a meeting.

Of course, the king and his Minister for War and Foreign Affairs were often obliged to go into conference close to midnight, such were the demands on their time. Or at least, on the minister's time, for José was rarely over-burdened by affairs of state. That is what ministers are for, he would say, as they set out for the hunt together, or examined the latest acquisition in the royal collection of musical scores or discussed plans to invite one of the great castrati of Europe to sing for their Christmas celebrations. Or, when it could not be avoided, appeared before the common people at a newly commissioned opera, decked out in satins and silks, instead of their hunting garb. Was it not the function of ministers to relieve the monarch of the dullest tasks of the workings of government, that the king and his queen might indulge their shared passions, their intimacy?

Until that intimacy had waned.

Despairing of finding sleep, Mariana Victoria cast aside the cover and slid from the bed, her bare feet cold on the marble floor. She reached for the shawl which she kept draped upon her pillow on the nights when the king did not come to her bed. Which was often. In recent times, most nights. The fine wool wrap, a gift from her mother, warmed her bare skin as her fingers traced the threads of intricate embroidery whose every swirl and lozenge her hands knew by heart even in the dark, the fabric tinged with the aroma, the textures of home.

If sleep would not come, she would write to her mother.

Though late, the darkness was incomplete. The maidservant had left a shutter part-open, so that a sliver of moonlight cast its pale gleam across the floor, across the bed and the mantelpiece, where a few candles were hidden behind the clock. Mariana Victoria padded across the room and retrieved two of them.

With a few paces, she traversed the anteroom and opened the door to the main corridor. Two lamps fixed on the wall at head-height emitted the faint, smoky hiss of whale oil. Glancing along the passageway, assured that she was not observed, she reached up to one of the guttering wicks, its faint glow receding in shadow. This light would not last until morning but it flickered still, just enough to permit a weak flame to catch on the wick of the candle she held aloft. Having captured the fire, she made her way back to her bedchamber, one hand cupping the flame, and sank into the chair at her escritoire. She tilted the lit candle over a marble dish, allowing a trickle of warm wax to drip and pool in the base. With a steady hand, she pressed first one candle, then the other into the melted substance until both stood upright and firm.

Now seated before the half-open shutter, contemplating the ripples of moonlight quivering on the dark waters of the Tagus, she allowed the desolation to soften while she followed the current of the river, immersed in those deep waters that brimmed with possibility. How pleasant it would be to steal along the passageway, descend the wooden staircase, slip out into the garden towards the jetty where the royal barge was berthed, clamber into one of the little boats moored there, row with all her strength up the mighty Tagus, against the current, across the entire country, back to Spain, through Talavera, Aranjuez, Toledo where the river narrowed to a trickle and home was but forty leagues distant…

A draught from the river rattled the shutter. It swung open, tipping one of the candles off-centre. In her haste to catch it, she almost knocked it to the floor. Frozen in fright, she sat immobile until her pounding heart steadied. Although the Palacio de Ribeira was built of stone, every room, corridor and staircase was adorned with intricate wooden carvings, the walls covered with tapestries from Flanders and canvases of the great masters: Raphael, Caravaggio, Titian and more. Irreplaceable journals from the Voyages of Discovery were housed in the library, original charts annotated by Vasco da Gama, first editions of Os Lusíadas, the national epic wherein Camões immortalised the journeys of those great explorers that had made Portugal the richest nation on earth. The absolute prohibition against naked flames, especially carried by night, was from the lips of His Majesty himself.

Hands shaking, she moved the two candles from her writing desk to a marble slab beneath the mantel and watched them burn down, light pooling in a corner of the room. As she stared into the flames, her better judgement returned. This was not the time to write to her mother. What could she say to the great Elisabeth Farnese, who in her day had commanded not only her husband, the king, but the entire court and nation of Spain? Whereas her daughter could barely command the slightest consideration from her own spouse. What could she say that was so very different from the tales of infidelities José had inflicted upon her from the earliest years of their marriage, more than twenty years ago?

That this time was different.

That this was no slight dalliance, to be cast off after a few weeks or months, when he would weary and return to the arms of his queen.

That this paramour was no silly girl but a woman, a married woman, only a few years younger than herself.

That this was a person of consequence, born of one of the noblest families in the land, and the daughter-in-law of one of her closest friends.

Of all the betrayals, the abyss that the king's adventure with Dona Teresa of Távora had driven between herself and Dona Leonora of Távora was the hardest to bear. The marchioness was one of the few enduring friends she had made across the long years, almost three decades since that day, as a little girl of barely eleven years old, perched on a platform over the river Caio, her Spanish retinue handed her across the border to wed the young Portuguese Prince José in exchange for his sister Bárbara, who would marry her brother, Prince Fernando of Spain. Two princesses, each destined to be a queen in a land that was not her own, bartered across the border like two parcels.

And now, since Leonora had returned from India with her family a few weeks ago, her old friend would not look her in the face. Perhaps it was true that in that exchange of princesses long ago, Spain had got the better bargain.

'You are no longer that little girl,' Father Malagrida had reminded her the day before, when she had confessed the sorrow and yes, the hatred in her heart, 'but a queen, mother of four princesses, one of whom will reign as queen in her own right.'

Yes, four princesses out of eight pregnancies and no surviving son. How much easier might things have gone for them, for her husband, for the kingdom, if she had borne just one male heir. In earlier times, even today in other countries, that failure would be sufficient cause for her husband to put her away from him. Or worse. Those English queens. As it was, they now had the burden of finding a husband for Maria who would not be a usurper, a king consort who would not attempt to rule or worse, bring an invading army. A foreigner prince was out of the question, they must…

'This is not the moment to discuss matters of state.' Father Malagrida made the Sign of the Cross over her. 'In many ways you are fortunate, for in most affairs you have the ear of the king, even though it may not seem so. I do not doubt that he will find his way back to you.'

Were it not for the counsel and comfort of Father Malagrida, the desolation of these years would be unbearable. Both outsiders, they sometimes remarked on how difficult it was to understand these strange people, their language on the surface so close to her own Spanish tongue and the padre's native Italian, yet the nasal tones, the swallowed vowels, so many odd sounds that disguised familiar words, recognizable yet so reluctant to yield up meaning. And their secretive ways. This was a people whose habitual demeanour was governed by unnatural calm, their thoughts and feelings turned inwards, their intent hidden deep within the self, a muted landscape of words and feeling impenetrable for a young girl whose native land brimmed with unmediated exuberance and joy. And how unjust that these people should so easily read her, both her person and her language. Yes, Father Malagrida shared the same burden. How fortunate to have a confessor who understood her so well.

'Do not expect too much of the marchioness, Your Majesty,' he advised. 'Things have not gone well for her family since their return from India.'

He said no more than that. But it was true. The Távora family no longer enjoyed her husband's favour, for what reason she did not know, as he no longer entrusted her with such confidences. When she enquired of him whether Dom Francisco would soon be elevated to the promised dukedom, he had made no answer. And worse, Leonora's oldest son, her Luís Bernardo and the light of her life, was destroyed, a shadow of the man he had been, on learning that the wife he had left behind during those years in India had been – and continued to be – the mistress of the king. The weight of what remained unsaid between the two friends, queen and marchioness, remained an insuperable barrier.

There was no doubt that they all knew of the affair, all her intimates of the court. They had known from the beginning. Some, like Carvalho e Melo, must be colluding with her husband in concealing it from her. Was she really expected to believe in all these midnight conferences? A wave of resentment at the minister gripped her, more, hatred, that he should be closer to her husband than she was herself, not only in matters of state but in daily life. For while the minister treated José and herself with appropriate deference, at times he embellished his bows and respectful tones with exaggerated flourishes that amused the king; which impertinence should by rights provoke exasperation, even rage. You are king, or queen, his smooth humility said, but I am clever and know how to bend you to my will. How, why, her husband did not see this, was a mystery.

There was the question of the Jews, for example. The jolly tale of how the minister had corrected his king's proposal for identifying his Jewish subjects.

'I suggested that we command them to wear a little white cap,' José recalled. 'And I instructed Dom Sebastião to see to it.' The minister had not disagreed, though it was only later, José realised, that nor had he agreed. Instead, he marched into their next conference holding aloft a black velvet cushion upon which were displayed two scraps of white fabric. José had thought it another one of the minister's ideas for establishing new textile factories and wondered why Dom Sebastião had thought it fitting to bring him samples to approve.

'Can you guess what they were? Two little white caps!' José shouted with laughter.

'"One for you, and one for me, Majesty," said he, his countenance serious, his bow rather deeper than the usual. Which should have alerted me. My face must have been a picture, for I observed his lower lip tremble, as though he could not contain his mirth. "For there is no member of the court, Majesty, or of your family or my own," intoned the minister, with perfect gravity, "in whose veins does not run Jewish blood!"'

'How did you respond, Papa?' asked Maria. Yes, she would one day be queen but for now she was in need of a husband. Almost twenty and no match yet found for her. She was no admirer of Carvalho e Melo, any more than her mother was. The girl fretted constantly about who would be her chosen husband and who would do the choosing.

'Did you reprimand him, Papa? As he had failed to carry out your command?'

Of course, there was no reprimand. As usual, the minister had crafted his actions as a clever turn of phrase, an entertainment, so that José barely noticed that his orders had been subverted. Or if he did, had not minded enough to object.

'Is it wise, my love,' she had said that night after the princesses retired and they were reading an opera score together in the library, 'to yield so easily to the minister's will?'

A rare direct criticism of Carvalho e Melo, and a mistake. As soon as the words left her lips, a hooded look clouded her husband's eye, his only answer an irritated wave of the hand as though she were a troublesome courtier whose words merited no attention. A response most unaccustomed, for in temperament José was ever pleasant and equable. Except on the subject of his Minister for War and Foreign Affairs, on which matter he was immovable. And on that other topic, upon which she had given up remonstrating, it being the single subject guaranteed to rouse him to real anger.

'Father Malagrida.' The question escaped her before she could bite it back, 'is my husband's immortal soul in danger?'

The old priest clasped his hands before him in a prayerful gesture. She had presumed, that motion said. He was not Dom

José's confessor and even if he were, the seal of the confessional forbade disclosure of confidences.

Yet he answered, and with an urgency she had never before heard from his lips.

'It is not merely his own immortal soul that is in danger, Majesty. Also in peril are the souls of his subjects, his family, all those who know and love him. For this entire city, the whole nation, is in the grip of wrong-doing and sin...'

Could this be true? To her foreigner's eye, Lisbon had the air of a city, and Portugal a nation, remarkable for piety and devotion, even more than her native Spain. Priests and nuns from dozens of religious orders thronged the streets daily; above one-tenth of the population was a religious. The spires of churches, of which there were multitudes, jostled the skyline as the masts of ships sailing from the mouth of the Tagus jostled the horizon. Not for nothing was Lisbon known as the city of a thousand spires...

'...of frivolous distractions, merrymaking, theatres, opera...'

Here she had blushed, she was certain of it, the opera and music-making being two of her own favourite pastimes. Which she shared with the king.

'...carousing and fighting,' Padre Malagrida went on. This was true. The capital in recent years had become a dangerous place, especially at night, with gangs roaming the streets, many of them young members of the finest families.

'...fornication and adultery.'

At these words, she lowered her head, the better to conceal her humiliation. Father Malagrida's sweet, deep voice intoned the Portuguese tongue that came more easily to him than to her, imbued with the sing-song rhythms of his native Italian.

'Your Majesty, you must do all in your power to put an end to this situation.' He had no need to explain what he meant. 'So many people are harmed by what the king chooses to see as a dalliance, an indulgence, his right as king.'

She kept her head bowed, the better to restrain the anger she felt mounting, at her husband for his actions and yes, perhaps a little at Father Malagrida, too, for obliging her to confront them. But this was his way of helping her, she could not do without him.

'I have tried, Father.' Her voice shook. 'Many times. Too many. He will not be told. He feigns not to hear my words.'

'Then you must shout them in a voice that he cannot ignore.'

'That I have done also, Father!' Mariana Victoria found the rage abating to sadness. 'He became angry, very angry. I have never seen him thus.'

On the last occasion when she dared to confront him, his countenance transformed as though possessed by an alien mask, his entire demeanour calling to mind those curses of the evil eye which old village women were said to cast upon those who crossed them. She shrank back, resisting the urge to make the Sign of the Cross as he thrust one hand before her face and spat out a single word.

'Enough!' This was not the harsh word of a husband spoken in anger. It was the command of a king.

Since that day, not long before his mother died, she had not crossed him, nor made mention of the lady, but instead endured sleepless nights, pacing the floor, wrapped in her mother's Spanish shawl.

'I will pray for Your Majesty, that God give you fortitude to endure, and courage to lead the king from his wicked ways.'

She looked up, startled to hear Father Malagrida criticise her husband in such terms. This was not proper, she should intervene, chide him. And yet why, when he was stating aloud her own fears? But the priest was not yet finished.

'He must cease to put his family, his country, in danger. For the wrath of God will descend upon him, in one form or another.

Of that you may be sure.'

As he made the Sign of the Cross and led her act of contrition, his words, instead of bringing her the customary comfort, fanned the embers of her suppressed rage.

'*Ego te absolvo, in nomine Padre...*'

For which sin did she require absolution? For excessive devotion to the husband who humiliated her? For dedication to her daughters and their future wellbeing? Or affection for an old friend who was obliged to discard her?

Was there really nothing to be done?

Before he reached the door, she called out to him. 'Father Malagrida.' Perhaps, if he had an answer to one final question, it would bring her some small relief. 'Now that Queen Maria Anna is dead.' The priest inclined his head and waited. The old lady had been greatly devoted to him, she had summoned him from across the ocean when she felt death approach. Unfortunately, she had also been greatly smitten by Dom Sebastião José Carvalho e Melo, who would never have been permitted to take a wife of the high Austrian nobility without her intervention.

'Is it possible that Carvalho e Melo's influence over my husband will wane?'

Father Malagrida paused at the door. 'I regret to say that I think not, Majesty.'

Of course, he was right. Since the death of his mother a few weeks before, Dom José had depended even more, if that were possible, on his minister. And if Carvalho e Melo were minded to indulge his king in this affair... But Father Malagrida's response surprised her.

'I do not believe, Majesty, that Dom Sebastião José Carvalho e Melo, in spite of his dislike of the nobility, of my Order and of me in particular, is responsible for encouraging Dom José's adventures. Nor do I believe that he approves of the king's behaviour.'

'I did not know that you favoured the minister, Father Malagrida.' A tone of reproof crept into her words. 'I believed that you considered him dangerous.'

'I do indeed, Your Majesty. I believe Carvalho e Melo is a danger not only to our Order, but to the place of the Church, to the court, perhaps to the very authority of the king. And this, because of the misplaced confidence with which the king – begging your pardon, Majesty – favours him. But it is important to know our opponents. Their foibles, their obsessions. Neither to overestimate, nor underestimate their strategies and strengths.'

'He does what he pleases, Father. Whether my husband will it or no.'

'He will not oppose the king, Your Majesty. Not on matters on which the king is determined. Carvalho e Melo is a family man, he may even privately disapprove of His Majesty's…behaviour.'

Here, once again, he gave a little bow of deference, as though to compensate for his earlier temerity in criticising his monarch. Whose conduct was the height of indiscretion. Open carriage rides through the city, expensive gifts of which the lady boasted shamelessly, that white palfrey…

'But he will not challenge the king in any of his fundamental wishes. For his position depends on maintaining your husband's favour. And on ensuring that no other influences,' such as a wife, he did not say, 'will weaken his sway.'

He lingered at the door, awaiting permission to leave.

'Then what must I do, Father?'

Father Malagrida took a few paces towards her, his breath uneven as though preparing to launch into a sermon of great power, but his words were gentle. 'You must pray, Majesty. If all else has failed, all that remains to us is prayer. There is no greater power.'

'And that is all?'

His eyes appeared to fix on a vision far beyond her. 'Prayer is all, Majesty. If we petition our Saviour with a pure heart, He will answer and there will be a reckoning. As night follows day, my lady. As night follows day.'

Mariana Victoria leaned forward and blew out the flickering flames. Clouds had drifted across the moon, the room was plunged into darkness, the bright fingers of the dawn were yet to creep over the horizon, across the river and the sea far beyond.

This was the darkest moment of the night. Yet change was on the way. As day follows night, a great change was coming. They must pray that it come to pass, and soon.

A Musical Interlude and the Perils of Eavesdropping

November 5th, 1754, Palace of Queluz, Lisbon

An uneasy silence descended on the assembled audience, all chatter hushed as Dom Pedro entered through the southern portico, followed by the five illustrious performers: Queen Mariana Vitória; her oldest daughter, Maria, the Princess of Brazil, then Mariana, Doroteia and Benedita, Maria's sisters. The royal retinue processed the full length of the hall, six pairs of heels clacking on the newly laid *azulejo* tiles whose flashes of brilliant blue and green and white shimmered across the floor like river waves, while the sea of swaying bodies – marquises, counts, dukes and duchesses – parted to make way for the prince and his entourage.

According to protocol, Dom Pedro should have come last in the procession, being only the king's younger brother and therefore outranked by his nieces, who all preceded him in the line of succession. But here at Queluz such niceties were rarely observed. Although barely three leagues distant from the Ribeira Palace, in ambience Dom Pedro's estate was a world removed from the royal court. Visitors, eager to partake in the concerts and entertainments and general merriment for which the Queluz palace was renowned, often observed that Dom Pedro's domain epitomised the most congenial qualities of the man himself: amiability, conviviality, serenity, a touch of indolence, a dash of chaos, this last reinforced by the endless construction works of the last seven years which had not ceased since old King João gifted the ramshackle palace to his younger son.

'What is it this evening?' whispered M Martin, the new attaché to the Embassy of France.

'L'Orfeo,' answered Mr Stanton, Second Secretary at the British Embassy. 'Monteverdi,' he added, as though that intelligence would make the next few hours any easier. His pronouncement was soon confirmed by Dom Pedro himself, who was even now climbing the four steps to a temporary dais which had been raised beneath the great window in the eastern wall. With a genial smile, he bowed to the audience before turning to bestow kisses upon the hands of his sister-in-law and his four nieces, reserving a fervent handclasp and a tender glance for the oldest princess.

'Well?' M Martin murmured. 'Is it settled yet? Do you know?'

'Shhh,' answered Mr Stanton, shaking his head. 'No. Not yet. No one knows.'

The long-awaited announcement concerning the nuptials of the young Princess of Brazil was a topic that excited great interest amongst the entire diplomatic corps in Lisbon. Everyone knew that Princess Maria would have to marry, and soon. But to whom? The fond looks exchanged between the princess and her uncle, the prince, seemed to confirm that despite the difference in years, their affection was indeed mutual. And there was no doubt that Dom Pedro's late parents, the old king and queen, had favoured the match – the Portuguese nobility admitting no taboo regarding unions of uncle-and-niece, or aunt-and-nephew, the only requirement being a papal dispensation, which was almost always granted.

So why delay? It was puzzling. By the time Dom José had ascended the throne upon the death of his father five years earlier, the question of the princess's marriage – and therefore, the identity of the future king consort – seemed to have been brushed aside. Still, there was no knowing what negotiations might be underway behind closed doors. It was the dream of every junior diplomat to bring word, any tasty morsel on the subject, to his ambassador, who could in turn report back to their government on this crucial matter. Though such gems of insight had so far eluded them all.

And yes, here was Dom Pedro explaining his curious decision to mount this spectacle, barely three months after the death of his own mother. While he spoke, discreet looks were exchanged amongst the members of the audience, their unease at being invited to attend this performance at a time when both he and the king were in mourning little assuaged by the prince's complicated reasoning.

He began by thanking all present for their attendance, mentioning several by name: the Duke of Aveiro, various counts and countesses, a sprinkling of members of the clergy. Not Father Malagrida, of course. Though a frequent visitor and spiritual confidant to the prince and to the queen and to many of those gathered, the old Jesuit did not permit himself such worldly pleasures as attendance at music-making spectacles. As everyone knew, he did not approve of them. The pronouncement provoked a trickle of indulgent laughter, for they had all heard the holy man preaching against most entertainments but especially, against singing and dancing. Even so, almost everyone present felt blessed to be acquainted with him, to have heard words from the lips of such a holy man, a prophet. He was probably a saint. For a chosen few, he was the confidant to whom they could confess their sins and repent of their frivolities, thereby sparing themselves the pain of renouncing them.

When the respectful laughter had abated, the prince went on to commend those in attendance for the restraint in their attire, which this evening showed a decorum that lent a special dignity to the occasion. The habitual ostentation of dress, especially of the ladies, was subdued. All frock coats, all hose, all gowns, all shawls, were in black or shades of grey, at most enlivened with a few trimmings of white, and not a décolleté in sight, which absence of colour lent the proceedings a sombre air.

They – Dom Pedro, the queen and her daughters – after careful reflection, had considered the tale of Orpheus a fitting tribute to their beloved mother and grandmother, as the mythical bard and musician accomplished what no mortal had ever achieved: descended to the Underworld and convinced Hades to return his beloved Eurydice to the land of the living – only to lose her again. And, just as Orpheus was ever after compelled to live with his bitter loss, they all must continue their life's path in the sad absence of their lamented queen. Was this sublime work not therefore a fitting celebration of one who, like Eurydice, had been so loved in life by all the people of Portugal?

While his introduction faltered to a close, six chairs were carried in by footmen, of which five were placed on the raised dais and one positioned at its base. This last was swiftly occupied by Dom Pedro himself. Each of the five ladies, clutching her score and her fan, took her seat in a stately manner, yet all the guests remained standing. They had no choice. Chairs were never provided, not tonight, nor for any of the concerts which Dona Mariana Vitória and the princesses regularly performed at Queluz, Dom Pedro being convinced that prolonged periods of sitting were bad for the humours and that standing encouraged conviviality. This sombre occasion warranted no exception.

'How many acts?' Mr Stanton inquired under his breath.

'Cinque,' came the gloomy reply from another young diplomat, Signor Castiglione from Savoy, who was a lover of opera and familiar with many of the works which the Dona Mariana Vitória and the princesses had performed at Queluz.

'And how many will we…?'

'All five,' came the reply from the doleful Savoyard, 'with no interval.'

Having digested this unwelcome intelligence, Mr Stanton turned to his French colleague. 'François, where's your ambassador?' he asked *sotto voce*, upon which the three young men burst into snorts of laughter which each tried, with limited success, to disguise as coughs and sneezes. A few of their neighbours turned and frowned. By a happy chance, none of their superiors was close by. The ambassadors had the habit of seeking out a comfortable spot at the back of the hall, in some shadowed corner or beside a ledge upon which they might sit or lean. Which discreet indulgence served them well, until one evening the Count of Atouguia, answering a call of nature, slipped out of the great hall and almost tripped over the French ambassador who was lying stretched out on the floor of the anteroom, his eyes wide open, staring at the ceiling. When the count had stopped laughing he gravely informed the ambassador that on the matter of his feeble incapacity to stand for a mere two, at most three, hours in the interests of diplomatic harmony, the French nation could depend on the count's discretion. Which must not have been reliable, for the tale had passed into diplomatic lore, sometimes invoked by subordinates behind the ambassador's back and more often to his face over a glass of port wine.

While the little band of musicians behind the dais tuned their instruments – and yes, they enjoyed the privilege of chairs – the queen stood. Her voice vied with the strains and blasts of the tuning of two violas, a few violins and at least one cello, soon to be accompanied by sundry wind instruments, a cornetto and two or three recorders. Although they were but five singers, she explained, the opera required ten roles, five male and five female, therefore she and her daughters would each sing two parts, one female and one male, *en travesti*, with some slight adjustments to the key, to accommodate their voices. Each performer would hold aloft a mask to identify which role they were singing at any given time. She herself would take the roles of La Musica and Orfeo; the Princess of Brazil would sing Eurydice and Eco and the three younger princesses would divide the remaining parts between them. This did not, of course, include the various nymphs, sprites and shepherds of the chorus, when they would all chime in to create the required effects. It had gone beautifully in rehearsal.

As soon as the queen sat down, the little orchestra struck up the overture. A startling, lively melody blared from trumpets and cornettos, an air that resembled nothing other than a jolly dance tune. Once taken up and swelled by the strings, the resulting ambience could not have been further from the sombre mood which the prince's introductory remarks had promised. There he was, tapping his foot and beaming up at the dais with an eager pride peculiar for a man mourning the recent death of his mother.

And yes, the princess seemed to like him, although her mien this evening was unhappy. The queen stood to launch into the Prologue, a robust recitative from La Musica celebrating Orpheus's gift in charming the birds and making the stones weep, while the princess looked on with the dejected aspect of one who would prefer to be anywhere but upon that dais.

And with good reason. When the strings took over from the noisy wind instruments, the cadences softened to a melancholy hum carrying a darkness that foreshadowed inevitable victory of Hades over the living, she considered the assembled company, drab in their various shades of grey and black in tribute to her dead grandmother. Granny would not have liked it. She would have preferred a celebration, ladies decked out in their feathers and finery, marquises and counts in their gaudy frockcoats, to this sombre display. And yes, Dom Pedro would have been her own dear prince by now, if only Granny's wish, her own wish, had been fulfilled. Now that she was gone, her father and his advisors and yes, her mother, too, would prevail. They never would be married.

This was her cue: the few solo passages when her voice could sparkle and soar, until joined by the vivacious chorus that brings the first act to a close, the purest expression of sheer joy of the entire work in anticipation of the wedding scene, brimming with a gaiety as yet untainted by the sorrow that must follow. Perhaps it was ever thus – the expectation of happiness always yielding a rapture so much greater than its consummation, doomed to be extinguished forever by the poisonous snake bite in the second act that would send Eurydice to Hades and Orpheus mad with grief. Was it not ever thus? Did not the shadow of death hover over every life, even at its most joyous, only awaiting the inevitable sorrows to come, from which there was no escape?

Marriage to her dear Pedro had promised some measure of joy, a deliverance, or at least a respite from these dark thoughts that often plagued her, even now, as she surveyed the smiling faces of her audience.

Would their papal dispensation never arrive?

According to Father Malagrida, the delay was not surprising. If the intelligence from his associates in Rome was correct, the document had been withheld for reasons which must be evident to anyone aware of the conduct of the Portuguese state – of a certain representative of the state – towards the clergy.

'Princess, you must ask the queen,' he advised when she encountered him outside her mother's chambers, after he had heard the queen's weekly confession. 'Or your father.' Of course, this chance meeting was an ambush, but she was the heir to the throne, therefore not lightly dismissed. Waiting for her to step aside, he raised one hand, half in blessing, half in warning.

'If – when – you do speak with His Majesty on it, be sure that you are in private conference with him. At a time when he is not distracted by the presence of his courtiers. Or ministers.'

'Without Dom…?'

Father Malagrida pressed a warning finger to his lips.

'Remember, your intelligence regarding the fate of the document of dispensation – somehow withheld due to the conduct of a certain functionary – did not come from me.'

The heavy emphasis on the word 'functionary' left no room for misunderstanding. What a boon it was to have this holy man as an ally. Small wonder that dear Granny had sent for him when she knew she was failing. And Father Malagrida had also accompanied her grandfather, Dom João, on his final journey. How fitting that he should guide her, too, on her life's path, which surely must lead her to marry Dom Pedro.

Her mother's rich, sweet voice swelled in volume on reaching the high note at the end of La Musica's aria. Orfeo has just discovered the snake bite, there is consternation, thank heavens this is a concert performance, which relieves Eurydice of the obligation to collapse bodily or be carried away, feigning lifelessness. All that was required of her for most of the next act was silence, until Orfeo, anguished and enraged, would storm the Underworld, strike his bargain with Hades, feign indifference to his dead bride's futile pleadings that he turn and look at her as he strides away, while she weeps bitter tears, convinced that he no longer loves her.

Why had their papal dispensation been withheld? Did they even wish for her marriage to her dear uncle, brother of the king? Both her mother and her father had been as indifferent to her pleas for a declaration as Hades had been to Orfeo's first entreaties, but without even the glimmer of hope which the Lord of the Underworld had promised the grieving husband. Rather the opposite. During the last year, a procession of alternative suitors had been presented: the Duke of Lafões, who had left the country; and the Duke of Cumberland – the Butcher of Culloden, they called him –an Englishman, and as a foreigner, constitutionally prohibited from marrying a future queen. Why was he even considered?

Then the most puzzling and infuriating suitors of all – not one, but two, of the Palhavã princes. Dom José, the Grand Inquisitor; and Dom António, a Doctor of Theology, both ready and eager to give up their lofty positions to marry her. Yet if the king's full brother, Dom Pedro, was not considered a suitable match for his daughter and heir to the throne, then why were these two half-brothers deemed worthy?

As Dona Mariana Vitória intoned the final bars of the third act – now singing the role of Orfeo, to which the paper lyre she held aloft attested – a strange new thought occurred to the princess. Perhaps her mother did not want her to marry at all. Oh, she must marry, of course she must, as the oldest daughter whose husband would be king consort when Dom José was gone. But in her deepest heart of hearts, could she bear to see her daughter attain a joy that she herself had been denied?

'I should have been Queen of France,' her mother would say in her most bitter moments, reverting to that childhood state, a little girl, barely seven years old, sent away from the French court because some Bourbon Duke was persuaded that the daughter of the Spanish monarchs would not, after all, be a fitting wife for young Louis. The humiliation. The shame. And to be dispatched, years later, to Lisbon and exchanged for another princess, to marry a man who would be a faithless husband. Small wonder that Dona Mariana Vitória was bitter.

Securing a private audience with her father had not been easy. After several days of observation and conference with trusted footmen, she at last found the king alone in his office. He greeted her with a smile and a kiss. Taking a step back, he contemplated her visage.

'Are you well, my petal? You have grown thin.'
'Quite well, Papi. A little tired, that is all. The rehearsals…'
'Ah, yes. Your next performance is…'
'Orfeo. Monteverdi.'

There followed an awkward exchange during which Dom José questioned her in detail, too much detail, about the forthcoming concert. What interest had her father ever displayed in their costumes? Or the composition of the orchestra? As his conversation darted from one topic to another, leaving no space for the princess to insert her own questions, she had to admit that he did not want to speak with her. Or, that there was a particular subject which he was anxious to avoid.

'Papi, I must ask you. The papal dispensation permitting my marriage to –'

Her father stood and turned his back to her, his attention devoted to the balcony window, whose handle he several times tried and failed to move. 'My sweet, could you? This heat…'

'Granny wished for our marriage. Grandfather, too. All that is required –'

Dom José's fleshy countenance, flushed pink, turned a deeper red.

'My darling girl, there are matters behind this delay of which you are not aware. Of which I cannot speak. Not yet. But soon. It will arrive, you will see. All in good time.'

'But Papi, I do not understand why these other suitors…'

The quick clack of heels announced another presence: Dom Sebastião Carvalho e Melo, of course it was, emerging from a little alcove at the end of the L-shaped room. With a humble bow, he excused himself. He had left important documents behind. Might he impose? An amiable nod from Dom José signalled permission to approach. The minister affected to look around before approaching a shelf from which he removed a sheaf of papers, before removing himself. Out of sight, concealed in his little alcove. Where a curious footman, or minister, might linger.

Thus, the conference proved to be as vague and fruitless as every other attempt to engage her father on the subject, Dom José being insensible to the depths of her distress. As the pale muslin curtain billowed in the breeze behind her father's desk, the screech of gulls wheeling over the river far below was accompanied by invisible currents of that silent presence, that intractable will which hovered on the air. Her heart deflated in silent misery. Defeated, she retreated from her father's presence and on reaching the door, came face to face with Carvalho e Melo, who had emerged from his alcove. Making a courteous bow, he opened the door, for the footmen were nowhere to be seen, no doubt banished for the duration of her conference with the king. Without a word or a glance, she stalked past him.

For a long moment she lingered in the empty corridor, her thoughts racing. A shaft of sunlight speared the wall ahead, its rays reaching into the depths of the passage, illuminating the darkest corners. Her breathing stilled, she approached the warm sunbeams. Yes, somewhere ahead a door was ajar.

It was a small salon, sumptuously appointed, a tapestry from the new workshop at Tavira glowing blue and green on the far wall. A balcony, which could be accessed through a glass door identical to floor-length window in her father's office, spanned the full length of the building. Voices from the adjoining room were audible, their contrasting energies unmistakable, one urgent and rapid, the other deep and measured, though their words were indistinct.

If it were not locked... Holding her breath, she grasped the little wrought iron handle and pressed down. It moved but a fraction. But no, it was not locked and after a few attempts, it yielded. A gust of wind rattled the glass but the rhythm of the two voices continued unchanged, their words floating free on the air, Dom José's speech light and rapid, the minister's tones precise and measured, punctuated by frequent pauses as though he were weighing the heft of each word before parting with it.

'Have your people in Rome any news of the progress of the dispensation?'

'The situation has not changed, Your Majesty. The Vatican

thinks to force a softening of our policies in relation to the Jesuit missions in Grão Pará and Maranhão by withholding permission for the Princess Maria and Dom Pedro to marry.'

'Blackmail.'

'Indeed, Your Majesty. Which will not succeed. It must not, for we have no option but to put an end by one means or another to Jesuit domination of the lands and peoples of the Amazon and the River Uruguay. They are obstructing the implementation of our hard-won border treaty with Madrid. They have repaid the many privileges – those vast estates and handsome commercial concessions! – by protecting the Guaraní indians, and probably training and arming them too, in their resistance to relocate west of the Uruguay in accordance with the treaty. It is unconscionable, treasonous and it cannot continue. We may soon be obliged to make common cause with the Spanish to vanquish them.'

There followed a brooding silence. So it was true. The hatred that this devious minister bore the entire Jesuit order, not only Father Malagrida, had infected her own father, who had thereby incurred the displeasure of the Vatican. Permission for her marriage would never be granted, not while Dom Sebastião José Carvalho e Melo retained control of the affairs of the nation.

'In any case, Dom Sebastião, I am by no means certain that my brother is the best match for my daughter.'

'But it is by no means certain that your brother is plotting to take your throne, Majesty.'

The princess stifled a gasp. Could her father really believe this calumny? And what could have caused the minister to attribute such wicked intention to Dom Pedro, the sweetest, the most tranquil of men?

For Carvalho e Melo's conciliatory words, although they stated the exact opposite, had somehow suggested that this treasonous intention was yet a possibility.

'Then why is he in such frequent conference with my nobles,

above all, with those who have always opposed me, out there in his ruin in Queluz? That ruffian Aveiro is always visiting. And Francisco of Assis with his wife, that gorgon Leonora of Távora. And their son. Father Malagrida, even, and all the others, whose names you know. For what possible purpose would such a band gather, but to plot sedition?'

'To hear the musical ensembles, Majesty?' To which grave pronouncement Dom José responded with a shout of laughter.

As the princess felt her cheeks colour and her little fists clench, she longed for the day when she would deliver that upstart of a minister the reward he deserved. It could not come soon enough. But then, it would come only when her dear papa was gone and at that moment, she hated the minister a little more for provoking her to wish for the mild, infuriating, disloyal, affectionate father whom she loved, to be dead.

The minister continued, the earnestness of his tone unchanged. 'Majesty, may I speak frankly?'

Some kind of silent assent was given

'While I truly believe it unlikely that Dom Pedro himself harbours aspirations to rule – he has neither the temperament nor the inclination nor, forgive me, Majesty...'

'Continue, do not hold back.'

'...nor the intellect...'

It took all the discipline at her command to stifle a cry of outrage. How dared they? That he had not the temperament or inclination to usurp anyone's position, least of all that of the brother whom he loved, was true. But not for the reasons this most despicable minister had claimed. Pedro was not an ambitious man. In a second son born never to rule, that was surely a boon, was it not, the simplicity of his nature a sign of good character, not lack of wit. Why should he not be satisfied with the entertainments and pleasures that life in his Queluz palace allowed him? Yes, his time and thoughts were lately absorbed in reconstructing the palace, it was something of a ruin, but would soon be the most magnificent of dwellings, a national treasure, a fitting legacy for the second son of whom so little was expected.

Most of all, Dom Pedro would be remembered for his kindness.

Did it not occur to her father, or to his dreadful minister, that people might visit Queluz out of fondness, affection, even love, for Dom Pedro?

'Yes,' her father replied. 'He can decide nothing for himself. He accomplishes nothing on his own initiative. And yet he thrives, for he is surrounded by people who treat him as though he were a child of ten years old.'

'That is exactly my –'

'And yet our father always favoured him. And because of it, when we were boys he always disdained me.'

'Which disrespect may be used, manipulated, by others more calculating than he.' A warning note had crept into the minister's tone. 'For even if Dom Pedro himself has no intentions to usurp Your Majesty's throne, there are others who might consider installing him as a puppet monarch. One they could bend to their own will.'

The princess sank into a chair. If her father, or rather, her father's most trusted advisor, believed that her uncle presented a threat to the throne, together they would do all in their power to diminish Pedro's prestige, to encourage those who already saw him as a laughingstock, someone not to be taken seriously as a suitor. Head in hands, she closed her eyes. Would that she had never heard this exchange.

'If he married my daughter, there would be no need for any insurgence. He would be king consort soon enough.'

'He is but three years your junior, Majesty, and you are only forty. You can expect many more decades to live and rule.'

And of course, Dom Sebastião José Carvalho e Melo would stop at nothing to preserve her father's reign. For if her father were to lose his crown, Dom Sebastião José Carvalho e Melo,

Minister of War and Foreign Affairs, would lose everything. His position. His influence. He would cease to exist.

And therefore: for as long as her father lived, they would never be rid of Dom Sebastião.

The cue for the final act approaches. Orfeo has descended to the Underworld, dared to challenge Hades, demanded the return of his beloved from that place whence none may be delivered; and the Lord of the Underworld, mesmerised by the bard's great gifts, moved by his terrible grief, has relented. Eurydice may return to the land of the living. But the conditions of the bargain are harsh, Orfeo must leave without looking back, he must provoke the sorrow of his beloved wife, he must endure her despair. The burden of her grief proves too great to bear, and it cleaves them forever.

While the princess's voice soared, the countenances before her beamed in smiles that were perhaps a little forced now. Might Dom Pedro be persuaded to permit seating for the next concert? After the bows, a few of the most eminent guests seemed disposed to approach the dais to congratulate the performers. Was Dona Teresa, the young Marchioness of Távora approaching? She had married her brother's son and was therefore aunt to her own husband. Clearly, their papal dispensation had not gone astray.

For how long had that lady's dalliance with her father the king been an open secret? The brazen audacity of the woman, to attend a concert performed by her lover's wife, and now presume to offer congratulations.

'What am I to do?'

'Nothing, Majesty.' Carvalho e Melo took it upon himself to offer a reply. 'That is, very little. I recommend keeping Dom Pedro and his entourage under observation. I have people who can assist with that. We must learn who are his most frequent visitors and what they discuss when the singing and dancing and merrymaking end. And perhaps it would be wise to confine the prince to Queluz for some time,' he added. 'A few weeks. Or months.'

'Excellent.' Her father's voice had gathered strength. 'The less we see of my brother and his entourage in the Ribeira Palace, the better.'

As the performers stepped down from the dais, Dom Pedro placed one hand across his heart, his kind eyes moist. Her own heart beat a little faster, whether from affection for dearest uncle or rage at those who were keeping him from her. A hum of animated discourse arose from the guests, who, in anticipation of refreshments and a comfortable seat, had recovered their good temper.

Which among them might be spies for her father's minister?

Whether she would ever marry the man of her heart's desire, who could know? But one thing was certain: she would one day be queen. And when that day came, Dom Sebastião José Carvalho e Melo would face a bitter reckoning.

4

A Carriage Ride and a Brief Encounter

November 6th, 1754, The Streets of Lisbon

Although the enclosed space retained a little of the heat of the day, the late autumn sun having set but an hour before, Dona Teresa of Távora shivered and drew a fine silk fichu around her shoulders. The heavy velvet curtains admitted no draught of evening air, yet the impulse to cover herself was compelling. If only he would sit opposite, as was proper, and not beside her. If only he would not accompany her at all. When Pedro Teixeira had first arrived to escort her to His Majesty, years before, he had made no response to her first haughty instruction to remove himself. Nor did he understand when he was being put in his place, or even what his place ought to be, when addressing a woman of her rank. He merely smiled and explained that his presence, both travelling to and from her rendez-vous with the king, was essential to ensure her safety.

But did he have to sit so close? And beside her? On that first occasion, she had attempted to order him to sit on the bench opposite, but he merely answered that he did not care to travel backwards. Disconcerted by his insolence, she bade him exchange places, to which order he replied with a shake of the head, his bony hand hovering above her shoulder as he took up his seat on the bench beside her. Of course he stopped short of touch, for it is forbidden to lay hand upon the lover of Caesar and, notwithstanding the handsome young husband she had left at home, she now belonged to Caesar, if it were not too fanciful to equate their flabby monarch with the great Roman general who might himself have become king, had he not been so cruelly cut down by his enemies, and his friends.

In the gathering dusk, the carriage had the ambience of a closet or a tomb. Recalling the visit she had endured that morning, she shivered again. The movement drew Teixeira closer, as an iron file drawn to a magnet.

'Are you quite well, my lady?'

By way of answer, she wrapped the silk fichu around her, covering her décolleté cut low in the French style as the king liked, while the valet or whatever he was looked her straight in the eyes.

'Our journey this evening is but a short distance,' he soothed, then, after a pause, 'unlike yesterday.'

Her face burned. How could a man feign respect and leer at the same time? More, why did the king have such a creature as his intimate, no one knew. Teixeira called himself 'secretary' but he seemed to carry out the duties of footman and valet and errand boy and keeper of the king's secrets, especially his not very secret assignations. It was said he was privy to all the most underhand dealings in the royal household, especially those which Dom José wished to keep from his wife. It was said that he was as bad as, possibly even worse than that other upstart, Carvalho e Melo.

Yesterday. An afternoon assignation, therefore unusual from the start.

When the carriage had rattled to a stop on the edge of some out-of-the-way estate, instead of pulling back the curtains, opening the door, jumping down from the carriage and assisting her to descend as was his habit, Teixeira had left the curtains drawn and closed the door behind him. On the next instant, a figure clad in a voluminous black cloak – sinister and strange in the sunlight – climbed in and for a moment stood quite still, surveying her. When she shrank back into the furthest corner, Dom José, for it was he, her lover and king, cast off his cloak, laughing and contrite to have startled her. It did not seem to occur to him that she was truly frightened. In an instant he was beside her, running his finger along the plunging neckline, drawing aside the white muslin kerchief she had tucked in to preserve her modesty, begging her pardon in a coy whisper.

'Did you think Teixeira had sold you to the pirates? He is not such a rascal as all that.' His eyes roved across her face, her body, his full lips moist.

'Where to, Your Majesty?'

Was that Teixeira's voice? Had he taken over the coachman's seat?

'Wherever you wish,' Dom José called, leaning over to fasten the curtain, come undone from its grip upon his dramatic entrance. The scattered rays of the low autumn sun, which for a few moments had spilled through the open door, vanished, the only illumination now a narrow finger that penetrated a vent high in the carriage wall.

Straightway they set off at top speed down the rua de Janelas Verdes, careered along the Avenida Carlos I, rattled over the cobblestones, bounced up and down, up and down, lost pace, slowed before the statue of Camões, regained momentum and picked up speed along the rua da Junqueira Praça da Armada, the horses panting then faltering a little, slowed again and shuddered to a halt whereupon Dom José gasped, 'Drive on!' and the coachman's whip cracked to the rhythm of his groans accompanied by the voices and laughter of Teixeira and the coachman, the carriage resuming velocity over uneven cobblestones, bouncing ever higher, momentum ever more violent as they rattled along the Avenida Brasilia at a fine pace until the Sol Dorado crossroads where the carriage made a sharp turn and sped downhill, horses at the gallop now, the coach shaking from side to side in rhythm with their exertions, bouncing hard, now fast and regular, now slow, slower as they crossed the bridge of Setúbal, faltered, before the carriage once again came to a shuddering halt at the calçada da Boa-Hora, 'Drive on, drive on!' shouted Dom José in fury, the coach eased through the narrow gate of Aurora, sped along the Avenida da India close to the riverbank and the sea, the sounds of screaming gulls echoing their thrusting forward motion towards the rua Sol Aurora, the horses whinnying, carriage rattling, swaying side to side, up and down until the praça da Alegria, where momentum dislodged the carriage curtain which flapped open in the breeze allowing the sun to pour in and the wind to whip up her white kerchief, whirl it around until it flew out the window at the very moment of Dom José's deepest sob, his final groan as he collapsed on to the bench, resting his head upon her exposed breast.

As his breath returned, the voices of the coachman and Teixeira stilled and, with a great effort, Dom José sat up and retrieved his hose from the carriage floor. Having arranged himself, he planted a final, deep kiss on her lips and with a flourish, wrapped his own kerchief around her neck.

'We must ensure that you are properly covered,' he said, his lips still moist.

Where had he got the idea? Was it from some story book, some tale of fevered and lascivious love, some opera or work of the theatre, to ride through the city thus in an enclosed carriage? Perhaps he had it from his father, who was as incontinent as he, more, even. But no, the old king would never have taken such a risk. How did Dom José dare? And why?

Teixeira's eyes were upon her.

'Not like yesterday,' he repeated, his visage in shadow.

Her skin prickled. She should inform Dom José, your valet, your secretary, he looks at me in a way I do not like, but she would not. How would the king respond? Would he believe her? Would he care, even if he did? Not for the first time, she wondered at the warring impulses jostling in her lover's heart: ever commanding secrecy, their assignations so often planned for evenings when the queen was occupied with her retreats or with her friends or making her confession, or when the king was supposedly in conference with his minister. The unmarked carriage, the obscure meeting places, his discretion, coexisting with a contradictory desire to display her, to traverse the city in open carriage, to perform gallantries at the opera in the presence of his wife, to kiss her hand, exchange glances for all to see, to shower her with ostentatious gifts. That white palfrey. It had been a mistake to ride it through the park of Palhavã, her brother Francis had erupted in fury and Luís Bernardo left their bed and moved to another wing of the palace because of it.

That morning at first light, when her body was still aching and aflame from the carriage ride of the day before, Teixeira had appeared at her palace bearing a small parcel wrapped in fine wool. He waited, appearing to expect that she would open it in his presence. Or perhaps hoping she would give him a gold coin for his trouble. Having dismissed him, she ordered the footman to see him out and ran up the sweeping stone staircase, the gift concealed in the folds of her gown, hidden from servants' prying eyes, and slipped into her dressing room. Her own domain, which Luís Bernardo never entered.

It was the silk fichu, the like of which she had never seen. A shawl, really, the fabric of uncommon delicacy. She could spread it wide and cover her shoulders or fold it many times to make a triangle that fitted neatly into her bodice, covering her bosom in vibrant hues, blue and green spirals that drew the eye, jewel colours that perhaps had attracted Teixeira's impudent gaze.

But no. For some time past, so many people now looked at her askance. Not only Queen Mariana Vitória on the rare occasions when their eyes met at the opera or at court, but her family, too. Dona Leonora, the old marchioness. Her brother Francisco. And Luís Bernardo of course. Most disturbing were the glances from women whom she had known since childhood, whom she had thought her friends, the same women who as girls would nudge her and giggle whenever the handsome young Prince José made eyes at her across the room or kissed her hand or asked her to dance, oblivious of the frowns of his own parents. The very girls who would interrogate her on the softness of his skin and the hardness of his member, to which mild obscenities she would answer with a toss of the head and an exclamation of astonishment, *Goodness, I have no idea what you mean, I could not possibly comment on such matters,* with just enough of a sly twinkle to let them know that she knew very well and one day, just perhaps, might reveal all.

When had her intimacy with Dom José ceased to increase her standing but rather, begun to diminish her? At the start of their relations and for some time after, she had felt herself admired, envied as the chosen one, the beautiful young wife of the handsome Luís Bernardo whom she had known all her life and to whom she had been betrothed since both were infants, their birthdays being just a few weeks apart. Perhaps they knew each other too well, perhaps that was why she found him unexciting, dull. If even one of the pregnancies had come to term… but there was nothing to be gained by dwelling on such matters. It was hard enough to know that those same friends, those silly girls whose teasing had embarrassed and delighted her so, who now had husbands and babes, would avoid meeting her eye but greeted her instead with a friendly coolness that pierced her heart.

Had she erred in agreeing to remain in Lisbon after her husband and brother and Dona Leonora had departed for India? Even though she had not recovered from the most recent miscarriage, she could have followed them, she could have insisted. Dom José would not have commanded her to stay. Would he?

She would never know, for she had offered no resistance. Life in Lisbon was so pleasant, free of her mother-in law's critical glare, assignations with Dom José were so exciting, all the more for being illicit, almost everyone treated her, had treated her, with special deference and regard.

Dom José's tone was part solicitude, part rebuke.

'You are pensive!'

His flesh was soft, his skin very pale except where it was red, too often exposed to the sun while out hunting with the queen. If only he would cover himself. The thought must have penetrated his mind, for he gathered a sheet around him, covering his fat thighs. His stomach spilled over the folds. Always playful in humour after his exertions, he tugged at a corner of the blue-green shawl which she had wrapped around herself, the diaphanous fabric a comforting caress on her skin, for the night was dark and a chill breeze had drifted into the bedchamber from the river.

'I hesitate to trouble Your Majesty.'

Dom José released his grip on her shawl.

'Trouble me? If you have a trouble, my dear, you must tell me.'

Would this conversation assuage her misfortunes, or multiply them? All day she had thought of nothing else. But it was too late to retreat.

'I received another visit from Father Malagrida this morning.'

Dom José sat up.

'Malagrida has called on you before?' He leaned across her to retrieve his robe. 'And you did not think to inform me?'

Still shaken by the words and icy denunciations which the old Jesuit had hurled at her that morning – and in her own home! – Dona Teresa held back tears. Had the holy prophet heard of yesterday's carriage ride?

'Majesty, I informed Dom Sebastião of Father Malagrida's visits some time ago. From the very first. He said that I should not trouble you, that he would deal with… the situation.'

Of course. Dom Sebastião had called upon her the day after Father Malagrida's first visit. Why had it not occurred to her before now? The minister must have spies in her household.

'Ah. Yes. Indeed he did. That was some months ago…'

'About a year ago, Majesty. The padre has called on me two or three times since then.'

'Two? Three?'

'Three, Majesty. Or four, I am not sure, I cannot –'

'Three, four, it is no matter,' he soothed. 'With what purpose?'

'To…discourage me, Majesty. From…you…our…'

'What did he say? Tell me his words.'

Why were these tears spilling over now, when she had remained stony and upright and outwardly defiant in the face of Malagrida's most recent onslaught?

He had gained entry to her home early that morning, just after Teixeira had left, on the pretext of bringing a message from her confessor, anticipating that without some pressing motive she might decline to admit him. She was breakfasting alone on the terrace when a footman informed her that Father Malagrida awaited at the door. Clenched by a feeling of dread, for she knew his purpose, her heart pounded. Had he encountered Teixeira on his way to her door?

'Inform Father Malagrida that I am indisposed.'

'My lady, he says to tell you that if you are occupied, he has urgent business to impart concerning your confessor. He says he must speak with you. He brings a message that you will be eager to hear.'

She closed her eyes, felt the morning sun on her shoulders and a tear trickle down her face. This was no mere request. It was a display of might, a demonstration that the conventions of etiquette – the correct hour at which to visit, the correct response if rebuffed, whether one might visit at all, if not invited – did not apply to him. Now that he had insisted, she dared not oppose him further. He was God's representative on the earth whose spiritual guidance her mother-in-law and so many of the great families followed without question. The queen, too, of course.

He would not stop until she had done his bidding.

When she entered the anteroom and he turned to face her, she was surprised to see a conciliatory smile playing about his thin lips. His white mane glowed in the sun, suffused his head with a divine aura. He took a step towards her.

'Dona Teresa, you are aware of the reason for my visit.'

When she made no response, he raised his palms in mock pleading, his bearing more cordial than on his previous visits.

'His Majesty has a wife and four daughters. You have a husband. The example you are setting to the court, to the whole nation, brings the king, the very monarchy, into disrepute. Are you willing to be the cause of –'

He had not even attempted to pursue the fiction of bringing a message from her confessor.

'Father Malagrida, I cannot discuss this matter with you. You must address yourself to His Majesty. Or if he cannot see you, to Dom Sebastião Carvalho e Melo, who will explain to you in detail the king's wishes and desires.'

Was it the mention of the detested minister that unleashed the unbridled fury in the old priest? For there followed an onslaught of vituperation the like of which she had never heard, words she was determined to forget but which surfaced in her mind unbidden. Spawn of Eve, Whore of Babylon, others, all the more terrible for being enunciated in a low hiss murmured through gritted teeth.

Dom José became very still,

'What were his exact words?'

'He insists, Majesty…he says I must put an end to our…relations. He says that I have ensnared you. He says that I am to blame, that my immortal soul…'

The king's pleasant, fleshy features all at once were transformed to an alien mask, a stone visage contorted by a terrible wrath. She shrank back at the sight, her voice fading.

'And?'

Her tongue refused to bring forth the rest, those terrible names but there was more, of course there was, everyone knew of the fiery sermons Father Malagrida preached in the Rossio and on the Cais de Sodré and anywhere a crowd would gather to hear him denounce the sinful ways of the people of Lisbon.

'He says that a terrible punishment will be visited upon me, upon the kingdom, upon us all, that there will be a reckoning…'

'Did he, indeed.' His voice was tense with a coiled anger the like of which she had never seen in him. 'What kind of reckoning? What kind of punishment?'

'He did not say, Majesty. Only that it would be a manifestation of the wrath of God, that my immortal soul –'

But Dom José was not interested in Dona Teresa's immortal soul. He raised a hand to silence her.

Was it time to get dressed?

So Dom Sebastião had not told the king of Malagrida's meddling in his affairs? Or perhaps he had and Dom José really had forgotten. But no. That alien stone mask which for several terrifying moments had transformed his face, now melting back to the familiar fleshy features, was a manifestation of a fury born of new intelligence.

Also, the minister had not said that he would tell the king about Malagrida's visits. Only that he would deal with him.

Dom Sebastião's head and shoulders were hunched forward, as

though to avoid towering over her.

'You must pay no heed to the padre,' he had assured her. 'He is an old man, a foreigner, who has spent too long in the missions. He has lived too long among the savages of Grão Pará and brought back some of their bad manners.' His eyes twinkled. 'I am told that some of them tried to eat him once. But he was a fast swimmer in his youth, apparently. More's the pity.'

She pursed her lips to suppress a smile.

'He insists that I must end –'

'My lady,' Dom Sebastião brought his hands together in prayerful supplication. These were not his words, or not only his words, but came from the lips of the king himself, they expressed what the king would say, were he party to this dialogue.

'Father Malagrida may not insist on anything. He cannot. He is a guest in this country, he and his entire Order. They are all guests of His Majesty. And like any guest who behaves badly....'

His words trailed off as he cast a sympathetic glance upon her. She glared back at him. She would not be comforted by an individual of his rank. How dared he presume?

'My lady, you must be aware that the members of that Order make trouble in so many ways. For example, in his dealings with members of your own family.'

She gasped. The audacity.

'Forgive me, Dona Teresa. I know that Father Malagrida is confessor to your family...'

'To my mother-in-law, Dona Leonora. Not to me.'

'...and that he is held in great esteem by her. And by many of the great families. Also, by the old king and queen.'

'That is why his denunciations of my behaviour...'

'Dona Teresa, please listen. In attacking you thus, in such disgraceful terms, Father Malagrida is foolish, very foolish. He is playing a dangerous game. Your – behaviour – as he so impertinently calls it – could not be conducted without the approval, more, the enthusiastic participation of one who is not bound by convention or law. Of one whose word is the law.' His earnest gaze betrayed not a shred of lechery and once again she had to bite her lip to supress a smile.

'Father Malagrida says that he answers to a higher authority than the king.'

'Yes, I had heard that he was in the habit of making such declarations. But never before from such a reliable source.'

And now, he presumed to compliment her!

'You are quite sure? He used those very words?'

'Those exact words, Minister.'

Dom Sebastião clasped his hands together, took a few paces forward and backwards before turning on his heel to face her. His countenance, now absent of all vestiges of humour, was possessed of a new gravity.

'Dona Teresa, Father Malagrida's attack on you – and yes, I do not hesitate to call it an attack – is the last desperate attempt of an old man who has lost his influence because his patrons are dead.' His meaning was clear. He referred to the old king and queen, devoted followers of the old Jesuit. With the new king on the throne, he no longer held such sway. 'There is only one person who can insist on the ending of your relations,' the minister continued. 'And it is not Father Malagrida. Think on it no more.'

'And if he should return?'

'I would be surprised if he did not, my lady. That old Jesuit is nothing if not persistent. He has judged – wrongly, I know – that of all those who are intimate with His Majesty, you are the most susceptible to threats.'

He touched her elbow, another impertinence. She should object but did not, for the minister's words had alarmed her. If Father Malagrida's attacks on her were implied criticisms of His Majesty, this was no longer a simple matter of the heart, or the family. It was a matter of state. Dom Sebastião had not breathed

5

An Unexpected Guest and a Resolution

November 7th, 1754, Mouraria Palace, Lisbon

Dona Leonora of Távora glided across the floor towards the long, south-facing windows and, without waiting for the footman, opened the shutters herself. Straightaway the room was flooded with light that illuminated hosts of hitherto invisible motes floating on the air, flecks in the brilliant noonday sun which momentarily dazzled her two companions. Both turned away, hands raised to shield their eyes from the glare.

No matter. If there was to be any hope of unravelling the tangle of rumour and innuendo that had ensnarled this family since their return from India, light and clarity would be essential. There must be no equivocation, no deception, neither of the self nor of others. Small wonder that the ambience had the air of a funeral rather than celebration of a homecoming. Gossip concerning this affair would inflict, perhaps already had inflicted, irrevocable damage upon the reputation and influence of one of the oldest families in the realm. It must be stopped, by any means necessary. Fortunately, significant resources were at their disposal: her own judgement; Francisco's insight into the machinations of the court; and – regrettably – the influence of their odious brother-in-law, José Mascarenhas, now Duke of Aveiro.

Who, as usual, was late.

Ah, the duke.

Would there be no justice from this new king? No recognition of loyalty, no recompense for unparalleled service to the Crown? It seemed not. The elevation of Mascarenhas to the rank of duke was a triumph of sycophancy and low manoeuvrings, a sure sign that respect for courage and loyalty, so greatly prized by the old king, Dom João, was a thing of the past, at least where members of the Távora family were concerned. Since their return almost two months before, Francisco had every morning awaited the message from the Riverside Palace to attend the king, that Dom José might bestow upon him the promised dukedom. Every evening, the sun had set on his disappointment.

Today, such distractions must be avoided. The dukedom was a matter of enormous importance for the family, true. But the need to put an end to this scandal was of immediate urgency.

A footman entered to announce the Duke of Aveiro. Dom Francisco and his son Luís Bernardo rose to greet the visitor, who strode into the room and looked about him, his small, sharp eyes flitting around with a regard of frank appraisal that settled upon the person of Luís Bernardo. It was a look that pierced his mother's heart with a dart of sorrow and rage.

As the duke bowed his greeting to the young man, the aspect of her son as he must appear to a stranger rose before her. In that instant, two versions of the young marquis were simultaneously manifest to Dona Leonora's devoted eye: his customary smooth complexion, his bright eye and dark blond hair, burnished with a pleasing reddish tinge, rather like her own had been in youth; and this ruined shell, a foresight of the old man their son would one day become, decades from now, when she and Francisco were long dead, buried with honours in the family crypt, their beloved son now Marquis, perhaps Duke of Távora after all, the two images mingling until the vision faded and all that was left was this wreck, his countenance gaunt, cheeks hollow, dark shadows smudging his eyes.

Oh, if only those harbingers of age and distress had been etched by the burdens of the military duties the young man had fulfilled in India in company with his father, who had accomplished what no Viceroy before him had ever accomplished: the quelling of those vicious native rebellions, the capture of the pirate king and so much more. In those premature, ageing shadows there would at least be honour.

But no. This decline had begun only since their return, the flesh fallen from the young man's bones, his sunken eyes betraying many sleepless nights. How dare those miscreants cause her boy such pain!

But what was the source of that pain? Who was the true culprit?

Having greeted his hosts, the duke eased his lithe frame into the armchair which Dom Francisco had just vacated and tilting a hand towards his lips in the manner of one supping from a glass, nodded to the footman, who in turn glanced at Dona Leonora.

'Tea has just been ordered.' The servant bowed to her and left the room. Not yet noon and Mascarenhas, who seemed to think he had the run of her house, was demanding port wine, like the English. They would all need clear heads for the conversation that must follow. But the consultation could not begin in earnest until their final guest had arrived.

'An awkward climb for the horses.' Mascarenhas was no doubt irritated that his demand for port wine had been thwarted. 'We had to leave them by the Praça do Graça. I don't know why you've chosen this hellhole to meet.'

Of course he did know, and very well. The little Mouraria Palace had the peerless advantage of discretion. Tucked amongst these winding streets and alleys, its situation allowed occupants and visitors to enter and leave without the fanfare of a carriage and four careering up a driveway. In truth, there was no reason why the Marquis and Marchioness of Távora should not meet with José Mascarenhas – the Duke of Aveiro was their brother-in-law, after all, and might be expected to commune with relatives recently returned from a four-year absence. But the coldness between their two families was widely known. Added to this, the lukewarm reception from Dom José, the absence of any official welcoming reception on their return, the conspicuous evasions during the few audiences His Majesty had granted when the subject of the promised dukedom had been raised, above all, this scandalous intelligence which Mascarenhas had reported with unseeming relish, together conspired to create an unaccustomed sense of unease. In such circumstances, an excess of caution seemed prudent.

'Hardly a hellhole,' she retorted. 'You should have known better than to attempt to bring a carriage all the way to this door.' And, injecting a note of condescension into her voice calculated to infuriate, she added: 'A short climb from the Rossio is surely a small price to savour the delights of this historic quarter.'

The charms of this *bairro* were lost on the Duke of Aveiro, whose tastes ran to opulence and ostentation, ever indifferent to the colourful, chaotic patchwork of roofs and spires that fell steeply to the Rossio far below, then rose again to the Bairro Alto and beyond, to the silver gleam of the Tagus winding its mighty way to the sea, affording a spectacular vista from the very centre of the city.

'I suppose the fewer people who know we are assembling, the better,' he conceded.

So this was not a secret meeting, quite. But nor would it be announced. Those who were acquainted with the ebb and flow of relations between members of the high aristocracy – and it seemed that the Minister for War and Foreign Affairs was troublingly well-informed – must know of their long-standing property dispute with Mascarenhas and would wonder at a new rapprochement that had seen the two families confer several times during the last month. Though were it not for the scandal, on which Mascarenhas seemed to be excellently informed, it would be preferable not to see him at all.

But there could surely be no truth in such vicious gossip. At most, exaggeration, misunderstanding, wilful slander put about by enemies at court. That was the way of the world. It had ever been the lot of a young, charming, above all, beautiful woman to attract attention, then envy and, all too often without cause, opprobrium and calumny. A woman had to be careful in all matters, a lovely woman doubly so. Unfortunately, Luís Bernardo's alluring wife had never been renowned for discretion. Since a girl, she had always been troublesome in her conduct, which had not improved since her marriage. Rather the contrary, for she had not only failed to give Luís Bernardo an heir but had given him no child at all.

And why had Dona Teresa chosen to remain in Lisbon for the entire duration of their mission in India, even after her state of health had improved? Recovery from a series of miscarriages took time, this was true – Dona Leonora herself had endured six. But might other considerations have dissuaded her daughter-in-law from joining Luís Bernardo and the rest of her family in India, from fulfilling her duties as wife to Luís Bernardo, as the future Marchioness of Távora?

The gossip recounted by Mascarenhas was intolerable.

In a carriage?

'Will the young marchioness be joining us?' The duke knew very well that she detested hearing her daughter-in-law referred to thus.

Luís Bernardo flushed and looked away. 'Dona Teresa is receiving a blessing from Father Malagrida this morning. She will join us later.'

Dom Francisco looked from his son to his wife and again to his son, half-rose from his chair, sank back in it, his fine, square jaw clenched.

'A blessing from Malagrida?' He rose again and approached his son, who was perched on the edge of a chaise longue. 'Luís Bernardo. You say *your wife*,' he almost spat out the words, though he could as easily have said *my sister*, 'is receiving a blessing from her confessor? This very morning?' The young man raised his head and looked his father in the eye.

'He is not her confessor, he –'

'Fransciso.'

The marquis shook his wife's hand from his shoulder. 'Do you take us for fools?'

Luís Bernardo made no answer. For a long moment, the silence brimmed with a growing awareness that could no longer be denied.

In a carriage.

It could not be true. Rumour, gossip, the smallest detail, the slightest misunderstanding, had a way of infiltrating minds and tainting judgement, as the smallest drop of ink colours an entire pitcher of water. Mascarenhas was a vicious manipulator, a liar who could not bear to hear of Dom Francisco's successes and glories as Viceroy. He had determined to sully the joys of their homecoming with these scurrilous accusations.

'She will join us when Father Malagrida has bestowed his blessing,' the young marquis repeated, 'and conducted the spiritual exercises he has prepared for her,' he continued, refusing to meet his mother's imploring gaze that he be silent, that he not compound his humiliation.

The duke snorted. 'So that's what they're calling it these days.'

This was intolerable. An attack on Dona Teresa, however justified (but it could not be!), was an attack on Luís Bernardo, on Dom Francisco, on the great house of Távora. It must not be countenanced. Even though the troublesome woman was her son's wife and her husband's sister, there could be no truth in such insinuations, no more than inventions of the spiteful minds of the court.

As though responding to her thoughts, the duke moved in for the kill.

'And is Father Malagrida attending the young marchioness at your own palace even as we speak?' He addressed his remark not to Luís Bernardo, but to the young man's father. Dom Francisco turned pale, as he did when overcome with an anger he was struggling to suppress. 'Or was perchance a carriage sent for her?'

Luís Bernardo was rescued by the entrance of two footmen bearing trays loaded with cups of tea made in the English fashion, the leaves brought from India by Dona Leonora herself. In the presence of the servants all discussion ceased, lest any be in the pay of the minister, who seemed to know everything. He must not hear of this reunion for, once Dom Sebastião José Carvalho e Melo learned of it, his master the king would too, and they would all have questions to answer.

Formalities completed, footmen withdrawn, Mascarenhas placed his teacup on the marble mantle and spread his hands, directing a glance of enquiry towards the young marquis.

'Well?'

As Luís Bernardo made no answer, the duke turned to Dom Francisco. 'I assume that Luís Bernardo is unaware of the full guest list for this assembly.'

The young marquis frowned but made no response, leaving a silence heavy with insinuation until the duke visibly lost patience. 'Come now, Luís Bernardo,' he said testily, 'you must be frank with us.'

The young man bowed his head, oh do not weep, my son, not tears, not even a glitter of them in the eye, not in the presence of this gloating ruffian. But Mascarenhas was relentless.

'For is this not the reason we are gathered here today?'

Luís Bernardo leaned towards the little table at his elbow, grasped a porcelain cup which he raised to his lips. His tea must be cold, would that she had ordered port wine after all but his eyes were dry and his voice, when at last he spoke, was steady, his countenance resigned, a model of quiet dignity.

'She left before breakfast. And yes, in a carriage. Unmarked,' he added, his fair skin flushed with shame that he, Dom Luís Bernardo de Távora, heir to the great Távora title, husband of the beautiful Dona Teresa de Távora, son of Dom Francisco and Dona Leonora, the most illustrious family in the nation excepting the royal family and possibly even greater than they, was reduced to skulking in corridors and peeping from behind curtains to spy on his wife.

The duke was merciless. 'And was she accompanied in this unmarked carriage?'

The young man's voice was barely audible. 'An unliveried escort assisted her into the carriage. I believe it was Teixeira.'

Which pronouncement was received with varying response from the three listeners. Dom Francisco remained very still, his eyes fastened on the pinched countenance of his son, who continued to contemplate the teacup cradled in his hand. Mascarenhas sighed deeply, clasped his hands behind his back. The marchioness clutched her husband's arm. For Francisco, this affair was a double sorrow, Teresa being not only their son's wife, but his own sister. A double insult, therefore – no, triple, for the affair degraded her name too. A multiple offence. The honour of the entire family was compromised, perhaps irrevocably.

'Teixeira.' The duke's flat pronouncement did little to conceal his triumph. 'I think that settles the matter. Does it not?'

It did. His intelligence had been correct. In every detail.

But did he have to take such pleasure in his pronouncements? Must he torment Luís Bernardo so? All present knew, for it was common knowledge, that Pedro Teixeira was no ordinary servant but rather an unofficial secretary who managed those of Dom José's activities that demanded the greatest discretion, assignations of which neither the official secretary nor the queen was aware. That such a low-born, disreputable wretch should escort the young marchioness in an unmarked carriage known to belong to the royal stables was intolerable, as intolerable as the taste of this new king for the confidence and counsel of adventurers of little or no standing. Scoundrels such as Teixeira and that upstart Carvalho e Melo who, it seemed, now enjoyed Dom José's exclusive confidence. It was hard to know which was worse – the Minister for War's veneer of exaggerated respect, which failed to conceal his contempt for their caste, or the frank impudence with which Teixeira, emboldened by his intimacy with the king, addressed his betters.

So those accounts of assignations, or one assignation at least, in a carriage that drove through the streets of Lisbon in full daylight, were all true.

Was this how such loyal service should be repaid? That Dom José, as prince, now king of the realm, should take as lover the wife of the most illustrious young noble in the realm, and the sister of the bearer of the ancient title of Távora?

That this new king had no respect for their family and indeed, the most open hostility, could no longer be denied.

Dom Francisco arose from his seat and paced about the room. 'Now that we know,' his breath had become shallow, as it often did when he was overcome by emotion. 'Now that the matter is certain, we must decide what course of action to take.' He came to a halt in front of his wife and sat down beside her.

'For action must be taken.'

'Action will be taken.' She clasped his hand. 'But we must tread carefully. We must consult with our confessor first, for the king –'

'Nonsense!' Since his elevation to duke, Mascarenhas had fancied himself head of the family. 'The principal decision, the only question, is how to ensure that our families secure the greatest benefit possible from the king's…regard…for the young marchioness.'

'Our sister…' Dona Leonora refused to look him '…my son's

wife, is not for sale. Nor is the honour of this family.'

The duke grimaced. 'Yet mine is a reasonable question.' He sighed, as though despairing of making the blockheads who were his relatives see sense. 'This is a situation best regarded with equanimity or resignation, not resistance.'

The worst of it was, from a pragmatic standpoint, he was right. Other families in other countries conducted their affairs thus. But not those bearing the great Távora name.

'If the honour of your own wife were in question...' All present turned to regard Luís Bernardo, who had said not a word since Mascarenhas had forced out of him the humiliating intelligence of Dona Teresa's most recent assignation. '...you might not view the trade with such equanimity. Or resignation.'

Mascarenhas took a step towards Luís Bernardo, his face contorted with rage. Dona Leonor rose quickly and stood beside her son, who had settled himself in a deep chair, unconcerned and oblivious of the effect his words had produced in the duke. A violent reaction. An interesting response. Had Luís Bernardo hit a sore point? This was not the time to reflect on marital discord in the house of Mascarenhas but if Dom José's indulgence had extended beyond dalliance with the young marchioness, such knowledge could be useful in future negotiations with the king. His own father, old King João, had left behind a flock of bastards. The three he had recognised, the Palhavã princes, were all out of mothers of no real consequence: nuns, the wife of a low-ranking *fidalgo*, the best of them an abbess. He had stopped short of tupping the wives of his highest nobles, not because such indulgence was prohibited – to the monarch, all was permitted – but because it was bad statecraft.

Once again, the duke, whose rage had subsided, was following her train of thought.

'A king with four daughters and no male heir would be unwise to exercise his royal prerogative with such incontinence.' He laughed.

Did he speak in earnest or in jest? In either case, he spoke true, for even the staunchest allies of the monarch could, if circumstances warranted, become his enemies. Perhaps Dom José had overlooked this. Perhaps he did not care, believing himself invulnerable.

Was Mascarenhas the buffoon he appeared to be? Or was his presence here, his interest in their family crisis, calculated to pursue some advantage of his own?

A single rap at the door interrupted the uneasy discussion. A footman entered.

'Father Malagrida.'

The arrival of a newcomer, clad in a sombre cassock adorned with the cross of the Society of Jesus, was received by those present according to their deepest desires and fears. The colour drained from Luís Bernardo's countenance. Dona Leonora, making a deep curtsey, reached for the bony hand the padre extended and kissed it. Thus she remained until, obedient to a murmur from him, she arose, her head lowered in an attitude of reverence. Dom Francisco stood beside her, head bowed in respect but otherwise maintaining the upright, military bearing that befitted a marquis of the realm.

Only Mascarenhas showed no sign of awe, though he did make a bow, not very low, as one disposed to show respect but with no intention of making obeisance. Not that he had any objection to the wily old fellow, in fact, he admired him, he knew how to worm his way into the confidence of everyone who counted. Including old Dom João and his queen, too, both ridiculously devoted to him, their final journeys apparently eased by the presence of their trusted confessor. The ladies, including Queen Mariana Vitória, were especially devout.

And here was the fearsome Leonora de Távora, doe-eyed, awaiting the old chap's blessing or words of wisdom or perhaps another tale of his exploits in Brazil. There was the time he was determined to convert a tribe of natives who chased him to the banks of a crocodile-infested river, which he swam for his life. Under the protection of the Virgin and the Almighty Himself, of course. Soldiers made up yarns all the time, but this cunning old priest was the best he had heard, those bright pins of eyes gazing off into the distance as though communing with higher beings, communicating the string of prophecies he pronounced. Quite a few of them came true. But as they were mostly about the deaths of people who already had one foot in the grave, he was bound to get some right. Clever. Oh, there were many ways to stamp your authority on a gathering! What better than to convince people you were in direct communion with the Almighty Himself? And so many of his disciples seemed to believe it: the last king and his wife and the present king's wife and his own wife and the old marchioness and the devil alone knew who else. As a military man, he could admire the physical bravery and endurance, the fire and determination burning in those eyes. But all this hocus-pocus gave him a headache.

Was the old chap waiting for him to kneel?

'Your Grace...' he began.

'Father will suffice. I am not a bishop, but a simple servant of God.'

'Father Malagrida,' the duke said. 'Welcome. We thought you were occupied –' A glare from the marchioness exhorted him to adjust his next pronouncement. 'With early Mass.'

'It is past noon, my lord. Early Mass is long over!'

'Will you give us your blessing, Father Malagrida? Before we turn to discuss...'

Were those tears glittering in the eyes of the haughty marchioness? And had the padre just laid his hands upon her head?

'Let us pray.'

So there was nothing for it but to kneel after all, while the padre intoned a decade of the rosary which he rounded off with a rambling blessing that invoked the power of prayer, of submission to the Almighty and his messengers here on earth, and finished by railing against the weakness and decadence into which the court and society and the whole of Lisbon had fallen and which would surely be punished with the wrath of God.

Fortunately, all the footmen had withdrawn before the padre had begun to speak, for these words of blessing were best not uttered abroad. They were the words of a politician, one whose tools were the workings of the spirit and the mind. But a politician nonetheless. Like all the Jesuits, they made good allies but bad masters, very bad indeed, too many of them ended up employing their cunning to direct the monarchs they had pledged to serve. Look what they were up to in Brazil and New Spain, replacing the authority of the Crown – in fact, two Crowns, for the Spanish were having the same trouble with them – building cities, training the natives in the arts of war, claiming territory. If they got half a chance they'd overrun the whole continent. Father Malagrida, I have my eye on you.

'How could this have happened?' The marchioness had moved on from her prayers to more pressing matters. It was not so difficult to understand. Yet the old priest devoted another interminable speech to the regrettable influence of the young woman, the weakness of His Majesty in yielding to temptation, the decadence of Dom José's life since a young man, his only devotion to the opera and to hunting and general dedication to the pursuits of pleasure. The current plight of the Távora family being an inevitable outcome of such decadence, which found its source in the behaviour of the father of the nation. His Majesty, Dom José.

Dom Francisco listened to this speech with increasing agitation and more than once attempted to interrupt.

'We are not here to criticise the king, Father,' he insisted, when at last the old fellow stopped for breath, 'only to determine how to recover the good name of my sister and our family.'

'And the return of my wife to our marital bed.'

All present turned towards Luís Bernardo. The marchioness

gasped.

'Why did you not tell us this, Luís Bernardo? It would have...'

She did not continue. She did not need to. Such intelligence would have all but settled the question of the young woman's conduct. For it was scarcely credible that a wife, after such a long absence, would deny her husband. But perhaps she had motive?

'Padre Malagrida, is this a matter in which you might assist us? As you are a confessor of the queen herself? Surely she may exert influence upon her husband, who might in turn ...'

The old cleric remained silent. When he spoke, his words were barely audible. 'I regret, my lady, that the queen's influence regarding her husband's indiscretions is null. She says – and I am not breaking the seal of confession in divulging this to you – that it is the one topic that provokes his anger. She has tried to discourage his dalliance with the young marchioness.' He bowed towards Luís Bernardo. 'And his other mistresses. But to no avail.'

Dom Francisco and his son gazed at the cleric, frozen in shock. That Dona Teresa should be but one of many lovers of the king, albeit his current favourite, but yet a plaything, the cost to their peace of mind and the family honour so carelessly used... It was not to be borne.

'Might the Minister of War be approached?' Luís Bernardo suggested. 'His word has great influence –'

'Never!' Not for the first time, Dona Leonora wondered at her son's poor judgement. 'That man is of no standing. No member of the Távora family will petition him. On any matter.'

'But if the end result–'

Malagrida raised his hand.

'I fear that the marchioness is right, albeit for the wrong reasons. There is nothing to be gained by approaching Dom Sebastião José Carvalho e Melo on this matter. Whatever his private opinion of His Majesty's conduct, he will not risk incurring the wrath of the king, who is the source of his position and power, by opposing him in this matter.'

Dona Leonora turned to the priest. 'Padre Malagrida, you are aware that my daughter-in-law is not…fecund.'

The young marchioness was no longer so very young. Thirty-one years old, and several years of marriage – and presumably, years of relations with King José – had produced no issue. Perhaps that was an attractive quality to the king – there would be no bastard son to distress the queen.

'Given the circumstances – betrothed to my son from infancy yet not blessed with children, having refused to accompany her husband, my son, to fulfil her wifely duties in the colonies; and above all, her conduct of sinful relations with His Majesty'…that the sin was the young woman's and not the monarch's, she was careful to imply… 'in justice, the only valid course of action is for this marriage to be declared null, and struck out.'

'Annulment.' For the first time, the voice of elderly cleric wavered. 'The quest for a Catholic annulment is a difficult process. Most difficult. The English king was unsuccessful. His attempts resulted in the fracturing of the Catholic Church and the establishment of a heretical sect.'

'Henry's first wife – his legitimate wife – was the daughter of Ferdinand and Isabella, the *reyes católicos*,' Dona Leonora insisted. 'How could he have deluded himself that such a woman, with such a heritage, would bend to his will and permit that she be put aside?'

Of course, this was not the whole, simple truth, for the lady herself had desired that her first marriage, to Henry's deceased brother, be declared null. Most important, there had been strong evidence that that early union had never been consummated. Whereas Dona Teresa's several miscarriages proved the opposite.

'In any case, Dona Teresa is no Catherine of Aragon,' Dona Leonora continued. 'She is a silly woman whose head has been turned by the attentions of a prince, now a king, a marchioness-in-waiting who failed to protect her own virtue and her family honour as she should. As any good and wise woman would.'

'Very true, sister,' the duke put in. 'None of this would have occurred had not the lady been willing.'

Contrary to her own words, Dona Leonora knew this to be untrue. Many such adventures were pursued when the lady was unwilling. In this regard, she was not without sympathy for her daughter-in-law. Once a beauty herself, she well remembered the care which a woman, above all, one who excited men's appetites as Dona Teresa did, must employ in rejecting the attentions of a suitor. A straightforward refusal might be ineffective and indeed, could provoke unpleasant consequences. The higher the rank of the would-be seducer, the greater caution the object of his attention must employ; for true resistance – as opposed to the feigned reluctance so often part of the chase – had a way of transforming the most passionate declarations of love to vicious retaliation.

From an early age, clever women, wise women, had to learn secret ways, some called them wiles – a tone of voice, sweet words, sighs, eyes turned away in sorrow for what might have been, were it not for…ill health, a dying relative, an infectious disease (but this only if the lady were married, for if that got about she would never find a husband) – to indicate her deep yearning to yield, to succumb to the attentions of her illicit suitor, her frustration, no, her deep sorrow that their love could never be consummated, always noting that a husband, even one who was beloved, was not sufficient reason for refusal. So that eventually – and it could take many weeks or months for the suitor to understand that this was not an exaggerated extension of a courting ritual, where the lady was desirous that the pursuer should persist, but on the contrary, really did expect him to withdraw – if she were skilful enough, the gentleman would retire with grace, convinced that relinquishing the pursuit was his own wish, that the lady was after all not worth the trouble.

And the lady could expel a sigh of relief as she bade him a wistful goodbye.

Had Dona Teresa ever learned such strategies? Almost certainly not. The woman was too innocent or too vain, perhaps she enjoyed such attentions too much to discourage them. At best, her indiscretion indicated a failure of education, at worst, bad character. Whatever the reason, it made no difference, the situation had gone too far. All that mattered now was that this union had cast a blight on the Távora name, exposed the entire family to ridicule, inflicted anguish on Luís Bernardo.

The marriage was dead in all but name. Whatever the obstacles, all that remained was a decent, formal, unequivocal burial. If the others could not or would not fight for this marriage to be annulled, then she, Dona Leonora de Távora, would do so, even if it meant incurring the wrath of Dom José himself.

Part 2

1755

6

Living the Shock

November 1st, 1755, City of Lisbon and Environs

Rossio Square, Lisbon

Fire first finds Dom Francisco of Assis, Marquis of Távora, when he leaves the Palace of the Inquisition on Rossio Square, where he had intended to secure an audience with Dom José, the Grand Inquisitor himself. He hopes that support from Dom José, the king's half-brother, might persuade His Majesty to fulfil that sacred promise made long ago: to elevate the present Marquis of Távora to the rank of duke.

Marquis. Duke. To the flames, smouldering slyly within the ruins of the Hospital of All Saints, it makes no difference, the hospital ovens being all fired up and filled with bread baking for the patients' midday meal, the fire thereby lighted and ready to do its work. Years before, a magnificent conflagration had devoured much of the Hospital, this new construction a manifestation of the foolish vanity of men that endeavours to pit human will against the elements.

No, Dom Francisco. The Grand Inquisitor is not here this morning, he is at home in his palace in Palhavã. As the marquis starts to protest, put this insolent fellow in his place, a convulsion of the marble floor knocks him off his feet. For a moment, or is it an hour, the world is black and still but the silence does not last. Are those shrieks from the throats of humans or animals? Or from his own? His fingers brush the cold hand of the cleric who kept him waiting in an anteroom for a full quarter-hour, he is sprawled alongside him, head crushed by a fallen statue. On all sides black, towering shadows loom, debris is scattered around, there is no possible egress yet he stretches one hand, it finds a space through which an arm, both arms can labour, head and torso, his legs are uninjured, on all fours he can push, lever his body through a narrow opening in the rubble, coughing, eyes stinging. In the open air all is darkness, the weak winter sun is blotted out by a foul-smelling dust that renders the day black as night. Perhaps it really is night, perhaps he lost consciousness and woke in the small hours. He struggles to his feet and almost at once, the great entrance archway behind him groans and crashes to the ground. A second tremor.

There must be shelter, some corner or cellar, no, a place in the open air, the very centre of the square, perhaps, where tumbling debris may not reach. But now, through the swirling darkness, the skeleton of the Palace of the Holy Office of the Inquisition, this place which has passed judgement upon the final days of so many heretics, is lit up in glimmering spangles of yellow and orange. That vicious north-east wind fans the flames born in the kitchens of All Saints, chases them along wooden beams and balustrades, across the great staircase within. Soon, little tongues leap the great distance across the square to dance along the heavy oak panelling in the entrance hall to the Palace of the Inquisition, singe the tapestries, ignite the pews in the oratory, nibble on the thousand books and manuscripts in the library, a domesticated beast relishing sudden freedom, its power not yet wholly unleashed but soon, soon. Fire is no stranger to these parts, this is the home of fire, these are its people.

Dom Francisco, Marquis, not yet Duke, of Távora, has seen battlefields in flames, of course he has. But he has never before known fire to leap such distance unaided by human hand, this single spark that soars from the smouldering beams of the Hospital of All Saints to alight on the wheel of a cart on the western side of Rossio Square. As the flames creep towards him, from east and west, from north and south, his fears are not for himself, or not only for himself, but for Leonora and the children, for his young sister Teresa, for his whole family, fear for what will become of them all.

Távora Palace, Belém

Dom Francisco's young sister, Dona Teresa de Távora, trembling in her boudoir on the first floor of the Távora summer palace in Belém, although in no immediate danger, is in a state of terror.

As the walls of the chamber begin to sway, she straightway understands that the world is ending, that the Apocalypse is come, that the hastening of the world towards the End of Days is her doing, the inexorable consequence of her great sin. She has long expected this moment. Oh, she alone is not culpable. But her actions, and her failure to put an end to her scandalous behaviour, to obey the exhortation of the prophet, the holy man who foretold this disaster, has brought forth this roar of rage from the Almighty. The convulsions of the earth shaking the foundations of her home, the great Távora house, are all her doing. It was prophesied. She could have prevented it, and now it is too late.

It begins with a fallen mirror. As this is a feast day, she rises late and spends a quarter-hour before her glass in contemplation of her countenance, seated on the sweet little gilt chair that matches exactly the gilt dresser that Luís Bernardo ordered from France when they were first married. Hers is a rare beauty, the lustre of her creamy skin, wide eyes and rosebud mouth as yet untainted by the passage of time. People often remark that she resembles her brother around the eyes, though Francisco is much older, of course. And Luís Bernardo being her brother's son, it is not surprising that as husband and wife – also nephew and aunt – the family resemblance between them makes for a most handsome couple.

But recently, since her thirtieth birthday a few months before, faint lines have appeared around her eyes and mouth, most visible whenever she is afflicted by the melancholy that comes upon her from time to time since the most recent miscarriage. A light pressure upon both temples, and the lines vanish, only to reappear when the touch is released, restoring the inexorable marks of time that will, sooner or later, strip her of this loveliness and the many privileges it confers. The image of her mother-in law flashes before her mind's eye and she shivers. Is not Dona Leonora's ageing, ruined beauty a portent of her own future? Small wonder that the old Marchioness of Távora could not endure being in the same room as her, Dona Teresa's famous beauty no doubt a constant reminder of the loss of her own youth.

Although Dona Leonora had agreed to the match between her precious firstborn and her husband's young sister long ago, when they were infants, she had never hidden her dislike for her son's betrothed, which became ever more intense as Dona Teresa grew into womanhood. But the marriage took place all the same. Luís Bernardo was handsome and kind, they had known each other their whole lives. Perhaps they had known each other too long. Yet despite everything – the scandal, the ill-will of her mother-in-law – they were still together.

First, the looking glass falls to the floor. She jumps up from her little gilt chair in fright, gapes at the swaying walls, the tilting floor. A Chinese vase crashes to the ground. Without thinking, she reaches into the silver casket she keeps in a secret compartment of the dresser. Nestling within is a bundle of letters which she gathers up and clutches to her breast, as a talisman perhaps, while murmuring an Act of Contrition. She reads these missives often, too often. With a sob, she falls to her knees and joins her hands in prayer, as though Father Malagrida's words, brimming with accusations, might confer belated absolution for her great sin and allow her to save herself, prevent the walls from crumbling, right all wrongs.

At that moment, their wedding portrait falls from the dresser. Another gift from Luís Bernardo. It lies on the floor, face down, the frame shattered. Another omen. Can she ring for a footman to gather up the pieces of her cracked mirror and retrieve the broken portrait while the floor is tilting and the window frame has moved off square and that rumble and crashing of falling stone could be one of the chimneys tumbling to the ground? A downstairs footman appears in the doorway, breathless, covered with dust. Dona Leonora is in the garden with the young marquis and the rest of the household, excepting only Dom Francisco, who is in the city on business. She will require assistance to descend the staircase, for it is unsteady. They must make haste.

She struggles to her feet, the letters burning her hand as though she had just thrust it in a fire. The footman must wait outside. She crams the little bundle of papers into the silver casket, which slides easily into the secret compartment. There is no knowing if these letters from the holy man can protect her from the wrath of God, but they will not save her from her mother-in-law's fury. That much is certain.

Rua Formosa, near the Bairro Alto, Lisbon

By a half-hour after ten o'clock, the ubiquitous eye might observe Dona Eleonor gazing across the land and sea from her perch in the attic, while the bones of the city emerge through a faint glimmer of sunlight. She covers her face with a handkerchief and tries not to breathe, for the grimy particles of dust, though lighter now, swirl in the air still. But no flimsy cloth can suppress the foul odour the earth has disgorged through every open fissure.

Was her husband's counsel wise? Would they not be safer at ground level, or even outdoors, in the garden, than on the first floor as he had commanded? The attic window affords her a view of every point of the compass: the river and the sea, the city entire, the fields beyond.

Those rippling movements on the coast road, do they presage new tremors? And if so, how will Sebastião make his way to Belém, to the king's summer palace, and how will he make his return, if he is obliged to traverse such shifting, swaying ground?

No. This is no motion of the earth.

People. Hundreds, perhaps thousands, a snaking procession of survivors far below, fleeing the city, their progress a sinuous movement brimming with intent. But will their journey deliver them from danger, or cast them into even greater peril?

Leaning out of the window, she scans the river road for a lone horseman galloping alongside the throngs making their way on foot towards Belém. He must have taken another route, inland, through Alcântara, perhaps. She steps down from her perch and as she reaches up to close the window and casts a final glance southwards, where the sandbar separates the river from the sea beyond, her throat constricts in a silent scream, the sight before her more horrifying than anything she or her husband or the thousands of afflicted souls in this wretched city have yet seen on this day, or ever will see in the whole of their lives.

Mouraria Hill, Lisbon

Seated at a table outside a café not far from his lodgings behind Rossio Square, Mr Edmund Stanton is enjoying a morning free of his duties as Second Secretary to the British Embassy, when the tea in his cup begins to ripple. He frowns, but nothing can dampen his mood on this fine autumn day as he basks in the blue sky and mild ambience that make Lisbon one of the most pleasant of cities, where a young man might linger outdoors and watch the locals, rich and poor alike, spruced up in their best clothes as they stroll to one of the hundreds of churches and convents with which the city is blessed.

These religious festivals, of which the people of Lisbon are so fond, provide occasional respite from the working week for the British community of merchants known as the British Factory, and young diplomatic officials alike, especially those from the Protestant countries. On the most important feast days, high-ranking diplomats endeavour to leave the city for fear of risking forcible baptism in the street by their zealous hosts. This is not an idle fancy: one friend from the British Factory who decided to take a stroll around the Terreiro do Paço last Good Friday, soon found himself surrounded by a noisy procession of devout penitents. On hearing him speak English, they pressed him to submit to a baptism that would relieve him of the twin burdens of heresy and eternal damnation. He escaped their well-meant, but terrifying, ministrations only by a whisker.

Such are the final amused reflections to cross Mr Stanton's mind on this day, indeed the last carefree thoughts of his life, when begins a trembling of the earth, and on its decrease, a rumbling motion like the waves of the sea, so violent he can scarce remain in his chair. Turning his head round towards the castle on the high hill behind him, he perceives something tumble, the castle wall, perhaps, and the houses around him opening from top to bottom.

Immediately he feels himself falling and afterwards, but he cannot tell how soon, is sensible of a difficulty in breathing. He finds himself lodged between two walls not three feet asunder. He gets his body out of the rubble, which he climbs until it gives way and he slips. Finding himself under an arch, which he squeezes through, he tumbles down some steps that lead to a narrow street, it might be rua de São Mamede which leads down from the castle to the Rossio. He attempts to traverse it either up or down but cannot for the path is blocked either way, that observation being his last coherent thought before losing consciousness.

When he comes to, he finds himself propped up against a wall, eyes stinging, almost suffocating with the dust, bruised all over, the flesh scraped off part of his forehead and a large cut under his chin and a wound of some kind in his right leg. But he manages to struggle to his feet and stumble through the rubble, skirting an abyss in the ground at least fifteen feet wide. There are bodies of people, men and women and children in the street, some not yet dead. His senses are assailed by the noise of groans and cries, the swirling black dust, the incantations of priests intoning rosaries or trying to carry the wounded and the dead.

Having stumbled through a narrow street piled high with blocks of stone, he perceives his own habitation, of which only the upper storey has been demolished by the ceiling falling in. He next enters a wide square where the cathedral is burning. The streets leading from the square are thronged with people reaching up to receive bundles thrown from high windows. A little way down the same street, which is on fire on both sides, people are sitting on the bundles they have just retrieved from their ruined homes, apparently insensible of the dangers of the approaching flames.

Dazed, he sinks to the ground but is fortunately retrieved by a group of Frenchmen, acquaintances of his friend M Martin from the French Embassy, who assist him part of the way towards the Terreiro do Paço where they implore him to join them in making for the quayside in the hope of procuring a boat across the river. There is no time to lose, for in the lower part of the city the flames are gathering strength. But having a lifelong aversion to water and in any case no coin upon him with which to purchase passage, he resolves instead to make his way back towards the Rossio in the hope of finding a route by which he might ascend the castle hill towards the Alfama or Mouraria districts, for word is that the high ground has been less afflicted than these low-lying streets of the centre.

So it is that Mr Stanton, having dragged his injured body half-way up the winding streets of the Alfama towards the castle, by a quarter after ten o'clock has reached the edge of Mouraria hill on the eastern side of the city, where he stops to rest and gaze out over the city at almost the same moment as

Dona Eleonor looks out from her attic window on the rua Formosa to the west.

His heart freezes at the sight.

The riverbed is empty. Emptied, that is, of water. As far as the eye can see, the tides of the Tagus have retreated, withdrawn, rolled away as though a massive carpet has been dragged off, leaving the vast plain of the riverbed obscenely exposed. But the floor of the river is not empty, far from it, for the mud plain the waters have left behind is littered with wrecks: boats lost in recent times, ancient sailing ships which must have disappeared beneath the waves hundreds of years before, myriad items of debris impossible to identify from this distance.

And beyond the sandbar, something he does not at first understand: a huge, greenish tinge rising against the sky which is still grey from that foul dust, now tainted by a massive shadow that looms over the horizon, drawn back, balanced, impossible to know how high, but the figures on the bank, the miniatures of the lost boats marooned on the river bed suggest thirty feet, forty, more. The vast curtain draws back, sways, poised to sweep forward.

An immense wall of water sucked up from the riverbed has gathered all the waves of the sea beyond into a vast maw from whose open jaws thousands, millions of tons of water are expelled, rushing at the shore where hundreds of tiny figures have taken refuge on the quayside. It pursues a few horsemen who have understood what is coming their way and refuse to submit, galloping, urging their horses along the western bank of the river. Mr Stanton, too, sees that this gigantic beast, the yawning, gaping mouth, is about to sweep all before it, the riverbank, the city entire, while anyone, anywhere who is hopeful of finding safe passage must endure, paralysed and helpless, as the mountain of water delivers their fate.

Royal Summer Palace, Belém

Queen Mariana Vitória, in company with her family and most of the servants, is in the garden, shivering in her nightclothes, her teeth chattering from the shock of her narrow escape when one of the internal walls of the palace collapsed. There is yet no telling how extensive the damage to the whole structure is, but they are all present and uninjured, thank God, the household entire. Two of the servants who were dressed and carrying out their duties before dawn have ventured indoors to gather coverlets and cloaks. The valet Teixeira is pointing to the stables. He appears to be exhorting her husband to seek shelter in the carriages. A useful proposition, even if the man himself is detestable.

José is not listening. He turns a dazed, uncomprehending regard upon an approaching footman who bears a cloak in one hand and holds aloft in the other a decorative umbrella gifted to old King João many years ago by a long-dead British ambassador. He is looking at the cloak and the umbrella in puzzlement, as though surveying complicated machinery designed for some strange purpose that escapes him.

Mariana Vitória moves to approach him but a pitiful wailing erupts from one of the girls. Her daughters are frightened, of course they are, trembling and weeping and comforting each other, except for Maria, who until now has maintained an unnatural silence. Now her thin frame is shuddering with sobs, her shrieks of terror frightening her sisters, who are trying to pacify her. She will not be soothed. She needs a mother's solace.

The girl's distress has roused José from his paralysis. He takes a few steps towards his wife and daughters, turns back to murmur a few words to Teixeira, who listens and nods. And now he joins his womenfolk and they all embrace – poor Maria, little Dorotea, Benedetti, Anna, every member of the family weeping tears of fright and gratitude that they have all been spared.

Meanwhile, Pedro Teixeira has slipped away. He is taking

the road that leads down to the coast from the palace garden. If he chooses the path to the east, towards the city, that will mean that José has tasked him with finding a messenger to summon Carvalho e Melo. If not...

While her husband is calming Maria, the queen disengages from her family to scan the surrounding landscape. Teixeira is not on the eastern road. Yes, there he is, making his way towards the Távora summer residence. Of all the palaces, it has the best view out over the river and was always a favourite retreat of that family: Dona Leonora and Luís Bernardo, Dom Francisco's son and heir, the young marquis. And his wife, the young marchioness, Dona Teresa.

Even at this terrible time, her husband's thoughts are elsewhere.

Rato, Lisbon

Is it blasphemous, wonders Father Luís da Souza, to murmur the prayer of absolution for these several supplicants who are even now tugging at the hem of his cassock, while he is setting the thigh bone of a young woman whose leg has been broken in two places? As he intones the *ego te absolvo*, her eyelids flicker and she cries out in pain but only for a moment. Now it is done. He leans over that he might speak straight in her ear, for the air is rent by the howling of dogs, whinnying horses, the screams of injured and dying people trapped in the rubble, maddened with panic as they hear the crackling flames approach.

Perhaps not. God has spared him from being crushed by the collapsed roof of the church of Santa Maria Madalena, and from the fires that broke out amongst the ruins when falling rubble set hundreds of candles ablaze, and from the filthy, frothing waters that even now are sweeping through the great square. Therefore, He must have work in mind for His servant. Whether it be his mission to apply the basic knowledge of bone-setting acquired from his father's farrier, or to grant the comfort of absolution and last rites to the terror-stricken faithful, who could know? In this place, this nightmare from the Book of Revelation, this Day of Judgement, this Hell on earth, he can do so very little. And yet, that very little is what he must do.

Have the waters reached the Rossio?

At a half-hour after ten, the Tagus bursts its banks. For an interminable time after the third tremor, he crawls through the ruins of destroyed churches and buildings that struggle – straggled – up the hill towards the Bairro Alto, high above the western flank of the Terreiro do Paço. On the way, he tears his hands digging survivors from the wreckage, hears hasty confessions and grants hastier absolutions, often unable to do more than say a quick prayer over the dead.

As he makes his way past the burning Convent of Carmo and the newly built palace of the Count of Estoril, the structure already reduced to a charred skeleton, he rejoices that a pale sun is at last struggling to cast its weak light across the ruins. It is near one o'clock when he finally arrives, exhausted, at the convent near Rato. A gaggle of dazed women pass by, fifteen of them or so, a few of them young or in their middle years but most aged crones, stumbling around the ruins in bewilderment, remnants of the same coarse brown cloth barely covering their nakedness. Nuns. From an enclosed order. These women have not stepped foot outside their convent, may not have spoken to outsiders since they took their vows as young girls. What will they do? Where will they go?

The flood has not reached the Rossio. But that is a small mercy, perhaps no mercy at all, for all four sides are engulfed in flames. Leaping high in the air, they are devouring every morsel of floorboards, beams, window frames, every scrap of dry material integral to the construction of the edifices, grand and humble, every bench, table, carpet, curtain, tapestry, wall hanging, melting every glass or metal object, sacred or commonplace, silver plate, coins, golden altarpieces, artisans' tools, grills and gates, chalices, kitchen utensils.

Nor is the central space spared. Hundreds, perhaps thousands of survivors have gathered there. Many are laden with precious belongings salvaged from the wreckage of their homes or businesses: family heirlooms, items of furniture, paintings, money, jewels hidden in caskets and in the folds of clothing, the lot piled high in the middle of the square, anxiously guarded by their owners or by the servants of their owners. Their vigilance is in vain, for soon every last thread, coin, tapestry is become flame, offerings to the hungry blaze which gathers strength as the north-east wind carries smouldering ash from afar, sends sparks soaring high in the air, casts embers far over the heads of the frantic survivors, alights on roofs of the few buildings not yet aflame, the issue of errant sparks and ash feeding a malign will. Skirling flames fan out, scatter, commingle into one mighty conflagration while in the south-west corner, a whirling column of fire draws more and still more flames into its core, suffocates twisted bodies that lie at a great distance, writhing, choking on tides of poisonous fumes while smoke belches from this vast sheet of flame, an inundation of fire, a veritable Troy.

But now is a time for action, not contemplation. An entire family is trapped in the upper storey of a house whose gable has been ripped off. A mother and three or four children are cowering against the wall of an inner alcove. The floor could collapse at any moment. After some exhortations, a few of their neighbours agree to assist, but just as Father Luís is allocating tasks, they all fall to their knees, their collective gaze directed towards an unruly procession of rag-tag, half-maddened survivors, women and men, some carrying children, weaving their way through the debris, intoning the rosary at full voice. In their midst hovers a thin, ethereal figure, his shock of silver hair and white beard exuding an aura that gleams through the dust.

Father Gabriel Malagrida. Jesuit, confessor to the royal family, beloved of the nobility and common people alike. The people crowd around him, stop when he stops to preach, fall to their knees, grasp the hem of his cassock, plead for absolution. Some of his followers are injured, a child is screaming in pain. The old priest blesses the child, who goes on screaming while Malagrida continues to address his faithful. He is preaching damnation. The people of Lisbon have brought this disaster upon themselves by their sinful ways. The wrath of God is upon them. They must pray, for prayer and only prayer, true contrition for their sins, will save them from further visitation of the anger of the Almighty.

When Malagrida stoops to make the sign of the cross over one of his followers, Father Luís looks for his reluctant assistants, that he might resume instruction. They have vanished into the ruins, following the steps of the padre and his followers. Voices, ever more distant, continue to intone decades of the rosary while the trapped woman and her children, silent with terror, huddle on the third storey and watch their neighbours and friends follow Father Malagrida deep into the devastated city, towards the flames.

7

An Audience at Court and an Unexpected Encounter

November 3rd, 1755, Belém

Dom Sebastião alighted from his carriage and rubbed his back, his limbs aching from the hard bench he had been obliged to occupy during the journey along the riverbank road from the city of Lisbon to the village of Belém. It had taken almost two hours to cover the four leagues, a distance which, on good days, he had often made in under a half-hour. A blessed chance indeed that the royal family had been lodged at their summer palace in the hills above Belém when the earthquake struck. Even though the village had not escaped the effects of the disaster, the damage hereabouts was but a fraction of the destruction in the city, especially in the low-lying centre where so many of the grand government buildings and noble palaces were situated.

But the river told its own story. The waters, usually limpid and clear, were now sullied by filth churned up from the riverbed: jagged blocks of masonry, detritus stripped from the wrecks of ships, dead animals, bodies and body parts of victims crushed by the tremors or drowned in the battering waves or perished in the fires. Human remains drifted at the mercy of the tides, the Tagus now a turgid, frothing swell transformed to a roiling, alien substance. For two days, the river had ebbed and flowed according to its own mysterious rhythms, a turbulence that obeyed no natural law, impossible to predict.

And still the earth trembled, every aftershock a terrifying reminder that the shuddering earth was not yet done with the people of Lisbon. Perhaps His Majesty was right to fear that the disaster might yet engulf the whole country. The giant waves had already reached Setúbal to the south, a town of twelve thousand souls swept away entire, and Cascais to the west, with great loss of life. Already there were reports of massive destruction on the Algarve and as far afield as Tunis and Algiers, although these last were still to be verified.

Before making his way to the royal presence, Dom Sebastião gave instructions for his driver and the driver's boy to water the horses in the stables and seek refreshments in the palace kitchens. They would have the place to themselves, for most of the servants had accompanied the king, queen and their daughters from the summer palace to the new pavilion under construction in the garden, where the family were now lodged and where Dom José was receiving his messengers. Not two hours after the third tremor had brought down the Arab staircase in the summer palace, sending the entire royal household out into the garden in panic, still in their night clothes, the king had summoned artisans to build a lightweight structure where he, Queen Mariana Vitória and their four daughters might shelter until the risk of injury or death from falling rubble had abated.

Since Dom Sebastião's last visit – only that morning, though it seemed several days ago, so distorted was his sense of time – the pavilion had expanded. Tarpaulins that had earlier constituted walls and roof were now reinforced with sturdy rattan frames. New sections had been added and the lengths of wood he had ordered were easier underfoot than sailcloth, which had been the only groundcover a few hours before. While Dom Sebastião dragged his weary body uphill, a short, steep climb from the road that could only be navigated on foot, a dozen servants lumbered past, carrying choice fittings from the great hall of the summer palace – rugs, tapestries, a writing desk, chairs, no doubt borrowed from the boudoirs of the queen or her daughters. So the king did not intend his family to return to the palace for some time. Perhaps he had been listening to warnings of worse afflictions to come. Mariana Vitória was a great friend to the Jesuits and especially, to Father Gabriel Malagrida, who fancied himself a prophet. No doubt the holy man had taken it upon himself to advise her of what the future held.

While he climbed, Dom Sebastião gripped his walking stick and, with a savage blow, swept the head off a clump of thistles in his path. Those Jesuits had not only interfered with his attempts to instigate relief efforts in the last two days. They were actively obstructing the work, preaching to the faithful that only prayer and supplications and repentance for their sins and pleas to Saint Anthony and the Virgin could save them. A great pity that he himself did not have the power to silence the representatives of that impertinent Order. Perhaps an intervention from the Grand Inquisitor and the Patriarch would succeed where his own efforts had failed.

Few people seemed to have grasped that recovery from this catastrophe would require a massive, co-ordinated effort on an unimaginable scale, of which rebuilding the city was but one element. And that, not the most difficult. The imperative to rescue survivors, treat the injured, bury the dead, protect the populace from pestilence, establish order and discipline where panic, thievery, looting and even murder reigned, to enforce the rule of law where lawlessness had taken hold, required the entire reconstruction of a devastated nation. How could this be accomplished if some of the most powerful people in the country – the most influential members of the Church, the Jesuits – could not, or would not, assist? But instead, with the tacit assent of the idle, decadent nobles, they continued to preach that the terrified people, maddened with grief and loss, must fall to their knees and pray. When they all should be digging in the rubble, as he, Dom Sebastião José Carvalho e Melo, had done, to rescue the wounded and bury the dead.

The climb from his carriage to the door of the new pavilion had left him short of breath. Although well-made and strong, every one of his fifty-six years had begun to weigh upon him, and the exertions of the last few days had tired him. A sharp ice-prick of rain stung his face. At least this pavilion, which was taking on the aspect of a series of large, interconnected tents, was located on ground high enough to escape flooding, if another giant wave were to batter this part of the coast.

When he reached the new pavilion, a thick tapestry pinned to the door frame moved aside. A footman appeared and waited while Dom Sebastião removed his cloak and stamped the mud from his boots. Count Lourenço, not the worst of the high nobility but yet no friend to him, hovered inside the passage.

'His Majesty is anxious, Minister. You must not keep him waiting.'

Carvalho e Melo swept past without so much as a nod of greeting. The minister's standing with the king had soared when he arrived the day before in the immediate wake of the earthquake, armed with a list from which he intoned a litany of questions, while Dom José paced the room and flung out a despairing plea that someone tell him what must be done.

That had been Carvalho e Melo's moment, his demeanour modest and perfectly judged. Before anyone else could respond – true, no one else had seemed inclined to speak – the upstart minister stepped forward, inclined his head with suitable humility and declared: 'Heal the sick and bury the dead, Your Majesty.'

Since that instant, Carvalho e Melo had enjoyed Dom José's absolute confidence and sealed his position as the king's favourite. For now, at least. Yet those were not even the minister's original words – the Duke of Aveiro had heard the elderly Prime Minister da Mota mutter that very phrase on the day of the earthquake. For some reason, no one pointed this out.

Although not at all offended by Carvalho e Melo's brusque dismissal – the Minister for War and Foreign Affairs being a mere politician, of such inferior social standing that none of his words or acts could attain the weight of an insult – how intriguing that a government minister now felt at liberty to behave thus, even in private. Carvalho e Melo had obviously determined to make the most of the opportunities afforded him for as long as his favoured status should last.

Which, as the little scene even now unfolding confirmed, would be just as long as the immediate emergency endured and not a moment longer. No sooner had Carvalho e Melo swept past the footman than he was stopped in his tracks, face-to-face with Queen Mariana Vitória herself, accompanied by Maria, the Princess of Brazil. Such an encounter could never occur under normal circumstances in any of the royal residences. Carvalho e Melo was more startled than the two ladies, who both surveyed him as though he were an unusual specimen they had never seen before, while he made a deep bow. He could not have missed the queen's appalled regard fall upon his filthy boots and the trail of mud they had left on the exquisite, costly rugs scattered across the bare wooden boards. She responded to the minister's bow with a cold stare and no apparent intention to ease his discomfort, before relenting and bestowing a few words of gratitude that gave little appearance of sincerity.

'The city, the nation, is in mourning, Dom Sebastião. I thank you for all you are doing for our country. We are in your debt. '

Carvalho e Melo responded with another bow and a humble murmur.

'It is no more than my duty. Anything I can do to serve the king and your family is an honour.'

The queen inclined her head and gave a tight smile. Since the death of old King João three years earlier, this bumptious politician had been far too prominent at court for her liking. Her mother-in-law, Queen Maria Anna, had had a fondness for him and for his wife, to whom she was especially well-disposed, probably because both women were Austrian. Hadn't the wife –

Eleonor, was it? – been one of the old queen's ladies-in-waiting? And she had even been admitted to her own chamber, once or twice last year. Yes, she had been argumentative and had quarrelled with the Countess of Atouguia. And with Maria, too. No doubt about it, the standing of Carvalho e Melo's wife as a countess of the Austrian empire had done the man no harm at all. Had it not been for that leap through marriage into the high nobility and the patronage of old Queen Maria Anna, Dom Sebastião José Carvalho e Melo would have remained an obscure and not very successful diplomat who managed to live seven years as ambassador to England without learning the language, and five years in Austria, only to leave indebted and penniless, although at least accompanied by a noble wife. Who was he, after all? A failed lawyer. A failed soldier. A diplomat who knew not the first thing of protocols, who embarrassed himself and his ambassadorial office when he had the effrontery to kiss the hand of the Queen of Spain.

Carvalho e Melo's deference had never convinced her. Despite his apparent competence in his role, the Minister for War and Foreign Affairs had always had the whiff of an adventurer about him, an impression reinforced by his tall figure and handsome countenance. Although no longer young, he was still admired by some for his charming ways, especially by the ladies, with whom he enjoyed more favour than with other men. Yet her husband, no doubt influenced by his mother, had come to respect Carvalho e Melo's judgement and, most troubling, had acquired the habit of seeking and acting on the minister's advice in all manner of matters, many outside his official brief. Even before the earthquake, José had come to depend on him utterly.

He despises us, the sudden illumination flashed, as she led her daughter by the arm. All of us. Beneath the surface adherence to protocol, his humility is a mask. He is not a man to like. Certainly not a man to trust, neither in matters of the heart nor of the state.

When the footman announced the Minister for Foreign Affairs and War to the assembled company, the chattering voices fell silent. Some courtier had attempted to give the temporary dwelling an air of comfort by scattering around many valuable pieces gathered from the palace: carpets, which Dom Sebastião was careful to avoid, candelabra already filled with flickering candles – surely a hazard in this wooden structure? – cushions scattered over chairs and sofas, all unoccupied, for the king was pacing around the room, his nobles therefore obliged to remain standing.

Despite their conscious inclination, every man in the room looked towards the newcomer as though in hope of hearing some miraculous solution that would heal the fissures of the earth and their country and their lives. Before them stood a man, unusually tall, of proud bearing, his long, fine-boned countenance grey with dust from the streets and exhaustion from the last two nights he had spent camped in his carriage at the foot of the hill. He had resolved to be close to the king's quarters, the better to serve him, should His Majesty have some pressing matter to discuss with him during the night. Which Dom José did not. Beyond fretting about the rumours – for the most part accurate – of continuing tremors and fires still ablaze in many parts of the city, the king had no urgent orders to convey, for he had delegated all planning and execution of strategies to his Minister for War and Foreign Affairs, whose glittering, deep-set eyes, whose entire being, exuded purpose and readiness for action.

Dom José motioned him to approach.

The Count of Lourenço stood aside, detaching himself from the gaggle of helpless courtiers who had been in conference with the king since the disaster struck, today with one additional participant. The Duke of Alentejo, as everyone present was aware, had fled his palace to his country estates as soon as he had been able to make his way through the ruins of the city, his flight aided by an entourage of servants willing to risk their lives to assist him, or too terrified to disobey his orders. Not in the slightest intimidated by the assembly of his illustrious peers, he took up a prominent position alongside the Duke of Aveiro and the Marquis of Távora, the two most elevated nobles in the land. The affable nod with which he greeted the company betrayed not a shred of embarrassment that he had twice refused the summons, signed by the king himself, to return to the capital forthwith and assist in the relief effort – in short, to do his duty. His cheerful countenance gave no sign that his eventual acquiescence had been secured by a platoon of soldiers whose captain arrived at the gate of his country manor house bearing a letter with the seal of Dom Sebastiao Carvalho e Melo, which set out the duke's choices: to return to Lisbon of his own will, or under arrest. And here he was, shameless, engaged in serious conversation with the Duke of Aveiro and with Dom Gaspar, the king's half-brother and possibly the most influential of the three Palhavã princes.

When the footman announced Dom Sebastião Carvalho e Melo, Minister for War and Foreign Affairs, all present turned towards the new arrival. On every countenance a lip was curled or an eyebrow raised, each noble visage, excepting His Majesty's alone, displaying a haughtiness of bearing breathtaking in its arrogance. Not one of these parasites had made a useful contribution to the crisis, expressed an opinion, offered an idea or a plan with any practical application that might alleviate the misery of the people camped out in the wind and rain, mourning their ruined homes, their lost loved ones crushed to death or burned or swept away in the waves or drowned in cellars. It was left to this despised minor politician to take the lead, while the highest in the land debated and prevaricated and fled to save their own skin.

'Have you completed your inventory, Dom Sebastião?'

'It is not yet ready, Majesty. It is a work in progress.' He hesitated.

'You must tell us what you know, Dom Sebastião. Spare us nothing.'

The minister drew a folder from beneath the folds of his damp frock coat and extracted a single sheet of paper. It had taken him almost three days to gather this information, gleaned from his observations made while trudging around the city. This afternoon he had devoted several hours to distilling his notes into a dispassionate summary of death and destruction, unembellished and the more terrible for that. Every word written here was verified by his own eyes.

'The entire centre of the city has been razed, Your Majesty.'

His words were met with shocked silence, although all those present were already aware that he was right, having either escaped the earthquake themselves or heard reports from trusted servants whom they had sent into to the ruins of their city palaces to brave the fire and the flood and retrieve whatever valuables, jewellery and plate, could be salvaged from their city palaces. The minister took a deep breath.

'From the riverbank, through the Rossio as far as the Carmo, all is in ruins. Including the Palace of the Inquisition. The Castle of São Jorge is down, but much of the Alfama to the east and parts of the Bairro Alto to the west – not all, but much – has been spared. Not the Convent of Carmo, though.' He looked up, to see if he should continue.

'The Palacio de Ribeira?' Prime Minister da Mota. He was aged and would probably not live much longer. The shock of the last few days had weakened and would likely kill him.

'The Riverside Palace is a shell, Your Excellency.'

'But not destroyed? It survived the tremors?'

'It did. But not the fire. The structure still stands, but the interior...'

The room exhaled a collective gasp.

'The library?'

Dom Sebastião shook his head. The Count of Lourneço

groaned and turned away. He was known as a man of particular learning and culture. The loss of thousands, perhaps as many as a hundred thousand, precious books and manuscripts, city records, journals from the Voyages of Discovery of the explorers of the centuries gone by, maps and charts drawn by Magellan and Vasco da Gama, notes made in their own hand, would grieve him deeply. Dom Sebastião mourned those losses but the last days digging lost relatives and dead children from the rubble had convinced him that the life of one of those little ones was worth more than all those precious manuscripts put together. But no such bargain was possible, for they were all lost, books, children, families. So many thousands of people and their homes, with no way to know how many. The count seemed to read his mind.

'How many homes remain habitable, Minister? Of the common people?

'It is difficult to say at the moment, Excellency. Of twenty-five thousand – perhaps three thousand? No more.'

'And loss of life? Can we estimate…?'

For the first time, the minister's animation appeared to desert him. He extracted a handkerchief from a cuff and dabbed his eyes.

'Many thousands.' His voice trembled. 'Twenty thousand? More, perhaps. A full census will take time…'

'And the opera house?' The Duke of Aveiro glanced at the king.

'Burnt to the ground.'

Dom José sank into a chair. His proudest achievement, one of the most lavish constructions of the day, the magnificent new opera house, built to rival the greatest in Europe – destroyed in ten minutes by three tremors and a fire. All the expense, the magnificent paintings it housed, Caravaggios, Raphaels, so many others – gone. The king raised his hand, palm forward. He had heard enough. There was more, he knew, but not for now.

'Do you have any good news for me, Dom Sebastião?'

The Minister for War and Foreign Affairs drew himself up to his full, imposing height.

'Most of the edicts you signed into law yesterday and this morning have been, or are in the process of being enacted, Your Majesty.'

'A summary, Dom Sebastião.'

The customary timbre of his voice restored, Carvalho e Melo read out the proclamations of the actions deemed necessary to restore order. A ring of soldiers was already guarding the perimeter of the city to prevent able-bodied subjects from leaving and escort them back to the city to assist in the relief effort. Provincial governors had already been ordered to return any new arrivals to the capital in chains. Prisoners judged to be of no threat to the state had been released from the gaols. Rescue missions had been working throughout the night; reconstruction missions were created and were ready to start work as soon as sites were made safe, and materials available. However, no temporary rebuilding would be permitted until plans for reconstruction were drawn up. To facilitate administration of this and the many other necessary measures, the city was now divided into twelve districts. All as His Majesty had commanded.

'Excellent work, Dom Sebastião.'

The Duke of Aveiro and Count Lourenço exchanged glances. None present was deceived that a single one of the *Providências* from which the minister had read – drawn up, proclaimed and mostly executed already – originated from the pen, much less the brain, of the king.

'The new administrative structures will facilitate a census when the worst is over, that we may determine the number of dead. For the moment, this system will allow us to re-establish law and order. As I speak, Majesty, gibbets have been got up in each of the twelve districts. Miscreants accused of looting and murder and other crimes are tried by the local council and, if found guilty, hanged immediately.'

'Why waste time and valuable resources on trials?' The Duke of Aveiro's tone, as always, was belligerent. 'In these circumstances, thieves and murderers preying on the people deserve no quarter…'

'We must re-establish the rule of law, Excellency, not ride roughshod over it,' Carvalho e Melo retorted, before the king could speak. 'The trials will be swift but executions must not be summary. The eyes of the world will be upon us. The reputation of the kingdom, and therefore of the king, depends upon our conduct over the coming weeks and months, when knowledge of this disaster travels around the world. As it will.'

The king reached for the Royal Seal which lay on the ornate escritoire at his elbow.

'What more, Dom Sebastião?'

'Ships are forbidden to leave the harbour without a special pass, which is provided only following inspection.'

'Do we have inspectors?'

'Yes, Majesty. They are boarding every ship to search for stolen goods, criminals fleeing. And to obtain the grain we will need to feed the people.'

'This must be requisitioned.'

'Already in train, Your Majesty. We are purchasing grain from the ships; none is permitted to leave with their load. And tariffs for fish have been suspended.'

'Is it still possible to take fish from the river?' The Count of Lourenço's intelligent eyes widened in alarm.

'If we are careful, it soon will be, Excellency. But on that subject, there is a matter of great seriousness before us…'

'The disposal of the bodies of the dead,' the count murmured.

'Exactly. There are many thousands, as you know, and not all have yet been discovered. Some are rotting amidst the rubble as we speak. If we are to avoid disease…'

'There will need to be mass burials,' the count said. The king's eyes opened wide with horror.

'Probably at sea.' Carvalho e Melo paused. 'Beyond the sandbar so that the river is not sullied by the corpses.'

This declaration was met with silence. No one wanted to make the obvious objection.

'If I may have your approval, Your Majesty,' the minister addressed the count. 'Is this something you might raise with Dom José, the Grand Inquisitor? He must have influence with the Patriarch.'

The support of the Patriarch would be essential to secure permission for such unorthodox burials, which in normal times could never be allowed. His permission would be necessary, for as Archbishop of Lisbon and a Cardinal of Rome, the Patriarch was second only to the king himself in pomp, wealth and status, the granting of the elevated office a unique honour bestowed upon the kingdom of Portugal by the Pope himself, in recognition of the extraordinary pity of her people. And of the extraordinarily generous donations from the Royal Treasury to Rome.

'I am sure my brother will do whatever he can to assist,' the king murmured.

'If you provide me with a copy of a draft proclamation setting out the rationale and the procedures proposed for mass burials at sea, I will bring it to him,' the Count of Lourenço replied, adding: 'Signed by His Majesty, of course.'

Carvalho e Melo nodded and turned away, his thoughts already alighted upon other subjects, his energy swelled by an elemental life force within, released as the very earth was turned inside out. The greater the chaos that raged throughout the land, the steadier the minister's purpose and clarity of vision. It did not escape Count Lourenço, nor any of those present, that by means of these *Providências* – dozens of proclamations which Carvahlo e Melo had produced within the last two days, concerning justice, local administration, prisons, taxation, construction and now, burials – this obscure politician with a chequered past and no breeding had, with the unspoken agreement of the king, taken command of almost every arm of government. All except his own brief. But no, here he was, expounding on the threat of invasion from hostile forces – from pirates, from north Africa, from the French? – and how they must take steps to reinforce the defences of the kingdom.

Anyone would think that the king had abdicated in favour of his minister.

An impression of which Dom José seemed unaware or, if he was conscious of it, untroubled. Perhaps it was a relief. Before this audience ended, he even said as much.

'We are indeed fortunate that Dom Sebastião's house was one of those saved from the tremors,' he declared. 'The good Lord must have been watching over the rua Formosa to spare him for us.'

'But then, the rua Suja entire was saved, too, Your Majesty,' the Count of Lourenço quipped, the words out before he could stop himself. There followed a shout of laughter from the king himself and guffaws from the rest of the company, excepting only Carvalho e Melo. How elated they all were, that Dom José had no objection to a little jest in these dark times, that the survival of a street of brothels was as much on the Lord's mind as saving the home of the Minister for War and Foreign Affairs.

The tension broken, Carvalho e Melo smiled, though when the count tried to catch his eye, he found he could not. As the minister retreated from the room, the count felt a stirring of unease. It was a good joke, a little light relief in these terrible days. At the minster's expense, true, but harmless enough. Even so, as the long, lean form of Carvalho e Melo disappeared into the dark passageway, the Count of Lourenço found himself wondering if the joke, witty though it was, had been worth it.

8

Unwelcome News and a Request Rebuffed

November 5th, 1755, Rato, Lisbon

When the minister at last commanded that he enter, Captain Fernando da Oliveira was obliged to hoist himself into the carriage, the driver having forgotten to leave the step when he departed very early that morning.

'I told him to go home and sleep.' Dom Sebastião retreated from the narrow doorway. Stumbling, the young man blinked while his eyes adjusted to the dim interior. The minister drew open a curtain, allowing a shaft of weak morning light to enter and fall upon on two narrow benches strewn with papers. 'There is much work ahead, so we must take our rest when we can.'

Dom Sebastião's red-rimmed eyes and sunken cheeks attested that he had not taken his own advice. Had he really slept these past four nights in this cramped space, stationed in the garden of the royal summer palace in Belém? As soon as his sergeant brought the troubling news, Captain da Oliveira had galloped out to Belém from the city centre at first light, to learn that the minister's carriage had departed. But Dom Sebastião had left before dawn for the city, to continue the grim task of taking inventory of the damage and loss of life. The captain at last found his master – even though it was but four days since the minister had plucked him from the ranks, already he thought of him thus – in Rato, one of the few *bairros* close to the city centre which had suffered comparatively little damage.

'You have important information for me. Bad news.' It was not a question. Captain da Oliveira quailed under the minister's eye. Was it a blessing, or a curse, this ability to read so clearly the mood, even the minds, of others? A man who could see into the souls of his fellows must be a man who had no peace in his own.

'Indeed it is so, Minister.' He shifted on the narrow bench, cautiously moving aside some of the random objects and garments that had accumulated in the last days: a folded frockcoat and linens; a stack of files, papers and pencils; a spoon and an empty bowl.

'My wife brought me soup earlier this morning.' Dom Sebastião seized the bowl and spoon and placed them on the carriage floor. 'Like you, she was an hour or more looking for my carriage. I am sorry to say that the soup was cold when she found me. But I did not have the heart to tell her so.'

'If the minister wishes, I can bring food...'

'There is no need, Captain, thank you. Dona Eleonor also took the precaution of leaving me with provisions for the day.' He indicated a burlap sack at his feet. 'In any case, you would not find food in these parts, or anywhere in the city. There is no bread, for almost every bakery is destroyed. Those still standing whose owners have not perished cannot bake bread, for they have no flour, most of the millers being dead or having fled the city. And those few who are left cannot mill flour to sell the bakers, for they have no wheat. If we are to avert famine, we must straightway requisition wheat from surrounding regions, assist the millers and bakers in rebuilding their premises or provide temporary accommodation for their shops. And of course, enact measures to prevent them, and other essential workers, from leaving the city.'

Of course. But how would the minister accomplish that?

During the days since the earthquake first struck, anyone who could walk had fled the city, or tried to. And who could fault them? Those who had family in the country or in other towns far from the capital were lucky, for they, at least, had hope of refuge and shelter. The rest, thousands of miserable wretches, were reduced to sleeping in the fields around the city, watching it burn by night, haunted by the screams of the relatives and companions they had left behind, those too wounded or too aged to flee, while they, poor homeless unfortunates, shivered and wept, clothed only in what they were wearing when the tremors or floods or flames drove them from their homes, servant and nobleman alike, equal under the faint light of frozen stars.

He would use the army. Of course.

'But this is not your immediate concern, da Oliveira.' The minister was again reading his mind. 'And you have important information for me.'

'One of my sergeants heard Father Malagrida preaching in the Terreiro do Paço, Minister. He was present but a few minutes, for he was on his way to post guards on all public buildings and did not wish to linger.' He handed Dom Sebastião several sheets of paper covered in a small, cramped hand.

'Is this all?'

'No, Minister. These are fragments that my sergeant was able to recall when he returned to the barracks. I heard his account and transcribed it myself, as he cannot write very well. But he has an excellent memory. There was considerable disorder amongst the people who had gathered around Father Malagrida while he was preaching. Many of his listeners were in great distress, fallen to their knees or prostrate, wailing their prayers aloud, quite deaf and blind to reason. My sergeant ordered – tried to order – the penitents to arise and clear the way for the soldiers to cross the square and take up their posts, before looters stripped the public buildings bare. But the padre's followers were deaf to the pleas of my sergeant. Their minds and hearts were filled with Father Malagrida's preachings.'

'When did this occur?

'Yesterday in the afternoon, Minister. I heard of it myself in the early hours of this morning. I went in search of you as soon as I had transcribed as much as the sergeant could remember.'

The minister scanned the pages once, twice. This was worse, much worse, than he had feared.

'Know, o Lisbon, that the only destroyers of so many houses, palaces, temples and convents, the deaths of so many of her inhabitants, the fires devouring so many treasures, were not comets, nor stars, nor vapours, nor any phenomenon or contingencies or natural causes, but alone our intolerable sins.'

It was no surprise that Father Gabriel Malagrida's sermons in these last days had proclaimed hellfire and damnation to his devotees, among whom were counted humble commoners and the highest in the land, including the king's wife, Queen Mariana Vitória and their daughter, the Princess of Brazil. Nor that he declared the earthquake to be a manifestation of the wrath of God, and insisted that prayer – guided by Malagrida himself, of course – was the only hope for the afflicted. If God was so angry with the people of Lisbon, what could they do, but fall to their knees and beg for His mercy?

But this went far beyond religious fervour.

On the third reading he made a few notes in the margins, underlining certain phrases with such energy that the pencil point tore through the paper.

'Earthquakes have no other cause than Divine Intervention. All such great punishments are the effect of our own faults. <u>I know not how a Catholic subject would dare to attribute the causes to natural contingencies</u>. This is a scandalous and pernicious doctrine, for it diverts us from true penitence. The sword of fire wielded by Seraphim

with fire and iron is destined to exterminate the sinner. But it can, with the benefit of penance, become the key to open us to the treasures of misericordia. It tells us <u>to guard against those who try to assure us that these calamities are pure effects of natural causes,</u> and not the vengeance of a just God, visiting his ire on sinners. <u>I believe that the devil himself could not expound a doctrine so conducive to our own irreparable ruin than to teach this</u>. And yet the Court, <u>instead of seeking resolution, listens to poisonous words of the treacherous serpent…</u>'

There was no doubt. This sermon was an open attack on himself. It called into question his status as a true *Catholic subject*. It exhorted the people to disobey the crucial measures he had enacted, in the name of the king, that were so essential to establish law and order and set in motion the processes of relief and reconstruction that must follow. Which proclamations, according to Malagrida, instructing the people in urgent, practical action, were poisonous words and he was the devil, the treacherous serpent.

He had not expected that Malagrida would go so far.

But this paragraph near the end was the worst of all.

'We see it clearly, theatres, music, immodest dances, obscene comedies, streets filled with merrymakers and in the churches on holy days and apostolic missions, not a soul appears!'

Although Malagrida had attacked Dom Sebastião directly, he had stopped short of reproaching the king. For the moment. True, his words did not refer to the person of His Majesty. But they denounced those activities that were the king's favourite pastimes: music, theatre, general merrymaking. And this was only the beginning. In future sermons, he would be more explicit. Indeed, it was possible that he had already criticised the person of the king, for this document summarised only part of a much longer sermon that Malagrida delivered yesterday. As he was preaching all over the city, every day, it would not be long before he denounced the king and his (let us be honest) libertine ways. And spoke openly of the particular love affair that neither Dom José nor Dona Teresa had taken any pains to conceal.

Profiting from his reputation for piety and the devotion of the present king's father, Dom João, Malagrida had appointed himself confessor and judge of the city of Lisbon, of the entire country, of the king himself. Terrified people determined to stay on their knees pleading for God's mercy would never be persuaded to dig through ruins for survivors, bake bread, rebuild houses, as Dom Sebastião José Carvalho e Melo required and the king commanded. And it was only a matter of time before the nobles listening to these thundering denunciations of the people of Lisbon and their sins would question the fitness of a king whose progeny included not a single son, and whose conduct had brought down upon them the wrath of God.

Malagrida had to be stopped. Through official channels, if possible.

Taking a clean sheet of paper, he inscribed a few lines in pencil.

'Take this to the Grand Inquisitor, at the Palhavã Palace. Tell him to expect me within the hour. Or rather, request an audience with him on my behalf. Beg his forgiveness that there is no seal on my letter and explain this is due to the conditions in which I am living. You may give him this by way of authentication.' When the captain reached for the proffered ring, the Dom Sebastião closed his fist over it, before handing it over. 'See that he returns it to you before you leave. Those high nobles can never have enough baubles.'

To discuss this matter with the king's half-brother before reporting it to the king himself, was unorthodox. But if the Grand Inquisitor could convince the Patriarch to silence Malagrida, it would benefit not only the king, but the entire city of Lisbon and the whole country. Considering the generosity with which the king had treated Dom José and the other Palhavã princes, it was the least he could do to protect his brother.

The journey from Rato to the Palhavã Palace took close to two hours on foot. As the route wound through parts of the city he and his officials had not yet visited, it was necessary to stop every few minutes to make additions to the inventory. Reliable reports indicated that the great aqueduct at Alcântara on the north-western outskirts of the city was intact but engineers would have to be dispatched to verify this. It was a magnificent project, completed barely a decade before, created to bring drinking water to the people of Lisbon. They must hope that those initial optimistic reports were accurate.

On reaching his destination, weary from the journey, he was surprised to observe a throng gathered at the Palhavã palace gate. A guard explained that Dom Gaspar, Dom José and Dom António had decided to open their garden to as many of those made homeless by the earthquake as the space would permit. While he waited to be admitted to the grand reception hall, Dom Sebastião admired the façade of the exquisite little palace that nestled on the northern outskirts of the city, close enough for convenience of business but blessedly distant from the earthquake zone. The three Palhavã princes, the king's half-brothers, had all grown up here. Dom José, the youngest, whose given name he shared with his royal brother the king, had occupied the elevated position of Grand Inquisitor for almost four years. After the death of their father, Dom José, newly crowned king, had gifted his half-brothers – all out of different mothers – handsome positions in fulfilment of his deceased father's wish that they should be recognised as his sons. Had not that old goat tupped his way through every convent in Lisbon – the Grand Inquisitor's mother had been an abbess – a young cleric of such modest talents would have seen out his days as a parish priest in a remote corner of the Alentejo.

The Grand Inquisitor, a full twenty years junior to Dom Sebastião, greeted him with civility and a few words of commendation on his excellent work of the previous few days. Law and order for the most part was restored; the troops that would surround the city to prevent citizens from leaving were even now on the march; a system of maritime inspection, whereby all ships entering or leaving the port required a passport and were subject to inspection, was in place. Already, several ships had been detained leaving the port laden with treasures looted from public buildings. Seven seamen had been hanged – a Catalan, a Galician, three Spaniards and two Irishmen.

Having listened gravely to the minister's lucid summary of measures underway, Dom José took it upon himself to bestow compliments on these and the many other safeguards it had been necessary to put in place in recent days. The rapid progress made under such difficult conditions was a testament to the energy and strategic talent of the Minister for War and Foreign Affairs.

Dom Sebastião responded with a bow, though not a very low one, and countered with an equally respectful commendation of the Grand Inquisitor's efforts in providing shelter and food for the homeless in his own garden. As he spoke, Dom José regarded him with a narrow smile, well aware that the minister's purpose was not to commend, but rather to claim the right to commend. Nor was the prince convinced by the minister's declarations of admiration. This was a man who would gladly see him, his brothers and all members of his class join the earthquake victims in their watery graves beyond the sandbar. Yet as he listened to the minister's urgent petition, it occurred to him that this jumped-up *hidalgo*, far from intending to destroy their entire class, wished to become one of them. Perhaps the story about his ridiculous efforts to marry one of the Távora girls was true after all. It must be a matter of great distress for him to approach the hated Inquisition for assistance. Though these were far from normal times.

Dom José cast his eye over the pages which the minister had pressed upon him.

'Is this all?'

'No, Your Excellency. These are but fragments recalled by a sergeant who happened upon Father Malagrida while his platoon was attempting to cross the Terreiro do Paço. They were obstructed by his followers.'

'Not deliberately?'

'They refused to yield passage when ordered by a sergeant of the Crown. They remained on their knees, at prayer, in a state of utmost distress provoked by the exhortations of the priest.'

'Prayer is a great comfort in such terrible times.'

'It is indeed, Your Excellency.' It would not do to allow this whippersnapper to see that he had the power to disturb his equilibrium. 'And prayer in the company of action is the greatest comfort of all. For thus are the sufferings of the afflicted soothed and their wounds healed.'

'Father Malagrida is a man of the spirit, rather than action.'

Both men knew that this was far from true, that in his younger days, in the missions, Father Gabriel Malagrida had embarked on many dangerous adventures to bring the word of God to the most primitive peoples and on several occasions barely escaped with his life, a life lived very far from the tranquil destiny of a hermit or a monk. In his later years, his taste for adventure had been satisfied in the way of all Jesuits – by meddling in politics through the confessional. Every royal court in Catholic Europe was infested with them. The Grand Inquisitor was not making this easy.

'I do not deny the solace of prayer, Your Excellency, far from it. I applaud it. I am a good Catholic subject.' He tapped the document in Dom José's hand. 'Despite what some might think. But we need action in these terrible times. Builders. Bakers. Strong arms to pull the dead and the living from the ruins around our city. Gentle hands to care for the sick and the dying.

A people who are told to fall to their knees and repent – and do nothing else – is a people it is impossible to help. What can be done, if they will not help themselves?'

Dom José gave every sign of careful consideration of these words, his gaze fixed on a distant point on the wall opposite.

'I am not sure, Minister, how the Patriarch would view a request to censor the preachings of Father Malagrida. As you are aware, he is held in very high esteem by his Church brethren and by the royal family. Venerated as almost a saint. You know that he was at my father's deathbed and heard his confession in his final weeks.'

And there was a great deal to confess, Dom Sebastião did not say.

'To be honest, Minister,' Dom José continued, 'I am not convinced that it is my place to silence the voice of the man who was my father's closest confidant. And who was venerated by his queen, whose final confession he also heard. Dona Maria Anna summoned him back from Brazil especially to accompany her in her final days.'

Dom Sebastião bowed. He had never understood why a woman of such intelligence and good sense, his great supporter in the suit of his marriage, his champion at court until her demise less than a year before, had been duped by the charlatan Jesuit who allowed himself to be known as a prophet. Why the Inquisition had not denounced Malagrida as a heretic on that account alone was a mystery. For lack of anything conciliatory thought, he made no reply. At last, Dom José broke the silence.

'What says my brother the king?'

Ah, yes, he has read the final paragraphs.

'I have not yet apprised His Majesty of the contents of Malagrida's sermon. I was informed of it myself but two hours ago and came here in the hope that you – that we – might take measures that would spare the king unnecessary embarrassment.'

Leaning forward, Dom Sebastião again tapped the page

which the Grand Inquisitor continued to peruse.

'You see this, Excellency? These innuendos? It is only a matter of time before Father Malagrida moves from innuendo to overt criticism of the king's...frailties. And who knows what other factions could rally around this?'

Perhaps he had gone too far. But it was not a moment too soon to remind this privileged young pup that he owed his entire position, wealth and status to the half-brother whom he was now, it appeared, hesitating to protect.

'The threat to my brother which you perceive in these remarks... Is your interpretation perhaps exaggerated? Whereas the criticism of your own person is explicit.'

What of the fact, which he had already explained, that this document gives but an incomplete account of only one sermon; that there are no doubt others wherein Malagrida expresses himself with even greater clarity, or will do so. But why repeat arguments already made? He should not have come. The Grand Inquisitor had made up his mind before he arrived. If he could have turned on his heel and swept out of the palace without consequence, he would have done so. But this man's goodwill could be important in the future and so he contented himself with a wry smile and a nod.

'I thank Your Excellency for making your position clear. I have taken up too much of your time.'

'I will think on it, Minister. But I am not convinced that the Patriarch himself would have the power to silence Father Malagrida, even if he wished to.'

The king would have to be told after all. And if Malagrida persisted in his superstitious rantings among the people and the king's own court ... Well, there were other measures. Exile. From the court. From the capital. As far away as possible. He, Dom Sebastião José Carvalho e Melo, Minister of War and Foreign Affairs, loyal subject of his Majesty Dom José I of Portugal and Brazil, would see to it.

First Impressions and an Uneasy Alliance

November 6th, 1755, Rossio Square, Lisbon

Father Luís da Souza was beginning to wonder whether his strength would be sufficient to restrain this burly young man, who even now was bellowing and thrashing in pain, though the priest had yet barely laid a hand upon his injuries. Setting a broken arm and especially, a dislocated shoulder, were tricky enough manoeuvres at the best of times, requiring stamina and a degree of concentration to which the current chaotic circumstances in the Rossio – and less than two hours' sleep a night for several days – were hardly conducive.

Doing his best not to touch the arm, Father Luís knelt on the damp cobbles and raised the sleeve of the young man's tunic. It was a clean break and with luck should heal well, provided the lad did not move it for some weeks. Though it was difficult to imagine how anyone in this ruined city could find even a few hours, let alone weeks, of stillness. He bent to his task, senses assailed by the devastation the earthquake had wrought and by its aftermath: the howls of victims who still had strength to cry out, the weeping of grieving relatives as their loved ones struggled for their last breath, the stink of putrefaction on the air and – this, he tried not to think about – not only the horrendous end those poor souls must have endured, trapped in their homes by falling masonry and then drowned when the waves flooded the ruins, but the dangers their rotting corpses posed to those still living. With a great effort of will, Father Luís emptied his mind, shut out the sights and sounds of the suffering around him and applied his full attention to aligning the bone and calming the patient.

Thus he did not at first remark the figure approaching from the south-west corner of the square: tall, elegantly dressed, wrapped against the bitter wind and rain in a cloak sprinkled with a film of dust. An incongruous figure amidst the ruins, picking his way around piles of charred debris and clambering over a collapsed archway that had toppled into the southern side of the square.

When the figure came to a halt alongside him, Father Luís showed no surprise. Nor, having more pressing matters to attend to than conversation with an uninvited spectator, did he trouble to offer a greeting. He would have to set the bone with a makeshift splint but really, this young fellow, despite the agony he now endured, was extremely lucky to have come through the quakes with no more than a broken arm and a dislocated shoulder. Though whether he had acquired these injuries from a block of masonry that fell upon him while he was trying to dig a child out of the rubble, as he claimed, or in the course of other, possibly criminal activities, Father Luís preferred not to wonder. Certainly, these wounds were fresh, so could not have been suffered during or in the immediate aftermath of the earthquake, five days past.

He looked narrowly at the young man, who squeezed his eyes shut, whether from pain or to avoid meeting his benefactor's gaze, who could tell. There were rumours that nefarious persons were profiting daily from the prevailing chaos and terror by looting ruined, abandoned palaces, churches, even the humblest dwellings. It was said that some miscreants were setting fires in order to force survivors who had returned to their homes to flee yet again, leaving their belongings as easy pickings for the thieves. In a city where fire had wrought such destruction and still raged in many *bairros*, this must surely be condemned as an especially heinous evil. But it was not his business to decide whether this young man was one of the perpetrators of such a terrible crime. Later, perhaps, if ever his patients were to make their way to his confessional, he would attend to their souls. For the moment, he must heal their bodies to the best of his ability.

No doubt the imposing visitor who was now looming above him would take a different view.

'May I be of assistance?'

'You could hold him down,' Father Luís said, without looking up. And to the young man, whose good side was now pinned immobile to the ground by the imposing heft of the newcomer: 'This will cause you pain, but only for a moment. On the count of three, then. Are you ready? One, two…' Upon which, as the dislocated shoulder clicked back into its socket, the young man let out an almighty howl.

'Three,' the priest concluded, satisfied. It worked every time. A little distraction, and with luck, the pain was over before they knew it. Now to bind the arm and shoulder fast and they were done. A couple of unsavoury characters had appeared carrying a board on which they intended to transport their injured companion. There being no streets left to speak of, this was an unrealistic plan and in any case, the young man should be able to walk. Although in pain, he seemed eager to be gone. Perhaps he, too, had recognised the newcomer and wisely decided to absent himself before Dom Sebastião José Carvalho e Melo started asking questions.

'You must move that arm as little as possible,' Father Luís called after the retreating patient, who was making his way through the debris flanked by his companions, none of whom spared the priest so much as a backward glance. Father Luís had long ago ceased expecting thanks or even acknowledgement for his work and although this did not grieve him, it always troubled him to think that his efforts might be undone by the actions of careless patients who refused to heed his advice for aftercare. Perhaps fortunately, he heard of the outcome in only a few cases. This would not be one of them.

As he gathered up his materials, he noted that the newcomer showed no sign of leaving.

'You are a physician as well as a priest?'

The Minister for War and Foreign Affairs was making no attempt to conceal the admiration in his voice and regard.

'One can learn a great deal in the missions. I brought the people the Word of God. They taught me their ways in healing.'

'Including the setting of bones.' A sudden hesitancy came over the minister, as though he did not know how to proceed. When he continued, his tone was deferential, almost humble. 'I would speak with you on a matter of some importance.'

Father Luís responded with a glance around the square where misery and destruction abounded. A dart of despair momentarily pierced his heart. The sin for which there could be no forgiveness. In these terrible days, the only possible antidote to hopelessness was action.

While he recovered himself, Dom Sebastião followed his gaze, his next words surprisingly gentle. 'I can see that many others have need of your ministry. I ask only a few moments of your time. But if you will allow me to explain my purpose, I think you will find that the service I wish to ask of you will be of great benefit to the people of Lisbon.'

The young priest frowned, his countenance revealing the wariness and curiosity warring in his heart. After a long moment, curiosity having triumphed, he nodded and bade the minister follow him to a shaky little hut on the south-east corner of the square, constructed out of uneven bits of wood and remnants of tapestry and curtain, clinging to a fragment of wall which the tremors had spared.

'You sleep here?'

'For the moment. For as long as I must.' He drew aside a loose flap of fabric covering the narrow, makeshift entrance and retired a pace or two, allowing the minister to manoeuvre his long form, stooped almost double, into the dark interior, fashioned in haste out of whatever bits and pieces Father Luís had been able to get his hands on. Heaped along one side was a high pile of cushions, no doubt retrieved from one of the many ruined palaces around the square. They would make a comfortable enough bed but those remnants of tapestry would not keep out the cold, and certainly offered little protection from the rain.

'I would be happy to have some lengths of sailcloth delivered…'

'How may I assist you, Excellency?' Father Luís secured the entrance flap with a peg, allowing a weak shaft of sunlight to penetrate the interior, together with the chill and the fine drizzle. He indicated a low stool, upon which the guest gingerly balanced his long frame. Once settled, the minister produced a few sheets of folded paper which he covered with his hat, lest the rain cause the ink to run. He waited while the young priest sank on to a strip of tapestry set upon the damp cobblestones and took the proffered pages.

'During the last five days, Father Luís, I have made my way around as much of the city as I could reach under the present conditions. With my own eyes, I have seen the scale of devastation and suffering. I have spoken with the people, rich and poor, priests, nuns, noblemen and women and I have prevailed upon a number of trusted witnesses, people on whom I can depend to describe in detail, with neither embellishment nor exaggeration, what they saw, what they experienced, on the morning of All Souls' Day and on the days that followed.'

'So this is a full account…' Father Luís murmured, casting a second quick glance over the closely written pages, distracted and not a little disconcerted that the minister knew his name. It was said that Dom Sebastião José Carvalho e Melo had eyes and ears everywhere.

'Not quite. What we have learned about the earthquake and its aftermath has engendered many questions. Questions which I believe we must answer, to have any hope of recovering from this catastrophe. And...' he hesitated, '... to prepare for any future disasters of this nature.'

The priest looked up from his reading. It was not an unwarranted fear, for the earth was still far from quiet, its periodic trembling and rumblings not violent enough to destroy or kill, but sufficient to revive at any moment the terror and panic of frightened people in dread of yet more retribution from a vengeful deity.

The minister jabbed at the first page. 'A dozen questions or thereabouts. *How many tremors... Of what duration... Direction... Unusual behaviour of the tides... Unaccustomed behaviour in animals in the hours before the earthquake... Any other natural phenomenon unusual...* And more to be added.'

Father Luís pondered. Any reader of these questions could see that the minister was seeking to investigate not only the effects of the earthquake and the giant waves that followed but the causes, too. Yet according to many – some of his fellow priests, also Father Malagrida whom he had heard, on the very day of the earthquake, preaching the simplest of answers – Lisbon was destroyed by the wrath of God visited upon the city in punishment for the sins of her people. Salvation would be granted, if it were granted, by the mercy of God alone, according to His holy will and in answer to prayer and supplication.

In which case, what purpose could these questions serve? What did the minister hope to accomplish? He handed the pages back to his guest.

'Why have you brought this to me?'

Dom Sebastião regarded him steadily. Had he been perhaps misinformed about the character and abilities of this man? The deep lines etched around those eyes testified to the man's exhaustion, his tireless response to the call of the injured and dying, not with prayers and rosaries but with practical help. But who was this Father Luís da Souza? A Franciscan priest who was ministering to the people in the most devastated part of the city. A man who would construct a little shack with his own hand, that he may be present if needed during the night to succour the destitute people who had flocked to the square, those who had no resources to flee the city or who were in search of lost loved ones.

Like it or no, the people of Lisbon, rich and poor, simple and noble, listened to their clergy. Men of the Church, men of suitable disposition, would be needed to accomplish the colossal work that lay ahead.

Was this such a man?

'You are no doubt aware, Father Luís, that the city of Lisbon is now divided into twelve administrative districts, to facilitate rescue and relief efforts.' The priest nodded. 'In order to obtain the information sought here,' the minister tapped on the folded documents, 'I require the assistance of the twelve administrative districts. The active assistance, Father Luís. Not mere acquiescence.'

Amused in spite of himself, the young priest smiled. Everyone knew there were ways of evading government-sponsored measures, while technically adhering to the letter of the law.

'You will understand that once these questions are distributed throughout the twelve districts, neither I nor anyone else will have any real knowledge of the extent to which they have been explored, or indeed, whether they have been explored at all. And as we both know,' the minister's smile was both charming and complicit, 'there are those who consider these questions to be not only superfluous, but a personal affront to the Almighty.'

Determined not to succumb to the minister's levity, Father

Luís remained silent.

'I need one man to oversee the distribution of these questions, to persuade the clerics to gather this information,' he indicated the folded pages, 'and to ensure that the responses are returned to me. On the basis of their responses, I will refine the questions and then distribute them to the bishops, who will in turn have them put out to the widest population possible. May I count on your assistance?'

In the heavy silence that followed, Dom Sebastião watched the young priest consider his request and the possible consequences of acquiescence or refusal. In truth, this was not an assignment to be undertaken with reluctance. Unless Father Luís understood the importance, the necessity of this endeavour, better that he remain here, where at least he was convinced he was needed.

'This work need not take you away from your ministry for more than a few hours of a few days in the next week or ten days,' Dom Sebastião said. 'It is crucial that we obtain this information before people forget the details. Or die. And if I ask them...' he smiled bleakly.

Of course, the minister could never accomplish a task of this scale without significant help from members of the clergy who were working directly with the earthquake victims. And it really was an excellent idea, unique and daring, to conduct a systematic investigation of the circumstances that prevailed, before, during and after the earthquake, based on the experiences of those who had endured the brunt of the disaster. How gratifying – more, how thrilling – to have a role, however small, in such a novel undertaking, one that could be of immense future benefit...

'I do not even ask that you read the answers, Father Luís. Merely ensure that there is a comprehensive attempt throughout the twelve districts to gather the information sought, from as wide a range of people as possible – old, young, noble, humble, men, women. Is that something you think you could do?'

Father Luís suppressed a smile at the minister's strategy of appealing to his vanity. The question was not whether the proposed assignment was within his capabilities – of course it was – but whether in taking on this responsibility, for however short a time, he would become tainted as one of the minister's legion of informers.

'There are many ways of assisting in the relief effort, Father Luís,' Dom Sebastião continued. 'This,' he gestured toward the square outside, 'is of the greatest import. But there are less obvious measures, too, with a long-term impact that may be even greater. I assure you that this is a purely administrative role involving no secret or otherwise…distasteful tasks.'

In spite of himself, Father Luís burst out laughing. In the frequent whispered criticisms of the minister – his ambition, his influence with the king, his opposition to the Jesuits and all the restrictions he had placed on their activities – some even thought he would like to see them banished altogether – there was no mention of his wit and personal charm.

Correctly judging a shift in the young priest's mood, the minister smiled. 'If you are in agreement, my assistant, Captain Fernando da Oliveira, will visit you to discuss the practicalities in more detail.'

Father Luís found himself grasping the minister's outstretched hand. 'I will await his call.'

The words were barely out of his mouth than the minister was gone, his goal achieved, soon soaked through by the pelting rain. As he clambered over the toppled archway, he wondered whether Father Luís would accept a few lengths of sailcloth to improve his hut or if he would consider this a perquisite that would bind him irrevocably to the will of the Minister for War and Foreign affairs.

It was obvious that the young priest had been on the point of refusing his request. And not only out of concern for the pressing needs of his destitute parishioners. Oh, that was a factor, no doubt about it, he could have declined outright on those grounds alone. More likely he did not care to be associated with any member of the governing class – especially with Dom Sebastião himself.

This was not difficult to understand. Since his elevation to Minister of War and Foreign Affairs, since he had so fully gained His Majesty's confidence in all matters of state, including those far beyond his official remit, an interesting evolution had occurred in how people conducted themselves towards him. Some erstwhile opponents now cultivated him, their distaste for this upstart politician yielding to craven self-interest, in their public demeanour at least. A useful development, for the pursuit of personal gain or the avoidance of aggravation were rational motivations which rendered the behaviour of his adversaries, and sometimes their thoughts and intentions, predictable. Such people he could work with, bend to his will.

The idealists were another matter. Although few in number, they were troublesome, for it was difficult to get sense out of people who were willing to forgo personal advantage, to decline material inducements or career advancement for the sake of a belief or principle. There was no knowing what such people would do, how they would react to circumstances or threat. Some seemed willing to risk, indeed actively to provoke his rancour, the worst of course being Gabriel Malagrida. Even now, that reprehensible Jesuit continued to obstruct every particular of the relief effort, terrifying the people with his rantings about the wrath of God and prophecies of more earthquakes, exhortations to which, unfortunately, the many light aftershocks with which the city still trembled lent credence.

It was always intriguing – disconcerting, sometimes – to see oneself through the eyes of others, as though reflected in a warped mirror, especially those whose perceptions were based only on reputation rather than personal acquaintance. Although this Father Luís was not himself a Jesuit, he must wonder how any association with the Minister for War and Foreign Affairs would appear to his brethren of the cloth, should this longstanding dispute with the Society of Jesus escalate. Which it surely would. Yes, curtailing the activities of the Jesuits in Portugal would be a bold act no one thought possible. And it would not end there: forbidding them to hear confessions and say Mass would be just the beginning. Many kings and governments throughout Europe had long desired to rid themselves of the rapacious followers of Ignatius Loyola, for there was hardly a court that was not infested with Jesuit confessors to royal personages and statesmen. Such was their influence, their status almost that of an alternative government, an international enterprise whose tentacles snaked throughout Europe, through the colonies of Brazil and New Spain and the world entire, that no one had dared oppose them.

But he, Dom Sebastião José Carvalho e Melo, dared.

Perhaps Father Luís was also a little afraid of him. There was nothing to be gained by dwelling on the injustice of this. Effective leaders had to accept their actions being attributed to base motives, especially by those whose vested interests they challenged in defence of the common good. In truth, the opinions and judgements of the great majority of people were so clouded, so obscured by their expectations and desires, as to render admiration and ignominy equally meaningless. And of course, a minister of state who enjoyed the full confidence of his king need no longer court advancement or favour.

Yet it would be no bad thing to earn the trust, if not the respect, of this energetic priest, who was truly as much concerned about the bodily welfare of his parishioners as their souls. Was he indeed a pragmatist, though? Or one of those troublesome dreamers governed by vague notions of how the world should be, rather than how it is? Time would tell. Meanwhile, this Father Luís da Souza would make a useful ally.

Tired out by his exertions, Dom Sebastião leaned on a fallen pillar to catch his breath and look out over the little square adjoining what remained of the convent of Carmo. This was now an eerie, empty shell, some of the walls intact but the roof collapsed; those glorious soaring buttresses remained, etched like bones against the grey sky. The convent of Carmo was very far from being the most opulent or beautiful of the places of worship in a city that boasted so many, but this was his *bairro* where he felt most at home and the Carmo was a favourite of his, where he sought succour whenever he wanted to pray alone.

But why were its walls intact, when so many others lay in ruins? What had caused the roof to fall in, yet allowed those buttresses to withstand the violent tremors of the earth that had felled so many sturdier constructions? The Divine Will could not be so capricious as to destroy some edifices and see their occupants crushed to death, yet spare others; or to leave parts of one holy building untouched and others in pieces at his feet. Even for a good Catholic, to attribute such arbitrary effects to whims of the Almighty was an insult to intelligence and reason. It bore investigation.

The seed of an idea was taking root. Might it be possible to construct edifices that would withstand such convulsions of the earth that had brought down thirty-five of Lisbon's forty or so parish churches, drawing on the features of those buildings, and parts of buildings, that had survived? Some kind of internal frame, perhaps, that would reinforce and support the masonry around, allowing it to bend, like a young tree in the wind, rather than break? When his inventory was complete, he must summon General da Maia and his team of engineers.

Beads of sweat mingled with rain dripped from his brow as he paused, breathless from the arduous climb, and surveyed his street, the rua Formosa, blessedly undamaged, and the simple, elegant façade of his own home where Eleonor and the children, who had hardly seen him in the past five days and nights, awaited. Eleonor was anxious to move the family away from the city to safer ground. Which was out of the question, at least for the moment. As long as he had the ear of the king, he must lead by example, maintaining his family's household at the scene of disaster: this, a constant reminder to His Majesty and the court of the cowardice of those craven marquises and dukes who fled the city to save their own skin while the people perished. He gave three rapid taps on the door, gladdened to hear the eager patter of his children's footsteps. For the moment at least, here they would have to stay.

10

A Testy Encounter and a Glass of Port Wine

November 7th, 1755, Residence of the British Ambassador, Lisbon

The residence of His Excellency, Abraham Castres, was not the most magnificent of the mansions of the many wealthy British subjects long settled in the city of Lisbon, but it was very fine nonetheless. As well it might be, for English merchants and the representatives of their government constituted the most privileged community in the entire country, enjoying profits and living circumstances far superior to those of their Portuguese counterparts in England. Castres's predecessor, that devious upstart Benjamin Keene, had admitted as much, without a blush. But Keene, long departed, was now a thorn in the side of some unfortunate Spanish minister in Madrid. Although this new ambassador did not like him – Dom Sebastião was sure that Castres had lobbied against his appointment as Minister of War and Foreign Affairs – unlike Keene, the new ambassador did not relish open conflict. A frailty which might make him more responsive to persuasion than his predecessor.

The imposing wrought-iron gate stood half-open, unattended save for a single guard, a fair-skinned lad who approached without bowing and immediately offered, in halting Portuguese, to show Dom Sebastião to the ambassador's tent. Perhaps he had recognised him, for the minister had passed the greater part of the week trudging through streets and alleyways, scrambling over piles of debris, his cloak glistening damp in the rain, his boots coated with dust. Or perhaps the boy had orders to admit anyone who sought shelter.

Making his way towards the house, Dom Sebastião became aware of an insistent murmur, a dark undertone to the cacophony of city sound, ever-present since the disaster. It was the sound of nightmares invading the daytime: the barking of dogs, the whinnying of injured horses, the weeping and cries of people injured and in pain or despair. Here, beneath it all, many voices thrummed. The British ambassador had lent his weight and the resources of his country, Portugal's oldest and most faithful ally, to aid the afflicted. This, at least, was one argument with the British he would be spared.

Except for a large crack in the gable end, the handsome residence had suffered little damage. Several windows on the first floor were boarded up and a great pile of bricks lay heaped at the foot of the west wall, no doubt what was left of a collapsed chimney. The first storey, which housed Castres's sleeping quarters, was a good fifteen feet above ground level. The ambassador had been very lucky to have sustained no greater injury than a sprained ankle when he leapt from his bedroom window as soon as the tremors started. In any case, he had recovered sufficiently from his ordeal to pay a courtesy visit to the king in Belém two days before.

Dom Sebastião happened to know that another audience with the king would take place in a day or two; that it would be attended by both Ambassador Castres and the Consul General, Lord Hay; and that today, Consul Hay was unavailable to join today's meeting with the ambassador. This was a lucky circumstance, for Consul Hay was the spokesman and representative of the British Factory in all dealings with the Portuguese government – with Dom Sebastião himself, in other words. As the purpose of today's meeting concerned the practical response of the British Factory to the disaster, Lord Edmund Hay's absence would allow Dom Sebastião to confer with the ambassador without the inconvenience of Hay's usual pedantic interventions. For there was no doubt that when the two diplomats and the commercial interests represented by the British Factory heard his proposals, they would like him even less than they already did.

Ambassador Castres had set up a small tent in a secluded corner of his extensive garden, where he was able to conduct business in relative comfort. As the minister stepped into the shelter, his host attempted to raise himself from his chair, a difficult manoeuvre, for his left foot was bandaged and resting on a stool.

'Please, Excellency, do not exert yourself, you must rest your foot.'

Castres sank back in the chair and surveyed the gaunt features of his visitor who, on his invitation, lowered himself into the chair opposite. The minister had the air of a man who had not slept in days and who had no expectation of sleep in the near future. The ambassador pointed to the little table at his elbow where a teapot, two teacups, two glasses and a carafe of dark amber liquid were within easy reach.

'May I offer you refreshments, Dom Sebastião?'

The minister shook his head. 'I thank you, Your Excellency but I have been well provided for. My wife...' he smiled, before his brow puckered gravely. 'I hear that you have opened your home to very many survivors who are in great need of food and shelter.'

The ambassador had a harried air about him as though overwhelmed by the activity and chaos all around, for all that it was out of sight. Which was not surprising, if his people had orders to admit anyone who approached the house. The gardens, though extensive, could not accommodate unlimited numbers of people who had lost their homes in the disaster. The insistent hum of voices, a little muted by the trees in this secluded spot, suggested that the limit had been reached some time ago.

'We have upwards of two hundred and fifty, at the last tally.'

'So many! I had not realised…'

'I intend to shelter and feed every last one, of course, for as long as our provisions last.'

'I will see to it that your resources are replenished, Excellency. Please ask your secretary to send a note to my home on the rua Formosa with a list of your requirements. That is the best way to ensure an urgent message reaches me.'

'That would be a great boon, Minister. We have so many here, whole families…'

'All British subjects?'

'For the most part. English and Irish, the latter being of the poorer sort. And also, the household – the entire household – of M de la Calmette.'

'The Dutch ambassador, yes. Is it true that his family was saved from the earthquake by their pet monkey?'

Castres chuckled. 'Indeed it is. They were alerted some minutes before the tremors began. Its screeching got them out of bed, thus they were ready to flee at the first sign of the shocks.'

'The monkey started screeching before the tremors were felt? Are you certain?'

'According to Madame de la Calmette. You may speak to her, if you wish. You may even make the acquaintance of the heroic monkey. It is being treated as royalty.'

They both laughed, until Ambassador Castres's brow furrowed.

'Poor Count Peralada. A terrible loss.'

The Spanish ambassador had flung on a housecoat as soon as the tremors began and hurried into the street when the walls of his home came tumbling down around him – only to be crushed at his own front door by a massive concrete escutcheon that became dislodged and fell upon him. As relations with

Spain were delicate and complicated, finding the count's body had been one of Dom Sebastião's most urgent tasks, all the more so given that Queen Mariana Vitória was the sister of King Ferdinand of Spain.

The famous exchange of two princesses, one Spanish, destined to become Queen of Portugal, and Bárbara, the Portuguese princess, now Queen of Spain, had been intended to ease the hostilities between their two countries that had prevailed ever since the hated sixty-year unification with Spain had ended, more than a hundred years before. For all that the minister had never liked the Spanish count, the complex relations between the nations and their governing monarchs demanded particular respect for his person, even if in life his manners had always displayed the arrogance typical of the natural coloniser. Nevertheless, he did not deserve this horrible death.

The two men sat for a moment in a silence that was almost companionable, united in pondering the mysteries of the fate that had spared them and destroyed so many others: rich, poor, noble and commoner, all equal before the hand of chance, or Divine Providence, which had left one with a sprained ankle and crushed another to death. What great sin had Count Peralada committed to deserve such a dreadful end? And what of those who were spared? Were they especially virtuous? And what of all those poor wretches, hundreds, perhaps thousands of them, buried or drowned or suffocated or burnt to death? Of all the cities in the world, why had Lisbon been chosen for destruction?

'At this early stage, it is impossible to estimate the number of casualties, Excellency. Certainly in the thousands. Most likely, tens of thousands. And from your British community?'

'Not many, Minister, though of course, one death is one too many. Consul Hay is in the process of compiling a list. As far as we can tell at the moment, our dead amount to about seventy-eight, of whom forty-nine are women. And of those, only four, at our current reckoning, are from the Factory.'

Of course. Membership of the British Factory, both in Lisbon and Oporto being confined to the prosperous merchant class, represented the elite of the British business community in Portugal. Such people would not choose to be out and about on the streets of Lisbon on the feast of All Souls, or indeed any feast day, when the churches were thronged with worshippers and the Catholic faithful were suspicious of the English heretics who live among them. Even at the best of times, a well-dressed English merchant strolling along the Rossio on All Souls' Day would risk confrontation with keening believers brandishing rosary beads, hell-bent on forcing salvation on him, whether he liked it or no. Such amusing anecdotes made for entertainment over a glass of excellent port wine after dinner but the reality could be alarming. As such experiences, or the legends of such experiences, added to a general discomfort around the city at those times, most British subjects who had the means, chose to absent themselves from the city on religious feast days. This was a happy accident for those foreigners who had thereby escaped the wrath of God, which He had rained down on His faithful instead; a conundrum which many a spiritual leader would try to unravel in the coming days.

When sufficient meditation had passed, Dom Sebastião judged that it was time to discover how far the ambassador's compassion for the plight of the people of Lisbon would translate into practical support. He took a sip from the glass of water a footman had left by his elbow.

'You are perhaps aware, Excellency, that in recognition of the massive loss of life and property in the country, not only in Lisbon, cognisant of the enormous costs of rebuilding and re-establishing a commercial base, the Portuguese merchants of Lisbon have volunteered to pay an additional four per cent tax on goods as their contribution to the relief effort.'

Ambassador Castres was indeed aware but had no intention of making this easy for the minister. 'I did not know that but it is good news indeed.' He suspected that the term 'volunteer' was a liberal interpretation of how the Portuguese merchants' contribution had been extracted from them. 'Your British allies and friends wish to provide assistance to Portugal in her hour of affliction. To that end, I am pleased to inform you, Minister, that I have despatched an urgent proposal to our Prime Minister to provide clothing, food, building materials and a substantial sum of money in gold. I am fully expectant that the Duke of Newcastle and his government will agree, your country being our oldest and most valued ally. And I know you became acquainted with many members of our present government, such as Mr Walpole, during your time in England as ambassador. He held you in the highest esteem.'

In fact, Carvalho e Melo's reputation during his eight years as Portugal's envoy to Great Britain was mixed. He was said to be frequently in debt and got into trouble with at least one unsavoury character, to whom, it was rumoured, he owed a large sum of money. Of course, his sojourn had spanned a period of significant turmoil for Great Britain. Some members of the government, and the royal court too, viewed representatives of the Catholic nations with suspicion, lest they harbour covert support for the rebel Jacobites whose religious convictions they shared. The Young Pretender to the throne known as Bonnie Prince Charlie had been sent packing and his supporters executed in the year after Carvalho e Melo was recalled to Lisbon. As he never learned English, some of those government ministers who spoke neither French nor Portuguese did not know what to make of him.

'And I greatly respected him,' the minister replied, a declaration which Ambassador Castres was prepared to take at face value. Carvalho e Melo's admiration for English government, administration and the English people was well known. So, too, his great dismay at being recalled to Lisbon and sent to Vienna, a clear demotion. Though he had not done too badly out of that posting. He won the liking of the empress, no easy feat, and he found himself a noble wife. Once back in Lisbon, though, the new Minister for War and Foreign Affairs had been nothing but a stone in Ambassador Keene's shoe. From time to time, Sir Benjamin's letters from Madrid contained stern advice on how to handle this ambitious politician. With extreme care. Especially concerning his most recent venture out in the Americas, Grão Pará and Maranhão: a new company, a monopoly, founded not six months previous, which would put an end to the free trade in the myriad goods that had made so many men of commerce – not a few of them Englishmen – very wealthy indeed.

'If this Company of Grão Pará and Maranhão works as I think he intends,' Keene's most recent missive had warned less than a fortnight before, 'not only would it bring control of commerce in the colonies into his hands. He could, in theory, replicate the structure across every area of manufacturing – wine, ceramics, textiles and more – which would have serious consequences for the balance of trade between our two countries, and not in our favour.'

But first he needs a workforce, Ambassador Castres thought, to get gold out of the mines and sugar on to the ships. And out in Grão Pará that would not be easy, for the Jesuits control – or protect, depending on your stance – the native workers. It would be interesting to see how this tussle with the Jesuits developed. It was said that where the Society of Jesus was concerned, Carvalho e Melo could become a little unhinged. Though at present, he seemed to be in perfect command of himself.

'We are deeply grateful for all assistance your illustrious government has offered, Ambassador Castres. On behalf of the people of Lisbon and Portugal, I give you my humble thanks. I feel sure that Dom José will convey his gratitude, when you and Consul Hay confer with him.'

The ambassador smiled. Yes, the minister had intelligence of every move Dom José made. There was a pause, while Dom Sebastião looked into the distance and steepled his long, slender fingers.

'However.'

The ambassador waited.

'Notwithstanding Your Excellency's generosity in proposing such significant aid…'

This had obviously been discussed already with the king. Which meant that the terms which the minister was now preparing to propose had the approval of the monarch. Might this meeting, and the forthcoming audience with the king, be a strategy cooked up by Carvalho e Melo himself? Was he being tenderised, to persuade the British Factory to accept certain pre-ordained conditions? It was a pity that he had not thought to postpone this meeting until Consul-General Hay could attend and at least dilute the gimlet gaze of the Minister for War and Foreign Affairs, which was now firmly fixed on him.

'But Ambassador Castres!' The minister interrupted himself. 'How inconsiderate of me not to have enquired before now! How fares Lady Hay?'

Startled that his line of thought had been so closely intuited, Castres wondered for a moment if he had spoken his thoughts aloud.

'She is recovering well. She has had a great shock. Lord Hay is even now accompanying her to the home of a Factory colleague outside the city.'

The consul's wife, having given birth but a few days before, had had to be carried from her bed when the earthquake struck, by a nurse who was tending to mother and child, a woman who fortunately had physical strength and calmness of disposition sufficient to bring her charges to safety.

The minister's grave eyes showed concern. 'And the child?'

'A little girl, Margaret. She is well, along with her mother.'

'I am glad of it. Please convey my good wishes to Lord Hay and his family.'

His sincerity was convincing. The minister was known to be a family man. Had he not lost two children of his own, just last year? A newborn, and an older child of perhaps four or five years? In spite of himself, Castres found his heart soften, then harden again. Carvalho e Melo had known full well that Consul Hay could not be present at this meeting today. And why.

'To return to our question: Your Excellency will appreciate, given the scale of the disaster afflicting our city, our entire country, and the enormous cost of rebuilding and recovery, not only the edifices but caring for the injured, re-establishing commerce, compensation for small businesses which have been ruined...'

Like so many commercial interests of your allies, the ambassador did not say. The losses incurred by the merchants of the British Factory would be colossal. There was no doubt that the reverberations of the earthquake would shatter many English businesses and be felt in the coffers of the Bank of England. Even on the British stock exchange.

'As a nation, what we need from our allies is not gifts, however generous and however grateful we are for the offer. Not charity.'

Then what, the ambassador thought, for he knew what was to follow.

'What we seek is a just economic agreement: a reasonable levy on goods, comparable to that volunteered by our native merchants, in recognition of the great economic benefits and privileges which Great Britain has for so long enjoyed under the conditions of trade between our two countries.' To the extent that Portugal, economically speaking, was practically a British colony, the minister might have added. 'Now, in our time of need, this is surely a question of natural justice.'

It was a clever strategy, this appeal to the famed British sense of fair play. Would it not be churlish, in such circumstances, to insist upon the letter of the law in defence of the commercial interests of the British merchants whose trade with their host nation had so handsomely enriched them? Though defend them he must. While Ambassador Castres gathered his thoughts, he poured himself a thimbleful of dark amber liquid, that it might soothe his throbbing ankle, then wished immediately that he had not, for an ironic ghost of a smile was playing upon the lips of his guest. He nodded to the carafe at his elbow.

'Are you sure...?'

The minister shook his head. 'It is a little early for me, Excellency. But when I lived in England, I observed that for your compatriots, it is never too early for a small glass of our fortified wine. And indeed, why should it be, this great gift of our nation to yours.'

He smiled again and again the ambassador cursed his own lack of foresight. The word 'gift' was an open provocation. Carvalho e Melo had been attempting to renegotiate the tariffs on port wine since he took up office.

'But that is a subject for another day,' the minister swept on. 'For the moment, the question of a new tax on the goods of British merchants –'

'As you are aware, Dom Sebastião,' Castres cut in, 'the longstanding treaties between our two countries cap the levy on British goods at twenty-three per cent. Any attempt to impose an additional tax would be in breach of not one, not two...' He paused for dramatic effect. '...but three solemn agreements between our government and your own.'

That had not taken long. Every attempt to negotiate with the British Factory since his appointment as minister five years before, whether on rates of taxation, valuation of goods or conditions of trade, had been met by the same answer: selective appeal to those three wretched treaties that gave the English in Portugal such favourable conditions, not only of commerce but of living circumstances. This was a merchant class, represented by the British Factory, who guarded privileges which they had now come to regard as rights, the slightest of which they had no intention of giving up without a battle.

Well, Dom Sebastião Carvalho e Melo, Minister of War and Foreign Affairs, was equal to the fight. The protection of England's oldest ally and friend against the threat of invasion by Spain which had always, since the restoration of Portuguese independence, simmered on the borders, had come at a very high price. The conditions of those Methuen Treaties, the last signed half a century before, committed Portugal to a whole array of commercial agreements on massive importations from England of all manner of goods – goods that Portugal should produce herself! – in exchange for meagre concessions in tariffs on port wine imported to England. Of course, the imbalance had to be paid for somehow.

With Brazilian gold, of course. Which belonged to the English as soon as it landed, even before, long before, as soon as it left Brazil, indeed from the moment it was extracted from the mines of Minas Gerais. Nothing was more enraging than the smug congregation of British merchants who habitually gathered on the Cais do Sodré when the precious cargo from Brazil was brought ashore, complacent in the knowledge that it would soon be making its way to their English banks.

How such an unequal relationship had been allowed to continue for decades, nay, for close on a century, was a mystery. And in spite of all their privileges, their freedom of religion, their own church and cemetery – the exemption of British subjects from the judicial process of the host country! – at this time of crisis, they were still bleating the letter of those wretched Methuen treaties. It could only be explained by the indifference or sloth of old Dom João, the present king's father, and his incompetent band of advisors and courtiers. It could not continue.

'Those treaties were made at very different times from the present circumstances, as I have pointed out to Your Excellency on many occasions. For one, the treaty of 1654 was signed during the Protectorate, when Great Britain was governed as a Republic. It ought therefore to have fallen, or at least been renegotiated when the monarchy was restored…'

Castres was having none of it. 'And as I have pointed out many times, Minister, no country in the world – no civilised country, that is – would renege on an international treaty which has the status of law. The good faith of agreements made between nation states is the substance of diplomacy, and it is diplomacy that averts wars. A country that reneges on a solemn treaty has shown it cannot be trusted. By neither friend nor foe.'

Dom Sebastião glared at him. It was no small thing to accuse a government minister, in his own country, of attempting to tear up an international treaty. But he must not allow himself to be provoked.

'The letter of the law may appear to be on your side, Excellency. But I am convinced – and I am not alone in this – that the spirit of the treaties to which you appeal so eloquently is one of interpretation, rather than fact. And in these extraordinary times, our corresponding appeal to decency, which I know your nation so greatly prizes, is not the dereliction of a sacred vow you suggest. Rather, it is a sincere request for a just concession on terms, in our time of greatest affliction.'

If he had not been so irritated, the ambassador would have applauded the minister's skilful and devious change of tack. But he was not deceived. This proposal, now framed as an appeal to natural justice and the native decency of the British, was but one more concession which the minister was attempting to wring from the British Factory, one more assault on the bedrock of the British traders' vast commercial interests in Portugal.

The worst of it was, this canny Portuguese minister might well have a case. At least two of the greatest legal minds in England had conceded that the implementation of the Methuen treaties, as enacted, did not conform to the spirit of equality between the two nations to which they aspired. Until these anomalies in his eminent advisors' views were resolved, he would not engage in a futile battle of wills with this over-promoted politician who had proved himself ill-disposed to turn the same blind eye as his predecessors to the advantages his British countrymen in Portugal had enjoyed for so long.

'I will reflect on your proposal, and discuss it with Lord Hay, before our audience with His Majesty.'

Dom Sebastião smiled, confident of a favourable conclusion, if not immediately, then at some time in the future. But there was nothing to be gained, and everything to lose, in trumpeting confidence in victory: often, those who are obliged to confront their defeat may be spurred to unexpected, if futile, retaliation. It would do no harm to relax the formalities. He nodded to the little table at Castres's elbow.

'Might I accept your kind offer of refreshments after all?'

'Certainly.' The ambassador reached for one of the crystal glasses and raised the carafe. As the dark amber trickled gently, it gleamed in the last rays of the sun like liquid gold.

The ambassador raised his glass. 'To friendship,' he said. 'And to satisfactory conclusions. *Saúde*!'

Dom Sebastião held his glass high and summoned up his few words of English:

'Your good health.'

He would toast friendship with England, always. But satisfactory conclusions? In the golden depths of the rich port wine swirling in his glass rippled the vine growers, the tavern keepers, hundreds of casks on the quayside of Oporto, bound for the dinner tables of London… In his mind, he was toasting the first shot across the bows in a battle of wills that was very far from being over.

In truth, it had scarcely begun.

11

A Missed Appointment and an Unwelcome Visitor

November 15th, 1755, Távora Summer Palace, Belém

For the third time in a half-hour, the Marchioness of Távora laid down her quill and set aside the bundle of cards inscribed with invitations to a select group of like-minded people who would soon attend a discreet gathering in the palace. She rose from her desk and approached the floor-length window that dominated a panorama of the river Tagus, the Jerónimos monastery and the village of Belém. The Távora summer palace occupied an enviable location that surpassed even that of the royal family's summer residence close by, on the higher slopes of the hills. For once, Dona Leonora did not savour the vista, such was her mounting irritation, as the carriage she awaited from minute to minute failed to appear.

That her daughter-in-law would keep her waiting was already an impertinence. This could only mean one thing: that the king, in spite of Dona Leonora's solemn petitions, was clinging to the royal privilege of indulging his lust with whomsoever he pleased. Otherwise, the young marchioness – a designation of her daughter-in-law which Dona Leonora disliked, for it identified herself as the old marchioness – would never have responded to the urgent summons with such a brazen lack of courtesy. Her tardiness bordered on insult with every passing minute.

Although she would not admit it, Dona Leonora was anticipating this meeting with unease. The conversation would not be the one she had prepared, for the Patriarch had refused outright her pleas that the marriage of Dona Teresa and Luís Bernardo be annulled. That the young marchioness had caught the eye of the king while her devoted young husband was travelling in India with his parents – perhaps even before then! – and showed no inclination to end the liaison since their return, was intolerable. Francisco agreed that severing the marriage bond between their son and Teresa was necessary, to restore at least the appearance of honour to the family.

Why had the Patriarch refused to pursue this annulment on their behalf? No doubt because the king would not have it. Perhaps he found Teresa more alluring as a married woman whose husband was now close by. Perhaps he simply wished to remind the Távoras, however illustrious and powerful their dynasty, of the ascendancy of the royal will. Or might there be other influences at work?

A footman entered the room, bearing aloft a silver platter. A letter, sealed with her own family's coat of arms. Her own name etched in Teresa's graceful script. Dona Leonora retrieved a jewelled letter opener from her desk, the handle embossed with own initials entwined with those of her husband. That Francisco had not yet been raised to the rank of duke, nor she to duchess, despite the great service the family had performed for the nation in India, was incomprehensible. Intolerable. In spite of her tireless representations to the king, the promised elevation was repeatedly denied.

'Leave me.'

Taking three deep breaths to steady her breathing as Father Malagrida had taught her, for it was obvious who had written this letter and what it said, she slid the blade under the seal. Before she could catch it, the dark red wax split in two pieces and fell to the marbled floor.

The two lines of graceful script were polite, even friendly, and an outrageous presumption. Dona Teresa regretted that she would be unable to accept the marchioness's kind invitation. It had not been an invitation, but a summons, as the young hussy well knew.

Trembling and scarcely able to breathe, Dona Leonora sank into a chair by the fire, watching the last flicker of flame in the gathering twilight. This liaison with the king was but one manifestation, and the most public, of the contempt in which Dom José held her family. Five years before, they had had every reason to believe that if Francisco acquitted himself well as Viceroy to India, appropriate honours would be bestowed on their return. An understanding, yes, rather than an explicit commitment. But Dom João's intention was clear, and even had the enthusiastic support of Dom José, at that time heir to the throne. The then prince had even officiated, with great warmth, at that magnificent festival on the banks of the Tagus which his parents had arranged to bid the Távora family farewell, before they set sail for India.

What had changed? Too much. The old king was dead. Dom José had succeeded to the throne. And the first years of his reign had revealed the character of the man. Whether through lack of native wit or plain laziness, it was clear that their new monarch had not one scrap of the regal bearing or ability of his father. Although never openly stated – for that would be treasonous – several trusted intimates, among them the Duke of Aveiro, spoke *sotto voce* of the king's lack of interest in matters of state. While she and Francisco and yes, Luís Bernardo, too, were facing myriad dangers in India – quelling rebellions, consolidating relations with local rulers, even extending the national territory, in short, performing heroic service for their country – Dom José and Dona Mariana Vitória had been hunting and attending the opera. Neither had shown the slightest inclination to fulfil either their duties of governing, or their ceremonial roles. Which left the king plenty of time to pursue his many romantic liaisons.

But none of this explained the coolness of their reception when they returned home. The welcome was little more than a formal reception committee, a paltry display, in comparison to the fanfare that had celebrated their departure. What had changed to produce such a dramatic decline in the status and respect with which the family were regarded?

Sebastião José Carvalho e Melo.

The king's favourite. His most trusted advisor. Minister of War and Foreign Affairs, now Minister for Everything, it seemed. A minor politician, a failed ambassador in two jurisdictions, an adventurer who won his initial place in the government through low-ranking family connections. A man who gained a title and a fine fortune from his first wife and inveigled his way into the favour of the old queen, Dom José's mother, by marrying a fellow Austrian. A noblewoman, of course, her family held in the highest esteem by none other than the Empress Maria Teresa of Austria herself! To say that this nonentity had extended his influence into all areas of government through judicious marriages and a web of conniving supporters, was no hyperbole. Most sinister of all was his influence on the king, who consulted him on all manner of matters far beyond his remit. In the last fifteen days, His Majesty being called upon to respond to this terrible disaster, yet unwilling or perhaps unable to enforce the necessary policies himself, this interloper had assumed the reins of government.

And in the midst of such tragedy as had befallen their city, was the king even now continuing to indulge his appetites?

Dona Leonora crumpled the paper in her hand and let it fall to the floor. Whether Sebastião José had encouraged the king to continue the affair, emboldening her own daughter-in-law to decline her summons, she could not say. It was just as likely that the king wished to see her today on a caprice, and his whims, of course, must always be indulged. Still, were it not for Sebastião José whispering in his ear, assuring him of his rights to satisfy himself as he wished, Dom José would never have conducted himself thus. Nor would he have magnified the insult by offering inducements, money and honours – but not the dukedom – to overlook his 'sentimental attachment' to the wife of the heir of the house of Távora. It was the simple lusting of a fat old man for the charms of a willowy beauty with the creamy skin and red-gold hair that was the mark of her husband's family. As though the family dignity were for sale.

Her thoughts were interrupted by another footman bearing aloft the same silver platter, an engraved card at its centre. This, she declined to touch. A visiting card. Of the very last person she wished to see, under any circumstances. Who did this upstart think he was, to arrive at a Távora summer residence with no advance warning, no appointment, no invitation?

'Inform him I am not at home.'

The footman made no move to leave.

'Yes?'

The young man hesitated. Dona Leonora did not habitually take note of her servants' comfort or discomfort, but this boy's unease was irritating.

'That is a simple instruction, is it not?'

'Dom Sebastião said...'

'You refer to the Minister for War.' How well acquainted was this boy with the appalling Sebastião José? The boy stuttered an affirmative.

'Then instruct me. What did the minister have to say?'

'I beg your pardon, Excellency. The minister said to tell you... If you said you were not at home... That he comes on most urgent business. On behalf of His Majesty.'

The young man looked at the floor in misery, in preference to contemplating the countenance of the marchioness, who had become very still.

'That is well. Admit him.' Dona Leonora considered obliging the uninvited visitor to wait until she had finished inscribing her invitations but thought better of it. 'At once,' she commanded, returning to her writing desk, where she remained seated, occupied in adding her signature to her letters when the minister was announced. He stood just inside the door, his demeanour respectful, head lowered, as he waited for the instruction to advance.

'Minister.'

He responded with a deep bow, surprised when she gestured towards the little chair by the window. He had not expected to be invited to sit, for the marchioness was keenly sensible of the privileges of her rank and would surely take pleasure in obliging him to stand for the duration of their audience. Yet she was also an astute woman who no doubt had divined that strange unease experienced by many, regardless of rank, when a person of greater physical stature looms over them, whether standing or seated. She would not allow him that advantage. Her own chair was positioned to allow the side light from what was left of the evening sun to play gently on her handsome features, showing her profile to perfection.

'I am grateful that you have given me this time, Excellency.' He bowed his head again, careful to avoid looking at the uncapped inkwell on the marchioness's desk, the quill and the bundle of cards that teased his peripheral vision.

'As you can see, I am extremely occupied.' She waved a slender hand towards the papers, a brazen gesture under the circumstances. Did she think he did not know about her salons and soirées, supposed cultural events, frequented by every one of Dom José's opponents in the court, including several members of her own family, and presided over by the treacherous Malagrida? That their discussions were not confined to the Lusíadas or the opera had long been established. Nor was spiritual development the purpose of those gatherings.

'I come on a matter of some urgency, Excellency. Else I would not importune you at this most difficult of times.'

It would be extremely interesting to know the names of those addressed in that bundle of cards. No matter. For the moment, it was enough to know that the disaster that had befallen their city barely two weeks ago had not quenched the appetite of those high-born families for intrigue. And there was no doubt that Malagrida was still involved.

'It is a matter of some delicacy, Your Excellency.' The marchioness's unwavering amber gaze was disconcerting, as she remained steadfast in her silence, daring him to proceed.

He dared. 'It concerns Dona Teresa of Távora.' He coughed. 'Your daughter-in-law. Dom Francisco's sister.'

The marchioness remained impassive, determined not to assist him. It was said that Sebastião José was a prude in such matters, a family man who never indulged his appetites outside the marital bed. What must he think of his master, the king?

'And your son, Dom Luís Bernardo.'

'The young marquis.'

'Indeed. And... and... His Majesty.'

Her stubborn refusal to communicate confirmed his fears. The king's proposals which he was charged to convey would come to naught and might make a bad situation worse. Dom José had insisted on this approach – against his advice, there being no doubt in his own mind that the injured pride of the Távora clan would wreck any attempt at reconciliation or compensation. But Dom José in many ways was an innocent who often failed to grasp that the passions of his courtiers might lead them to act against what he, the king, perceived as their interests. Dona Leonora's compelling silence and unflinching gaze confirmed that this was a failed mission before it even began.

'Well, Minister? You come on urgent business. Speak, therefore.'

He considered prefacing the necessary harshness of his words with some flattering commentary on the marchioness's enduring beauty. At fifty-six, she retained traces of the allure that had made her one of the most sought-after brides in the court forty years before. But she was a woman little susceptible to flattery and would not indulge gallantry from him as she would from a man of her own rank. There was nothing for it but to plunge in.

'His Majesty is deeply grieved by the unhappy misunderstanding that has arisen between his royal person and your family.'

Which pronouncement she received with no change of expression.

'Dom José is cognisant that you and your husband...'

'...and my son.'

'...and your son, may have misinterpreted his... his...affection for the young marchioness as a slight upon...when on the contrary, his regard for Dona Teresa is a mark of his confidence in, and respect for, the Távora name...'

This was too much.

'Minister, Dona Teresa is neither a serving maid nor the daughter of a country squire. She is the sister of the Marquis of Távora, and wife of the heir to one of the oldest and most illustrious titles of the kingdom.'

Did this foolish woman not understand that what he had referred to as the king's 'grief' was, in fact, the king's deep displeasure? The marchioness and her husband and probably young Luís Bernardo too had elevated a trifling matter to a towering slur upon their dynasty. Kings had always taken the lovers that pleased them and the woman's family, if they were clever, regarded their ruler's fancy as an opportunity for advancement. But Dona Leonora and Dom Francisco had forgotten this unwritten, if unpopular, law of *droit de seigneur*. Furthermore, they showed little insight into the character of the king. They ought to know better. Easy-going and agreeable, he was rarely roused to ire, except when his will was opposed in his amorous adventures, especially at this time, when he was frightened by the earthquake, by the enduring threat from the river and the sea and tumbling masonry and by the damnation of all our mortal souls which the Jesuits, one Jesuit in particular, continued to preach. Even Mariana Vitória knew better than to oppose him on this matter.

Might he explain all this to the marchioness – that His Majesty was filled with panic and in need of comfort and pleasure, not censure – without betraying Dom José's confidence or, let us be honest, his weakness? But no. Impossible. Even now, Malagrida was preaching damnation to the people, repeating that the earthquake was God's punishment for the wickedness of the people of Lisbon. And this, but a short step to attributing the wrath of God to the wickedness of the king.

That scoundrel of a priest was a frequent guest in the Távora palace. And the Távoras and their intimates were frequent participants in the padre's spiritual retreats.

Retreats indeed.

No. The marchioness would never accept his advice as sincerely meant. However circumspect his words, she would use them against him. And of course, there were those vicious rumours which she had allowed to circulate unchecked for years: that in his youth he had made himself ridiculous by asking for the hand of one of the young Távora heiresses and been rebuffed as a vulgar adventurer with expectations far in excess of his station. Some versions of the tale even had him being physically ejected from their palace. Yet any inquiry as to which of the daughters or cousins he had supposedly courted, and when, was invariably met with nothing more substantial than smirks and raised eyebrows. If she had wished, Dona Leonora could have dismissed these rumours which even today, more than thirty years later, continued to follow and humiliate him. She had allowed the lies about him to multiply. Perhaps she had started them herself.

'Excellency, His Majesty has ordered me to confirm your acceptance of his gracious bestowal of the position of cavalier to your husband the marquis, and to his gifts of the famous emeralds of Goa for your own excellent person, in addition to the benefits of properties listed in the deed with which I furnished you at our last meeting.'

By way of reply, the marchioness rose from her chair. So. The audience was at an end. But not quite.

'Please inform His Majesty that the Távora family will not accept such benefits, when the honour of our young heirs is in question.'

The blind arrogance of these people was breathtaking. Their monumental self-regard eclipsed all sense of proportion and strategy. A wise matriarch would have accepted the situation, however distasteful, and received the compensations offered by the king with good grace, thus winning his favour or, at least, averting the rancour of her sovereign. They were living in the past, these relics, utterly blind to the new reality, of which even a monstrous earthquake had failed to convince them: that the epoch of their privilege and dominance was over.

She had not quite finished.

'Furthermore, please inform His Majesty, again, of our deep disappointment at his refusal to permit the marriage of our niece Luísa to the son of the Duke of Braga.'

'I will convey your disappointment, Excellency.' He hesitated. 'If you are sure.'

'I am.'

Oh, this was foolish. Dom José himself had straightway grasped that a union of the Távoras and the Bragas would establish a significant force which would rival the power of all other families and even, the might of his very throne. All credit for that particular decision belonged to the king himself. Still, it was both a duty and a pleasure to inform Dona Leonora that one more gambit intended to swell the already bloated influence of those two tribes had been thwarted. Perhaps the failure of this union, together with disappointment at not receiving the coveted dukedom, explained the anger which this appalling family had not troubled to conceal, even from the king himself.

As he turned to leave, his boot slipped on a crumpled paper. Before the marchioness could stop him – really, did he have to be told that the maid would clear it away, that a person born to rank would never stoop to pick anything from the floor? – he had retrieved it and placed it upon her escritoire. Into his pocket, unseen, he slipped two small pieces of wax scooped up along with the paper: the broken seal of the Távora family, embossed with their coat of arms.

Well, he had made an honest attempt to quell the fury of the marchioness and assuage the anger which her entire family bore towards the king. He had offered compensations as commanded; tried his best to deflect the king's displeasure; and all, as he had expected, to no avail. Pausing at the foot of the great staircase, he nodded to one of the footmen, not the boy who had announced him but another young man with a stronger stomach for such things, who nodded in return. All was well. The names of those inscribed on the marchioness's guest list would be divulged to him soon enough.

12

Two Troubling Interludes and one Alarming Order

December 15th, 1755, Bairro Alto

The streets of the Bairro Alto stir to wakefulness, as dwellers are roused from their slumber by urgent cries that echo through arid landscapes of uneasy dreams. A few stooped figures stumble into what is left of the streets, dragged from the respite of a little sleep into the shattered world that lies in ruins. Dawn has not come, nor yet even the faint glow that promises the end of night. But for the glimmer of a few unclouded stars, the darkness is complete. Trembling hands draw aside ragged curtains or bits of faded tapestry, rugs, sailcloth that cover the makeshift huts and carts and the few remaining window frames, a hodgepodge of fragile shelters wherein the homeless seek protection from the driving sleet and rain. One by one, gaunt figures venture from the flimsy structures which have afforded them refuge since the catastrophe six weeks before. Neighbours clutch at neighbours, all straining to apprehend the terrible warning.

Only the boldest among them dare light a candle or a taper. So many shrink from the faintest flicker of fire, their panic rising in recollection of the flames that consumed their homes. Some of the wreckage in this part of the city has been cleared, but the soldiers in charge of the relief effort have concentrated on removing cadavers, human remains, which are already cast into the sea. A watery, barely Christian interment deemed necessary to avert the spread of plague.

Seeking out the voice that roused them, the ragged wraiths summoned from uneasy slumber, soon gather to a throng. This cannot be the voice of a man but rather, the shriek of a wailing ghost, rasping words accompanied by the clamour and clatter of a stick banging on a metal bucket, a cruel parody of the chiming bells of Lisbon's thousand churches, now in ruins, their loved ones and treasures buried beneath.

'People of Lisbon, awaken! Do not remain within these walls, do not dare to stay beneath your roofs. Another calamity is about to befall us. Sleep beneath the stars tonight!'

As the words echo through the night air, fearful murmurs swell to a chorus of whimpers and cries. Candlelight flickers upon an uncommonly tall figure waiting in the shadows of a doorway, unremarked by the gathering crowd of women and men. Taking care not to attract attention, he slips out from beneath the arch, his movements agile for such a tall man. He clambers upon the wheel of a cart, thus attaining a vantage point which affords him a good view of the crowd and of individual countenances. Lamplight plays across gaping mouths and staring eyes that now and then are steeped in shadow, according to the vagaries of the wind. They had better attend to that wind, or no one here will see the dawn. Once satisfied that he has a sound grasp of the situation, reassured by the muskets carried by the dozen or so soldiers positioned about the place, he climbs down and returns to the shelter of the archway, his long face grey with tiredness.

A young soldier wearing the regalia of captain approaches. He remembers just in time that this is not the place to draw attention to the minister's presence by saluting him; then wonders why in any case he should salute the Minister for War and Foreign Affairs, who is not his superior officer. Dom Sebastião José Carvalho e Melo, for it is he, points to the speaker.

'Who is this man? Where did he come by his information?'

Captain Fernando da Oliveira raises the oil lamp he carries gingerly, still uneasy when this close to fire, having seen too many twisted corpses and blackened skeletons in the ruins of the city during these past weeks. His master's eyes, furrowed and red rimmed, have barely closed for more than two hours a night in the past forty-one days.

'His name is not yet known, Dom Sebastião. These neighbours say that he is a ship's pilot on the Tagus. They say he observed a similar phenomenon in the river on the very day before –'

The configuration of shadows is shifting as the multitude gives way to allow passage to a spindly silhouette who strides into their midst. As though awaiting some kind of greeting or obeisance, the newcomer pauses. A half-dozen people, men as well as women, fall to their knees. A few grasp the hem of his cloak and plead for his blessing. One arm emerges from the folds of the black cassock, rises, falls, rises and falls again. Soon, the words of the river pilot disappear beneath a sonorous chant.

'The rosary.' Dom Sebastião steps forward, out of the shadows. The newcomer does not observe his presence or, if he does, declines to acknowledge it. 'As if prayers tonight will serve them any better than they did on All Souls' Day.'

Captain da Olveira feels the comforting heft of his musket on his hip. Had he done right in rousing his master from his first night's sleep in so many weeks?

'One night's uninterrupted sleep, Captain, just one?' Dona Eleanor had not wanted to waken her husband. The captain bowed in answer, even in these terrible days elaborate courtesies not forgotten, and insisted as politely as the emergency permitted.

Dom Sebastião's attention is now fully alert, fixed upon the man in the centre of the square leading prayers and yes, even hearing confessions, out here in the open air, in the middle of the night. So those requests to the Patriarch – his advice, his pleas to silence this disruptor of the peace, his warnings of the consequences of inflaming panic among the people – went unheeded.

'What phenomenon has frightened the river pilot so much that he is determined to rouse the whole neighbourhood on account of it?'

'The tide this evening was two hours late, Minister. Or so this fellow says. And he says more. That never in his life had he seen such a strange occurrence on our river. Except …' He hesitates. 'Except on the evening of October 31st.'

Dom Sebastião makes no answer. His young companion stands beside him in respectful silence. Together they survey the scene. Impossible to believe that life had continued after the earth swallowed up so much of the city in just a few minutes, at the very time when the faithful were attending mass and saying their prayers on one of the holiest days of the year. But continue it had. Even the fear of the flames that had raged for weeks, consuming almost everything that the earthquake and the giant waves had spared, seems a little diminished, for those present are listening to the pilot's words by the light of candles and tapers held aloft, transfixed in horror, the hollows and shadows of their stricken faces illuminated by the ghastly glow. They could do no other. The night is dark, light is needed, fire gives light and the memory of the terrible destruction inflicted by the flames must yield to the continuation of life.

The ship's pilot, who had found himself a makeshift platform on the back of a cart, is speaking with growing urgency when the people drift away from him, distracted by a throng whose chants and prayers were ever more insistent.

'Leave now,' he cries. 'Take your children and belongings enough to keep warm and dry. Food if you can carry it. Find a patch of high ground – at Rato, perhaps, there are camps there, they may find space for you. Sleep in the open tonight, cover yourselves in nothing of greater weight than a tapestry or sailcloth, for this strangeness of the tides can mean only one thing.

Above all, stay away from the Rossio.'

Their attention ignited by those final words, for everyone present knows what happened in the low-lying centre, several of those gathered around the newcomer halt their incantations and turn to listen to the pilot. A few cease praying and begin to wail in response to the pilot's warnings. Fear has a life all its own, it spreads like fire and engulfs crowds in its waves. Soon, panic will reign and the city will be lost.

For a few moments, Dom Sebastião José Carvalho y Melo inspects the ever-shifting tides moving through the throng, his stillness brimming with intention. When he finally speaks, his voice is soft. It brooks no dissent.

'Apprehend that man.'

'Father Malagrida?'

'No. The river pilot.'

The captain hesitates. From his vantage point, he sees what Dom Sebastião perhaps cannot: that the hovering, spindly figure has ceased dispensing blessings and leading prayers and is making his way through the crowd to take up position alongside the river pilot who, on remarking the padre's presence beside him, falls to his knees before him.

'Dom Sebastião, the people are frightened, the pilot himself is receiving a blessing…'

'Immediately, Captain. Arrest the pilot and conduct him straightway to Belém. Have him detained in the tower until the danger is past.'

But which danger, wonders Captain da Oliveira? The peril of a renewal of tremors in the shuddering earth, whose rumblings have barely ceased in the last forty-one days? Fear of robbers and murderers who daily and nightly risk their own skin by picking over the ruins of what is left of the city and scavenging the remains of the dead and dying? The terror of the crowd which could soon become a mob? Though it is quiet enough now, for the people are kneeling before a prophet, who, they believe, will save their immortal souls.

'It is possible that the crowd will not permit it, Dom Sebastião,' the captain murmurs. 'While the padre is hearing the pilot's confession, he will not suffer to be interrupted.'

'In which case, shoot him. Shoot them both.'

The young captain gapes.

'Are you armed?'

'Yes, Excellency

Captain da Oliveira's musket is in plain view and he had the foresight to station his soldiers, hastily rounded up from the remnants of those who had tried to flee the city in the first terrible days, at strategic points around the little square. With the intention to maintain order, not to –

'How long would you have me wait, Captain, before putting an end to this spectacle? Very soon there will be panic here, then throughout the city and when that happens, the earthquake in people's hearts will destroy us all. There will be carnage, again. What would you have me do?'

The young man opens his mouth and quickly closes it. It has never been clear to him why Dom Sebastião José Carvalho e Melo should do anything. Under normal circumstances, Captain Fernando da Oliveira would not have hesitated to comply with an order from a superior officer, however distasteful. But Dom Sebastião is not, properly speaking, his superior officer. Still. These are not normal days. No one else has given an order, any order, no one else has any idea of what is happening or what to do. Yet somehow, with the apparent agreement, or perhaps as a result of the paralysis of the nobles of the court and the rest of the government, Dom Sebastião has assumed the full authority of a commanding officer of the army. And of the Treasury, what is left of it. And of any number of other institutions of the state. All of them, perhaps. It is said that he is the eyes and ears and is probably the brain of His Majesty, too.

The minister rubs his face and looks upon the young man

with a little more kindness.

'Act with decision and authority and you will have no difficulty. The people are longing to be delivered from these purveyors of doom. Order them to free themselves and they will obey. And then apprehend the pilot and remove him to Belém. Else this panic will spread all over the city.'

'And Padre Malagrida? Should we apprehend him also?'

The old Jesuit had not once looked their way, though he certainly must have observed their presence.

His master glares into the darkness. 'No,' he says. 'Leave Malagrida to me.'

The apprehending of the river pilot is accomplished smoothly, much more smoothly than expected. Dom Sebastião had correctly judged the mood of the crowd. When Captain Fernando da Oliveira strides into the crowd, shouting orders, not yet brandishing his musket, the densest section of the throng parts and when the river pilot clings to the captain's hand, pleading earnestly that the captain and everyone must heed his warnings, a firm grip pinning the frightened man's arm behind his back is sufficient force to overpower him.

'Go back to your beds,' Captain da Oliveira bellows. 'This poor deluded chap has had his mind shattered by the horrors we have all endured. I am apprehending him for his own safety. No harm will come to him.'

While the captain and his men guide the people back to their makeshift shelters, the agitated cries dwindle to grumbles and jeers and soon, to a few nervous mutterings. Dom Sebastião represses a smile to see da Oliveira address the crowd with an authority that is almost jocular, no doubt relieved to be spared the obligation of shooting anyone, at least for the moment.

'Go home. There will be no more earthquakes tonight.'

At that, the spindly figure emerges from the thinning crowd, raises a hand high and speaks, his voice deep and sonorous and sweet.

'The sword of fire wielded by Seraphim is destined to exterminate sinners! God reveals that he was greatly angered by the sins of the whole kingdom, and especially by Lisbon and consequently had to visit upon her a great affliction that cannot be attributable to natural causes, but to the indignation of God because of the vileness of our sins! Penance alone is the key that will unlock the treasures of mercy. Would there were as much determination and fervour for this necessary exercise as is now devoted to the erection of huts and new buildings! God undoubtedly desires to exercise His love and mercy, but be sure that wherever we are, He is watching us, scourge in hand!'

When the padre raises his voice, those closest to him hesitate, caught between the words of their prophet and the captain's command, terror rekindled by this new spark ignited by conflicting orders. A few women sink to their knees before the old man. When Dom Sebastião approaches, Malagrida continues to preach, head held high, his regard fixed on the darkness ahead, his hands reaching out, almost touching the heads of two of his followers who are gazing up at him in supplication as though he, and only he, can deliver them from the terrible fate that God has in store for them.

'If you must kneel, kneel before His Majesty the king and no other.'

Padre Malagrida ceases his preaching and at last, deigns to address the minister.

'Their immortal souls are of immeasurably greater import than their bodies. I am the representative of His Lord –'

'And I am the representative of His Majesty King José I, empowered to arrest or if necessary, summarily execute anyone who interferes with or obstructs the relief effort. Captain!'

Malagrida hesitates. Dom Sebastião watches the shades of calculation play across the old priest's features, his lips pursed as he weighs the heft of the threat and the minister's inclination and authority to carry it out. Oh indeed, Padre, you may dismiss my words as empty sabre-rattling. But there are fifteen new gallows set around the city from which are dangling already the corpses of thieves and murderers who have sought to profit from the disaster. You, you may be a Jesuit and in past days a confessor to our young king's dead father and to his mother, too. You may be a revered missionary, venerated as a prophet and therefore think yourself far beyond the sanction of an upstart minister.

But you are no longer sure.

For an instant, their eyes meet, Malagrida's diamond glitter and the minister's basalt gaze crossing like two rapiers glinting in the moonlight.

'Padre Malagrida,' Dom Sebastião makes no attempt to hide the contempt in his voice. 'This is not the time or the place to preach hellfire to the people.'

'It is exactly the time. Lisbon is paying for the sins of her people. Sins which brought the wrath of God upon us and –'

'Lisbon must be healed and rebuilt. Your sermons and blessings frighten the faithful into inaction. Cause them to flee, instead of assisting in the relief effort, ministering to the wounded, rebuilding the ruins. This is a time to inspire courage, not terror. I require that you desist. I speak with the authority of the king.'

Malagrida takes a step forward. 'And I answer to a higher authority. The highest. The Almighty Lord has his eye on you, Dom Sebastião.'

'And my eye is upon you, Father Malagrida.'

The old man's countenance is expressionless as he gathers his cassock about him and, in open defiance of the minister's glare, lays his bony hand on the heads of a couple of small children their mothers had thrust before him. He permits himself one final barb before vanishing into the night, trailing a few straggling followers on his heels.

'Let us see which of us prevails.'

Dom Sebastião watches him go. He sighs and rubs his face

again, overwhelmed by a tiredness that the activity of the last forty-one days has until now kept at bay.

'Will you return now to the rua Formosa, Dom Sebastião? You must sleep.'

'I must ride to Belém before dawn. The king will require a report on this occurrence as soon as he awakens.'

'And will you take the children with you? And Dona Eleonor? Will you require an escort?'

'Soon, Captain Fernando.' His own temporary pavilion still being under construction in Belém, it was not yet possible to move Eleonor and the children from the rua Formosa. They would have to remain in the city, while he slept in his carriage, close to the new pavilion in Belém, in case His Majesty should need him.

'What troubles you, Captain da Oliveira? You are uneasy.'

'Did we do right to let Father Malagrida go, Dom Sebastião? He makes the greatest mischief wherever he preaches. Your warning seemed to inflame rather than subdue him.'

Yes. The wily old Jesuit had got the better of him, and in public. This time.

'I can do nothing for the moment, Fernando. The Patriarch has refused to rein him in. But things will change.'

Strangely, the minister's mood seems to have lightened. He flings a comradely arm around the captain's shoulder.

'Let the old devil have the last word, this time, and enjoy his advantage. For it will not last.'

Da Oliveira salutes smartly, his heart chilled by the soft tones of his master's pronouncement.

'Not for him. Nor for any of them. I will see to it, Fernando, believe me.'

I do believe you, Dom Sebastião, with all my trembling heart.

Part 3

1758-1759

13

A Carriage Ride and a Heinous Event

September 3rd, 1758, Ajuda, en Route to the Royal Pavilion

It was most uncommon that the king would require his personal valet to share his carriage when returning to the Royal Pavilion following one of his amorous encounters. No doubt he enjoyed bathing in the solitary afterglow of sensual pleasure, especially when the lady was the luscious Dona Teresa of Távora. But this was a night unlike any other. This evening, the charms of the young marchioness had failed to lift Dom José's spirits or distract him from the sad news that had arrived from Madrid that morning.

In the aftermath of the earthquake three years previous, many courtiers had predicted that Dom José would renounce, or at least temper, the indulgence which for years had so grieved the queen and outraged the clergy, and worse, infuriated the heads of the greatest families in the kingdom. Of course, he had not. The love affairs went on, the queen continued to despair and the young Távora marchioness was still his favourite, though by no means his only, lover. Arranging these clandestine encounters with the discretion required to spare the queen intimate knowledge of details that could only anger and humiliate her was no small feat. Pedro Teixeira's mastery of the subtle manoeuvre, and the less subtle art of menace, had won him few friends at court; but these skills assured his success in overcoming the difficulties of ministering to His Majesty's requirements, challenges to which he, personal secretary and valet to the king and Knight in the Order of Christ, was more than equal. And even though he was detested and perhaps a little feared on account of the liberties which Dom José permitted him, facilitating the adulterous assignations of his king never failed to afford him a vicarious excitement.

Under normal circumstances he could have counted on the genial temperament of the king to acquiesce to his advice, his strenuous advice, that they should travel separately in two unmarked carriages, as was their custom. Tonight, however, Dom José shook his head and, without a word, climbed into his valet's carriage, indicating with a flick of the wrist that Teixeira should join him. While the carriage rattled across the rough terrain the king sat slumped, silent and morose, eyes now downcast, now raised, as he leaned forward to draw the curtain aside a crack that he might gaze upon the heavens where glimmered but a few faint pinpricks of starlight. There was a new moon, so tonight her silvery gleam was hidden. The air was warm and fragrant, a last hint of summer drifting in from the Tagus on a light breeze. The open window framed a night of almost total darkness, modulated by undulating shadows of the fields beyond the high walls of the Quinto do Meio. The chatter of little nocturnal creatures – chirruping crickets, the deep, ominous hooting of an owl – soothed the spirit, or would have, were it not for the heavy silence of the king's sorrow, which swelled and filled the enclosed space. After a few moments' sightless scrutiny of the passing shadows, seeing nothing of comfort in the darkness, Dom José pulled the curtain closed and sank back into his bench, as though seeking solace in the sweet, velvet obscurity.

He had always spoken fondly of the kind temper of his sister

Bárbara, of how he missed her since she left Portugal to marry Ferdinand, now king of Spain, and often boasted of her legendary musical talent. She was regarded as *maestra* in singing and for her skill on the harpsichord, even by the greatest musicians of her day. The temperamental Italian genius Scarlatti would take only Bárbara for a pupil and had followed her to Madrid to continue her lessons. She regularly sang with Farinelli, the greatest *castrato* of the era.

When the news arrived that morning, Dom José locked himself away in his office and instructed his valet to admit no visitors. On emerging two hours later, his voice trembling, his countenance grey, he declared a full week of mourning and the cancellation of all his court appointments. The death of his only sister had caused him to deflate, his corpulent body shrunken in a matter of a few hours. In silence he accepted hesitant condolences before returning to his office and locking the door. Yes, His Majesty was taking it hard, very hard. He would neither receive visitors nor leave the palace for the entire week. It was a terrible blow.

How astonishing, therefore, to be summoned only a few hours later and ordered to make ready the coaches for a visit to the young marchioness that evening. They were to leave at eight o'clock instead of midnight, the hour which Dom José usually preferred. Tonight, though, his expressed intention was to return to the palace by a half an hour after eleven. This was not only surprising. It was reckless, for it would not be easy to explain to Dona Mariana Vitória why her husband had no need of her comfort in the few hours between the end of dinner and bedtime, especially on this evening, when he was in particular need of solace. But as Her Majesty must know, did know, there were always important affairs of state to attend. This evening, an urgent conference with his minister would be needed to prepare for the king's absence from public life in the coming days.

Summoning Carvalho e Melo to these meetings was one of

the great pleasures of life at court, Pedro Teixeira being only the second person in the realm, after the king himself, with the power to command the minister, even if only on this single matter. Carvalho e Melo had never voiced any objection to his assigned role in these amorous deceptions, nor expressed the slightest disapproval of the king's nocturnal adventures, his observations confined to matters of discretion and security. Nevertheless, his countenance and general demeanour sometimes betrayed concealed unease; concealed, that is, from His Majesty, if not from his trusted secretary. No matter. A secretary-valet was obliged only to ensure that Dom José's wishes were fulfilled. It was the minister's business to worry about the consequences of the king's adventures. Tonight, therefore, the young marchioness had been instructed to rendezvous with His Majesty at the earlier hour.

Casting a furtive glance towards his sovereign, Teixeira considered offering a few words of condolence, but hesitated. Even though Dom José had seemed to crave company for the journey home, he now appeared disinclined to engage in conversation. As an alternative to words, the valet exhaled a deep sigh, hoping thus to convey his sympathy for the king's sorrow, without interrupting the silence which his royal companion desired. The carriage swayed from side to side, the horses trotted contentedly, the gentle rocking and the comforting, regular clip-clopping of hooves lulled the tired occupants to a light doze, undisturbed by tiny nocturnal scurryings of little animals hunting for prey or fleeing from predators. The king folded his hands across his corpulent stomach, his eyelids drooped, only to start open with a frightened look, as though he had just remembered his sorrows anew, before sinking back into a light sleep.

Now the quiet of the night is shattered! A thunderous blast and a shout, the voice of the coachman Custódio, the darkness is rent, a flash slices through the air, penetrates that heavy curtain, the horses are whinnying, they are frightened, will they rear? The carriage lurches, gathers speed, not on this terrain, Custódia da Costa, have you lost your senses, the beasts will stumble, their legs will break, we are about to smash into the wall of the Quinta do Meio, overturn, we will be lost, da Costa. How many of these thoughts are an internal scream and how many bellowed aloud? Thrown against the huddled figure of the king, clutching at the open window frame you fill your lungs, prepare to shout a warning but two more musket blasts tear through the night like the crash of waves in a storm. There is an anguished cry from Custódio, some ill has befallen him, a sick splintering of wood cracks the interior wall not a hand's breath from the king, is His Majesty injured? Those were musket shots, no doubt of it, the coach is shuddering, any moment now we will tumble into the ditch. Dom José is doubled over, his breath is shallow, he is gasping, there is a thudding of hooves, at least two, perhaps three galloping horses making a swift departure, you kneel at His Majesty's feet, has he been hit? Can you hear me, Your Majesty? Yes, he is wounded, his words are rasping, but his orders are clear, bellowed into the night.

'Da Costa! Are you hit?'

Yes, the driver is wounded yet the carriage speeds on, the horses have calmed, they are under control, the pace has slowed but this is still too fast for such a narrow, uneven road.

'Listen, da Costa. Do not take the road home. Turn right at the next crossroads, downhill, towards the rua Junqueira. It is the king's wish. Do you hear, man?'

Just in time, the words hit their mark. The carriage shudders downhill, Dom José is swaying on his bench, it is too dark to see his injury but his right arm and his right thigh are wet and that is the sharp scent of blood, yes, Dom José's cloak is damp with his own blood. At every ridge in the road His Majesty winces, he cries out once but is otherwise calm.

'We will soon reach the home of Dom António, Majesty. He will dress your wounds.'

'Such was my purpose, Pedro.'

In the midst of the chaos, Teixeira finds himself observing the scene as a detached spectator, astonished at the king's cool head, his immediate grasp of the situation and his quick thinking in choosing the single course of action most likely to save him – to seek immediate treatment at the home of the royal surgeon, in preference to returning to the Royal Palace first and sending for him later. That decision saved valuable time, possibly even His Majesty's life, so said Don António Soares Branolão when examining the king's arm. A man can bleed to death in a very short time with the wrong kind of wound.

While the surgeon dressed Dom José's injuries, Teixeira and the surgeon's apprentice eased da Costa out of his driver's seat and laid him on the ground. A storm lamp glowed in the velvet black of the night, the cold waves of the Tagus glittered dark silver, flecked with the tiny eyes of stars scattered across her surface. Da Costa lay on the damp earth, face up, drifting in and out of consciousness, unable to raise his voice above a whisper, exhausted from the effort of driving two frightened horses at a gallop with those grave wounds.

'Two attacks,' he breathed as the surgeon's apprentice moistened his lips with a sponge. 'The first shot came from a pistol, it misfired else I would be dead straight away.' He tried to raise his head. 'From a single masked horseman.'

'And the muskets?'

'Two. Behind the first. Two horses, two muskets, two more masked men.'

So they had been lying in wait: three attackers and two ambushes, in case the first missed its mark.

'Da Costa! The first carriage. Did they attack it too?' Teixeira made to shake him but the apprentice stayed his hand.

'There is little can be done for him,' he whispered. 'I will give him laudanum to ease the pain, should he awaken. He may not see the morning.'

Breathless and trembling, Teixeira got to his feet and strode into Dom António's surgery without invitation. The dressings on the king's thigh and arm were in place, the patient was comfortable but would have to rest for some days. All that remained was to convey the injured man back to the Royal Palace. There was much to be done. And one person who must oversee the next crucial steps.

Dom Sebastião was accustomed to being summoned on nights when the king was preparing for one of his assignations but had never yet been ordered to attend him upon his return. He was admitted to the king's chamber, where a disturbing scene unfolded before his eyes. Dom José lay stretched out on a chaise longue, his right arm and right leg extended, his garments in disarray and a wide strip of cloth wrapped around his arm. And kneeling by His Majesty's side, the odious Teixeira, white-faced but with a steady hand detaching a thick wad of blood-stained muslin from the king's wound. Dom Sebastião approached with an exclamation of alarm.

'I am in no danger, Dom Sebastião. I have a little pain, but it is a flesh wound only.'

'A robbery, Your Majesty?'

'I think not.' Teixeira's voice shook with emotion.

In that instant, the reality of the spectacle came into sharp focus: the wounded king, surprisingly calm, the silent, worried, hovering servants, the valet Teixeira in whose countenance he saw reflected his own shock and fear. Fear for His Majesty, of course but also for the fragility of his own position. In truth, his own status as one of the king's favourites was no better than that enjoyed by this unsavoury character, Teixeira. In a single flash, he sees the vista of his life's trajectory come to an end on the death of the king, a possibility he has never before contemplated. The king is still a young man, a decade and a half younger than Dom Sebastião himself, he was bound to outlive his minister by many years. Or should. But then, his younger sister, Bárbara, has just died, aged only forty-six. And now, this assault on his life. Which by the looks of things, almost succeeded.

'Well, Teixeira, apprise the minister of what we know so far.'

Dom Sebastião observed the king's cool demeanour with surprise. Were it not for his deep indolence and self-indulgence, he might have made a great ruler after all. But in that case, he would not have needed Dom Sebastião José Carvalho e Melo to do his ruling for him. Or Pedro Teixeira, to organise his adulterous comings and goings.

On hearing Teixeira's account of the events of the evening, Dom Sebastião made no response, his countenance immobile, mask-like, concealing his horror. Not one, but two ambushes, directed against the person of the king, on a quiet, narrow road, His Majesty's customary route from the Royal Palace to a certain discreet little residence he frequented when his amorous inclinations leaned towards the young Marchioness of Távora. The attacks carried out by at least three men on horseback, masked and armed, who had shot at and nearly killed the king.

'There is more,' Teixeira continued, his voice shaking. 'A third ambush, which we escaped for having taken a detour along the road to Junqueira, towards the home of the royal surgeon, instead of returning directly to the Royal Palace. The driver of our first carriage spied two men emerging from behind a gate. He did not know they were ne'er-do-wells, having no knowledge of the attack on us.'

'There was another carriage travelling ahead of the king? Unoccupied? And it was allowed to pass unharmed by all three ambushes?'

That Dom José frequented a certain mansion in which to rendezvous with the young marchioness was known to his intimates and possibly to others. The king's habitual route on his way to meet his lover would therefore be difficult to keep secret.

But the day, and especially the hour of this assignation – who could know that His Majesty would choose tonight of all nights, when the court was in deep mourning on the orders of Dom José himself, for a visit to his favourite mistress? Or that the assignation would take place some hours before the customary time?

And most disturbing of all, who could know that tonight the king would break with precedent and travel with his valet in the second carriage, leaving his own unoccupied?

'Why did you travel in the same carriage tonight?' To soften his peremptory tone, Dom Sebastião addressed his words to Teixeira, though his question was really directed to the king, who opened his soft eyes and blinked.

'Do not scold him, Dom Sebastião, I prevailed upon him, for just this one night.'

The minister glared at Teixeira. In any journey the king undertook without the protection of his full royal guard, there must be two coaches, unmarked: one carrying the monarch, the other a decoy. It was a principle of basic security, inviolable. Teixeira quailed, pale and trembling, as well he might, having survived unscathed an attack that had injured his king. Not so brave as the insolence of his demeanour suggested, then.

Might he have been …? No, there was no sense in that. Teixeira already enjoyed enormous privileges. His position could not be improved, there was no profit to him in causing harm to the king. Quite the opposite, for his power, which he flaunted to great effect at every opportunity, depended wholly on the unaccountable esteem in which Dom José held him, even if his brusque manner and outright rudeness to all who crossed him incurred the fury and hatred of everyone at court. More than once, he had had to be prevailed upon to temper his manners, especially in his dealings with the Duke of Aveiro, who detested him. Of course, the duke was a brother-in-law of the Távoras – yes, these people were all connected by an intricate web of family ties and intermarriage, by rivalries and jostling for position and the favour of the king.

Even by the standards of his class, the Duke of Aveiro was an unpleasant character, hated by everyone, including his own family, whom he had cheated out of various desirable properties and advancements. Dom Sebastião had long observed the progress of the former count, Dom José Mascarenhas of Silva and Lancastre, elevated, through a combination of legal sleights of hand, intimidation and sycophancy, to the rank of Duke of Aveiro. Beneath that veneer of aristocratic manners beat the heart of a common ruffian, ambitious far beyond his abilities or rightful expectations. Yet he had his supporters. Better, therefore, to refrain from antagonising him without good cause. This was a prudence which Pedro Teixeira declined to observe. Still, it was amusing to see the duke knocked from his perch from time to time, even if Teixeira's recent taunts, hinting at relations between the king and the duke's own wife, had gone too far. Pure entertainment for Teixeira, but it had sent the duke into fits of rage, all the greater for knowing that the impudent valet enjoyed the total protection of the king. Such baiting could only inflame the duke's temper and add to his many imagined grievances against Dom José.

'So there was no attempt at robbery. And the attackers had accurate intelligence enough to support three coordinated ambushes.'

'It would appear so, Dom Sebastião.' Dom José attempted to sit up.

'This was a conspiracy. Against the person of the king.'

Dom José turned to Teixeira and with a silent nod dismissed him from the room.

'And therefore, against the state.' His Majesty's countenance was milk white, his equanimity shaken. The lethargy that had engulfed him that morning with the news of his sister's death was replaced by a white hot, silent fury that the minister had never before seen, as though this brush with death – and at the hands of his own subjects – had revived him, instilling a rage commingled with a renewed sense of vitality, an intense awareness of being alive. The colour returned to his face, he enunciated his words with exaggerated clarity.

'Dom Sebastião. You must identify the perpetrators of this heinous deed, traitors who dared to make an attack on the life of their king. You have full powers to take whatever actions, engage whatever measures, you may need, to accomplish this. With the greatest possible speed.'

'Majesty, I counsel that we make haste slowly.' Yes, this crisis must be resolved, but definitively. The culprits must be found and dealt with. All of them. Any attack on the king was, directly or indirectly, an attack on Dom Sebastião José Carvalho e Melo himself.

'It will be of no benefit, Your Majesty, to arrest the three or four lowly ruffians who carried out this cowardly attack. Until their paymasters, the instigators and any and all of their supporters are rooted out, Your Majesty will never be safe.'

Nor would the king's minister.

'What is your plan, Dom Sebastião? I can see that you are hatching one. Although I need not know all the details.'

'Tomorrow, Your Majesty, we must make an announcement that the king is indisposed, having suffered a fall within the precincts of the Royal Pavilion. His injuries preclude him from managing the affairs of the state for, let us say, one week.'

'That would require the imposition of a regency…'

'Indeed. The queen will be regent for that week. Thus, we will convey that Your Majesty has sustained a grave, but not life-threatening, injury. Thereafter, we wait. We watch. Whilst I conduct my own clandestine investigation.'

'Who could be culpable of such a heinous act?'

Many suspects came to mind, for, painful though it was to acknowledge, Dom José was not universally loved. Nor was he greatly feared, for the most unpleasant measures – putting an end to that Oporto business last year, for example – were carried out on the authority of Dom Sebastião himself.

And yes, he had ordered fourteen of the rebels hanged, including women. Harsh. That he had ordered their bodies quartered and impaled on spikes around the city, harsher still. But necessary. Five thousand angry rioters, enraged that the new state monopoly on wine production was reducing their profits, attacking the home of the General Company of Upper Douro Viticulture. It was nothing short of an insurgence against the state. It had to be crushed.

And it was he, Dom Sebastião Carvalho e Melo and not the king, who bore the burden of responsibility. Even though that measure, and every single *Providência* enacted in the last three years, had borne His Majesty's signature.

'Time will tell.' His Majesty had just granted the minister extraordinary powers to pursue this investigation. He would use them all, to bring the miscreants to justice, to protect His Majesty, to protect the state.

From this moment onwards, no one was above suspicion. No one would be spared in this quest for the truth.

14

A Worrying Conversation and a Job Well Done

September 5th, 1758, Tagus harbour, Lisbon

On this balmy autumn day, as he strode across Rossio Square observing how his vision for the new Lisbon was taking shape in the construction of these straight, gracious streets and wide pavements, the foundations of buildings whose simple, elegant facades would soon rise on all sides, Dom Sebastião should have been in high spirits. The king was recovering well from his ordeal. The latest edition of the *Gazeta de Lisboa* reported that His Majesty had suffered a minor accident, a fall in the Royal Palace. As agreed, there was no mention of an assassination attempt. Already, just two days since the vile attack, the investigation was making rapid, if discreet, progress.

But his conversation with Father Luís had unsettled him. There was no obvious reason for this, as the young priest had responded with equanimity to the bad news the minister had decided to convey in person. His little hut where, for the three years since the earthquake he had heard the confessions of the poor, healed their ailments and sometimes distributed food, would have to be dismantled. The ruins of the hospital of All Saints which occupied that part of Rossio Square would not be rebuilt but must be torn down to make space for a new street that would connect the Rossio with another, grand square. The city engineers deemed that both the earthquake and subsequent fire damage had rendered the hospital structure beyond repair. Soon, a new hospital would be built on the hill overlooking the square and named for the king, dedicated to the care of the poor, with all the facilities and more for which All Saints had been renowned. Father Luís's tiny refuge would also have to be demolished.

'We can find you rooms in the convent in Rato. A spacious building, where you can more easily conduct your work.'

'I thank you, Excellency, but there is no need. I have been expecting this. We can simply rebuild our hut on the other side of the Rossio. That way, the people of the parish will know where to find us.'

Dom Sebastião resolved to send building materials and a few workmen to assist Father Luís in making the move, though he said nothing. The priest might decline a direct offer.

'You must think me a very bad man,' he once joked when Father Luís refused a significant gift of alms that would have fed many of his parishioners for several weeks. No doubt a man of the clergy had to choose his public allies with care. Unless the minister really was a bad man. Some people seemed to think so. Many had judged him harsh in the Oporto business. They were people who had never been tasked with making hard decisions that would serve the wellbeing of the entire population.

As he approached the Terreiro do Paço, pleased that he had left his sword at the rua Formosa along with his carriage and driver, his brisk stride slackened to a stroll. Although the reconstruction works were at an early stage, already in his mind's eye he could see the magnificent square, complete and entire as it would be five, fifty, a hundred years from now, the splendour of three sides opening on to the harbour, warm stone gleaming in light reflected from the river and the shimmering sea beyond. A renewed city, conjured into existence before his eyes, through his own endeavours. The fruit of long conferences with the king, arguments with architects and city engineers, hours, many hours and days and nights at his desk, scrutinising plans, organising competitions for proposals and counter-proposals: plans to rebuild the city exactly as it had been before the catastrophe struck; plans that would have abandoned Lisbon entirely and moved the court and capital to Oporto or even Brazil, for heaven's sake. He had battled them all, and he had prevailed. The city, his city, would rise from the ashes, a modern Lisbon built on the ruins of the corrupt, decadent old order, dedicated to the support of human endeavour and commerce.

Perhaps the time had come to rename the square, in recognition of the new order.

But today, the sights and sounds of industry all around did not improve his mood. It would have been better not to have taken his customary detour to converse with Father Luís, but he had wanted to give him the news about his hut before he read it in the *Gazeta*. As a rule, those talks with the priest, infrequent though they were, fulfilled his occasional need for a real conversation unencumbered by the conventions of the court or manoeuvrings born of self-interest. If Father Luís never tried to curry favour, nor did he oppose him for effect or in order to create an impression. He was one of the very few people who would tell the minister exactly what he thought, his singular views sometimes challenging, yet almost always providing food for thought. Perhaps he maintained this unusual acquaintance for that very reason.

Today, however, the conversation had provoked in him an unaccustomed state of turmoil. Yes, he ought to have made his way directly to the Cais de Sodré where a rowboat even now awaited to ferry him to the *Nossa Senhora de Adjuda* for the meeting with her captain. This encounter was crucial to the investigation and would have to be handled with great care. Permitting distractions by the ill-advised comments of an innocent young priest with no insight into affairs of state had been a mistake. The conversation had agitated his passions to a most unusual degree, to the extent that every sight that ought to have filled him with pride and satisfaction, now created the opposite effect. In the hard labour of the workmen rebuilding the city, hauling blocks of stone and sacks of sand, in the countenances of street vendors, women and children struggling to scrape a living selling fried eels and pastries in the square, he saw not a slow recovery of his country, but lives endured in misery and oppression.

How could such people, poor people, be so easily cajoled by their betters and convinced to take actions contrary to their own interests? That the work of his Oporto Upper Douro Viticulture Company would only benefit the common people in the long run, a child could understand. Controls on the quality of the wine, an end to price fixing, rules about how and when the precious wine could be sold and to whom – yes, such rules would reduce profit margins for the tavern owners and winegrowers but would also modernise the industry and ensure a living wage for all. They would even make the wine which the workers themselves consumed in those taverns cheaper!

Yet those were the very people who protested most, who had been incited to riot when the new regulations were enforced. His harsh response, declaring a state of siege, sending in the army, the executions of course, had been brutal. But necessary. And effective. Not a word of opposition to the Douro company had been heard from Oporto in the twelve months since. But the ignorance, the ease with which people could be inflamed... It was a tragedy that such firm action had been necessary.

An equally decisive response was called for now. A response proportionate to the offence. Attempted regicide. Lèse-majesté. Treason. As there was no greater crime than an attempt on the life of the king, the consequences for the perpetrators must be fearsome. Moreover, such was His Majesty's wish. While Dom José regained his strength and recovered from the attack, his rage mounted with each passing day, his equable temper gripped in a fury most alien to his placid nature. He had been shocked to learn that some opponents hated him enough to wish to be rid of him, even more disturbed that they had gone so far as to plot his assassination. And almost succeeded.

All opposition must be rooted out and crushed. The perpetrators must be brought to justice and punished to the full extent of the law, sufficient to ensure that this could never happen again. Else neither the king nor his minister would ever be safe.

'Do you truly see the hand of the Jesuits in this attack, Dom Sebastião? Why would they commit such a treasonous act?'

'They already have committed treason, many times.'

This was not the time to remind Father Luís of the perfidious work of the Jesuits in Brazil, who were, even as they spoke, rousing the natives to take up arms against the crowns of both Portugal and Spain. Their activities at home were betrayal enough.

'Since old Dom João died, the priests of the Society of Jesus have opposed almost every measure His Majesty has enacted. You know from your own observations, Father Luís, how Father Malagrida obstructed our attempts – your own attempts – to succour the wounded and homeless in the wake of the earthquake. Since then, they have not relented. Without exception, they have pursued the interests of their own Order at the expense of the people and the state.'

Not least in their attempts to have him, the king's minister, removed from his post. That devil Malagrida had the effrontery to make a direct appeal to the Pope, advising the king of Portugal to dispense with the services of Dom Sebastião José Carvalho e Melo! Were it not for the absolute trust and high regard in which Dom José held him, he might even now be languishing in the obscurity of his family estate. Or worse. At least that outrage had finally opened the king's eyes and convinced him to remove the Jesuits as royal confessors, and to exile Malagrida from court. Only to Setúbal, which, although some distance from the capital, was still close enough for his disciples to attend his regular meetings and retreats. At least the prohibition prevented them from assembling in the palace of Dom Pedro, the king's brother, in Queluz.

Could Dom Pedro have had a hand in the assassination attempt, that he might himself ascend the throne? Unlikely. Not only was the king's brother lacking in wit, he had also always been much too fond of the pleasant, opulent life he enjoyed in his palace in Queluz to aspire to anything as taxing as ruling a kingdom. But his weakness of intellect made him susceptible to flattery, and if he himself harboured no ambition to rule, he favoured the company of those who did, members of the old noble families who had shown little love for the king. And even less for the king's most important minister.

The Duke of Aveiro's presence at Malagrida's retreats, for example, was suspicious. An utter blockhead whose ambition was surpassed only by his stupidity, this unpleasant man did not have a religious bone in his body. No doubt about it, something very different from spiritual guidance was occurring at those gatherings. Furthermore, it was not credible that a person existed who was sufficiently deluded in his own capabilities, and imbecile enough to give prior warning of his intentions, to permit one of the tiny Azores isles to declare him king – and have coins minted in his own image! But such a person did exist: José Mascarenhas, the Duke of Aveiro, detested by everyone, including his own family.

Vengeful little people gathering in vengeful little groups, each nursing his – or her, for Dona Leonora of Távora must not be forgotten – personal grudge against the king. A dukedom withheld here, a marriage obstructed there, and of course a son cuckolded by His Majesty. And no end of grudges against Dom Sebastião himself.

No. Those so-called spiritual retreats were nests of vipers, plotting sedition. The attack on Dom José had been their first attempt.

It must not be repeated.

They must be crushed, all of them, no quarter given.

For which mission evidence enough was required that would allow the law to take its course. This visit to the captain of the *Nossa Senhora de Adjuda* was the first step in obtaining the required proof.

Not for the first time, the priest had seemed to divine his thoughts.

'Is there any real evidence that the Távoras were involved?'

So, despite the co-operation of the editor of the *Gazeta,* everyone in the city, including Father Luís, knew that an attempt had been made on the king's life. And everyone had a theory about who was behind it.

'I am not at liberty to reveal the names of our suspects, Father Luís. But we do have witnesses.'

'And is there evidence to corroborate their testimony?' The priest persisted, insensible of the sharp edge that had entered the minister's tone. 'For as we know, witness testimony is notoriously unreliable.' The young man hesitated, stopping short of pointing out that the veracity of statements gathered from interrogations in the dungeons of Belém might be tainted.

'We are in the process of gathering evidence in order to corroborate the witnesses' testimonies.'

'Or refute them,' Father Luís added, at last divining a coldness in the minister's silence. He pressed on regardless. 'It is hard to credit, is it not, that noble men, and men of God, would commit such a heinous act against their own anointed king.'

It is only too easy to believe, the minister could have answered, for regicide had been committed throughout the history of their nation, to manage rights of succession and shifts in the balance of power between kings and their nobles.

'One of the rumours on the street – and there are a lot of them,' Father Luís continued apologetically, as if he had started them himself, 'is that His Majesty was not the intended victim.

That his valet had quarrelled with someone, a member of a great house, who tried to exact revenge and attacked the wrong carriage.'

'Yes. I heard that rumour too.'

In theory, it was possible. Teixeira had many enemies at court and any one of them could be a potential assassin. The Duke of Aveiro, for example. The duke's haughtiness regarding Teixeira's humble origins had been ill-judged, for in the person of the king's valet, greatly favoured and indulged by His Majesty, he had met his match. When Teixeira's taunts went so far as to impugn the honour of the duke's wife – with the king! – the hot-tempered duke always rose to the bait. Such an insult, to such a man as José Mascarenhas, might well warrant the ultimate revenge. Nor would it be difficult. A dagger on a dark night. Poisoned wine. An unfortunate fall from a window.

But this attack – elaborately plotted, involving not one, but three separate ambushes, requiring several horses and horsemen, military grade weapons, the collusion of servants – no, such complex planning would not be needed to get rid of the likes of Teixeira. This was a sophisticated endeavour, informed by accurate intelligence, thwarted only by chance and the bungling of inept would-be assassins. Whoever had conceived and set this plot in motion had a first-rate mind for strategy, their only misjudgement being the practicalities of its execution. They should have paid more for professional killers who would have known how to adapt to the unexpected. They would not make the same mistake the next time, if there was a next time.

In any case, both of the witnesses had, in the end, been vocal and explicit. They had named names.

'You may be right. Perhaps Teixeira was the target after all,' the minister said. 'The investigation will pursue every avenue and all possible motives.'

'The witnesses will give testimony at trial?'

'They will, of course.'

Of course, they would not. They were to be hanged, in secret, that very morning. Most likely already had been.

On reaching the Terreiro do Paço, he stopped for a moment and allowed his eyes to wander across the cobbles to the mighty river, so vast that visitors often took it for the sea. The half-finished façades of three sides of the square were overlaid by wooden boards on which were painted images of the finished structures – lines of gracious, identical archways on the east and west sides, completed by three more magnificent arches to the north, whence wide, straight streets would one day lead, in pleasing symmetry, to the Rossio. Very different from the warren of pretty, but unsanitary mediaeval streets that had been toppled and swept away by the earthquake.

Oblivious of the elderly stranger in their midst (Was sixty elderly? Impossible! Probably!) a multitude of bustling workers engrossed in their labours was proof, he now saw as his mood improved, of a gradual recovery as the nation began to emerge from the ashes of catastrophe. In this, he had every reason to rejoice. Fishermen hauled nets bursting with sparkling silver fish, yelling instructions at their mates; carts packed with enormous bundles secured with canvas and rope rattled across the square, gulls swooped and screeched, a few merchants awaiting news of their ships hovered on the water's edge, youths selling sardines wove their way between the workers; all accompanied by a pleasing din and a medley of odours that signalled industry and the green shoots of prosperity for his country.

Nothing must be allowed to obstruct this rebirth. Nor would it.

A carriage bearing the insignia of the Royal Postal Service trundled past him and came to a halt at a certain spot on the quayside, alongside the berth where he himself was bound. The carriage door flew open. A burly lad leaped out, reached into the interior and dragged out two large sacks which he swung over the edge of the quay into a waiting rowboat where two foreign sailors, one red-haired, the other blond, reached up to catch them just as Dom Sebastião approached. Excellent. The first part of his plan was in motion. His conference with the captain of the *Nossa Senhora de Adjuda* would ensure that the rest would work just as smoothly. Father Luís had wanted evidence. Evidence was what Dom Sebastião intended to find. Though the young priest would not approve of his methods.

That was the trouble with idealists. Their moral certainty, their unshakable judgements concerning right and wrong, the integrity of their actions, were only made possible by the murky work which others carried out in the shadows. Their scruples were founded on illusions, luxuries in which no true leader, no intrepid explorer who ventured beyond the borders of the known world, could indulge. The spectacular discoveries of Portugal's finest navigators three hundred years previous, explorers who circled the globe, founded new colonies and brought vast wealth back to the Crown, had for a time made the Portuguese nation the greatest and wealthiest on earth, her expeditions into the unknown admired and envied by every country in the world. Such feats of bravery and daring could only be accomplished through sacrifice, by overcoming the terrors of facing the unknown, by plunging into the immense empty spaces which maps named only *Terra Incognita* with the fearsome warning that *Here Be Dragons*.

Sooner or later, every captain encountered that moment when others hesitated or trembled to advance. And when that moment came, when there was nowhere to go but forward, it was the captain's role, his duty, to rouse his people to bravery, root out cowardice and the threat of mutiny, for the sake of the entire crew and the glory of the nation.

Confronted by such moments, in the battle against decadence, superstition and sloth, Dom Sebastião José Carvalho e Melo had never yet faltered. How much greater was the need for decisive action now, when the king, the people, the very nation were in danger from a treachery that threatened to engulf all, utterly, more completely than the earthquake that had almost swept the city from the earth. Faced with his duty to protect the king, to protect them all, he would not be found wanting.

As soon as the rowboat laden with the postal sacks had vacated the berth and put out on the river towards the *Nossa Senhora de Adjuda*, another arrived to take its place. The oarsman stood, swaying as the little boat rocked in the waves, his cap twisted in his hands, surveying his illustrious passenger, a man no longer young but determined to descend the rickety iron ladder fixed to the harbour wall without help. He watched as the captain's visitor toppled from the lowest rung into the boat and settled on a bench. The water was calm with hardly a breeze across the surface, thus the journey from land to the ship took but a few minutes.

Captain Silva was waiting. He raised an arm in greeting and, without consulting his eminent guest in the rowboat, ordered the two young foreign sailors who had transported the post bags from the quays to climb down and assist their visitor's ascent. As Dom Sebastião clambered onto the ship, the thought returned that he might have committed his orders for the captain to a sealed letter, a notion he once again dismissed as being too great a risk. His two agents, who were already aboard and would accompany the *Nossa Senhora de Adjuda* to the Azores, had conveyed the relevant orders. But there could be no mistake in this. The captain had to hear them from the source.

Declining an invitation to descend to the captain's quarters below – two rickety ladders were more than enough to navigate in one day – he took Silva's arm and steered him towards the deck. This sharp-eyed captain had the look of a man who had navigated stormy waters on land as well as on sea and who had no time to waste.

'Your Excellency, the tide will turn in a half hour and if we are to set sail…'

'Indeed, Captain Silva, I will not long detain you. You received my orders?'

'I did, Excellency. But I am glad you are come, for…'

'I understand. I am not surprised if you doubted their veracity. That is why I am here. To confirm my wishes and ensure your full co-operation. Would you repeat them to me, as you understand them?'

'We are to put into São Miguel, as scheduled.'

The voyage had been planned so quickly that there had been no time to add it to the maritime schedule. Officially, there was no sailing today. But somehow, word had got about – or rather, he had instructed his people to put word about, having decided that a formal announcement of an unscheduled sailing might arouse suspicions in those who he hoped would be careless. The large sacks of mail now loaded aboard indicated that the strategy had been successful. Anyone with relatives in the Isles of the Azores, noble or commoner, would have taken the opportunity to pen a hasty letter.

'And when you put into harbour you will…'

'…have the mail bags taken from the ship…'

'By night.'

'Under cover of darkness, unseen, of course.'

'And then?'

'They will be taken to the office of the Governor of the Azores.'

'And in the morning, before first light, returned to the ship.'

Thus, His Majesty's subjects in the Isles of the Azores would receive their letters and parcels and bills and billets-doux – excepting only missives of special interest, those deemed relevant to the investigation.

So. The words of any conspirator unwise enough or reckless enough to pen a letter remarking the current state of Dom José's health, or the failure of a plot to kill him, would find their way to the minister's office; and eventually, to the eyes of the king himself. Some might doubt that anyone would be so reckless. But it was impossible to exaggerate the arrogance of the high nobility, typified by a sureness of self that so often induced blindness: it would never occur to them that a mere government official would dare to break the seal of their private letters.

'When does the next sailing return from São Miguel?'

'The first week of November, Excellency.'

Good. This gave him at least six weeks, perhaps eight, to advance the investigation, quietly, of course, for officially there was nothing to investigate. The king had had a fall, he had sustained a minor injury and was a little shocked, nothing more.

Could the criminals seriously believe that the assassination attempt had been dismissed? Possibly. Or else they would realise he was lying in wait, stealthy, like a cat waiting to pounce, for them to show themselves. Satisfied with his morning's work, his earlier agitation faded, he extended a purse to the captain.

'There is no need, Dom Sebastião. I am at His Majesty's service. Your service.'

'But it pleases me, Captain Silva. As token of my appreciation for complying with my unusual request.' In truth, it was not a request. 'And for your discretion.'

'That is understood, Dom Sebastião,' Captain Silva said fervently.

Maintaining secrecy only mattered until the trial. Though the captain would no doubt consider it in his own interests to maintain his silence ever after.

The short trip across the lapping waters of the Tagus from the *Nossa Senhora de Adjuda* back to the quays afforded a perfect view of the coast. Since the catastrophe, the skyline had changed forever, most of the thousand spires for which Lisbon had been famed now buried in fissures opened by the tremors of the earth or reduced to rubble, much of it still heaped about the streets. The roiling of the sea and the shuddering land on that terrible day had left scars on the city and on her people that would never be forgotten, not only by those who had witnessed it, but for all generations that would follow.

Leaning over the side of the little boat, soothed by the sound of the oars plashing gently through the water, Dom Sebastião stared upon his undulating reflection shifting and rippling in the waves, all thought faded from his mind, his senses brimming with the sounds of river and sea, screaming gulls, stevedores yelling from the busy quayside, the metallic clatter of chains scraping along the river wall, the thudding of crates lowered from ships. Taking a deep breath, he filled his lungs with the pure air of the bay and turned to gaze upon his city. This view of Lisbon from the water, although but a little way from shore, never failed to enthral him. The arms of her coastline enfolded him, gathering him in an embrace whose very distance seemed to draw him closer to the heart, to the people, than when he was on shore, in streets and squares thronged with people.

Was it possible to love a place as you loved a person? If so, he loved this city, this country in all her shabby imperfections, the crumbling buildings, once glorious in their splendour, the remnants of her broken streets, many vanished forever since the earthquake and worn away long before that by neglect and decay. The tired city and her ruined beauty inspired in him a protective affection, much as the ageing countenance of a loved one animates a fondness so different from the first flush of passion, but no less profound. He could not restore the bloom of youth to his wife's cheeks, nor would he, for in the blemishes and wrinkles of her worn features was etched the story of their shared life, their sorrows, their dead children and yes, their joys.

But if those who had conspired to do away with the king had their way, now or in the future, everything would be lost. This must not happen. His beloved, beleaguered country and her king, his city – he would return to their former grandeur and glory. He would deliver his country from the darkest of days and restore her to the light.

The little time he had spent on the water, the sea breeze and the good air cleansing his lungs left him refreshed, exhilarated, his thoughts steadied. Father Luís was an effective worker and a good man, much loved for his service to the poor and the homeless. Perhaps he was in need of a change. Some little parish in the Alentejo, or the Algarve, there were poor people everywhere. He would be missed, of course, but circumstances alter, times are hard and sacrifices have to be made. It would be for the best in the long run.

15

A Challenging Day and a Pleasant Dinner

December 23rd, 1758, Tower of Belém

Doctor Gonçalvo Cardoso stepped out of the darkness of the Belém Tower and lingered for a moment, his face damp from a spray the wind had whipped up from the Tagus, while his eyes adjusted to the pearly winter light reflected from the river. His best woollen cloak would afford him little protection from the needles of rain stinging his cheeks and eyelids, but he nevertheless wrapped it close around his body in the hope of imparting a sliver of warmth or comfort.

Making his way from the Tower towards the main square of the village of Belém, he approached the magnificent Jerónimos monastery, whose hundred windows, illuminated for the evening's Christmas service, twinkled like jewels in the twilight. The multitude of fantastical archways, stone carvings and impossible curlicues adorning the Jerónimos' towers and courtyards and cloisters never failed to dazzle him. But now, trudging alongside the great western door towards the Pateo dos Bichos, the old menagerie, his head was bowed. Having spent three days in dank, windowless rooms below the waterline, he was troubled to learn that the old menagerie had been designated an overflow site of detention. At the Pateo, they said, he would find

Dom Sebastião Carvalho e Melo, for the minister had been called to oversee some problem with a new batch of prisoners, for which reason he had been obliged to absent himself from the interrogation. As Secretary da Cunha and Judge Cordeira Pereira had both declined to act on the doctor's medical advice, it had fallen to Gonçalvo Cardoso himself to seek out the minister and convey to him his professional opinion.

The courtyard of the Pateo was thronged with people, all men, many attired with the ostentatious elegance of the nobility, others in the garb of servants of different rank – valets, coachmen, stable boys. As he drew closer, he became aware of an insistent hum, the subdued murmur of hundreds of people gathered together, yet evoking none of the animation habitual for such a throng – two, perhaps three hundred, some with heads lowered in resignation, others striding about the place asking questions, demanding answers, as though unable to believe their predicament.

Most placid of all were the servants, accustomed as they were to their fate being subject to whims and forces beyond their understanding and therefore disposed to submit without resistance, in the hope that things might turn out for the best after all. In contrast, many of the prisoners of aristocratic bearing appeared to be remonstrating with the guards and with each other. Dom Sebastião, standing at least a head taller than most others in the crowd, was easily spotted. And there was the Count of Lourenço, assessing the comings and goings in the courtyard. His regard came to rest upon the person of the minister himself, to whom he made the ghost of a bow. It was true what they said, that count was a bold one. The minister's gaze slid over him without expression and landed on the doctor. In obedience to a nod from the minister, Cardoso pushed his way through the throng, his forehead damp with a sheen of sweat. Upon finding himself face to face with Dom Sebastião, a torrent of words straightway tumbled from his lips.

'But has he confessed all?'

The doctor's voice quavered and fell silent. So, this too was required of him? Not only his presence at every interrogation which had taken place in the Torre de Belém during the last three days. Not only his silent acquiescence which, he could no longer deny, gave tacit assent to the proceedings. Not only medical intervention when the prisoners were on the point of losing consciousness. The questioning, the dank smell, the lapping of river water outside the tower walls an ever-threatening presence, all this – and now? Must he now interpret the words uttered by those unfortunates? This minister was a man not to be crossed. Whatever answer he gave was bound to be the wrong one.

'My area of expertise, Dom Sebastião, is not…'

'Of course, Doctor Cardoso, you are right, forgive me. Judge Pereira and the other members of the Special Tribunal will decide. That question is outside your competence and beyond the scope of your role. My apologies, I was distracted. These newcomers…'

He shrugged and nodded towards the throng behind him, palms raised in a gesture of helplessness as though lamenting the difficulty of corralling an influx of house guests arrived too early for a dinner. At times, it was easy to forget the charm of the minister's character. Or at least, of his conversation, for who can see beyond the façade constructed to conceal the person within.

'You are the medical man. Tell me, what is his true state?'

'Dom Sebastião, in my professional judgement, there is no doubt that if Dom Francisco is subjected to any further interrogation, his heart will give out.'

The minister gazed up at the sky, as though hoping to see a solution to this irritating intelligence in the grey clouds, which had begun to darken. He sighed. The doctor suppressed a sigh of his own.

He had no excuse. He might persuade himself that he could

not have foreseen the nature of this commission, which no one had forced him to accept. Rather, he had been persuaded, by financial inducements and hints of the promise of a minor title, that the work was well within his powers. It would have been madness to refuse. He might even be carrying out a necessary service, providing some relief to the prisoners from time to time. Besides, if he did not accept the job, someone else would do it, and who would gain from his absence? Not the unfortunates over whose fate he had presided these past days.

But the noises that nightly penetrated his dreams – the creaking of ancient timber, the sickening stretching of tendons, the agonised shrieks and perhaps worst of all, the soft, dispassionate voices of the interrogators, interspersed with the groans of their prisoners searching for the words that their tormentors required, even if those words would send them, send their loved ones, to the scaffold – who could have foreseen such barbarities, here, in Portugal? Was not this a civilised nation? Had they not left such methods behind in the Dark Ages?

Whether from the strain of his work in the Tower, or from fear to convey the bad news that the interrogation of Dom Francisco, Marquis of Távora, must be suspended, the doctor was shaken. Taking care to avoid looking at him and thus further agitating him, Dom Sebastião listened to the cadences and hesitations of the doctor's voice. At no moment since December 20th, when the king signed into law the special decree that permitted torture in the questioning of the prisoners, had this Doctor Cardoso wavered in his duty of ministering to the criminals under interrogation and, where necessary, reviving them to consciousness when, overcome by their travails, they slipped into oblivion. It was unlikely, therefore, that the physician's latest pronouncement was motivated by pity for the captive. Rather, he had most likely judged that an incomplete confession from the old marquis would be preferable to no confession at all from a dead marquis, who would thereby evade a just punishment that must be enacted before the whole nation. If Cardoso was prepared to stake his reputation – or more – on his diagnosis that the marquis was *in extremis,* it was safe to believe him.

'Very well.' He extracted pencil and paper from his sleeve. 'Inform da Cunha that he is to heed your advice and suspend interrogation of the Dom Francisco until I return, as I have written. Patch the marquis up as best you can.'

The doctor, white-faced, tucked the paper into his glove.

'And Doctor!' Cardoso stopped in his tracks.

'Thank you for your good work. You were right to halt the interrogation. I am grateful.'

With those reassuring words, the minister stepped away, his attention caught by some commotion at the gate involving a few unruly nobles. There would be a respite, of sorts, for the unfortunate marquis. But what torments awaited him on the morrow?

A half-hour later, Dom Sebastião and his soldiers had succeeded in putting order on that group of treacherous aristocrats who had not yet understood that their days of ascendancy and privilege were at an end. No matter. Thanks to Doctor Cardoso's intervention on behalf of the marquis, Dom Francisco's torments had been suspended, at least for a time. But it would be necessary to supervise the next stage. Covering his head with his cloak, which afforded but little protection from the rain, Dom Sebastião hurried across the square towards the Tower and arrived soaked through, the damp having penetrated to his frockcoat. Which he would have to change, lest he fall prey to a chill, for this week was no time to fall ill, given that the trial date was set for early January. Which left little time – two weeks, perhaps less – to assemble the evidence and present the case.

The thick oaken door which gave access to the lower levels of the Tower swung opened as soon as he knocked. No doubt the guards had observed his approach through the deep, narrow slits in the rear walls. To the south, the Tagus swelled, the rough boards of the little boats at anchor in the bay groaned and strained against their tethers. Once admitted to the tiny vestibule he blinked, his eyes adjusting to the dim glow of a single taper held aloft by a guard who saluted when the minister handed him his sodden cloak. It would not be easy to find a dry jerkin to fit that long, lean physique but find one he would, for Dom Sebastião was well-known for his generosity towards those who did him good service. And he did not want to be the man to send the minister back out into the dark, stormy night in his wet clothes.

'I will find one without delay, Your Excellency.'

Dom Sebastião grunted in reply and made his way down the rough-hewn steps, his fingers brushing stone walls dripping water and slime, guided by flickering torches set into iron sconces that must have been there since the Tower was built. The door to the interrogation cell swung open. He reached for his handkerchief. It did little to temper the stink of urine, excrement and blood to which da Cunha and Pereira seemed insensible, their work of the past days having accustomed them to the stench. Against the far wall, on a long, low table lay a broken body clad in soiled undergarments that had once, long ago, been of the finest white silk. The Marquis of Távora had always been a slender man but in the three weeks since his detention, the flesh had fallen from his body. During the last three days of special interrogation, all four limbs were splayed out at odd angles.

There being no need for closer inspection, the minister remained at the door. Don Francisco's head had lolled to one side, his tongue protruding. He did not appear to be breathing.

'Is he…?'

'Passed out,' said Judge da Cunha. 'Or perhaps sleeping. The doctor gave him a draught before he left.'

A flicker of pity kindled in the minister's heart. Really, one would not keep a wounded horse alive in that state, or even a dog. But there was too much at stake. The very life of the king, the royal family, the stability of the state, his own future, depended on the trial and what would come after it. Justice must be done. More, it must be seen to be done, most especially by anyone who might have future pretensions to attempt what Don Francisco and his co-conspirators had failed to accomplish. The marquis must stand trial, along with the other traitors, and take the consequences of his actions.

'We terminated the interview as soon as we received your note from the doctor.' Da Cunha nodded towards the broken body, no more disturbed than if he were speaking of an injured donkey. But then da Cunha was a military man, he had seen active service and must be accustomed to such sights. Pereira was another matter. A man of the law before his elevation to judge, the tools of his trade were dusty tomes and parchments, his peers were other lawyers and university professors, not those sinister brutes that awaited their orders in obedient silence at the foot of the rack. He could not be expected to have the stomach for this. Nevertheless, his presence was essential, for all branches of the judiciary had to be represented to ensure legitimacy of the proceedings.

'The marquis confessed all before losing consciousness,' Pereira's voice was shaking, 'as soon as the doctor left, before he slipped into blessed unconsciousness. He may have thought that things would go even worse for him without the doctor in the room.'

'I will need to know exactly what he said, Judge Pereira. And we should review all the evidence gathered during the last three weeks and establish the extent of the conspiracy. We must determine beyond a doubt exactly how many people, and which of the king's nobles and their households, were involved.'

Pereira's fleshy lips trembled, his eyes moist in the guttering light cast upon his countenance.

'Let us continue this discussion elsewhere,' Dom Sebastião said gently. They were all in need of fresh air and perhaps a glass of port to revive their spirits.

In any case, the confessions he and his team of interrogators sought from these key accused were by now confirmatory. Enough witnesses had come forward of their own volition to implicate the whole of the Távora household, as well as the Duke of Aveiro and several of his servants; more than enough to secure a conviction. And the return of the man-o-war from the Azores at the start of the month had yielded enough proof to convince any court beyond doubt. Within a day of the return of the ship, he had placed in the hands of His Majesty two dozen letters – from Malagrida, from the Duke of Aveiro, from almost every member of the Távora family – lamenting the failure of the attempt on the king's life and declaring the intention to repeat it. Dom José had straightaway signed all the orders for arrest with his own hand and soon after, the decree that permitted the temporary use of torture for the duration of the investigation.

During these last weeks, since the first arrests, they had all been working too hard. The sheer scale of the process, to round up all those who were implicated, was unprecedented, the Belém Tower having the capacity to harbour only a fraction of the hundreds of suspects who had been arrested. Hence the opening of the old menagerie to take the very significant overflow. However, practical considerations demanded that special sessions be conducted in the tower, so it was fortunate that only forty or so culprits had been deemed to possess information important enough to warrant enhanced interrogation. Extreme procedures, distasteful, which gave him no pleasure. But he would have given much to be present on the night his soldiers arrested those decadent leeches in their own palaces, at exactly the same hour, returning home their merrymaking at the British Factory Christmas Ball. To have seen the whole cabal apprehended, to have surveyed their countenances, one by one, as understanding dawned: that their days of privilege and impunity were over, that their rank would afford them no protection from the consequences of their crimes. Yes, that would have been pleasant.

However, the arrests had had to be conducted in the utmost secrecy, and as his presence at even one of the palace raids would have alerted the criminals and their associates to the danger closing in around them, it was a pleasure denied him. No matter. They were here, now, in the Tower, dozens of them, and in the Pateo de Bichos in their hundreds. Which for the moment would suffice.

Draped in a dry cloak borrowed from one of the tower guards, Dom Sebastião led the two judges across the square and the main thoroughfare to a side street, where he stopped and knocked on the rear door of a small tavern a short distance from the Pateo Dos Bichos. The proprietor, a short, rotund fellow, looked up as they entered, this door apparently not in general use. Obviously acquainted with the minister, he nodded to a discreet corner separated from the main tavern by a sturdy wooden screen. Once they had settled, the innkeeper brought a carafe of ruby liquid and three short glasses to the table.

'Leave us the bottle.' Pereira and da Cunha exchanged glances. Dom Sebastião was well-known for his abstemious character. No one had ever observed him imbibe more than a polite sip or two of wine or port but here he was, draining his glass and pouring himself another. Perhaps the work of the last days and weeks had shaken him more than he allowed.

'If we wished to eat…'

'Fried fish and newly baked black bread, Excellency?'

So they did know each other. It was difficult to imagine the fastidious Dom Sebastião frequenting such a place but perhaps the tavern-keeper was one of his spies. It was the perfect place to hear the local gossip. Both the Royal Palace and the minister's own lavish pavilion were but a league distant.

How could da Cunha and Carvalho e Melo even think of eating?

But when the servant-boy arrived with three plates of steaming fish, that and the comforting aroma of new bread, transported Judge Pereira back to happier days when, as a small boy, he would hover in the kitchen while Cook kneaded the dough. However much she scolded him to return to his lessons else his mother would blame her for his laziness, he would linger by the oven until the soft, dark bread was ready. Dom Sebastião laid a plate before him.

'Eat.'

The moment he took the first, obedient mouthful, he found that he was ravenous and descended on the tasty morsels of fish with unexpected appetite. The minister, hunched over his own plate, picked at his food.

'This is difficult work. Necessary, but difficult. For everyone – excepting alone those men, those strange beings who are fashioned of the hardest of flint that protects them from normal human feelings. Make no mistake, what we are doing extracts a cost, a great cost. To our sleep. Perhaps to our souls. Those of us with normal feelings of compassion for our fellow humans, however heinous their crimes, must make special efforts to strengthen our resolve in the knowledge that by our actions, however dreadful they may seem, we are protecting the king, the king's family, our very nation. We do not do this because we wish it. We do it because we must steep our hands in blood, that others may sleep easy.'

He really seemed to believe what he was saying. During this speech, conscious of every one of his own movements, Judge Pereira concentrated on his food, now as he speared a bit of fish on his fork and guided it to his lips, now as he tore a piece of dense, black bread from the end of the loaf, dipped it in sauce and crammed it in his mouth and then again, and again, he could not stop himself, while Dom Sebastião watched him, brows furrowed, his expression peculiar, perhaps a mixture of amusement and concern. At last the judge wiped his mouth with his handkerchief – it had been brilliant white just this morning – and leaned back, sated but still strangely empty.

'And what of Dom Francisco? His confession?'

'The marquis confessed all, Minister,' said da Cunha, 'a few minutes after Doctor Cardoso departed for the Pateo in search of you. As soon as the doctor left, the words began to spill out of him in a great flood.'

Dom Sebastião set down his fork. This was interesting. Dom Francisco, having resisted speaking until both he and the doctor had left the room, in his agony had perhaps imagined that those who had just left were the lesser of his tormentors and feared that in their absence things would go that much worse for him. However brutal the questioning from the other interrogators, and whatever physical trials accompanied them, the minister's own tones and inflections, ever soft and reasonable, sometimes lulled the prisoner into a sense of relief, of gratitude even, which imbued interrogations with an air of seduction as much as torment. As though Dom Sebastião, himself the tender rescuer, desired nothing more than to put an end to all this agony, if only the reluctant prisoner would allow him to do so.

'All?'

'He has named his entire family, Minister.'

Dom Sebastião leaned back in his chair.

'His wife? Children?'

'All of them.' Judge Pereira folded and refolded his handkerchief. If only that tremor would disappear from his voice. 'Both of his sons. Luís Bernardo, his heir, the young marquis. And his younger son, Jaime, who is only sixteen years old.'

'And the others?'

'His wife, the old marchioness, Dona Leonora. Also their brother-in-law, Dom José Mascarehnas.'

The Duke of Aveiro. This was no surprise. The duke and the marquis, two arrogant characters who shared a deep personal antipathy but were yet united in a hatred of the king, co-conspirators with a common purpose – to elevate themselves and their families at the expense of the king. Whose murder they had planned, and in which they had almost succeeded.

'The Duke of Aveiro has long seen himself as the next king,' da Cunha put in. 'For which treachery he has significant support. Especially from the islands.'

'And from the Jesuits,' the minister murmured. 'Did the marquis make any reference to the participation of the Jesuits in the conspiracy? Malagrida? Any Jesuit?'

Judge Pereira shook his head, with regret. 'No, Minister. But he did name his wife – and as Dona Leonora is a known disciple of Padre Malagrida and a frequent visitor to his spiritual retreats in Setúbal – in fact, I believe he may even be her confessor –'

'He is.' So the illustrious Marquis de Távora had at last implicated his whole family, his flesh and blood and the mother of his children, too, in this heinous conspiracy. A confession obtained under torture would be questioned, of course. But there were the letters. The existence of such robust documentary evidence of a conspiracy rendered these confessions purely confirmatory, for the most part.

'Did he name anyone else?'

'A large cohort of servants, Minister.'

Dom Sebastião poured himself another glass of wine.

'And the young marchioness?'

There. It was out. The question that had been in everyone's mind but never yet articulated. Until now. Dona Teresa of Távora: sister – to Dom Francisco whom they had just left, physically broken, in the tower; wife – and also aunt – to Dom Luís Bernardo, named by his own father as a co-conspirator; daughter-in-law – and by all accounts, thorn in the side – of Dona Leonora, the old marchioness.

And, of course, lover of the king.

Dom Sebastião had never understood the king's attachment to this silly woman. Her conventionally pleasing looks – the golden hair, the clear eyes, the body both slender and curvaceous, the habitual décolleté, plunging just enough to be a little daring while stopping short of vulgarity – could make no compensation for her vacuous manner and ostentatious behaviour. Her conversation, the little he had heard of it, was inane. Discretion was unknown to her. Upon receiving from His Majesty the handsome gift of a beautiful thoroughbred palfry, instead of quietly stabling the animal and enjoying such a magnificent gift in private, she had insisted on parading it through the estates of her noble relatives, boasting of its provenance, virtually within the hearing of her unfortunate husband. While at the opera, with Dona Mariana Vitória at the side of the king and Luís Bernardo on her arm, there were open flirtations, and the pair had been spotted more than once in a carriage on the outskirts of the city.

But the poor judgement of Dom José in persisting in this affair, even after the lady's husband had returned from his years of loyal service in India, reflected poorly on the throne, too. Notwithstanding his undoubted right, as monarch, to seek the attentions of any woman in the realm who happened to take his fancy, married or not, it surely demonstrated an absence of nobility of spirit to permit himself such indulgence when it meant openly humiliating the husband and compromising the lady's reputation in the process.

Yet this was an indulgence which Dom José's own father, the old king João, had permitted himself, often, and which had resulted in several offspring, of whom only the three Palhavã princes were recognised. No doubt there were more. This woman, Dona Teresa of Távora, who was by now well past the first flush of youth, had as yet produced no issue from her affair with the king – it was rumoured that she was barren, having miscarried several times. She must be exceptionally talented and energetic in the boudoir, for there could be no other explanation for the king's continued interest in her.

This was the woman who had been entertaining the king on the night of the attempt on his life as he made his way back to the Royal Palace, having just left her bed.

'Is Dona Teresa a witness, minister? Or a suspect?'

Well, Pereira, he did not say, that is the very question. One which so far, no one has been able to illuminate. Not one Ceveira, the glove maker who, several weeks before, came forward to report that an acquaintance of his called Ferreira had borrowed a musket on September 8th – and returned it *the day after the assassination attempt* saying: 'With this weapon, I did a better piece of work than I have ever done in my life'. Of course, this was before the attackers knew that the king had not died.

This Ferreira was a servant of the Duke de Aveiro, which further strengthened the evidence against his noble lord and indeed, others, most of whom were even now incarcerated in the Pateo dos Bichos.

But the one piece of information that most concerned him was the one that had not, so far, been forthcoming, not from Ferreira nor from any of the others: how did they know where to attack the king, the specific details of his route? And, even more important – how did they know the hour at which to attack? Very few people on that night had prior knowledge of the king's decision to leave the royal pavilion at an unaccustomed hour, on the day he had entered a state of mourning for the death of his sister.

Dona Teresa, of course, was one of them.

Were there others?

Or had the young marchioness, either knowingly or through her habitual indiscretion, revealed the details of her assignation with the king to the miscreants who had tried to assassinate him?

Perhaps the information came from a completely different source.

Witness or suspect?

'That remains to be seen, Judge Pereira. I will interview the lady myself, in the first instance. She deserves an opportunity to present her side of the story. She could be an innocent caught up in events of which she had no knowledge.'

As no doubt were at least some, perhaps most, of those unfortunates even now incarcerated in the Tower and the Pateo de Bichos. Dona Teresa would have to be treated with much greater consideration than they, lest the king insist on her innocence, regardless of what emerged as her role the conspiracy. Thus, the young marchioness would get her hearing – unlike most of the prisoners, noble and servant alike, possibly hundreds of them, some of whom were no doubt as innocent as the day was long.

But that could not be helped. In these dangerous times, with so much at stake, caution must prevail.

16

A Troubling Encounter

December 23rd, 1758, Convent of Santos, Lisbon

For a brief moment, Dom Sebastião considered postponing his interview with the young marchioness until the morrow. Night had fallen, the rain was turning icy with sleet, the inky waters of the Tagus were whipped up by a bitter wind that had swept in from the east while he had been taking fried fish and port with da Cunha and Pereira. He would dearly love to be making his way home to Eleanor and the children. She would be in the kitchen, for on the day before Christmas Eve she always made a special pudding with her own hand to a recipe from her native Austria. The house would be filled with the warm scent of cinnamon and cloves, the littlest of the children would be clamouring to help and to scrape the bowl once their mother, pink-cheeked from her unaccustomed exertions and the warmth of the stove, had finished mixing the dough and the dried fruits. No doubt his coachman had a similar domestic bliss awaiting him, if only his master would for once relent and allow them to return home before their children were abed.

The minister hauled himself into the carriage. This was getting more difficult with each passing month, the cracking of his limbs reminding him that his sixtieth year approached. He was not immortal, his endeavours to protect his country would last only as long as his life and good health, which thought spurred him to action and displaced all thoughts of Christmas festivities and family life.

That there had been a well-planned plot to assassinate the

king was beyond dispute. The most recent interrogations had yielded unassailable proof of the identities of some of the traitors, evidence that would certainly withstand the scrutiny of a trial. What was not yet clear was the breadth and depth of the conspiracy, and the extent of the measures that would be needed to bring the perpetrators to justice.

'To the Convent of Santos, Perez, if you please. We will not delay there long.'

This would be a very different conversation from his last meeting with Dona Teresa, which had taken place more than three months before, on the day after the attempt on the life of His Majesty. That interview had been conducted in the Távora summer residence in Belém. Today, she was a guest of the nuns of the Convent of Santos. Perhaps the news of confessions by members of her own family would encourage her to recall details she had withheld from him during their last meeting.

That morning, September 4th, he had been received coldly and obliged to wait in Dona Teresa's anteroom for a full fifteen minutes. When he was finally admitted to her presence, she did not invite him to sit. Her mother-in-law, Dona Leonora, had conducted herself in a similar manner when he had visited her for a very different purpose after the earthquake. No matter how these people quarrelled amongst themselves – and they did, for the favours of the king and his bounty were not limitless – in their dealings with outsiders, they were wont to display the same arrogance.

On that pleasant autumn day, the ambience of luxury evoked by the fine palace, the opulent reception room, Dona Teresa's jewels, the rich satins of her gown, the servants who attended her, all belied the fragility of her position. She had no idea that all this was about to end, that for all purposes had already ended, the external trappings but a gaudy shell embellishing the rotten interior of a way of life that would soon crumble to dust and be cast upon the air, as though it had never existed.

A faint stirring of compassion threatened to move him to pity but was soon extinguished. Not twelve hours before, His Majesty had risen from this woman's bed and minutes later, was attacked by enemies who meant to end his life. A less perceptive interrogator might have interpreted Dona Teresa's initial haughty demeanour as proof that she was ignorant of the conspiracy. However, he happened to know that earlier on that very day, she had received a visitor who was already of considerable interest to the investigation.

She knew.

But how much did she know? And when did she learn of the attack? In such circumstances, her demeanour took on the patina of dissemblance, rather than innocence.

'Dona Teresa.'

Startled that he should have the temerity to address her while she was occupied ordering tea from her own footman – who, correctly judging where the authority lay, scurried out of the room, closing the door with a soft click that resounded like the crack of doom – she rose from her sofa, bristling with indignation.

'Sit.'

'I...'

He repeated the instruction and this time she sank on to the silk-covered sofa, all colour draining from her rosy complexion. To her horror, the minister sat down next to her, much too close, this upstart, this Antichrist, so often vilified by her mother-in-law, by her brother, by their relatives and friends, all illustrious aristocrats, all deeply offended by his presence, by his very existence, this adventurer who had the ear of Dom José, who all but ruled the country, no, who did rule the country and to whom none of their rank, of her rank, must ever defer, but on the contrary must always put in his rightful place. Outside the door.

Yet here he was, in her best salon, sharing her Italian silk sofa, sitting close enough to touch her. Perhaps he was about to touch her, take her hand! He raised his bony, wrinkled fingers and for a dreadful moment it looked as though he really might reach for her own white little hand, such was the concern in his eyes, fear, almost, yes, these were the warm eyes of a kindly uncle, of a friend who was in genuine alarm at her position. Her heart beat faster, her indignation at the impudence of this man evaporated as a terrible awareness dawned: if this all-powerful First Minister – a person who, in his own way, was as intimate with her lover the king as she was herself, who had more influence over him than she ever did – if this man was so concerned for her well-being, how afraid should she be for herself? For her liberty? For her life?

While these thoughts were playing across her expressive features, Dom Sebastião permitted the silence to lengthen, allowing the young woman plenty of time to consider why he was there and what his presence might mean for her. He would not need to explain to her the precariousness of her position.

His words, when at last he spoke, were infused with genuine warmth.

'I wish to help you, Dona Teresa.'

She made no answer but her hands fluttered, clasping and unclasping of their own volition.

'You must tell me all.'

It occurred to Dom Sebastião, not for the first time, that great beauty in a woman could be more curse than blessing. How much better for this guileless young woman if she had never caught the eye of the king. She would have been a faithful wife, or not; might have indulged in harmless adventures with courtiers of little note; given her husband heirs or not, bickered and quarrelled with her mother-in-law, attended the opera; and never have found herself at the centre of the hurricane about to be unleashed, as violent and destructive as the earthquake that had destroyed so many lives less than three years before.

'What was the subject of your conversation with José Mascarenhas this morning, Dona Teresa? For what purpose would the Duke of Aveiro pay a visit to you at such an early hour?'

A single tear spilled over and made its way down her dewy cheek. At other moments, with other men, this might have been a calculated plea for comfort, but in her misery there was no coquetry. Her low murmur was almost inaudible.

'He wanted to tell me… it is my fault. I am to blame.'

'What were you to blame for, my lady?'

'Everything. Dom José… The king…'

And now she began weeping in earnest, her strangled words impossible to understand. He waited while she calmed herself.

'He said the king was attacked…last night, as he made his way back to the Royal Palace… on his way… from me.'

A storm of violent sobbing ensued, whether provoked by the divined injury to her lover, or for the mortal danger she now faced and perceived more clearly with every passing moment.

'Dona Teresa, the king lives. He has been injured, but he lives.'

'Yes, the duke told me.'

'Did he, indeed.' Now, how could Mascarenhas have come by those two pieces of information, and so quickly? First, that Dom José had been the victim of an attack. No word of the attempt on the sovereign's life had yet been published abroad, and nor would it be, until the moment was right. And secondly, that he had survived.

How could the duke know this – unless he himself, or someone he knew, had been present at the act? The young marchioness seemed not to have understood the nature of her revelation. Unless it was deliberate, and she wished to draw his attention to Aveiro. Might he have underestimated this woman? She had, after all, retained the fickle affections of the king for almost five years.

'How were you to blame, Dona Teresa?'

'It was foretold, Minister,' she said. 'Father Malagrida has said these years past that something dreadful would happen, many terrible things would happen, if Lisbon did not mend her ways and turn from her sins. And the greatest of them all was the sin committed by Dom José. With me. His Majesty sinned only because I tempted him and would not refuse him. And so all this has happened.'

'All what, my lady?'

'Everything! The earthquake, the waves, the fire, the destruction, the loss of life. It is all due to my conduct. Everyone says so.'

Ignoring her mention of the king for the moment, Dom Sebastião felt a surge of irritation mingled with compassion, that any person should carry such a burden. Was this woman so gullible?

'Everyone?'

'Father Malagrida, Minister. You have seen those letters he has been writing me these past years, denouncing my conduct and foretelling all manner of dreadful consequences. And one after another, his prophecies have come true.'

'Father Malagrida writes letters to me too, Dona Teresa, and has done for years, saying much the same thing. He calls me the Devil incarnate.'

His wry tone succeeded in eliciting a slight curve of her lips, not yet a smile.

'He writes letters in the same spirit to Dom José, too, you know.'

'Yes, I know.' Of course she would.

'For myself, I pay him no heed.' This was not true. On the contrary, he paid Malagrida and his disciples a great deal of heed, some would say too much, with the goal of devising a plan that would silence him once and for all. If the Jesuit Order declined to discipline their troublesome priest, then he would have to deal with the matter himself. 'Nor does the king. As you know.' In truth, Dom José was become ever more agitated at Malagrida's thundering denunciations, frequently made in public, and often asked why his own father, whose conduct had been little better than his own, had not received similar denunciations.

'But the prophecies! They came true! The earthquake. The death of the old queen…!'

The prophecies. Exactly. There was a fine line, and His Majesty was greatly sensible of it, between foretelling the future, and planning for it.

Between a prophecy, and a threat.

'Dona Teresa, Father Malagrida specialises in foretelling the deaths of many people who are old and infirm. He is bound to get a few right sometimes. That the old queen happened to be one of them was but a fortunate coincidence – for the padre, that is – which served to enhance his reputation.'

'The earthquake…?'

No, he had not underestimated her. It was baffling, this combination of humility and hubris that drove ostensibly rational individuals to believe that their actions, their petty sins, were of such monumental significance as to attract the attention of the Almighty to the extent that He would visit a disaster upon a whole city in retribution.

'What else did the duke say, Dona Teresa? How did he convince you that you were to blame for the attempt on His Majesty's life?'

He could see her weighing her answer, judging how much to say and what to omit, though he could not yet divine her purpose. To save herself? Or others?

While he pondered, she stood and drew herself up to her full height, looking down upon him where he sat on her sofa of Italian silk.

'He casts blame upon my family, Dom Sebastião,' she blurted out, spoiling her advantage by sitting down again and putting her hand on his arm. 'It is not true, Minister. My husband, my mother-in-law – my brother – yes, they were unhappy that the king…that Dom José…loved me. At first.'

To say they were unhappy was an understatement. The old marchioness for years had been agitating to have the marriage between Dona Teresa and her son annulled.

'But they grew accustomed to it. And there were benefits…'

She trailed off. There was no decorous way to express the exchange of the family honour, or what the Távoras had seen as such, for the material benefits of the new riches and property that had come their way in recent times. Though not, it must be recalled, the coveted dukedom.

He decided to take the bait.

'Is there any reason why the Duke of Aveiro should seek to implicate your family unjustly in this heinous crime, Dona Teresa?'

'I can only think of one reason, Minister.'

She seemed to believe it. Perhaps she did. And perhaps she was right.

Despite that first interview having yielded invaluable information – perhaps because of this, or from a native instinct to protect his sources – Dom Sebastião had decided against discussing it with his co-investigators or even acknowledging that it had taken place. Now, this very evening, he would learn whether the three months that had passed since that meeting, and her detention in this convent while members of her family were questioned in the Belém Tower, would produce any change in her story.

At first glance, her person glowed with the same intense vitality as it had three months earlier. But dark shadows under her eyes and in the sunken hollow of her cheek attested to many anguished days and sleepless nights. Her slender frame no longer filled out the satin gown she had chosen for this meeting – perhaps she had worn it in deference to his visit? Or more likely as a kind of armour, a relic of the life that was now in the past, to remind her of who she once was, a talisman that would protect her from the torments she feared might await. But the jutting collarbone and spindly arms inspired no awe for her station: rather, an uncomfortable compassion for her person. Had there been a shawl at hand, he would have gathered her up and wrapped her in it, as he had often swaddled his own little daughters, safe from the bitter cold.

'Have you news of my husband, Dom Sebastião?'

Luís Bernardo, the young marquis and cuckold, at that moment was occupying one of the cells of the Belém Tower. After a three-day interrogation, he too had just implicated his entire family – including his wife – in conspiring against the life of the king.

'He is well, Dona Teresa. He is assisting us in our investigation. He asks that I convey his warm affection and tell you not to worry on his account.'

A single sob escaped her. Things must be very bad. It had been so long since Luís Bernardo had offered a kind word, let alone an expression of affection, and who could blame him. She had humiliated him, she had no right to expect anything from him, much less warm feelings. The threat of more sobs subsided and a profound tranquility washed over her, such as she had not experienced in the three and a half months since she had been escorted in bewilderment from her palace and brought to this convent, for her own protection, they said.

She did not believe him, that much was clear. Perhaps it was for the best. There were people whose resolve crumbled in the face of direct threats. But others, and Dona Teresa might be one of them, responded more to fears they invented for themselves, once they understood the gravity of their situation.

He moved closer.

'My lady.' And now he really did take her hand, the impertinence of that gesture, no matter how kindly meant, an unmistakable signal of the reversal of fortunes between them. She closed her eyes while he spoke, her breath stilled while she absorbed his words, low and insistent.

'I think you did not tell me quite everything, when last we met.'

She opened her eyes and looked down at her hands. The minister's gnarled fingers hovered above them.

'Dona Teresa, you *must* tell me all that you know of what happened on that night. The night of the attack on Dom José. And everything that went before,' he added. 'Things will go much better for you if you do.'

She covered her face.

'The visit from the Duke of Aveiro?'

'It was as I said. He told me nothing of any conspiracy. Only that I was to blame for all the ills that had befallen our family. And the country too, probably. Because of my conduct with the king.'

'But you suspected him?'

With no hesitation, she raised her head and, with a single nod, assented. In fact, no corroboration of the duke's involvement in the crime was necessary, for all the evidence required to condemn the arrogant and detested José Mascarenhas, Duke of Aveiro, had already been extracted from said Miguel Ceveira, the glovemaker who had approached the office of the minister some weeks before with interesting information. On the day before the attack on the king, an acquaintance of Ceveira had borrowed a musket. He returned it the next day, remarking 'with this weapon I did a better piece of work than I ever did in my life.' Dom Sebastião had taken the precaution of confining this Ceveira to the attic on the rua Formosa to ensure his safety.

The fellow who had borrowed the musket, named Ferreira, was a servant of the Duke of Aveiro, this fact providing unshakable evidence as to the identity of those who carried out the attack.

But it was not enough to know who had committed the deed.

For such an action to have proceeded so far – and it had almost succeeded, would have succeeded, were it not that the musket had misfired – there must have been a vast network of supporters involved in planning, financing or otherwise supporting the plot; and an army of conspirators who had known of it and failed to denounce it.

It was just as important, no, more important, to discover who they were. All of them. And ensure that they all paid the price.

'Your assignation with His Majesty on that night, Dona Teresa, was at an unaccustomed time.'

'Dom José always determined the time and place of our meeting. He was in mourning, having just received news that Bárbara – his sister – had died.'

And yet His Majesty had slipped out of the Royal Pavilion all the same, to spend a few hours with this woman, while his wife lay abed and his sister in her grave.

'How did you receive notice of His Majesty's intentions? A message delivered by a page-boy?'

'A note.'

'With an unbroken seal?'

She gaped in shock. With reason, for it was unthinkable that any page or servant would dare to break any seal that bore the imprint of the monarch's ring. But in these strange times, so many unthinkable things were happening.

'Of course.'

'Who else could have known of the arrangements? Your husband?'

She shook her head vigorously and some colour returned to her wan countenance.

'Luís Bernardo was not at home that day. He had not been at home for some weeks.'

This was true. The young marquis, it was known, had absented himself from his marital home some time before.

'So there is no possibility that Luís Bernardo could have known anything of the details of our meeting...my rendez-vous with His Majesty. But others...' She turned towards him, as though a new thought had just illuminated her mind. 'My mother-in-law! Dona Leonora! She knows everything that occurs in my house, I am sure of it. I think she has spies in my household. Any one of the servants could have told her of my movements on that or any other night, for I would be obliged to give orders for which dresses to prepare, when to draw my bath, whether or not I needed a carriage...'

Was Dona Teresa a very cunning woman, or a stupid one? It was hard to decide whether she understood what she had just done. In attempting to protect her husband – the husband she had humiliated and cuckolded for years – she had just implicated her whole household: every servant, every page and indeed, her own brother, Dona Leonora's husband, as well as Dona Leonora herself.

'Is this your formal statement, Dona Teresa? Are you aware of what you are saying?'

Trembling, she nodded, the enormity of what she had just done perhaps beginning to dawn. And perhaps also the understanding that her testimony had by no means exonerated her husband after all. Rather, the reverse.

Unless. Was that her intention?

Her next question chilled him to the bone.

'What will happen to me?'

What, indeed? She was still a suspect and indeed might have had much to gain, had Mascarenhas succeeded in ousting Dom José from the throne: a return to the favour of her family; a monarch well-disposed, unlike the present king, to her brother and her husband.

Were the decision his and his alone, he would be conducting a very different kind of interrogation. However, His Majesty might see things differently. It was possible that Dom José would choose to convince himself of the innocence of his former lover.

No. This was one suspect who would have to be managed with the greatest of care.

17

Exciting Insights and a Fruitless Endeavour

January 12th, 1759, rua Formosa, Lisbon

It had been surprisingly difficult to obtain permission for a timely audience. No matter that his appointment as Defender was confirmed less than a week before, and that his Instructions arrived just this morning – though the trial was on the morrow! No matter that said Instructions contained a number of inconsistencies and outright errors which would make it impossible for him to conduct the defence he intended. Nothing less than a forceful reminder that he had been chosen by the king himself had persuaded Dom Sebastião's secretary – a petty tyrant, as functionaries of powerful men so often are – to find a space in his master's busy schedule.

Doctor Eusébio Tavares Sequeira raised himself from one of the many gilt chairs that graced the anteroom to the minister's office. As he paced the gleaming tiled floor, his portly figure advanced towards him, reflected in full-length mirrors adorning a pair of double doors, beyond which Dom Sebastião conducted his daily business. The pleasant, inoffensive countenance, a little less plump than usual, bore unaccustomed lines of worry, etched during the last week, since the day the minister summoned him to this very office to inform him of the great honour bestowed upon him.

He had lost no time in spreading the news abroad, to his

family and of course to his colleagues, who would be sick with envy that he, above all the lawyers in the city of Lisbon, had been chosen to perform this prominent role. But his wife's troubled countenance gave him pause. Even as he spoke, the reality of his new commission dawned in her fearful eyes. As her slender hand flew to her lips, his voice faltered and fell silent. Dear Lucia, too discreet to speak aloud what he ought to have understood himself, even before the wily minister had greeted him with such deference – that this was a poisoned chalice. To conduct the defence of such miscreants – so clearly guilty, without the slightest chance of acquittal or mitigation – would cover anyone associated with the case in ridicule.

But what could he do? No subject could refuse a request from the king. There was nothing for it but to carry out his role as Defender to the best of his abilities. During the first day or two of his work on the case, while he pored over the bundles of witness statements and summaries of strategy which the minister had sent to his office, he found himself slipping into a state of near paralysis, such was the futility of his task. And the shame of association with criminals who had conspired to assassinate the king and topple the government! His professional standing would never recover. Small comfort that the commission, though of short duration, was exceptionally well-remunerated.

When did his spirits begin to reawaken? How many days of immersion in those sad, horrifying accusations and confessions to plotting and murder had he endured out of painful duty, before he found himself rising an hour, two hours earlier than his custom, reading far into the night, ignoring calls for luncheon and even missing dinner, in growing excitement at the questions that called to him from between the lines he was reading?

Perhaps it was the end of the third day when the first glimmer of doubt was kindled, then flared to a blazing certainty: that beneath the story created by the myriad accusations and confessions from prisoners and servants, in the city markets, of a brazen attack by two illustrious families who had conspired with the fanatical priests of a renowned Order to do away with the king, was another story altogether. One that he, and only he, was equipped to tell, to prove, to declare to the wider world. Was there a Divine Providence at work here, that had guided His Majesty to select the person who would discern the pattern beneath the evidence and bring the truth to light?

But they had given him less than a week to prepare the defence! And until this very morning, there had been no certain intelligence concerning which of the accused would be formally tried. Seven or eight, he inferred from his reading: the Duke of Aveiro, certainly, who had confessed all and named many accomplices; the Marquis of Távora and two of his sons; several servants and, of course, priests of the Jesuit Order. The glaring weakness in this evidence being that many statements were made under torture! This surely undermined the case for the prosecution and would be a major element of his strategy for the defence. That much was clear.

However, the procedures drawn up for the conduct of the defence were far from clear and must have been drafted by a young clerk, an apprentice at best, for the process they described could not be correct. A brief meeting with Dom Sebastião would, must, set things to rights, for it would be impossible to conduct an effective defence otherwise: hence his present imposition on the minister's time. This would be a delicate undertaking, for in questioning the Instructions, there was no telling whose work, and therefore, whose person, his implied criticism would challenge. His questions, his doubts should be expressed with firmness, yes, brooking no opposition, while conveying respect for the illustrious office – this office – where they originated.

Quick footsteps from the corridor interrupted his musings. The outer door leading to the vestibule opened and a footman stood aside to allow a tall, thin gentleman, familiar of countenance, to enter. The newcomer looked around the room and hesitated, as though undecided about where he might sit. He chose an ornate, rather uncomfortable sofa set alongside a window that looked on to the street. The early morning light illuminated his troubled features, as he lowered himself gingerly on to the sofa, looking neither to the right nor the left. The footman closed the door but instead of leaving the room, took up position at the side of the mantelpiece, eyes focused on the middle distance.

Doctor Eusébio glanced at the visitor. Certainly, the countenance was familiar. As the eminent newcomer – for his attire, his carefully powdered wig and general bearing gave every indication of eminence – showed no inclination to speak, after some hesitation, Doctor Eusébio stood, bowed and introduced himself. Before he could elaborate on his role and his business with the minister, his lugubrious companion interrupted.

'You are the Defender, lawyer for the defence. Appointed by the king himself.' Startled, for he was not accustomed to his reputation preceding him, Dom Eusébio stammered an affirmation.

'I believe we may have met?'

'Doctor João Marquis Bacalhau. I am afraid we must take care not to converse.'

Of course. This was one of the five Tribunal Judges who would hear his defence of the accused on the very next day! How strange that a judge should seek conference with the minister on the day before the most important trial the country had ever seen. Surely there must be strict separation between members of the government, who were prosecuting the case, and the presiding judges who would have the fate of the accused in their hands? Perhaps, like himself, Doctor João was obliged to clarify a pressing matter of procedure; for as counsel for the defence, his own presence in this place, at this time, for similar reasons, was no less irregular. Overcome by an urge to explain himself, he set about assuring the judge that his audience was not intended to make representations on behalf of the accused, but concerned important practical aspects of the –

'I am sorry, Doctor Eusébio, but I may not speak with you. Neither concerning the trial, nor any other matter.' The footman continued to hover by the marble fireplace, paying no attention to the exchange. 'We should not even be in the same room.' Despite the sharpness of his words, his tone was polite. Notwithstanding his exhortations to discretion, he drew in a deep breath and seemed about to speak but hesitated and lapsed into silence. At that moment, a merry, bell-like sound chimed from beyond the mirrored doors, which swung open to reveal another footman who, lingering on the threshold, bowed to the judge and informed him that Dom Sebastião would see him now.

While the judge was in conference with the minister, there remained but a short time in which to rehearse anew the observations and questions which Doctor Eusébio had deemed in need of clarification. His first comment must comprise a formal objection to the speed of the entire process of the investigation, prosecution and trial.

Minister, barely one month has passed since the accused persons were arrested, which commendably rapid progress in the investigation has, however, left no time to test the veracity of the evidence against them.

True, there was evidence aplenty, for the investigation had commenced – in secret – on September 4th, the very day following the assassination attempt. But none of the evidence gathered during that time had been made available to a defence of the accused until a week ago, for until then, no defence had been appointed. The first arrests were made on December 9th and interrogations of the accused commenced on December 14th, barely one month ago; and on the 20th was enacted the infamous change in the law that permitted the use of torture – torture, in Portugal!

During the three weeks that had passed since then, a flood

of testimonies had poured from a few highly vocal witnesses; and especially, from the accused themselves, who not only admitted to the charges, but incriminated dozens of servants, friends, even members of their own families, in all manner of treasonous acts that ranged from actually having discharged a pistol at the coach in which the king was travelling, to providing practical support for the heinous act, or – and this of greatest concern to His Majesty – to having planned the entire endeavour. Now recovered from the minor physical injuries he sustained in the attack, but shocked to learn that opponents of his reign were so determined to be rid of him as to deprive him not only of his throne but of his very life, Dom José had determined that the full force of the law must fall, not only on the perpetrators, but on all those who had planned or conspired in the treason, or even had the slightest advance intelligence of it. And if the law had to be changed to accomplish this, then so be it.

Which strategy gives rise to the second observation:

Testimony extracted under torture may not be accurate and therefore must be corroborated by independent evidence.

The use of such methods in a civilised nation must be regarded as a regression to barbaric practices of the distant past and the worst excesses of the Inquisition. Yet even the Holy Office conducted interrogations in a manner circumscribed by clear limits and regulations. Such limits, as far as it was possible to determine, were not observed during the questioning of prisoners in the Tower of Belém or the prison of Junquiera. Far from it.

Much had been made of the confessions of the Duke of Aveiro and the Marquis of Távora. But would not many people – perhaps most of us! – admit to any crime, if subjected to unendurable pain? And even go so far as to incriminate our loved ones, if such compliance held out the promise of respite from the agony, however brief? Of the principals of the two families, only the younger of the Távora sons, a lad of barely seventeen, did not break. Neither the rack nor the knife extracted from him any admission of his own or his family's involvement in the conspiracy. Perhaps his youth endowed him with reserves of physical and mental resilience denied his elders. Or perhaps Dom Francisco and Dom José Mascarenhas, Duke of Aveiro, really were guilty. But without corroborating evidence, how could any judge determine the veracity of their incriminating testimonies?

The practice of detaining and conducting violent interrogation – torture – upon some witnesses, and rewarding others, calls into question much of the witness testimony on which the case against the accused is based.

This was the most delicate of the observations that the minister must hear. It would have to be expressed with great delicacy.

In truth, few facts concerning the events of the night of September 3rd were undisputed. That His Majesty had left the assignation with the young marchioness, Dona Teresa of Távora, at around eleven in the night, yes, that much was certain. Likewise, that contrary to his custom, he had travelled in an unmarked carriage in the company of his valet, Teixeira; that perhaps sensible of the impropriety of indulging his carnal appetites on the very day when the entire royal household had entered deep mourning for his dead sister, he had travelled without his customary escort; that the carriage had been ambushed, twice, on a narrow road at a point halfway between the residence where the assignation with the young marchioness took place and the Royal Palace; that the skill of the coachman and the quick thinking of Dom José himself in redirecting the carriage to the home of the royal surgeon in Junqueira, instead of following the route home to the Royal Palace, had saved them. For, a little further along their original route, a third ambush had lain in wait.

Beyond those bare facts, all was obfuscation and confusion. Did the would-be assassins know that the carriage was occupied by the king? The two ruffians who admitted discharging the shots, Ferreira and Talvora, insisted under torture that they did not know His Majesty was a passenger in the carriage they had attacked. Yet this part of their testimony had been ignored. Perhaps, as the notes in the Instructions argued, the miscreants pleaded ignorance of the traitorous intent of their evil deeds in the hope of a more lenient sentence – or at least, a less painful death than that which a verdict of treason would merit. Yet the fact that they did not change their story, even on the rack, surely justified investigation of this aspect of their confession. (But when? For the trial was on the morrow!) If they spoke true, then the king was never the intended target and neither the attackers, nor their paymasters, were motivated by treasonous impulses. Murderous, yes. Vengeful, perhaps. But not treasonous.

One individual who had no shortage of enemies, of course, was Teixeira, His Majesty's valet, a nasty specimen who profited greatly from his proximity to the king. Including the perquisite of using one of the royal household's unmarked carriages for his private business…

Every page of those testimonies, every detail of the facts – as opposed to the conjecture and interpretation embellishing the facts – called into question the version of events set out in the Instructions. And those letters intercepted by the captain of the *Nossa Senhora* on their way to so-called co-conspirators in the Azores, they would have to be scrutinised with a neutral eye, for it was those secret messages which had revealed the identities of the conspirators in the early stage of the investigation and provided the evidence for their arrest. So many of the various stories swirling around the affair, bloated by rumour and gossip, evaporated like smoke in the wind as you tried to grasp them, which suggested…

'I will not.'

The mirrored door dividing the anteroom from the minister's office flew open and Doctor Bacalhão appeared, his face white and his jaw set. He paused on the threshold and advanced a few paces towards the startled Defender, who made a hesitant bow.

'In answer to the question you put to me earlier – yes, I am a judge of the Tribunal of Inconvenência. But for how much longer I cannot say. For I have refused to accept the sentence.'

What sentence?

'I will not accept it.'

As he spoke, those strange words enunciated through gritted teeth, a wayward muscle in the old man's cheek began to tremble. And yes, the reserved gentleman who had entered the minister's private office not a quarter-hour before, perhaps a trifle arrogant but kind with it, had emerged shaken, the lines of age etched more deeply around his mouth, his eyes sunken with an unhealthy glitter. He turned and moved stiffly towards the door, resting one hand briefly on Dom Eusebio's shoulder as he passed by him.

Of what sentence did he speak?

'The minister will see you now.'

The interior office where Dom Sebastião Carvalho e Melo conducted his daily business had the air of a private parlour, with none of the grandeur of the ante-room where petitioners and those summoned to meet him were obliged to await his pleasure, in contemplation of the many signs of opulence it boasted: rich tapestries adorning the walls, an escritoire and several chairs in the French style, no doubt chosen to inspire admiration or awe.

This room, where the minister most likely spent the larger part of his working day, was modest, frugal by comparison, its proportions no more imposing than the best room in Dom Eusébio's own home. Family portraits and small, domestic items, including one or two children's toys, such as that spinning top in the corner, were scattered around, infusing the room with a comfortable, domestic ambience. The handsome portrait above the mantel depicted a richly dressed lady, plain but with a sweet regard, who must be Dona Eleonor, though it was difficult to be sure, for Dom Sebastião's wife was rarely seen in public. A series of miniature paintings of children of various ages were lined up on the minister's massive oak desk. Here is a man who works tirelessly on behalf of the nation, the room said, but a family man, too, with human cares and woes, a man who sometimes is obliged to take harsh decisions to protect the country and his family, his little ones but a staircase away.

'I really should not be meeting with you, Doctor Eusébio,' the minister said, but his tone was genial. He rose from behind his desk and made his way to an armchair opposite, beside the fire, which was already lit in spite of the early hour, the better to dispel the January chill.

'I am sorry to disturb Your Excellency and I am sensible that the propriety –'

The minister waved away his protestations with a finely manicured hand. Why did the sight of that soft skin, those carefully shaped nails, fill Dom Eusébio with unease?

'You are here now. And allow me to congratulate you on your appointment. You are aware, of course, that His Majesty selected you himself.'

'It is a great honour, Excellency, and I would be most grateful if...'

Dom Sebastião raised both hands, as though in defence against an anticipated attack.

'You know that I cannot discuss the case, Doctor Eusébio. In fact, I must admit to a certain discomfort that you asked to see me on matters which I assume must be connected to the trial you are to defend tomorrow.'

Despite the implicit rebuke, the minister's regard was warm, even inviting.

'I assure Your Excellency that the matters which bring me here are purely procedural. They concern mainly the nature of my instructions and certain aspects of...'

The minister sighed heavily. 'Mainly!'

But his tone remained affable, as though disposed to indulge a favoured protégé or colleague, if against his better judgement. But before Doctor Eusébio could take advantage of the pause, his host swept on.

'I do hope you are not here to complain about the speed with which the investigation and trial have proceeded, Doctor Eusébio. Others have expressed that very concern, and we have answered it in detail. We have no choice but to identify and punish not only the perpetrators of the crime, but all those who conspired to conceive and support its execution, before they make another attempt. Or flee the country to regroup.'

This was a clever line of argument, to which Doctor Eusébio had no answer. At least one suspect, Policarp, the Duke of Aveiro's shield bearer who, it was believed, was one of the main perpetrators, had managed to flee the duke's country residence when he and his master spotted a military guard approaching in the distance. But – if the duke really were guilty of this attack on the life of the king, and in no doubt about the punishment that such a crime would merit – why had he not taken the opportunity to escape at the same time?

'With respect, Minister... notwithstanding the wisdom of your concern... I was allocated less than a week to prepare the defence of the accused. And my specific Instructions arrived only at first light this morning.' In fact, it had been dark when the messenger hammered on his front door and deposited a bundle of files in the arms of the maid. 'Until this morning, I was not even sure of how many accused I am to defend.'

'Exactly, Doctor. Hence my surprise that you are here, and not in your office, writing your defence.'

Making a determined effort not to glance down, the Defender clutched at the scrap of paper where he had made rough preparatory notes for this meeting, now crumpled and damp in his palm.

'Permit me, Minister, to bring to your attention certain matters of procedure – crucial matters – which are so far unclear to me. And which are so irregular –'

The minister made no response at his hesitation. He did not bid him continue, but nor did he bid him be silent.

'– which are so unusual, that I feel sure there has been some error in drawing up my Instructions. And some questions I have concerning....' At the mention of the word 'error', the minister stood up from his armchair and, leaning one arm on the mantlepiece, turned to observe Dom Eusébio, who was now obliged to look up at him, Dom Sebastião being uncommonly tall and this chaise longue being uncommonly soft and deep.

'Minister, the name of Dona Leonora, the Marchioness of Távora, is included on the list of accused, which I received this morning. I had understood that she was detained as a witness only, not as –'

'She was one of the first to be arrested, Dom Eusébio. The warrant was signed by the king himself.'

Dazed, Dom Eusébio remained silent for a few moments. There was too much to ponder. His voice, when it returned, sounded strained and weak to his own ears.

'But there is no evidence against her.'

'Her association with the Jesuits, in particular the agitator Malagrida! The letters intercepted on the *Nossa Senhora*! A full account of which is contained in your Instructions. Had you examined your Instructions closely, you would be well aware of the extent of the evidence against her.'

With difficulty, Doctor Eusébio rose from his chair and stood to face Dom Sebastião.

'I should like to have sight of those letters, Minister. If I am to defend the marchioness and the other accused, the originals are a necessary –'

'The original letters are in the hands of His Majesty the king. Who charged me with creating a summary of their contents, to form part of the Instructions to the Defence. Your Instructions. Really, Dom Eusébio, is that so difficult to understand? I assume you do not wish me to rebuke His Majesty on his chosen strategy for bringing his attackers to justice?'

Many years before, there was a rumour abroad that the Marchioness of Távora had ejected Dom Sebastião from her house, dismissed him as an upstart adventurer who had had the impertinence to seek the hand of one of her daughters in marriage. However, no one ever said which of the daughters was the object of the attentions of the young Dom Sebastião José Carvalho e Melo. In any case, the story seemed unlikely, for the marchioness and Dom Sebastião were of an age; and in those far-off days, her children, the four who survived infancy, must have been little more than babes. None of the people who were in the least acquainted with the parties involved took the story for anything more than a scurrilous rumour put about to humiliate an upstart who did not know his place. And if the marchioness herself were not the author of the rumour, she had never corrected it.

Could such a wound, inflicted on the pride of a man such as the minister – haughty, ambitious, quick to take offence – motivate him to exact such a terrible vengeance, almost forty years later?

No. This could not be. The king himself had signed the warrant for her arrest. It was well known that since their return from India, Dom José had little love for any of the Távoras – the young marchioness excepted, of course – and that his normally equable temperament was often roused to fury at this arrogant woman who seemed to consider herself and her family his equal, or better. Nor did her intimacy with the Jesuit Malagrida, who regularly prophesied disaster, endear her to him.

And then there was the business with the young marchioness, Dona Teresa, another slight on the honour of the Távora name and source of conflict with the throne.

'Do you have any further questions, Dom Eusébio, or are you ready to get back to work and prepare your defence of the accused? They will have need of every scrap of your skill.'

If both the minister and the king were aligned against Dona Leonora, she was lost. They all were. But he had come this far. He would not now retreat.

'A very few, Minister. The witnesses who gave testimony against the accused. I should like to speak with them.'

'Impossible, Dom Eusébio. With just a few hours remaining before the trial…'

'Exactly.' His words were soft but for a few seconds, Dom Sebastião appeared to deflate a little.

'Or, if that is not possible —'

'It will not be possible. Most are detained. Outside the city. For their own protection.'

Since when did it become customary to detain not only suspects in a crime, but also the witnesses providing the testimony?

'Then I can put my questions to them during the trial itself.'

The minister gave him a hard look. 'As your Instructions specify –'

'The young man who heard, who claimed to have heard, the voice of the Duke of Aveiro outside the stables, after the attack.'

'A key witness. He clearly heard the duke declare that the king would die some day, if not on that day.'

'"No matter, for he will die some day,"' read Doctor Eusébio. 'In answer to a remark by the young Távora boy. Alleged remark. That the king had escaped.'

'So you have studied the Instructions, Doctor Eusébio. I am happy to know it.'

'What puzzles me, Minister, is how this young man, who was

not a member of the household of either the duke or the marquis – I believe he was waiting for an assignation with one of the serving maids of the house? – how he could recognise the voices of two men, noblemen, whom he had never met. Their paths could never have crossed.'

'Their countenances are well-known…'

'It was the night of the new moon, Minister, in an unlit courtyard by the stables. A pitch-black night.'

Dom Sebastião received these observations in silence.

'And where is this young man now, Minister? Will he have safe passage from his place of detention to the trial tomorrow, that I might put these questions to him in person?'

'He is not in detention, Doctor Eusébio. In fact, he has left the country. Fled. For fear of persecution, and with good reason, I would say.' The minister picked up a sheaf of papers from his desk. 'Which is immaterial, Defender. For there will be no questioning of witnesses, neither the young man nor any of the others. Not today. Not tomorrow. Never.'

I refuse to accept the sentence.

What sentence?

Would Doctor João Bacalhau be one of the five Tribunal Judges on the morrow?

The minister uncurled his long body from the armchair and got to his feet.

'I regret to say that our conversation has far exceeded the boundaries of proper discourse between us, Doctor Eusébio. You have your Instructions. Everything that passes next falls within the limits of the law.'

The law. Which was changed not three weeks ago to permit torture. And changed again, just two days ago, to permit the judges to deliver a sentence of severity untold in this country for centuries.

The minister's kindly hand weighed heavy on the Defender's shoulder as he steered his visitor towards the door.

'Just do your best.'

The merry chimes of the little bell rang out. The minister must have positioned it on his desk, concealed behind one of the miniatures of his children. The footman reappeared and opened the door wide. By the time Dr Eusébio turned to make his bow, Dom Sebastião was already seated, head lowered, dipping his quill in his handsome silver inkwell.

On this crisp January morning, Doctor Eusébio made his way down the hill on foot towards the Rossio where his carriage awaited to take him to the Junqueira, and thence to the Torre de Belém, where his clients awaited him, desperate to hear his strategy for their defence.

18

The First Reckoning

January 13th, 1759, Market Square, Belém

From: Edmund Stanton Esq
        rua da Janela
        Lisboa
        February 5th, 1759

My dear brother,

    Please forgive my tardiness in responding to your letter, and especially for my failure to provide you and our father with news of how matters stand at the embassy, concerning which I had promised to make a report early in the New Year. I have no legitimate excuse, David, beyond the unaccustomed disturbances of mind which have plagued me ever since I witnessed, a little over three weeks ago, a series of terrible events in this city, news of which may not yet have reached London. Since that day, January 13th, I have had no heart for work, nor for pleasure, nor for aught else. Even the agreeable chore of penning my weekly missive to you is beyond my feeble energies. I write these words now only at the urgings of Caroline, who, I think, is becoming frightened to see her husband retreat into a morass of dark thoughts, in the hope that, as I refuse to speak to her about that day, I might achieve some small relief by writing of it to you. For I dare not utter my thoughts aloud to any person in this city, thronged as it is with spies who regularly inform the authorities of agitators and rebels, a designation which I fear any expression of my horror would earn me, were I to let slip my opinions in the wrong company.

I am rambling, I know. You will think your brother has lost his wits. If so, we may thank Sir Edmund, for he it was who bade me attend the spectacle and write an account of all that transpired, that he might convey the information to our government. Which report I have completed and despatched to London, under Sir Edmund's name, of course, who declared that he himself had no appetite for witnessing such barbarities as public executions.

Did he think I had?

Yes, brother. On a single day, in a spectacle that lasted from dawn to dusk, seven members of the most illustrious families in the kingdom, together with four of their servants, all found guilty of conspiring to kill His Majesty King José, were put to death in the public square. I enclose for your perusal an extract from the *Gazeta de Lisboa* published in the week following the executions, which summarises the bare facts of the case (please excuse my imperfect translation, which I append below) but conveys nothing of the horror of the butchery, the gore, the groans and shrieks, of which the mind and soul, once polluted, can never be cleansed. For the brutal sufferings inflicted on the condemned went far beyond depriving them of life but were contrived to inflict the greatest torment and humiliation, to strip the unfortunates of all dignity and inspire terror and fear in all who witnessed them.

From the Gazeta de Lisboa, Friday, 18th January 1759

Of the terrible events of the night of the 3rd to 4th of September, which will linger in the memory of all readers, as will the infamy of the authors of those events, the Prime Minister being charged with the duty of bringing the perpetrators to justice, which duty he discharged with admirable prudence and wisdom, and in so doing those incontrovertibly identified as the aggressors of this execrable crime, the Duke of Aveiro, the Marquis of Távora, his wife, two of his sons and his brother-in-law, the Count of Atouguia, and thus were sentenced by the Junta da Inconfidencia to be stripped of their lands, properties and titles, declared strangers to this Kingdom and known as vagabonds and refugees; furthermore it was ordered that Leonora Tomasina, she who was known as the Marchioness of Távora be decapitated and that José Mascarenhas, he who was called Duke of Aveiro, and Francisco of Assis, known as the Marquis of Távora, and Luís Bernardo who had the same title, and Jose Maria adjutant and Jerónimo of Adaide, named Count of Atouguia, their arms and legs to be broken, their chests shattered with hammer blows, all to be garrotted, their bodies burned, including that of Leonara Tomasia and their ashes cast into the sea. All their houses in which they lived to be demolished and the land on which they stood, salted. All their lands, titles, properties to be confiscated by the Royal House. This sentence was carried out on the 13th day of this month in the place that lies between the quay of Belém and the palace which belonged to the Duke of Aveiro. On the same day, in the same place, were put to the garrot Manuel Alvares Feirreira, gentleman of the chamber of José Mascarenhas, and Braz José Remeiro, footman of Fracisco de Assis and João Miguel, footman, whose bodies were burned, together with the effigy of José Policarpe of Azevedo (who escaped capture and upon whose head is a bounty of ten thousand cruzados to whomsoever will hand him over to justice) and their ashes cast into the sea, with those of Antònio Alvares Ferreira, gentleman of the chamber of Jose Mascarenhas, who on the same day and in the same place was burned alive.

Dawn had not yet broken when I arrived in Belém. As I approached the market square, the bells of the Jerónimos began to toll, their mournful knell accompanied by the pounding of hammers on wood and the cries of artisans whose work on constructing an imposing scaffold at the northern end of the square, facing out towards the Tagus, was not quite complete. In fact, it was the news that workmen were occupied throughout the night building a mysterious structure in Belém which alerted Sir Edmund to the possibility that some serious act was afoot. For, despite rumours that a trial had taken place, all was conducted in such secrecy that no one knew which members of the Távora family were accused, nor even that an execution would take place. Thus it was with the entire affair, of which whisperings and suspicions abounded in the final weeks of last year. Not until a few days before Christmas was there any official acknowledgement that a crime had been committed against the person of His Majesty (it was claimed that he had merely suffered a fall at home). Only then did public notices signed by the Minister, Dom Sebastião José Carvalho e Melo, appear. These described the treason perpetrated and offered substantial rewards to anyone who would provide information about the attack on the king, as well as threatening terrible consequences for those who had any intelligence of the crime and did not come forward.

So it was that for those few weeks, before and immediately following Christmas, the city was pervaded with an air of unease. The people trembled, lest an acquaintance or neighbour should decide to profit from the minister's inducements and threats by recalling – or inventing – some morsel of information that would see innocent people cast into the cells of Junqueira or the Belém Tower. And thus it must have transpired, for I have learned since that the prisons are overflowing with suspects, both nobles and commoners, who have been detained on the flimsiest of grounds, or no grounds at all.

As to the accused, in spite of the rumours that members of the Távora family were implicated in a conspiracy to kill the king and replace him with the Duke of Aveiro, so many hundreds of people were detained that not even Sir Edmund was able to discover the outcome of the trial – if there had been a trial – or even which persons of the family had been found guilty. Certainly, there was no sure word that there would be executions. That is, until one of Sir Edmund's people rushed to his house in the middle of the night to inform him that an enormous scaffold was going up at that very moment – this was the early morning of January 13th – in Belém village square. Which messenger Sir Edmund then sent to my house, with instructions that I must go to Belém immediately and make a record of all proceedings on behalf of our masters.

Which order I of course obeyed. However, I had great difficulty in getting close to the square itself for, even at that early hour, three sides and the streets beyond were thronged with troops, many on horseback, who, in addition to keeping order among the thickening crowds, appeared to be escorting several groups of richly garbed individuals who were processing towards the square in complete silence. I later learned that these were illustrious members of the noble families, who had all received orders to witness the execution of their peers, many of them their own relatives.

The scaffold was an imposing platform raised about twenty feet above the ground and therefore visible from afar, but as the troops kept spectators at a distance of some hundred feet, once dawn broke I realised that I must secure a better vantage point, to be sure of having sufficient detail to pen a comprehensive report on the proceedings for Sir Edmund. Would that I had contented myself with a more distant view of what transpired during the six hours or more that followed. But I was foolishly anxious to do my best. Thus it was, in my halting Portuguese, I explained my predicament to a sergeant, who said that while he could not allow me to approach, were I to make my way to the quays and find a pilot willing to take me in one of the rowboats moored close to shore, the kind used to ferry passengers out to the ships anchored in the bay, he would not object. Upon which advice I acted and was happy to secure a position on a small craft close to the riverbank, which as you know, forms the fourth side of the square. It was the perfect spot from which to see, and hear, all that would happen on the scaffold, which loomed but a short distance from where my little vessel bobbed upon the gentle river waves. And you will recall from our days fishing as boys, David, how clearly sounds travels across water.

The morning was grey and chilly and drizzling rain, as is customary for Lisbon at this time of year. The old pilot was pleased with the few coins I pressed into his hand. While the bells of the Jerónimos continued their ominous chimes, I closed my eyes and allowed the gentle swell of the waves to lull me, comfortable and warm, wrapped in my good cloak, to a state of tranquility.

Just before eight o'clock, a commotion on the eastern flank of the square roused me from my meditations. A solitary soldier on horseback was making his way through the crowd, which parted to allow passage of a small, covered sedan drawn by a single black horse. While it processed at walking pace, accompanied by two friars in dark habits, one on each side, the people fell eerily silent, until it halted at the foot of the scaffold before a rough set of steep wooden stairs. Out stepped a woman of elderly mien, tall and dignified. The crowd roared.

I recognised her immediately. David, this was the matriarch of the greatest family in the kingdom. The Marchioness of Távora. Forgetting where I was, I leapt to my feet, setting the little boat a-rocking and startling the old sailor, who barked a rebuke and pointed to my bench. When I had resumed my seat, he nodded towards the scaffold and drew one finger across his throat. Thanks to my diligence, which I was by then regretting, I was close enough to observe one of the friars offer the lady his hand as she paused at the foot of the scaffold. She paid him no mind but with a steady foot mounted the steps unaided, her skirts raised in a practised manner as a lady accustomed to navigating awkward public appearances in unusual places.

Having reached the platform, she turned to a priest, to whom she addressed a few words. I imagine she must have been asking permission to make her confession, for immediately she began to speak, during which time the crowd became restless and started calling and jeering. The distance was too great for me to hear more than a few fragments of her speech, my command of the Portuguese tongue being very imperfect, although her clear, authoritative voice carried well. I managed to discern only a few words: *inocencia, lealdtad, crimen, familia*. Which I took to mean that the marchioness, about to be executed for treason like a common criminal, was declaring her innocence, and that of her entire family, of the crimes of which they were accused; and declaring her loyalty to their king.

When she had finished speaking, a tall, burly man, who, I soon realised, was the executioner, grasped her arm and marched her around the scaffold, that the baying crowd might get a good look at her. Several times he halted and leaned forward to speak in her ear, his words accompanied by lively gestures that indicated various items arranged at regular intervals around the wooden platform: several enormous wooden crosses; a long-handled hammer such as a workman might use to demolish a wall; several blunt, sturdy objects, possibly wooden sticks or metal bars, I know not which; a number of cords or ropes. And kindling for a fire. I did not at first understand that these were the instruments by which the other condemned souls – several members of her own family – would soon be put to death. I cannot say if she shed tears. But her erect posture remained unbending, until the executioner led her to a stool at the front of the platform, in my direct line of vision, to which she was tied and then blindfolded.

Thus it was that my view of what happened next was unimpeded. David, I wish I had had the foresight to avert my eyes, but the baying crowd, the flourish with which the executioner gathered up her long hair and wound it around one hand while brandishing a cutlass in the other, imbued the entire scene with an air of the theatre, as though we were witness to some horrible opera, which seemed to cast a sickening trance upon my mind and compel my attention. I would never have thought myself capable of being a willing observer to such a spectacle, but when the moment came, when the cutlass was raised, when the weak rays of the sun struggled out from behind a cloud to flash for a second on the cold, silver metal as the executioner's arm swept an elegant arc through the air and with one blow, severed the marchioness's head from her body – I could not look away. In spite of myself, I witnessed every motion, such slow motions, David, as the lifeless body toppled over and fell sprawling on to the platform, bound still to the stool, as the head rolled a little way away from it. There was a moment of silence, a stillness that echoed through the square louder than the loudest clap of thunder, and then a collective gasp, followed by cheering and screaming and howling from the mob.

    I must have swayed or perhaps lost my balance – when had I got to my feet again? – for I felt a firm grip on my arm and my pilot pushed me on to the bench, where I sat down heavily, waving away the leather pouch which he was thrusting in my face. Thinking I did not understand, he removed the plug and from a height, poured into his mouth a stream of dark, purple liquid. Once again, he pushed the pouch towards me and when I again shook my head – it being not yet half-eight in the morning and the sun barely up! – he began to enunciate slowly, insisting, as far as I could make out, that what we had just seen was only the beginning, and I would need this and more before the day was out. Notwithstanding my reluctance, I held the wineskin aloft as he had done and swallowed a mouthful of the rough wine, for which I was immediately grateful, as the warm current that coursed through my veins steadied me a little and imbued my vision with a slight haze, a transparent film that separated my eyes from was happening upon the scaffold.

As you know, brother, I have had no military experience or training, so the sight of weapons and torsos and severed heads is no small thing to me. Nor can I fathom the minds of those who would derive pleasure from a spectacle where human beings, even traitors, are butchered for entertainment. Are we no more civilised than the tyrants of Ancient Rome, or the barbarian hordes that defeated them? This, after all, is the eighteenth century, not the eighth! Yet despite the fearful reticence that pervades the city, I am sure that I was not the only one sickened by what happened on that day. Perhaps that is the true purpose of such spectacles. Perhaps they are intended, not so much as entertainment for the people, as warnings, strategies to inspire terror and warn others of the consequences of opposing the established order?

What I have described, David, was only the beginning. The old sailor spoke true. A little after half-eight, the crowd along the eastern side of the square parted once more to reveal the return of the covered sedan. Once again, it halted at the foot of the scaffold and from it emerged a young man whom the two black-clad friars half-carried from the carriage towards the platform. As he was dragged up the steps, it was clear that he had to be supported, not because he was struggling, but because he was in no condition to walk, both his legs being bent at unnatural angles and unable to support his weight, I suppose the result of long hours on the rack. This was José Maria, the second son of the marchioness whose headless torso remained sprawled on the scaffold without so much as the dignity of a sheet to cover it.

I later learned that of the many, many accused who were put to torture, only the young José Maria refused to confess to any of the crimes of which he and other members of his family were accused. A youth of seventeen years, on the scaffold he conducted himself with great dignity and resolve, offering no resistance to his fate. But on seeing the headless body of his mother, he wrenched himself free of restraining arms, fell to his knees and remained thus for a few seconds, head bowed in an attitude of prayer, until two assistants of the executioner seized him and dragged him to one corner of the platform, where lay an enormous wooden cross, the diagonal sort that we call the St Andrew's Cross, because of the nature of the martyrdom of that saint.

First, they blindfolded him. Then they stretched his body so that each limb lay along one arm of the cross, to which his ankles and wrists were fastened. What happened next was not random, as I first thought, but must have been mandated by the court judgement, for the process was repeated exactly, for all but one of the condemned. Most terrible was the methodical, calculated demeanour of the two assistants, who administered the beatings with neither anger nor frenzy, but with care: two blows of the metal bar to each arm, two to the legs, from both men in turn, I suppose to ensure that neither tired before the job was complete. And then a single, final blow of the hammer to the centre of the chest.

Even more shocking than the sight of such brutalities was the accompanying sounds. Once this first beating started, the baying of the crowd subsided and an absolute silence fell, as though every spectator were filled with a kind of reverence for the young man's suffering, as the dull thud of each blow landed on the twisted limbs, followed by the most horrendous, heart-rending shriek. And this accumulation of sound, the dull thump of a blow on bones, the cry of pain, a few moments' silence before the next blow, the next shriek, the rhythm, is imprinted on my mind, in my dreams, a terrible drumbeat whose silences, whose brief moments of respite offer no relief at all, for every instant that is not a moment of torment is filled with anticipation of the next blow, the next scream, so that the horror of silent expectation is even greater than the actual cries of torment.

And since that day, it seems to me that such is the condition of our very lives. That we endure, as best we can, the blows that come as we are dealt them, and though we be deafened by the groans of suffering, our own or those of others, the intervals of peace between are but illusory for we know that more torments will surely follow. And thus we live, our lives a stream of suffering, whether from the blows of Fate, or bracing ourselves for the next, ever recovering from the last disaster or awaiting the next. Yet before that day such thoughts were never in my mind, and now I cannot get them out.

But do not imagine, David, that the beating put an end to the young man's suffering. For he lived still and would have lived, perhaps for hours more, had he not – by a mercy – been sentenced to be garrotted. His limbs thoroughly broken, they dragged him to a stool attached to an upright post, where a cord fixed at head height was fastened around his neck and pulled tight. But there was some interruption, for it seemed that the cord broke when he was only half-strangled and had to be replaced, in order that the garrotting be completed. At least I was not close enough to see the contortions of his face, though the gurglings and groanings carried all too clearly across the water.

Most horrifying to me, and I know not why this detail should intrude upon my peace of mind more than other, more terrible, sights of that day, was the wheel. When the young man was properly dead, the two assistant executioners untied his poor broken body and lifted it up to one of seven identical contraptions which were placed at regular intervals around the scaffold, and whose purpose had until then escaped me: several wooden wheels, positioned horizontal and raised high on sturdy posts, each being a little larger than a card table and so of insufficient size to accommodate the body of an adult male. After they had hoisted the body of young José Maria and laid it upon the wheel, that the multitude might have better sight of it, his legs and arms hung out beyond the circumference. But the executioner, apparently dissatisfied with the effect, approached and folded the limbs across the body, which now lay heaped upon the wheel, the corpse so broken and contorted that it resembled more a pile of rubbish than a human being.

It now being past ten o'clock – for the business of untying the corpse of young José Maria and displaying it to greatest effect took some time – the executions of Luís Bernardo and his brother-in-law, the Count of Atouguia, followed, according to the same brutal ritual. They, like all the condemned, were paraded around the scaffold and shown the mutilated bodies of those who had died before them, while the mob bayed and jeered. First came Luís Bernardo, commonly known as the young marquis, the older brother of the lad who had just been put to death. Luís Bernardo was husband to Dona Teresa, the woman whom the king had taken as a lover, which insult to the Távora family is widely thought to have provoked the whole dreadful business of plotting to get rid of Dom José. Though of this interpretation I have my doubts, for I have always thought it unlikely that a dispute of such magnitude would be motivated by an insult that in our country would be considered a private offence. But I own that I do not understand how the concept of family honour preoccupies these nobles, who will marry their daughters and sons to uncles and nephews, nieces and aunts – Dona Teresa is also the sister of her husband's father, the old marquis, also condemned – rather than permit an outsider to obtain by marriage their titles and lands.

After the Count of Atouguia had been put to death, the executioner set upon the servants: Manuel Alvarez Ferreira, João Miguel and Braz Romeiro, all liveried servants of the Marquis of Távora or the Duke of Aveiro, all found guilty of various crimes against the king, from procuring the weapons, to actually firing them and wounding His Majesty. It is said that they all confessed under torture. Also, that they all retracted their confessions before they died. The execution of the servants on the same platform as their noble masters, on a roughly built scaffold, was an insult of the greatest magnitude to a proud aristocracy, a humiliation of the greatest families in the kingdom who had dared to perceive themselves as equal with the monarch.

You may find this difficult to believe, David, but at midday the executions were paused, and the bells of the Jerónimos tolled – for prayers! A priest mounted the scaffold and led the mob, the soldiers, the executioner and his assistants and anyone else of a mind to participate, in reciting Hail Marys, before the bloody process recommenced. A short while after two o'clock, the Duke of Aveiro and Marquis of Távora suffered the same fate as their loved ones, except that the duke was not accorded the mercy of the garrot, but was left to die on the scaffold for the remaining hours of daylight, moaning and whimpering and sometimes shrieking in torment, from the dreadful injuries inflicted from the beating he had got on the cross. Likewise the old marquis, but Dom Francisco fell silent soon after they untied him from the cross. I later heard that his heart gave out, or perhaps one of the blows to his chest ended his suffering, either by accident or from an impulse of pity from one of his tormentors.

The most horrible spectacle, David, which I cannot bring myself to describe, was the final execution, of the fourth servant, António Ferreira, a brother of Manuel who had died that morning. He had been found guilty of firing the shot that hit and injured the king. The kindling piled up on the scaffold was for him. He was burnt alive.

When that bloody commission was complete – dusk was starting to fall, the daylight fading soon after four at this time of year – all of the bodies were gathered up like so much rubbish and thrown upon the pyre where António Ferreira had just expired in agony. I will not describe to you how the flames danced or how the wood crackled and sang, as the flesh and bones of those who had been the flower of the Portuguese nobility, and their unfortunate servants, were consumed, melted and turned to ash, or how the sickening smell of roasting meat drifted on the air.

As that fire began to subside, darkness having fallen almost completely, I indicated my wish to disembark, but the pilot became agitated and gestured me to sit, repeating, *'Perigo!'* – the only word of his babbling I could understand. And soon, the danger he referred to became apparent, as I perceived the outline of shadowy figures, soldiers positioned at each corner of the scaffold, others clustered beneath it, intent on some frantic task. There must have been a signal, for all at the same moment, a line of torches positioned along the three sides of the platform blazed into light and a few seconds later, disappeared briefly, as they were tossed beneath the wooden platform, which quickly caught fire. Soon the flames mounted and roared, sparks and little fragments of burning ash floated towards us on the darkness and my old sailor, ever alert, quickly rowed us away from the shore. We did not wait to see the scaffold collapse, nor for the ashes to be gathered and tossed into the Tagus, for, with a sober mien, he indicated the intention to pilot his little boat along the river to the Terreiro do Paço. To this I gladly acquiesced, relieved to be spared the long walk from Belém to the city and my home, and especially, as the sentencing had decreed, the ritual casting of the ashes of the eleven people who died that day into the water, that their physical remains be wiped from the earth, that no trace of their existence remain.

But David, it is not so easy to obliterate even one human body. Those ashes were indeed cast into the Tagus, yes, and the ashes and charred wood from the scaffold, too. But I have heard that when the tide is right, gory remains come floating in on the waves and refuse to disappear, haunting the shore, just as the memories of the dead invade my dreams and, I fear, will haunt the reign of this king, this country, my own soul, for many days and years to come, perhaps forever.

Part 4

1775-1782

19

A Birthday Celebration and an Important Book

June 9th, 1775, rua Formosa, Lisbon

Dom Sebastião José Carvalho e Melo, First Minister and trusted confidant of His Majesty King José, having sharpened his quill with a little silver knife, dipped the nib in the fine silver inkwell, a gift from a grateful, now very wealthy, Oporto merchant, and hesitated. A drop of purple ink – the most refined colour for personal notes – fell upon the oaken desk, pooled, spread. If not removed straight away it would make an indelible stain.

This was the time to reflect upon every element of the greatest festival of His Majesty's reign, an event in which he, Marquis of Pombal, had assumed the roles of both author and protagonist. Three splendid days of celebration in honour of Dom José's sixty-first birthday! And, as everyone knew, a triumphant affirmation of his own service to the state during these tumultuous times.

Twenty-five years since the king appointed him to office.

Almost two decades since the terrible earthquake that devastated the city and country, from which catastrophe he, Dom Sebastião José Carvalho e Melo, latterly Count of Oeiras, now Marquis of Pombal, delivered the nation.

Eighteen years since his own might was fully realised and rendered unassailable by means of the punishment visited upon those treacherous nobles, their entire caste humbled upon the scaffold at Belém.

He had led his country out of darkness into the light, just as he had promised. This was indeed a time to rejoice.

The dark purple stain had already seeped into the grain of the wood, its contours expanding, blurring his vision, clouding his thoughts, creeping ever closer to the hand which had dropped limp upon the desk. He started to his feet and reached for a handkerchief. Wiping his smudged fingers, he approached the window.

The guards were still there. Four of them, as he had ordered on Friday, the morning of the first day of the solemn jubilee that marked the pinnacle of his work and his life. Yet here he was, peering from his study window towards the coach house below, his achievement tainted by the heinous acts of those who would do him, and the nation, harm.

Eleonor would have to be told. That they had apprehended the criminal, one of them at least. That the plot had been foiled. He would inform her himself after breakfast, when his mood had improved.

He took a few paces about the room and his spirit lightened, as it always did whenever he installed himself in his office, which had been the children's nursery. There was no doubt, this was the most delightful part of the house, for the window faced south-east and caught the first rays of the sun. And here, lined up against each wall, were stored the material products of his labour of these past five-and-twenty years: hundreds, no, thousands, of documents, state papers, most of them in his own hand, crammed into specially prepared barrels from the winery at Oeiras. He could have built a formal library, of course. But in this large, bright room, what pleasure it was to improvise, to make use of materials to hand, in particular those which symbolised his greatest achievements of the last three decades.

And what achievements! Companies dedicated to manufacture and trade in a multitude of goods and natural resources:

textiles, ceramics, tobacco, wine and more. The monopolies had made it possible to wrest control of the nation's commerce – and profits – from the hands of adventurers and Jesuits and smugglers and the British; the Upper Douro Viticulture Company, of course, being closest to his heart. It seemed fitting that the company casks, once scoured and cut horizontally, should serve to hold the records of government business.

His thoughts calmed, he returned to his desk and, taking care to avoid the damp purple stain, dipped his quill in the ink for the second time that morning. The proceedings of the last three days must be recorded for posterity. This report would reach His Majesty's hands before the week's end.

An historic occasion lasting three days: 6th, 7th, 8th June, 1775 in the city of Lisbon, the festivities concentrated on the newly constituted Praça do Comércio, formerly the Terreiro do Paço; the jubilee centred upon the inauguration of a colossal equestrian statue of His Majesty, unmatched in grandeur and costliness, its manufacture the making of senhor Bartolomeo, cast in eighty thousand pounds of molten bronze, the ceremonial unveiling performed by the Marquis of Pombal, the act accompanied by gun salutes firing in unison from the Castelo do São Jorge and warships anchored in the bay, upon which signal the great veil rippled and slipped to the ground, revealing the gleaming figure of His Majesty astride a plumed stallion, gazing west towards Belém, the snakes of misfortune and treachery trampled beneath his horses' hooves.

And set into the pedestal beneath, by royal decree, a noble bust of the Marquis of Pombal.

Three full days of celebrations. Splendid balls in a vast salon, so superbly decorated as to outvie every preceding event. A magnificent supper in another hall, at which supper no fewer than four hundred persons were seated and served with the greatest luxury and delicacy, on the most costly and beautiful national plate, without using one article from abroad. The rooms of the Junta da Comércio fitted up with every article that taste and riches could procure. All the tribunals of the court and all the various companies of the city, striving to exceed each other in the costliness of their preparations and the richness of their entertainment. The chief magistrate of Lisbon and his deputies having erected seven allegorical triumphal cars, significant of the great occasion. All the windows of the nobility and gentry teeming with costly ornaments, with splendid diamonds and precious stones. The streets rendered impassable by the extraordinary multitude of rich and sumptuous carriages. The whole population gaily and richly dressed, from the nobility to the humblest individual, showing the capital and kingdom in the highest state of prosperity and opulence. Speeches extolling the greatness of the king and the virtues of his minister, the Marquis of Pombal. Fireworks. Acclamations, declamation of poetry, odes and sonnets written to exalt the occasion. A solemn procession of city dignitaries, nobles, His Majesty and His Majesty's court.

His hand trembled and smudged the last few words, which were now illegible. Breathing deep and steady, the better to govern his movements, he extracted a pristine, fine-wove page from his writing case and began anew.

The Marquis of Pombal was not given to apprehensions of horror. But the recollection of that great procession provoked tremors in his body and mind. It was only thanks to the diligence of his own people that the calamity had been averted. He closed his eyes. Perhaps Eleonor's scruples would be assuaged, to see the work of his informants thus vindicated.

Two wax models of the key to his own coach house. Drawings of the ground plan of the house. Three wooden barrels filled with gunpowder, destined for the undercarriage of his own coach, or so the Italian blackguard had confessed. An evil contraption, never seen in the country, designed to produce maximum death and destruction. Worst of all, an incendiary device attached, set to burn for several hours, primed to ignite the powder during the solemn procession of His Majesty's ministers, judges, military and court, as they traversed the square.

The explosion would have killed him. Along with dozens, perhaps hundreds, of His Majesty's entourage at the moment of greatest rejoicing.

Had the miscreant been working alone?

Impossible. That contrivance must have been smuggled into the country from France. And how could a foreigner have gained access to the keys of the coach house of the most powerful of His Majesty's ministers? Answers must be found, and soon.

Should Eleonor be apprised of all this intelligence? Or should he keep his counsel, that she might sleep easy? He would decide later and tell her what she needed to know while they had breakfast.

But first, they would recall the magnificence of the festival. Their proudest moment, the one they would remember forever – Henrique, as he presented commemorative medals to each member of the diplomatic corps, gold for the ambassadors, silver for their *chargés d'affaires*. Their elder son and heir, now Count of Oeiras, charged with performing the most symbolic act of the entire jubilee!

And how perfectly accomplished was the desired outcome of the spectacle! To have produced a favourable impression of the country, and most particularly on the foreigners present; to have shown Portugal on a par with nations who hitherto imagined themselves superior. To have manifest the national worth and consequence, the continuing expansion of the national defences, the power of the military and the strength of the country's alliances.

Ah yes. Alliances. The greatest satisfaction of all, when the British ambassador received his gold medallion from the hand of the Count of Oireas. And the few words he had managed to exchange with Mr Walpole, while his subordinate accepted the silver medal from Henrique. The pale-eyed Englishman handled it as though it were a stick of dynamite and not a valued memento of the most significant jubilee celebration of the era.

'Dom Sebastião, Mr. Stanton is our esteemed *chargé d'affaires.*'

The angular countenance, nondescript in the way typical of his countrymen, revealed no sign that he had been introduced to the most illustrious personage in the procession.

'He speaks excellent Portuguese.' Mr Walpole's remark contained the ghost of a rebuke, which prompted a reluctant response from the melancholy Englishman.

'You are too kind.' The pale eyes remained fixed upon the silver medallion, which looked to be burning a hole in his palm. Only when Henrique's entourage had moved on did he raise his head. Watery blue eyes flickered over his ambassador's countenance, then slid off to contemplate the middle distance. Not a very diplomatic diplomat. The only discordant note of the day, not for inclusion in the official account.

Which must include a summary of the process by which the national achievements of the past quarter-century had been accomplished.

His Majesty has dissipated the darkness that reigned in his kingdom and repaired the ruin in which he found it buried.

A good introduction, yes, that could stand. A fitting opening to a solemn record of the exact measures taken which have so much astonished both natives and foreigners.

Item One: Handwriting – the acquirement of a correct and intelligible hand is now common amongst the great majority of respectable people, which skill had been a great rarity prior to 1750.

Item Two: The Mechanical Arts – native factories are now furnishing works of gold, silver, wool, silk, glass, steel, as well as everything required for the dress and ornament of men and women alike, as well as items of all kinds required for the furnishing of houses, all products which had formerly entered the port of Lisbon from foreign countries.

Item Three: The Liberal Arts – we now boast numerous excellent paintings by our distinguished countrymen, including portraits of His Majesty and of his First Minister; to which may be added the many sumptuous and well-built edifices of Lisbon; the colossal equestrian statue of Dom José now gracing the Praça do Comércio and the superb pedestal on which it is erected; as well as the marble bust of the Marquis of Pombal, created by order of His Majesty and set into said pedestal.

Item Four: Literature – This nation may now boast a multitude of Works, both in prose and verse, presented to the Board of Censure in Portuguese, Latin, Greek, Hebrew, Arabic, written with an elegance and purity of style worthy of Homer.

Fingers cramping, he set down the quill. When had his capacity for work diminished? Unsurprising. He had passed his seventy-sixth year. And perhaps the burdens of so many weeks' preparation for the festivities were taking their toll. He should permit himself a little ease. But there was so much to be done. And being a decade and a half older than His Majesty, there remained so little time in which to complete his mission: to leave the country in the best possible state, in anticipation of the day when Dom José would be obliged to rule without the assistance of his First Minister.

His spirit soothed by the odour of old paper mingled with a whiff of tannin and oak, which never failed to transport him to the vineyard at Oeiras, he yawned and stretched. Of course, his winery was a source of dispute and envy, his vines being permitted to supply the Upper Douro company for the manufacture of port, in spite of the geographical inconsistency – Oeiras being located in the Tagus valley, rather than the Douro, as regulations required. A small matter, a perquisite of his position, and it earned the estate a very pretty sum for every pipe. Complaints from the naysayers could be disregarded, for the Upper Douro Company had enriched enough merchants and suppliers to stifle any voices of opposition.

This draft must be finished before breakfast.

Item Five: The Higher Sciences – advancement especially seen in the restoration of the University of Coimbra, in new syllabi, scientific laboratories, botanical gardens and a new spirit of enquiry; also in the creation of numerous new posts of professors, to support the development of special studies.

Item Six: Domestic trade – noting that every article displayed in the streets, squares and windows of Lisbon during the entire three-day jubilee was the product of the national manufactories.

Item Seven: Foreign Commerce – including, but not confined to, the lucrative extraction of diamonds from Brazil, and from our colonies, vast supplies of sugar, tobacco and hides, salt, and at home wines, produce of the Douro, fruits exported by foreign vessels, supply of cocoa, coffee, rice, cotton, cloves, spice and other products of Pará and Maranhão, from which places His Majesty now derives profit.

Item Eight: Social harmony is preserved between the high nobility and the middle classes, as also between both with the lower orders. And when over one hundred and fifty thousand of the commonest rank assembled together on this late joyous occasion, not one voice was raised either of complaint or clamour.

Item Nine: Wealth of the people as a result of all the above measures, and the effects of this upon the national spirit – equality, respect, prosperity, stability.

A pity that a most significant achievement would have to be excluded from the record, for Dom José's conscience had started to bother him. In one bold swoop he, the king's First Minister, had rid Portugal and all her colonies of every member of the Society of Jesus, thus liberating the nation from the noxious influence which that reprehensible Order had wielded over every institutions of the state: education, even in the illustrious university of Coimbra, whose curriculum they had limited to ancient languages and canon law, confining that seat of learning to the Dark Ages; abuse of commercial privileges; enormous profits generated from vast estates in the colonies; secret machinations, which included making common cause with the enemies of the state for their own dark purposes and colluding with disgruntled nobles who sought to overturn the reign of the king and the office of the king's First Minister. Not forgetting their wilful obstruction of the recovery efforts after the earthquake.

Worst of all, they had fomented rebellion in South America among the native population of Grão Pará and Maranhão, having trained and probably armed the rebels, too.

How, and why, the queen and the Princess of Brazil and their followers remained so devoted to Jesuit confessors, whose only loyalty was to their Order, was a mystery. Which afflicted not only Portugal. The whole of Catholic Europe had suffered the same infestation, yet not one crowned head had dared to challenge their ascendency, much less expel them. But he, Dom Sebastião Carvalho e Melo, had dared. In this measure, the Bourbons in Paris and Madrid and others had been instructed by him and followed his lead. Even the Vatican had suppressed them at the last, though it had taken almost two decades and a long breach between Lisbon and Rome to accomplish this. A mercy that His Majesty had kept his nerve during those nine years and shown that it was possible for a nation to be estranged from Rome and survive. And thrive. Now the institutions of the state were governed by the proper authority – His Majesty and his appointees. National sovereignty was restored. All Europe thanked him for it.

More was the pity that this accomplishment would have to be omitted, since His Majesty had become susceptible to the manipulations of the queen and the Princess of Brazil. They stuck to him like limpets, exaggerating his minor ailments, bewailing their fears for his immortal soul.

Having completed a rough draft, he blotted the last few paragraphs – that purple stain had migrated to his white linen sleeve – and read the document in its entirety. No reader, neither His Majesty nor the unknown readers of the distant future, could fail to be impressed. And he was not finished yet. Retirement? Withdrawal to his Oeiras estate to enjoy the fruits of his work after a lifetime of loyal service? That time would come. But not yet.

No conspiracy, no attempt on his life, or on the life of the king or on his own people, would stop him from completing his work.

20

The Second Reckoning

February 26th, 1777, Belém and Lisbon

Royal Pavilion, Belém

Four days since he left them, two days since they buried him, and at last she could breathe again. How strange that the death of a beloved husband should bring relief from the feeling of suffocation that had gripped her these past weeks, ever since the last attack felled him. The final blow of many that had confined him to his sick bed in Sintra for months, his physical powers waning until he lost even the power of speech, eyes wide with fear as he contemplated his approaching end. At least during those months she had managed to govern attendance in the sickroom and bring him the solace of confession he needed to calm his mind and spirit.

Suppressing a sob, for the servants were solicitous and might enter at any moment, she stepped out on to the little oval terrace set into the hillside where they had planted a garden together, years before, when the Royal Pavilion was first constructed in the months and years after the earthquake. It was luscious in high summer, a riot of colours splashing on the hillside and even now, pretty spring flowers, purple and yellow and orange, peeped out of the foliage. A light drizzle sprinkled droplets of rain on her cheek and mingled with her tears. She did not mind. The rain on these bright days was always a comfort, perhaps because there was so little of it in her native Castile.

She had thought she would have him for much longer. He was not yet sixty-three years old. She should have done better. Loved him more. Fought him less. Endured without rancour all those sleepless nights waiting for him to return from some assignation. And now a sob did escape her. Why had she quarrelled with him so, when she could have dismissed all those hussies as the gaudy playthings of a silly boy, soon to be discarded?

She could have forgiven him.

No sooner had the thought occurred, than there rose in her mind's eye the alluring countenance of the young Távora woman as she had been almost two decades before.

Some things could not be forgiven. Terrible transgressions, not in her gift to pardon.

Leonora de Távora. Her entire family.

She had pleaded with him. Maria had too. But he was implacable. Utterly convinced.

Convinced by whom?

She would not think on that. Not today. All that mattered now was that he had found his way back to the holy Church. To God. In these last weeks, as his body failed and the peril of his immortal soul loomed large, he had requested a confessor. A mercy that he did not hear the murmured words of one impudent courtier when the priest was called:

'It will be a long confession.'

If she could not forgive him for the dreadful acts in which he acquiesced during all those years, the Almighty Lord would. The Patriarch had assured her of it. His confessor had comforted him. It was their great consolation that he had died in the arms of Christ, that he had found his way back to her. As Father Malagrida had said he would, long ago.

But the wise prophet had not warned her they would have to endure so much evil in their lives and in the kingdom, before that came to pass.

Father Malagrida should have been there to ease the journey of his king to the next world, as he had eased the passage of Dom José's father and mother, long ago. Oh, he would have been a very old man, had he lived... No, no man could live so long. But the manner of the holy man's death. Imprisoned for years. Stripped naked. Confined in darkness until his mind broke and he lost his wits. The dignified, pious teacher become a raving madman, his end on the scaffold an abomination. All Europe knew of the barbarity. All Europe condemned it.

What that man, no, she would not name him, what he had to answer for.

His letter wilted in her hand. When had she retrieved it from her escritoire? Why had she not consigned it to the fire? The audacity. The delusion. Did he think she had forgotten? The day he forced the court entire, their nobles, servants, her own girls, to watch the butchery of their relatives on a public scaffold in Belém? Maria had collapsed, suffered attacks of panic for years after, perhaps she had never recovered.

Others imprisoned. Hundreds of them. Thousands, for all anyone knew. For eighteen years. Women. Children, too.

At least they had persuaded him to spare the women and children from the garrot and the cutlass and the flames. Though not from gaol or convent.

The Society of Jesus. Gone. Every last one of the Jesuits expelled from the country, from the colonies. And lately suppressed by the Vatican, too.

At least Maria had been permitted to succeed to the throne. Her position remained secure, even though she had long been left to languish in the palace at Queluz with Dom Pedro and their children and denied any part in any public affairs. Despite that man's efforts, her succession was accomplished.

Count. Marquis. Every title, every scrap of land that man had acquired, bought with the blood of her countrymen and women.

Would Maria be equal to the demands of ruling over the kingdom and its colonies? It had been her father's wish, in the end. And she would have her mother to guide her.

The clouds darkened to grey, drops of rain trickled down her cheeks, her arms, they would soon drench her. The fine-wove page, grown limp in her hand, dripped purple ink on to the tiles.

The time for change was almost upon them.

Convento dos Santos, Lisbon

During the last eighteen years, Dona Teresa had from time to time received news of His Majesty, often when the royal barge was passing. They had given her rooms overlooking the river, bright and airy, pleasant enough, in compensation for her seclusion. However, she was not permitted to step beyond the convent walls, although she was allowed unlimited access to the cloisters. His Majesty did not wish her to live in discomfort.

Mother Superior entered the room without knocking. The gravity of her mien was sufficient to reveal the sad news. Her mask-like countenance remained unresponsive to the tears that welled in Dona Teresa's eyes and slipped down her pale cheeks.

'When?'

'His Majesty passed away four days ago. He was interred the day before yesterday, in the Church of São Vicente da Fora.'

Outside the old city walls, close to the Alfama. One of his favourite parts of the city where they would often drive, incognito, in an unmarked carriage driven by his valet, what was his name, the one who always leered at her.

Of course she had not been permitted to attend the funeral, or even to observe the cortège as it passed by. Had it passed by? It had, of course. That was why they had not told her. For fear that she might try to show herself. As if she had ever, in these eighteen years, rebelled against her fate.

During those days after the trial and the executions, terror had yielded to relief when they told her that she would not join her husband, her brother, her mother-in-law and the others on the scaffold, nor languish in a dungeon, like Father Malagrida; but instead would take up residence in this convent. She had been fortunate. The Convento dos Santos was home to several young, widowed noblewomen who had decided, or been informed, that they would not marry again. It was not a bad life. Some guests were allowed to receive visitors, even lovers, it was said. No, she was not in prison, the minister had assured her when first she was installed here. Rather, she had been granted refuge. For her own protection.

'His Majesty wishes you no harm.'

It was many months before she understood that although Dom José wished her no harm, nor did he wish to set her free. But was she here by order of the king? Or of the minister? Of course, he was marquis now. Perhaps that was why he had not been to visit for such a long time.

There was always news from the outside. A gossipy seamstress. A novice who had connections in the Royal Pavilion. Some years before, the marquis – he was just a count then – had given her reason to hope. He had arranged for the succession to bypass the Princess of Brazil and settle on her young son instead, the Prince of Beira. If His Majesty were to die...perhaps the minister would become regent, and she might be permitted to return to the world. But his plan had been thwarted. And if it had succeeded – would he really have granted her freedom? Even today, so many years after that terrible day in Belém, the minister's judgement of her was still a mystery. Did he consider her guilty, yet another conspirator determined to do away with His Majesty, fortunate to have avoided the scaffold? Or as an innocent victim of circumstances? Oftentimes, she scarce knew herself.

But lately, the stream of gossip from the world outside had become a trickle. Mother Superior, no matter how cold her demeanour, was now the only source of information.

'Will the marquis…?'

A hesitation. The silence lengthened.

'We will not be receiving any more visits from the marquis.' Another silence while the surly old woman weighed her words. 'It is possible that Queen Maria will bring charges against him.'

Dona Teresa received this intelligence with a gasp and sank into the nearest chair. How would these new circumstances affect her own standing, her own life? The Mother Superior would not say, perhaps she did not know. But there was no one else to ask.

'Do the charges concern his actions against my family?'

The Mother Superior's countenance betrayed no shred of sympathy or compassion, not even for a woman who had lost everything, including her liberty. No, not quite everything. For she lived still. For which bounty she ought to be grateful.

'I cannot say. I understand that his acquisition of lands, fortunes, properties will come under scrutiny. As will the conduct of his business interests.'

There was nothing more to say. But yes, one final question remained.

'Is his position in danger?'

'He has already lost his position, my lady. Whether he escapes with his life remains to be seen.'

Dona Teresa remained immobile as the Mother Superior quit the room. If Queen Maria had decided to pursue the man who had been her father's minister for almost three decades, might she turn her attention to other former witnesses?

It was a question with no answer. One that she must live with for now, and for the rest of her life

Royal Pavilion, Adjuda, Belém

For all that she had buried her father only the day before, now was no time for the indulgence of tears. Too much work lay ahead. Still, she was not yet ready to begin the myriad tasks that awaited. She turned the Royal Seal over, as she had often watched her father do. It weighed heavy in her hand. Yesterday, Princess of Brazil; today, Queen of Portugal. If tears began to flow, they would never stop and now was a time for restraint, to consign to memory Papi's hoarse whisper, his poor parched lips moving, his eyes wide with terror in the knowledge that his time had really come, that the fear that had plagued him his entire life was now upon him.

What did he need? His confessor?

One of the courtiers brought paper and a pencil which he grasped in clawlike fingers, hand shaking as he guided the point across the page. He wished to confess. And he wished her to know that she would succeed to the throne.

'Of course I will, Papi. That was a misunderstanding. Resolved long ago.'

She clenched the Royal Seal ever tighter.

That was a terrible day, years before, when she burst into his office, having managed to avoid his footmen and valet, for she had not been granted an audience, and threw herself at his feet. He started in horror and bade the servant leave. For once he was alone, pale and pacing nervously. He had understood immediately.

She knew.

'Papi, I am come to beg for my throne.' She had burst into a storm of sobbing and a tirade of retributions. The betrayal! To remove her from the line of succession. To declare the Prince of Beira – her own son! – as his successor in place of his oldest daughter!

And she knew, they both knew, who was behind this plan. The poison that that man had dripped into her father's ear these years past. Hinting that Dom Pedro was plotting to dethrone his own brother. And now, scheming to deprive her of her birthright, in favour of her own child. Of course, he would be better able to command a child, a very young man, if Papi were to die.

But he would not. He could not die so soon.

The spirit of Father Malagrida must have guided her steps that day, provoked the tempest of tears, invoked her words. For Dom José relented. Made her a solemn promise that she, and no other, would be his heir, had ever been his heir. It was all a scurrilous rumour. A misunderstanding.

So earnest were his utterances, his countenance, his bearing, she almost believed him.

'From whom did you learn this intelligence, Maria?'

At first, she could not recall. Then, she remembered but could not say. Most uncommon to Papi's temperament, he insisted.

'This was not a matter for discussion outside this room, Maria.'

So it had been discussed.

'Papi, will you promise me that no harm will come to him if...'

That was the second solemn promise her father made her on that day.

The first, concerning her succession to the throne, he had kept.

She replaced the Royal Seal in its case and took up position in her father's chair – now her chair, behind the desk which was now her own desk, and rang for the footman.

'Summon the Marquis of Angeja.'

He must have been awaiting her call. One of her loyal, if discreet, supporters in recent years, the marquis arrived within the quarter-hour. He had earned her gratitude, having arranged and executed every detail of her father's obsequies.

Where to begin?

'See that Dom José de Séabra da Silva is recalled from Angola.' It was the least her loyal subject deserved. He had paid dearly for warning her of the plan of to deprive her of her rightful place as successor to the throne, all those years ago.

'Immediately, Your Majesty.'

'Have the prisoners been released?'

'Tomorrow, Majesty. We have alerted the prison authorities…'

'Tomorrow.' The people, her father's subjects, now her own subjects, incarcerated on the orders of that man. Hundreds of them. Did anyone really know how many? Nobles, their servants and horsemen, in gaols all over the city… Those who had been children when first detained, now adults; those who had then been in their middle years or elderly, now aged and sickly, or dead. They had tried, she and her mother had done their utmost, and they had failed. The prisoners remained in the gaols, the Távoras and their relatives and servants had died on the scaffold, her pleas and prayers had been ignored.

There must be a general amnesty, immediately. The Távora name must be restored.

'Have you found the transcript of the trial?'

'Not yet, Majesty. We believe that the original may be lost. When pressed, the Count of Oeiras owned that his father, the Marquis of Pombal, might have copies…'

The tremors began in her hands, coursed through her entire body. The Marquis of Angeja, ever discreet, turned his eyes away but those gasping, staccato breaths alarmed him, he approached…

'Are you quite well, Your Majesty? Some water…?'

Struggling to inhale, she nodded and accepted the cup from his hand. Small, frequent sips. A few deep breaths, as Father Malagrida instructed long ago, until the trembling heart is quiet.

That letter. Cream, fine-wove paper inscribed in purple ink, lay unopened, beside the Royal Seal. Her mother had received a similar missive.

'Marquis.'

'Yes, Your Majesty.'

'I do not want to lay eyes upon that man ever again. Until

we have conducted our investigation, he must remain distant from my presence. Twenty leagues distant. At least.'

The time for a reckoning, so long awaited, was at hand.

Rua Formosa, Lisbon

The funeral cortège which accompanied His Majesty to his final resting place earlier had, by all accounts, been a magnificent spectacle. Yes, it was a matter of great sorrow to Dom Sebastião that he had been unable to accompany the king on his final journey. Notwithstanding his great personal desire to bid farewell to the man who had been his master and friend these twenty-seven years, under such circumstances, attendance was impossible. He had made no formal objection to the slight but had had to be content with sending his regrets on the day. He was indisposed.

Oh, he had not expected to be charged with the direction and oversight of his Majesty's obsequies. At seventy-eight, he ought to have retired long ago. And he was the first to acknowledge that with the ascension of the new queen to the throne, his position must change.

But so soon? And so brutally?

'You have nothing more to do here, Your Excellency.'

That cardinal. And His Majesty but a few hours dead. Such brutal words. To dismiss thus the man who had commanded the court for nigh on three decades.

When had his situation declined? When His Majesty's health failed, of course. As long as His Majesty lived and commanded, the position of his First Minister was secure, the service which Dom Sebastião José Carvalho e Melo had rendered the nation recognised by all. A circumstance that would last at least until his retirement, and probably for the rest of his life, the minister being a decade and a half older than Dom José.

Who could have expected such a reversal?

Oh, while His Majesty's power of speech remained, while he still had his wits about him, no one dared deny his faithful minister entry to the sickroom. But the moment his condition worsened, when everyone knew that Dom José would not recover from the last stroke, the man who had been his confidant and his friend was no longer welcome. No longer was he considered a trusted intimate; rather, an intruder, admitted but grudgingly. And then, once Mariana Vitória was elevated to Regent just three months earlier, from that day onwards he never saw His Majesty alone. The wife and daughter ever by his bed, the sickroom swarming with a battalion of priests and clergy. Had His Majesty been in his right mind, they would never have been admitted.

'Your Excellency, you have nothing more to do here.'

The public humiliation of his allocated position in the funeral cortège, more than halfway from the head, between the Gentleman of the Bedchamber and that fool the Marquis of Tanquin. An intolerable insult.

Worse, Eleonor had warned him he must not leave the house, not even accompanied by his guard. Bands of ruffians were gathered in the street chanting his name, calling for his blood. Of course, this was their opportunity – the old nobility, crawling out from beneath the rock to which he had confined them these last decades, drumming up agitation against him. Some had even paid actors to dress as humble people, working people, the people whom all his tireless efforts of the years had aimed to benefit, baying for his downfall, for his blood. Some of them were burning effigies of him. It was not credible.

But the Marquis of Angeja as Master of Ceremonies to lead the funeral procession! A slippery customer. Always affable, always agreeable. Never showing his hand. No experience whatsoever. But close with the Princess of Brazil, a regular visitor to her and Dom Pedro and their brood at the palace at Queluz.

Was this really His Majesty's final wish?

In truth, it was impossible to know what His Majesty had wanted in his final days or weeks. Had he really asked for confession? For the sacrament of Extreme Unction? In his weakened state, no longer able to speak, he was powerless against those fanatics who had recovered their grip on him. And when the Patriarch appeared, after the ceremony of Extreme Unction, a formal occasion organised and executed in the absence of Dom Sebastiao José Carvalho e Melo, without his knowledge…

During those last weeks of Dom José's life, in their increasingly sparse interactions with his intimates, many courtiers had adopted an insolent tone towards the First Minister. Others declined to meet his eye. These were people who owed their positions, their fortunes, in some cases their very lives, to the patronage of Dom Sebastião, now doing their best to shun him.

That there would be a transition, of course, had always been clear, and it would be a difficult one. The new queen and her advisors had not the slightest knowledge of the machinery of state. In anticipation of the complexity of the process, the proposal he had crafted several months ago, before Dom José had quite lost his faculties, addressed every aspect of the workings of government. Included were several reasonable requests concerning the manner of his departure: to be permitted to resign; to retire to his estates; to work with his successor, or successors, in handing over responsibilities. A logical strategy, for there was no one more qualified, no one qualified at all, to prepare the new administration to take over the functions he had performed for nigh on three decades.

Mariana Vitória had not replied. Nor had the Princess of Brazil – the new Queen Maria – answered his second letter, which set out his proposed strategy in even more detail. But she had just buried her father. It was possible, even likely, that she would soon see the wisdom in his offer of help, put aside her personal antipathy, and act in the interests of the nation. He must await her response. For the first time in many, many years, he could do no other.

21

A Final Return

March 30th, 1775, Rossio Square, Lisbon

The last time Father Luís crossed Rossio Square, the heart of his parish when a young man, was the saddest moment of his life: September 22nd, 1761, almost fourteen years before, the day he buried his mother in the graveyard of a tiny chapel high in the Bairro Alto, the only mourners being himself and his two sisters. They were both angry with him: first for his absence, that their mother had endured her long illness without the solace of her only son, who, thanks to his reckless babblings, had been all but banished to the Algarve. Angrier still that he had returned for her funeral – without permission – a little more than two years later, fearful that his illicit presence would bring the wrath of the authorities down upon them.

Although there had been no formal order of exile – rather, he was 'reassigned', as his superior Father Bernardo had told him – he was not so deluded as to imagine he had a choice in this new posting.

'You must have offended someone very important.' Father Bernardo held up one hand, silencing any explanation the impetuous young Father Luís might wish to make for his words or deeds. Better he did not know. The faintest criticism of the investigation into the attack on the king, the slightest doubt expressed concerning the innocence or guilt of the Távoras, was sure evidence of disloyalty. Treason. Considering which, a reposting to a quiet parish near Tavira might be considered a stroke of luck.

When he arrived in Lisbon the night before, exhausted from two days' travel in rickety carriages, he had neither vigour nor inclination to explore his old parish in the dark. But morning found him much recovered, in part from the congenial company of Father Bernardo, now a very old man. In the morning, he crossed the square, carried along by the animated streams of people, young and old, noble and humble, who, like himself, were making their way towards the riverbank in hope of finding passage to Belém. Some raised their voices in song, others capered about in excitement, not a few shed tears. The streets beyond the Rossio hummed with an air of liberation. The new, wide pathways were unfamiliar, as were many buildings, newly constructed: handsome palaces, a new hospital, simple facades, all emanating from the mighty will of the man to whom he owed his 'reassignment'. He stopped at the corner where he had built his little hut almost twenty years before and recalled the person he had been in those far-off days: a young man filled with fire and passion to serve the poor and injured and dying.

How different would his life have been, had he not, on that balmy November day, incurred the wrath of Dom Sebastião José Carvalho e Melo, the king's First Minister, Count of Oeiras, now Marquis of Pombal? Viewed through the prism of so many years, those conversations with the minister crackled with the impertinence of a young man convinced of his own probity in speaking truth to a man of power. Such foolishness. And a colossal error of judgement. In his arrogance, he had imagined he understood the minister. That a mutual respect, even liking, bound them. That virtue would protect him from any consequences which his audacious remarks might provoke.

But was it virtue which had prompted him to express his thoughts with such liberty? Or wilful, culpable innocence? For he knew, or ought to have known, that virtue is seldom rewarded. Virtue had not saved Father Malagrida, who, everyone knew, lived a life of astonishing austerity, drank only water, ate neither meat nor fish, took nourishment only from nuts and fruit and a few herbs, slept only on a hard surface for a few hours after passing most of the night in Church in prayer before the most holy sacrament, his body continuously laden with instruments of penitence. He lived and breathed only for the glory of God and the health of the souls with which God had entrusted him.

What misfortune it had been, then, to have witnessed the poor old Jesuit's agonising end upon the scaffold, here, in this very square, along with fifty-one other unfortunates, a bitter end to his years of imprisonment. Had Father Luís known of the auto-da-fé in Rossio Square, set to dispatch those fifty-two wretched souls to their maker on that same day, the very day of his mother's humble burial, he would have demanded to remain in the home of his sister for one more night and braved her husband's ire.

His mood plunged into gloom as the joyful crowd jostled around him. Overcome with weariness, he halted. Padre Malagrida had died on a scaffold raised at this spot, fourteen years before. Never would he have chosen to attend such a spectacle. But he had been distracted. By grief at his mother's death. By harsh words from his sisters. By his exaggerated care in navigating the steep downwards incline of the cobbled streets from the Bairro Alto to Rossio Square, for though he was not yet forty at that time, the twinges in his knees had already started to trouble him, hence his anxiety that he might stumble over the jagged paving and curbs.

Thus, he had no forewarning of the vast, silent crowd gathered on Rossio Square. Puzzled and anxious on his own account, for soldiers were stationed at each corner, he joined the edge of the eerily quiet throng, whose grave faces were turned towards a platform erected on the eastern side. All present, women and children too, were listening to a functionary read aloud the offence for which the fifty-first offender had been sentenced to death. The condemned man stood, composed and dignified, facing his accuser, who pronounced him guilty of declaring the Inquisition to be corrupt, of claiming that every high office was occupied by usurpers, appointees of unscrupulous government ministers whose wishes and will they were paid to fulfil.

'One minister,' a voice breathed. Concealed in a shadowed archway, two soldiers armed with muskets surveyed the crowd, their eyes lingering on individual faces. He must leave before he was spotted and questioned. Before the garrotting began. Or rather, continued, for it had gone on all day. But the crowd was dense, there were soldiers on every side, it was impossible to push through without attracting attention. Progress was slow, very slow.

He had just reached the foot of the scaffold when the functionary announced the guilt of the fifty-second condemned man.

Father Gabriel Malagrida.

The scarecrow who mounted the scaffold, unaware of where he was or why, was barely recognisable as the man who had commanded the streets of Lisbon in the weeks and months following the earthquake, leading his ragged band of followers, intoning the rosary and preaching to the multitude. He must be near eighty years now, perhaps more. Even so, the emaciated body, the bare countenance shorn of his beard, the face a death's head, the contours of the skull clearly visible, bore blemishes of greater injuries than those wrought by the passage of time.

Neither his virtue nor his reputation had saved him from the dungeon of the Belém Tower. There he had rotted alongside so many of his fellow Jesuits, no one seemed to know how many, for the crimes of treason and lèse-majesté, ever since the Jesuits had been declared authors of the heinous plot to kill His Majesty, Dom José. And he, Gabriel Malagrida, was declared the prime mover behind the treasonous acts of the Távora clan.

'Not a whit of evidence against him.' An elderly woman

close by clutched her rosary, body shaking with quiet sobs as her neighbours cast furtive glances towards the soldiers and tried to hush her. Most likely she was right. News did sometimes reach the little backwater of Tavira and no one there, nor in Lisbon nor the Alentejo nor in any part of the country, believed those accusations; nor that the mere fact of his intimacy with the Távora family could ever furnish sufficient evidence to condemn him.

And yet, here he was, on the scaffold, answering for those alleged crimes with his life.

While the functionary intoned the charges, faint whispers in the crowd became murmurs, murmurs swelled to cries and audible weeping. The glares of the soldiers as they scanned the throng grew ever darker, it was only a matter of time, they would approach, detain him as a sympathiser, once identified, he…

Yet against all good sense, while the functionary finished reading the condemned man's crimes, he lingered. The original charges for which Father Malagrida and his fellow priests had been cast into dungeons around the city years before were not mentioned. But the sentence, yes, the grim sentence was clear. He was condemned to be strangled, thrown into the fire, his ashes cast to the wind. For crimes committed while in the prison of the Inquisition.

Heresy. Being leader of a heretical sect. Immodesty. Indecency. Being a false prophet.

Nothing of the original charges of treason and conspiring to kill the king for which he had been thrown into gaol in the first place.

'Indecency?'

A burly, upright fellow in front of him half-turned his head.

'It's said the old man lost his wits when he was inside.' The speaker had not troubled to lower his voice. 'Thought he was in communion with the saints. Who knows what that means.' He glowered and spat. 'They planted a spy, a false confessor, to inform on him, you know. They'll say anything.'

And now he really must flee, the soldiers are pointing to those murmuring dissent. A few mourners are wailing at the sight of Father Malagrida on the scaffold, the gag on his mouth is kept upon him while his crimes and the sentence of death are read. The strangeness of the reverence of the crowd, the Father's fortitude, his modesty, his saintly demeanour, provoke many more tears in the spectators. When the gag is removed, being free at last to speak, his wits apparently restored, Father Malagrida declares that he is innocent of the offences of which he is accused. He begs forgiveness of God for his sins, as he forgives his accusers and the judges.

The immense gathering of people listen to his words in the most sombre silence, which is periodically interrupted by stifled sighs and tears. More spectators sob while the padre speaks. Soldiers approach. Father Luís bows his head, pushes his way through the crowd before they come for him, before the garrot, before the old man is tied to the stake, before the pyre is lit, before the shrieks begin…

A lively, fair-haired young man accompanied by two elderly women came to an abrupt halt beside him, their joyful demeanour returning Father Luís to the present.

'A day to rejoice, is it not!'

One of the woman, being very aged and in need of rest, grasped the young man's arm while sipping from a flask of water her daughter held for her.

'We tried to persuade her to wait at home.' The young man stroked the old woman's hand. 'But she insisted. After eighteen years, she said she must be there when those gates are unlocked.'

'Is it…?'

'Her son,' answered the young man. 'My father. I don't remember him. I was only two years old when he was taken. For my grandmother, this is the happiest day of her life.'

'And your mother…'

'I am his aunt,' the younger of the two women said. 'Pablo is my brother. Aurelio's mother died last year, the Lord have mercy on her soul. It is our great sorrow that she never saw her husband again, after that night.'

For a moment, the three family members stood in silence, their animation dimmed as each contemplated the deprivations they had suffered from the loss of a father, a brother, a son, to the Junqueira prison.

'Father, will you bless us, and our endeavour, to bring our dear Pablo home?'

But how much of the Pablo they had known would remain? And what of Eugenio and Pedro, sons of his dearest friends whom he had promised to find and bring home to their parents? He had never met the two boys, for by the time he arrived in Tavira, destitute and afraid, the minister's vast net had already scooped them up, two young fellows just arrived in the capital, eager to make their way. They lived still, grown men now in middle age, that much was known. But who were they now? Having endured eighteen years incarcerated, like so many hundreds of others, what remnants of their being, their spirit, would remain?

Having taken his leave of the little family, he made his way at a leisurely pace towards the Terreiro do Paço, marvelling in spite of himself at the wide, straight streets, the gracious facades whose simple, classical contours rose from patterned pavements, many only partially complete. He lingered in front of an imposing archway that bristled with scaffolding, the pillars of beautiful honey-coloured stone supporting a triangular pediment of the same colour, the entire design fit for the triumph of a Roman emperor.

And the river – in his youth, never had he made this approach towards the quays without a catch of the breath that bade him pause, contemplate this grandeur, this beauty – the sparkling water, the sandbank and the horizon beyond. But what a shock to see the Riverside Palace gone. How foolish. The flames devoured it and everything around, he had seen it himself; the last time he tarried here in daylight – the very day of his final, ill-advised conversation with the minister – the site had been piled with rubble. Now, wooden boards decorated with painted archways extended the full length of the square, evoking the stately contours of cloister-like colonnades that would one day grace the perimeter entire. An enormous equestrian statue of Dom José in the centre was new, its plinth damaged, as though some adornment had been hacked away from the stone.

Having reached the quay wall he decided to sit a while, enjoying the cool air and the weak sun on his face, wondering whether to seek a place in a cart or in one of the small boats that were taking passengers along the river to Belém.

As he contemplated the river waves lapping the walls, little slivers of light sparkling upon them like trembling stars, lending the river and the sea beyond the aspect of a spangled carpet reaching out to the horizon and the sky, a light mist shimmering like the cloths of heaven, a blessed calm descended upon him. For the first time, it came to him that perhaps his life in Tavira had not, after all, been a mistake, a deviation from what should have been his true path; or, if it were a mistake, a fortunate one. Had he remained in Lisbon in that little hut on the Rossio, ministering to the sick and sparring with Dom Sebastião, what manner of mischief might have befallen him? In what iniquities might he have become embroiled, perhaps even undertaken?

Or, if he had endeavoured to resist, at what cost?

So many possible responses. So many impossible choices.

To remain silent in the face of tyranny and thereby acquiesce in its continuance.

Or to work covertly for the good, light a candle in the darkness, yet each step advanced through compromise, small deceptions which, however vital to the greater cause, would destroy a fragment of the soul with each complicit act.

To resist. And endure all the risks resistance must bring.

Who could judge others for the choices they made?

He would not. He did not have that right. For he had not been tested. Exile to that little parish in the south had saved him from it all. From agonies of conscience, corruption, bodily danger, even from death.

And if he had no right to judge others – might that permit him to lay down, at last, the burden of judging himself?

Were those years of turmoil – the fear on his sisters' faces, being shunned by old colleagues and friends – not after all a disgrace, but rather, a gift of Fate, or Divine Providence? Not a punishment, rather, a deliverance? As the mist faded in the sunlight, the miasma of sorrow which had tainted his spirit for so long that he had almost forgotten it was there, dissolved. For the first time in decades, brow unfurrowed and heart light, he felt free.

When a pilot from a little boat called and waved up to him, he leapt to his feet with a sprightliness uncommon in a man approaching sixty. Yes, a short river trip would be pleasant. This was a joyous mission, a fitting service to his beloved hosts who had opened their home to him when their own two boys were caught up in great events of which they knew nothing, for the simple crime of being in the wrong place at the wrong time.

He would find them. It would be a fitting farewell to the city of his birth. They would leave together, homeward bound to Tavira, and never set foot in Lisbon again.

22

The Past Revisited

March 30th, 1775, Market Square, Belém, Junqueira prison

Caroline had been right. He ought not to have come. Moreover, there had been no obligation upon him to do so. He could have instructed one of his ambitious young subordinates in the embassy to attend Junqueira and make a full report on the occasion. At least a half-dozen of them would have relished the opportunity to distinguish themselves and impress the ambassador by finding the best vantage point and recording the event in meticulous detail. As he had done, in his day.

But no. He must be there. Bear witness with his own eyes to the righting of a great wrong.

For the dead, of course, nothing could be righted.

'Those nightmares,' Caroline said.

In recent years, the terrifying dreams had abated. Although he rarely visited Belém, and never of his own volition, only when official business demanded, today would be different. This would be a joyful occasion, sure to lay his ghosts to rest forever.

She had offered to accompany him. She had tried to insist. But he demurred. This was more than official business, more than a report for the ambassador, to be received by some bureaucrat in England, scanned and consigned to a shelf in a windowless office. The events of this day would herald the end of an era: the collapse of a régime whose oppressions and cruelties had blighted the last two decades of his life. He owed it to himself, he owed it to the many hundreds of souls incarcerated in Junqueira and the other gaols for so many years, to see those gates flung open, to witness the restoration of the lives that had been stolen from them. As his own had been.

Was it a frivolous comparison? Of course it was. Of what relevance, of what interest, were his own sleepless nights? Or the many promotions he had refused, out of dread that the duties of high office would necessitate liaison with the authors, with the single author, of that dire spectacle? The very thought nauseated him. Even so, his own miseries were as nothing beside the agonies which those prisoners had endured.

He would not think on that now.

Having set out with time to spare, he had thought to secure himself a spot close to the massive iron gates that separated the prison courtyard from a large area of parkland, but as his chaise rattled towards the village of Belém, he realised his mistake. Little groups of people were hurrying alongside the carriage, bound for the same destination. Before long, the crowd was so great that the chaise could proceed no faster than walking pace. When the market square came into sight he stepped down and ordered the driver to wait for him beside the Tower.

Carried along by the crowd, he observed many people of advanced age, some of them very frail, bodily supported by younger family members. There were no children but most noteworthy was the lack of distinction of rank, age or class. Ladies in silk day dresses brushed shoulders with maids in their service garb; soutane-clad priests jostled men of patrician demeanour and artisans alike. The mood was animated but anxious, and when the prison came into view, some of the sturdiest members of the crowd quickened their pace until a good many were running towards the gate. Of course, all the relatives were desperate to be reunited with their loved ones, innocent people who had been rounded up, detained and forgotten by all but their families; and not only those of the noble class but their servants, too, and even acquaintances of their servants against whom someone had spoken.

Given the size of the crowd there would no merit in positioning himself close to the gate as he had intended, where bodies would jostle on all sides. A tavern located on the eastern flank of the square suggested a solution. At an open window on the second storey sat a balding fellow in a striped apron, enjoying a perfect view of the prison courtyard and the parkland beyond.

'What time will the gates open?' Mr Stanton called up to him.
'Eight o'clock, they said.'

A brief negotiation ensued, following which he entered the tavern through a side door and climbed a narrow flight of stairs to the second storey. The innkeeper met him at the top of the stairway, where he stood, planted, until coins were counted and laid out on the windowsill.

'You must have been here when these poor souls were incarcerated, all those years ago?'

'I was indeed. Day after day, dozens rounded up. Hundreds. Families wailing at the gate. Bad for business. Very bad.'

'It is said that most of them had no knowledge of the events of that time. That anyone who happened to be acquainted with a person being questioned, or who even resided in the same house, was detained too. And forgotten.'

'Who knows?' The innkeeper shrugged. 'They must have done something. No smoke without fire.'

'Some of the interrogations were conducted across the way, I believe?'

Yes, his chaise was there still, waiting for him beside the Belém Tower. Such a beautiful, stately structure, the honey-coloured crenelations ever recalling the adventures of kings and the explorers of old. It was said that the dungeon was below the waterline.

'I wouldn't know.'

'Perhaps you were acquainted with him? Served him, even?'

'Who?'

'The minister. The Marquis of Pombal.'

The innkeeper's jaw hardened. 'Never met him.' He scooped up the coins from the windowsill. 'Now if you'll allow me. I have work to do.'

How many times had he requested to be reassigned to the London office, even at a lower rank? Caroline had agreed. But he had always been refused. He was too useful, they said. His knowledge of the language, of the country and its customs was of such value, the information he supplied so accurate, his analyses of events, his judgements so perceptive, he was indispensable to the Lisbon Office. He had no choice but to remain. Had he insisted on returning home, he would have been obliged to leave the Service.

So here he had remained. Gathering information. Interpreting facts. Analysing events.

Information was never lacking. On the contrary. Dispatch after dispatch, month after month, year after year, emanating from a multitude of sources, official and unofficial channels, pronounced on any number of subjects, but always with a single goal: to laud the latest achievement of the day. Another grand street whose edifices were declared to be resistant to any future earthquakes, the fruit of years of investigation and application of the best scientific minds and skilled engineers. The city centre reconstructed around elegant, classical facades in wide, regular streets leading straight and true, towards the Rossio, that modern agora, resurrected from the ashes of Ancient Greece. Lighting and sewerage systems, created to make the city brighter and cleaner and safer for the people.

Not forgetting radical improvements to the institutions of the state. All of them. Education: a new curriculum for the University of Coimbra that included modern languages. Foreign Affairs: delicate negotiations of great diplomacy and skill with France and Spain that averted invasion and war, while maintaining the long alliance with England. Defence: reorganisation of the army, to ensure adequate protection of the national territory, in the event that diplomacy should fail in the future. Commerce: the creation of a state-sponsored company to manage the production of port wine, ensure its quality, maximise the revenue from trade with England. Manufacturing: gleaming new factories producing all manner of goods created from locally sourced materials. Not forgetting the employment that flowed from these many innovations. All of it out of the brain of one illustrious minister, ennobled long ago to count, now elevated to marquis. The king's right-hand man.

Until His Majesty's demise a few days ago.

What would become of the marquis now?

For, notwithstanding that avalanche of dispatches and presentations which the marquis's office rained upon each of the embassies, all was not as it seemed on the surface. Any visitor could see with their own eyes that talk of a city risen from the ashes was so much fantasy. Buildings toppled by the earthquake were still there, almost two decades after the catastrophe, heaped around the city in piles of broken masonry. Many of the streets beyond the grand squares remained impassible. To this day, some of the old disaster zones were unstable.

And all those new factories and industries of which the marquis boasted – was he still a marquis? – turning out, as everyone knew but never said, lumpy ceramics and textiles of such inferior quality that the people would not buy them but turned to the English and French products they had been destined to replace.

The Jesuits gone, of course, long gone, Portugal liberated from their vice-like grip – if liberation meant the expulsion of six hundred old men, dragged from their monasteries, stuffed on to barges and sent off to be decanted into the Vatican City, those who survived the journey, leaving the schools bereft of teachers and the hospitals deprived of the skills of healing and caring for the sick. To be replaced by – what? Brilliant innovations based on the ideas of the great thinkers of the day, Voltaire, Rousseau, Montesquieu, Kant and Smith?

Well, no. Contrary to his oft-proclaimed determination to wrest the national psyche from superstition and atrophy, to drag the country into this enlightened century, the minister, then count, now marquis, had instead looked into his own heart and seen there, writ large, what the people needed and did not need. And instructed the censor accordingly.

Which was not difficult, the censor being his own man.

During the course of his decades in the embassy, Mr Stanton had come to appreciate, if not admire, the efficacy of a really good *trompe l'oeil* which, like the Nossa Senhora da Vida *azulejo* tiles in the Church of San André, by sleight of hand and careful craft, convinced the viewer of hidden, entirely fictitious, depths.

Just as a lie, repeated often enough, becomes the truth.

So many lies.

The Távoras received a fair trial!

Let us not dwell on the lack of evidence against them; nor on the absence of a proper defence; nor on the use of torture in the extraction of witness testimony.

Father Malagrida's fate – judgment and sentencing by the Inquisition, then death on the scaffold – was proper and just!

Let us not mention how the Grand Inquisitor – beg pardon, the previous Grand Inquisitor, he who was the brother of the king – refused to condemn the old man, only to be himself arrested and dragged off to gaol with his brother. Yes, two of the three Palhavã princes, natural brothers of the king, cast into exile, the replacement as Grand Inquisitor a brother of the minister himself.

Father Malagrida's trial was conducted by a panel of independent judges!

It would be unseemly to allude to the disappearance of those judges, soon after the trial. Yes, every one of them vanished, never to be seen or heard of again.

And so on. And so forth.

A mercy that it was beyond the remit of a middle-ranking diplomat to draw conclusions from these facts, much less make open comment on any anomalies in the official record. Instead, it fell to the ambassador to listen with a straight face as the minister-count-marquis presented his ridiculous pamphlets, commissioned to peddle whatever fiction would varnish the most recent dubious policy or murky bargain; to nod and smile, as though the contents of the latest handsome, hollow publication corresponded in the slightest to reality.

No one believed a word of it.

Yet once a lie is pronounced with sufficient boldness and frequency, when the penalty for doubt is sufficiently brutal, falsehood becomes truth. Those who reveal a flicker of uncertainty – neighbour, spouse, child, brother – are traitors, on whom you will not hesitate to inform. Else suffer the penalty for treason yourself.

But the events unfolding today would lay the ghost of all that. For once, his report would contain nothing but the unambiguous truth: good news of loved ones reunited with spouses, children, brothers and sisters. And more: an end to tyranny, the toppling of a dictator, concluding with a prediction: that one day soon, the tyrant and all who had abetted him, would be held to account.

Was this really what he had expected? That the gates would fly open and joyful prisoners would bound out, eyes shining, hair streaming in the wind as they rushed into the arms of their loved ones?

Perhaps.

But this? This, he had not expected.

It was not, at first, a multitude. Rather, a trickle. The first prisoners to take their faltering steps towards freedom were the oldest and most infirm. Shaky on their feet, they advanced in twos and threes, some leaning on the shoulders of companions, others half-carried, legs dragging on the ground, their clothes flapping around emaciated limbs, for not all families had had the means to supplement the meagre prison rations or pay the bribes require to ensure that their loved ones received adequate provisions and attire. Ragged, infirm, broken wraiths stumbling towards freedom, tottering out into a world they did not recognise and which did not recognise them. He gazed down upon them from his vantage above the square, the blood in his veins turned to lead, a familiar chill gripping his heart.

As the exodus gathered momentum, most of those who followed were able to walk unaided, some looking neither to the right nor the left, as though convinced that their friends and relatives were long dead or had abandoned them. But the majority scanned the throng in hope of a glimpse of a beloved countenance. Before long, the guards were unable to hold the line. Relatives rushed forward to mingle with their liberated kin. Cries of recognition, of joy and of sorrow were indistinguishable. One fellow in his middle years, stooped almost double in the manner of a much older man, clutched at the hand of a very aged woman while a ruddy-faced lad with a mop of blond hair looked on. Another man, a pitiful wretch of indeterminate age, in the thirties or forties perhaps, his wild black hair framing a gaunt, yellowish countenance, peered hollow-eyed at the remnants of his family gathered around him. One man – a brother? – had locked him in a desperate embrace. A woman cradled his face and whispered to him, while he gazed at her and at each face in turn, a body emptied of the soul, yet obedient to the guidance of his sister. She is not yet cognisant that he does not know who they are and perhaps does not know who he is himself.

He called down to a captain of the guard.

'The Count of Lourenço?'

'He remains inside the prison, senhor. He says he will not leave until he is exonerated of all wrongdoing.'

The ambassador would be disappointed. But not surprised. At least he would be relieved to learn that the count was alive and his irreverent spirit, always a favourite with the king and with the diplomatic corps, remained undimmed.

Notwithstanding this morsel of good news, the familiar dread, the paralysis, swept over him. He had seen enough. As he wove his way through the crowd, across the square towards his chaise, he came face to face with an elderly priest whose mane of white hair framed gaunt, anxious features.

'Please, senhor, can you tell me, how I might find…' He held aloft a card bearing a few words: PEDRO EUGENIO TAVIRA. 'Their parents said they do not read well. At least, they did not when last…'

'Desculpe, padre, não falo português. Ask him.' Mr Stanton pointed to the captain of the guard and hurried on.

Yes, the chaise awaited him on the bank of the river, alongside the Tower. Caroline was right. He should not have come. She had understood, as he had not, that no matter how much time has passed, there are things that can never be undone, for which there is no remedy, for which there can be no healing, not now, never.

23

The Road Back

March 7th, 1777, On the Road to Oeiras

Dona Eleanor shifted on the wooden bench and reached for the cushion she had brought from home. It was a poor substitute for the deep, upholstered seats, the purple velvet interior, the painted nymphs and coat of arms which embellished their own carriage, both within and without. Eyes moist, she held fast to her reticule in which she had stored the best of her jewels. The Amoreiras reservoir and the aqueduct beyond flashed by. Shuddering and swaying, the hired coach rattled over the rough terrain, but the springs seemed sturdy and the horses fresh. If they continued at this clip, they would reach Oeiras before nightfall in time to dine with Sebastião.

When had they first travelled this road? Eighteen years before, the whole family together. In those days, it had been little better than a mud track pitted with hollows and strewn with loose stones. This would not do, Sebastião said. Now that His Majesty had bestowed upon him the title of Count of Oeiras, they must have a proper road, one that would assure swift travel between their home on the rua Formosa and the dilapidated edifice in Oeiras, from which he had promised to create a palace, a noble seat worthy of a noble family.

And so it had come to pass. He had transformed it all: the house, renowned for its rare magnificence, now graced with sweeping stone staircases, magnificent halls and turrets reminiscent of an Austrian castle; formal gardens furnished with statuary, intricate paving, waterfalls. And the surrounding lands! Working farms of a modern agricultural estate where only the finest equipment and the latest methods were employed, vineyards which yielded their very own wine, mulberry bushes with their own silkworms, workshops for the manufacture of their own silk. Every innovation, every scrap of reconstruction, overseen by Sebastião himself.

And this was still the best road in the country.

The children had been little when it all began. Henrique was eleven. Now he was a handsome man approaching thirty, Count of Oeiras these seven years past, since his father was elevated to the rank of marquis. Was that not a fine thing? To have garnered such titles, such lands, their great house at Oeiras and more, many more properties and estates, to be handed down to their heirs in perpetuity? Bounteous rewards, in recognition of Sebastião's loyal service to the king and to the nation.

No more than he deserved.

And was this now the end? What more could be taken from them? Their noble titles? The palaces and houses? Her own jewels?

His life?

Slipping her reticule under her shawl, she shivered. If truth be told, harbingers of the decline in their position had appeared some time ago, if only they had been minded to heed them. From the moment His Majesty fell ill. Perhaps even before then.

At first, Sebastião did not believe it. Dom José was suffering another spell of weakness and would soon rally, as he had rallied many times. Sebastião believed himself immortal and so his king must be immortal, too; or at least, being so very many years younger, would not, could not, predecease him.

And so they had not thought on it. Nor on the misfortunes that would overtake them, if such a calamity should occur.

'I ought to have known when the Count of Lourenço's family

stopped petitioning me for his release,' he admitted the day before, while the servants were preparing the hired carriage for his solitary journey to Oeiras.

The ambience of the house on the rua Formosa had begun to change some time before. Little by little, her weekly gatherings had fallen into quiet disfavour. This was a refined salon, where the wives of nobles loyal to Sebastião and young ladies recently presented at court would congregate, in company with spouses of government ministers, to be served tea in the English style and a particular Austrian cake she made with her own hand.

When had the young wives of up-and-coming courtiers ceased to press their influential friends for introductions? She had ignored the signs, failed to remark the new currents, the sinister forces at play in the shadows.

The sky darkened. A pelting rain battered the carriage roof. Still, the driver was unconcerned. Despite the change in weather, he said, they would be sure to reach Oeiras before dusk, where Sebastião awaited, having made the journey alone the day before.

They would spend one last night in their most beloved estate, where they had planned to live out their final years.

Intentions that would never come to pass. For on the morrow, by order of Her Majesty Queen Maria, they must depart Oeiras forever, bound for the village of Pombal. And there they must remain. The queen had made no answer to Sebastião's written proposal for his transition into retirement; nor had Mariana Vitória replied to his previous letter, wherein he set out his recommendations for the administration of the realm upon his departure. The only communication from the Royal Pavilion had been the decree that Dom Sebastião José Carvalho e Melo, Marquis of Pombal, faithful servant of the king for nigh on three decades, must depart into exile. A proclamation served less than one week after His Majesty's death.

Dom José would not have approved of such treatment of his

old confidant and friend. Nor of his daughter's decree that Sebastião must not approach within twenty leagues of Her Majesty's royal presence. Nor her insistence that he must be ready to remove himself from the district, if ever her travels bring her close to their new home in Pombal – a man nearing his eightieth year!

The new queen, it was said, suffered fits of rage whenever Sebastião's name was mentioned. She had been a troubled young woman and now she was a troubled queen, a circumstance that would bode ill for the nation.

Yet with all that had passed and was about to pass, could they be certain that the family's fall from grace was ended there? Most disturbing of all were Henrique's words of warning. At least he had kept his position at court, though many of Sebastião's associates and protégés had already been removed. Others, said Henrique, had distanced themselves from all communication with his father; and those, not only his enemies, but people he had considered friends. It was possible that some of those individuals would act against him, eager to curry favour with the new monarch and save their own skins.

But what more injury could they inflict upon him? He had already lost his position, his estate, and must now endure exile in the backwater of Pombal. For the rest of his life.

Though he did not wish to alarm her, Henrique had judged that she must be apprised of the danger.

'Mama, he must not seek an audience with the new queen. She will not grant it. But if he does seek to meet her, and if she does agree, he must not accept the invitation. He must not return to court. On no account.'

'But does he not deserve –'

'Some of his enemies are threatening to take matters into their own hands, if the queen does not act against him. Some speak of exacting vengeance for Trafaria…'

'The fisherfolk of Trafaria brought that disaster upon themselves! Harbouring rebels. Refusing to yield up their military-age men for conscription. Defying the authority of the state.'

'Mama, calm yourself. I do not criticise. But the events of that day are so recent, they loom so large in the minds of the people...'

It was true that most of the villagers died in the fire or were cut down when the army surrounded their homes. Hundreds of them. Women and children, too.

'He had no choice but to exercise his authority, Henrique.'

'I know, Mama. But he has no authority now. We must therefore take steps to avert any possible danger to him. Present or future.'

He lapsed into silence. But he had always been easy to read.

'I must know everything, Henrique.' She waited and watched, while he made up his mind how much to say an how to say it.

'There is word that the new queen intends to investigate other...difficult...decisions Papa was obliged to make over the years. Not only Trafaria.' Again he hesitated. 'Oporto. And the Távoras. Her Majesty has spoken of examining the case. The investigation. And the trial. There is even talk of exonerations.'

Henrique was too young to recall the details of the Távora business. It was so long ago. But she had not forgotten. Nor had the new queen; nor her mother, Mariana Vitória. Both women had exercised all their powers to undermine Sebastião's investigation, to question the basis for the trial and especially, the sentencing. Time and again, they appealed to Dom José, attempting to bully him with wiles and weeping and threats, into showing mercy. In which, where the conspirators and assassins were concerned, they had failed. But the families – most of the women and children – were saved from the scaffold. And now their progeny, almost two decades later, had stepped out of the shadows and were preparing their revenge.

'To what purpose would she set about reopening old

wounds, Henrique?'

'It is probable that the new queen will commence proceedings against him, Mama. There is talk of an investigation into his conduct. Perhaps even a trial.'

'On what grounds can she do such a thing?'

'No grounds are necessary, Mama. She is queen.'

'She has always hated us.'

'There are those who are urging a more – permanent – sentence than exile.'

A capital penalty?

'Be easy, Mama. It will not come to that. Papa has always insisted that every one of the legal instructions he enacted was signed by Dom José himself. Once the new queen has verified the truth of this… It is true, Mama?'

'Of course it is true! The wine caskets in your old nursery are filled with government documents that will verify the king's responsibility a hundred times over. A thousand, ten thousand.'

'Then let us find them. Once Dom José's signature is verified, every action will be deemed to have been on the orders of the king, and Papa but an instrument of his royal will. Which will render it impossible for the queen to act against him without implicating her own father.'

The bright, airy room retained a familiar whiff of wine mingled with old paper, an aroma which Sebastião always claimed was soothing to his mind.

'Should we ask father…?'

'Later. Let him sleep. His carriage will depart in a few hours. He must rest before the journey to Oeiras.'

They began by emptying each individual cask of all documents, the better to identify the subject of each pronouncement. Sebastião had imposed some general order upon the vast collection of papers, each casket containing those pertaining to a single year. Leafing through dusty pages, they gave special scrutiny to those from periods when significant events had occurred.

Two hours later, Sebastião opened the door and stood in the doorway.

'Papa, we are looking for the most important *Providências*. Those most likely to… here is one, concerning Oporto, January, 1767. The signature of His Majesty is writ clearly upon it, just as you said.'

'Did you doubt it?'

'Of course I did not, Papa…but others… This is an excellent morning's work. I can convey these papers to the queen's private secretary and he…'

Dona Eleanor took the page from his hand.

'Henrique, you will remove nothing from this house. These papers are evidence that every one of the actions your father carried out for twenty-seven years were in accordance with Dom José's royal will. If they were to be lost…'

'Mama, these are government papers. They will certainly be removed in their entirety to the office of Her Majesty's secretary. Her agents may even come today to transport them.'

'Let them have these.' Dona Eleanor extracted a half dozen pages from the bundle. 'They are decrees on less contentious matters than…These will suffice to verify His Majesty's signature.' She handed the page to her son. 'This one, for example, orders the exile of two of the three Palhavã princes. And here is the decree ordering the removal of the bishop of Évora from his post. And another for the exile of José de Séabra da Silva to Angola. More than enough to provide verification. But these,' she gathered the remainder and passed them to her husband, 'and any others your father deems to be of particular significance, will remain with us.'

Faced with his mother's brisk instructions and his father's questioning smile, the young man had no choice but to nod his acquiescence.

'There is one other matter of importance, Papa. I have not been able to find the documents from January '59. The Távora trial. Her Majesty particularly demanded to see the transcript. If I can bring it to court, things will go well…'

'We can certainly find a transcript to fulfil her requirements.'

'The original? She is seeking the original, Papa.'

Sebastião draped an arm across Henrique's shoulder.

'It will be better, son. Even better.' He placed a finger upon his own lips. 'She will find it more than satisfactory. You will see.'

Those documents bearing the king's signature signing into law the most difficult measures Sebastião had had to take in the last three decades, she had slipped into the false bottom of his old portmanteau and placed it at his feet herself, before the carriage set off. Papers that would travel with him into exile and only be brought to light if danger threatened. In which case, the contents of that old portmanteau would exonerate him from all wrongdoing.

Which made his recklessness recounted by Leo all the more puzzling. Their most trusted servant, Leo had just returned from Oeiras, having followed Sebastião on the outward journey in the decoy coach they had hired for extra protection. The marquis arrived safely at the Oeiras estate, he assured her, a little before nightfall, and was installed in the guest wing of the palace, where he had slept. He had deemed those modest quarters preferable to opening the master suite for such a short visit. Dom Sebastião eagerly awaited her arrival.

'You reached Oeiras just before nightfall? Why so late? Even by hired carriage, with those inferior horses, the journey should not take above three hours.'

He bowed his head. For the first time, she remarked strands of grey in the blue-black hair.

'Leo.'

His square, open countenance flushed.

'For how many years have you been in our employ?'

He continued to survey the ground 'Twenty?'

'More, Leo. Long enough for me to know when you are withholding information. With the best intention, I do not doubt. But whatever is troubling you, I must know of it. Else I will not be equipped to…' She stopped. She would not speak of comforting her husband before a servant, no matter how trusted and beloved.

It was worse than she had feared. Despite the precautions they had agreed – that he would travel a day before her in an unmarked carriage, accompanied by a decoy coach – he had been observed, and recognised. In Belém, having ordered the driver to take that road. As his carriage was crossing the market square, and in direct opposition to every measure they had agreed, he opened the curtain a crack and peered out. And that instant, he was seen.

Why would he do such a thing? Why risk his safety thus, when they had all decided – the children, their few remaining advisors, even Sebastião himself – that he must make this journey in complete secrecy? Such caution being all the more critical, in the light of the item of luggage at his feet, the portmanteau crammed with secret papers crucial for his defence, should Henrique's intelligence of the new queen's intentions be accurate.

Perhaps, having finally understood that he was leaving Lisbon and her environs for the last time, the city which he, through his own force of will had raised from the ashes, he had simply longed to contemplate the market square where he had brought those traitors to justice. Or perhaps he wished to gaze upon the coastline whence Vasco Da Gama and Magellan set off long ago into the unknown, to face great peril and accomplish great deeds, uncertain of their fate, not knowing whether they would return triumphant or perish.

He had triumphed. Step by step at first and so gradually that few, if any, believed he would amount to much. Until his moment had come and he delivered the country from a terrible catastrophe; no, two catastrophes, of which either one could have destroyed them all. Only when those traitors lay broken on the scaffold, their bones and possessions set ablaze, turned to dust and cast upon the river waves, could his work truly begin.

A little group of artisans, most likely drunk, had observed him lean out of the carriage window. They greeted him with taunts and roars. Soon, a small crowd had gathered, jeering, and chased his carriage, pelted it with stones. They would soon have surrounded him, had not the driver spurred the horses on and taken a detour through the Quinto do Praio, a circuitous route to Oeiras that added hours to their journey but had thrown his tormentors off the scent.

Most troubling of all: these were working men, humble people who, but a few weeks previous would have greeted the carriage of the Marquis of Pombal with bowed heads and respectful applause in gratitude for the many benefits he had brought to their lives in these twenty-seven years. A new city, the streets purged of open sewage and crime. Decent homes. Fair prices for bread and fish and wine. New industries and employment. Teachers, to instruct their children in reading and writing. Deliverance from slavery. Liberation from the clutches of the Society of Jesus whose grip on the schools, the confessional and the monarchy had tyrannised the nation and its colonies for nigh on a century.

The carriage slowed and shuddered to a halt. One of the front wheels was snagged in a cavity, the driver said, but it would soon be freed, and they would make up the time. Sebastião must hear of this, he would take steps to ensure that the road…

No. Sebastião would take no more steps to ensure anything ever again. Since the pronouncement of the new queen, delivered by messenger to the rua Formosa without so much as the courtesy of a private audience, he was but a subject of the realm. An old man obliged to make his final journey alone to the loveliest of all his houses, stripped of his splendid guard of six, which for so many years had accompanied his magnificent carriage wherever he went, the person of the minister deemed to be under greater threat than the king himself.

Now, since word of his dismissal was published abroad, those soldiers were required elsewhere: to defend the house on the rua Formosa from angry protestors, a rabble who bayed and spat and burned effigies of him on the street, a mob of ruffians who seemed capable of burning their house down…

It was time to leave. First, to Oeiras, where he awaited her. And on the morrow, the last stage of their journey together, to Pombal, his final place of exile, and her own.

24

In the Gathering Dusk

The Village of Pombal, May 7th, 1782

The repairs on the road to Oeiras ought to have been completed long before now. Dom Sebastião José Carvalho e Melo, His Majesty's First Minister, Count of Oeiras and Marquis of Pombal, surveys the vast terrain from his vantage in the hills high above Adjuda, such fertile fields extending to the west and to the east, the coast road winding towards Belém and beyond, towards Lisbon's thousand gleaming spires, thence to Oeiras and Cascais to the south.

He would have to take action. A note to the city engineers. Or to His Majesty. Or both.

While pondering the various permutations of phrasing best suited to the purpose, Dom Sebastião savours the caress of sunlight upon his skin, rejoices in a radiance that illuminates every step of the road that brought him from the rua Formosa through the city, along the riverbank where hundreds of ships are jostling in the harbour, past the burning Riverside Palace to the Royal Pavilion where he slept in his carriage at the foot of the hill during those dreadful nights after the earthquake, towards the procession of traitors mounting the scaffold at Belém, and on into his future.

It was a worthy road. A noble road. Though bristling with traps, obstacles, hidden dangers.

Those repairs must be accomplished without delay. It was

not fitting that His Majesty's First Minister should be obliged to endure such a bone-rattling journey, jolting and shuddering over rough terrain pocked with cavities where the horses' hooves could snag or the carriage wheels sink into patches of marsh. The matter was especially urgent ever since His Majesty had honoured him with this guard of six. How little Francisco loves to watch them, delighting in their straight, military bearing and brocaded uniforms, how he thrills to lean out of the carriage window, whooping and waving to those six brave men mounted on magnificent stallions, brandishing swords that glitter in the sun!

So many carriages, so many adventures. Too many. Did not Dom José and the young marchioness once… He had counselled against a reprise of that episode, but where Dom José's amorous affairs were concerned, he would not be guided. And that night, returning from an assignation with the same woman… If His Majesty had not travelled in Teixeira's old coach for the journey home – what caprice could have possessed him to do such a thing? – his reign would have come to a bloody, premature end. And with it, the position of his First Minister. Whose enemies would have triumphed. Since the Távora business was settled, they had gone to ground. But their descendants and supporters remained, lurking in the shadows. This, His Majesty understood. Hence his decree that the First Minister must not traverse the country, nor even the city, without the protection of this guard of six.

No harm must befall Eleanor or the little ones because of their father's work. And Eva would make her communion soon. She was no longer a baby but now a proper little girl, her papa's favourite. But what if their carriage should overturn on this dreadful road? They were obliged to make this journey so often, the building and restoration work at Oireas requiring supervision at all times. The creation of an ancestral home. A worthy legacy. So much time. The enormous cost. Yet every cruzado a sum well spent.

At the approach, there is always a thrill of excitement as the carriage speeds alongside the meadow, approaching the working farms and the estate, taking the downhill curve of the driveway at a fast clip, slowing to a halt alongside the courtyard wall. And when they pass through the massive oak doors and the groom guides them across the cobbled courtyard toward the double escalier that sweeps up to the entrance hall in two gracious, dramatic curves, down he leaps, ever sprightly and, disdaining to use the step, he hurries up the stairs, eager to escape the midday sun, leans against the cool *azulejo* tiles that already half-cover the walls, lingers a while in front of the gigantic granite fireplace, strides through the great hall whose massive windows open on to the formal gardens, that project is not quite finished, it must be completed before Henrique's confirmation.

Meanwhile, a carefully worded note delivered to Teixeira will remind him that something must be done about the road. Eleonor might assist, her turn of phrase for these delicate communications being so much prettier than his own.

'He is trying to speak. Papa, can you hear me?'

Who is this young woman? She is close, so close her breath caresses his cheek, she is someone he knows well, someone from long ago...

'A sip, my darling, just a little, please Sebastião.'

Eleonor seems uncommonly troubled, there is a quaver in her voice and what is this liquid dribbling on his chin, where is this shadowed room, and now there is another voice, a different woman.

'Moisten his lips with this sponge, Mama.'

Eva?

And yes, his lips that were parched and cracked are fine and damp now, shadows are playing on the ceiling, a flickering candle illuminates the dark corners of the room, a humble room of modest proportions – not Oeiras, then, of course, it is the little manor house in Pombal, four rooms, a single servant, but the bed is comfortable, piled with pillows and cushions. Figures emerge from the shadows, someone is weeping. Maria? Yes, she always was the most sensitive of the girls. How they are grown, Eva and Maria and even little Amalia, young women now and those fine boys, Henrique and Francisco, all gathered around, trying to smile, but their faces are serious and streaked with tears.

'Dom José?' His voice is a cracked whisper.

'What is he saying? Papa?'

'Is there something you need, my love?'

'He is asking for Dom José.'

Good lad, Henrique, ever attentive to his father's every word, always the one who understood him best. Eleonor kneels so that her lips are close by his ear, her words fluttering like moth wings brushing his skin.

'His Majesty went to meet his Maker some years ago, my love. Do you know where you are?'

'He understands, Mama. See, he is awake. Has the effect of the laudanum faded? Might he be in pain?' This from Amalia, the youngest and always the kindest.

There is no pain, my lovely girl, he says but only a croak emerges. Perhaps if he sat up they would stop looking so serious, he could reassure them, make them laugh, this is a colossal effort, nothing happens. Not a single limb stirs, not even a finger. As in the dreamworld, you are desperate to awaken, certain that someone or something is in pursuit, you try to flee, you know you are dreaming, you order yourself to wake, an exercise of the will bids your limbs move but they refuse to obey, leaden, the blood in your veins is turned to warm milk, weighs you down, no matter how much you struggle there is not the slightest movement...

Someone is murmuring a prayer. Eva. She has always been

the most religious of his girls, a faith she has passed on to her own daughter. Little Leonor. Their first granddaughter. Is that not a fine thing! How old is she now? Twelve? Thirteen? Memory is wavering, an effect of the laudanum, yes, she will soon be of age, another three or four years, this cool, damp cloth on his forehead restores clarity. No. Not quite twelve. But still, it is never too early to plan for her future, the shadows have receded, the room is bright, well-stocked candelabra on every surface illuminate the anguished expressions on the children's faces.

'Yes, he awake.' Francisco takes his hand. He will need his mother in the days to come. 'Mama, he is lucid.'

'As he has always been,' Henrique says and Eleonor has turned away to hide her tears, there is no call for weeping, my dears. Yes, he has lived a life of great lucidity. Everything has always been clear, every path, every course of action unfolding like a map upon his inner vision. All those muddles, tangles, threats of chaos or actual chaos, scattered in disorder, like a puzzle which reassembles in his mind's eye to create a pattern that never failed to show the solution, clean, efficient, elegant as those smooth, intricate *azulejos* on the palace walls.

Though it was not always possible to manifest his solutions. Especially in the beginning. Too often, people stood in the way, driven by ambition, by their hunger for power.

Which misfortune had produced his own fate. Banished from the capital on the death of the king, to this backwater of Pombal. Forbidden to approach within twenty leagues of the new queen – she is not so new now, and things are not going so well for her. Of course not, she has dismantled the best innovations of the last three decades. She was always fragile, never had the temperament to be a ruler. No more had her father, but Dom José at least had Dom Sebastião José Carvalho e Melo to help shoulder the burdens of kingship. And for his thanks, here he was. Forbidden to live out his days in his own fine palace, so that the high-strung queen would be rid of him.

But she had sent her investigators. Two years of questioning and interrogations. A mental torment for Eleanor.

They got nothing out of him, of course. Queen Maria was furious, it seemed, for in the end she could find no grounds on which to proceed against him. Even so, she would not exonerate him from wrongdoing. Had the presumption to decree a pardon instead. Bestowing mercy on a sick old man no longer in his right mind, she said. Still, he had got the last laugh. Two years' interrogations, and they left with nothing.

Another chuckle, a prolonged fit of coughing, and, while they minister to his crumbling body, his spirit is suffused with peace and the most tender desire to advise them, to reassure them, to distil the wisdom of his eighty-two years to a few words. Children, the first five decades are the worst. No Maria, I am not in distress, just the opposite.

There was a time when his great abilities were unremarked, when his vision, his facility for achieving progress was dismissed and mocked, when the world had not yet understood this gift for creating order from chaos whenever danger loomed – an earthquake, a rebellion, an invasion or the threat of invasion. Always, he could see what was right and just and what needed to be done.

But he was past fifty years on this earth before he had the power to make his vision reality, and that only thanks to the perspicacity and trust of his king. Of whom Dom Sebastião José Carvahlo e Melo, Count of Oeiras, Marquis of Pombal, was but a humble servant, privileged to implement the king's royal will. They accused me of severity, but I was compelled to be severe. When danger threatened, it was necessary to use force.

But children, there is always blame cast upon those who dare to manifest great events. For there are two kinds of people in this world: those who live quiet lives, safe and prosperous if they are fortunate, precarious and poor if not – the majority; and the others, few in number, very few, who know what must be done, what changes must be effected to restore order and remove obstacles to progress. To this great mission, few are called and of those, fewer still accept the call, so heavy is the load, so fleeting and uncertain the rewards, so fragile the greatest illusion of all: that of being author of momentous happenings, and not a mere leaf cast forth upon the wind, a ripple on the tide, a flash of sunlight that fades too soon in the gathering dusk.

As the shadows close in and the prayers and quiet weeping of the children recede, it is the sweet young face of Leonor, Eva's daughter, that appears – yes, she will soon be of age and that young Count of Eveiro, a grandson of the Távoras, is just a year older.

'Is he smiling? Papa?'

It will be an excellent match, young Leonor betrothed to a Távora, that will be a fine thing, will it not, I will see to it and all will be well.

Acknowledgements

There is a vast literature on the Great Lisbon Earthquake of 1755 and on the life and times of the Marquis of Pombal. This includes both scholarly and popular works, which draw on a myriad of sources ranging from eyewitness accounts of the disaster to critical analyses by seismologists, scientists and political commentators, writings which span the period from the 18th century to the present day. Much of this work explores the complex political situation in Portugal and her colonies in the 18th century, and especially the role of the Marquis of Pombal in the aftermath of the tragic events of November 1st, 1755.

Although I have consulted many of these sources, I will mention only a few of them here, lest a comprehensive bibliography suggest that this novel aspires to the authority of an academic study or biography. I make no such claims for *Aftershock*. This is a work of fiction, based on historical events and the role of real people in them – seasoned with the imagined drama, interiority and subjectivity which distinguish the novel from the historical text.

With that caveat in mind, these are some of the works I found most useful in their accounts of the earthquake, and the life and times of the Marquis of Pombal. They make for fascinating reading, and I am grateful to their authors for their many insights into a wide and complex set of topics. They are, of course, not responsible for any inaccuracies or errors in *Aftershock*. Any such inaccuracies or errors, if discovered, are all my own.

About the Marquis of Pombal

Azevedo, J. Lucío (2009) *O Marquês de Pombal e a Sua Época,* Lisboa: Alfarrábio.

Cheke, Marcus (1938) *Dictator of Portugal, A Life of the Marquis of Pombal,* London: Sidgwick & Jackson.

Maxwell, Kenneth (1995) *Pombal: Paradox of the Enlightenment,* Cambridge University Press.

Sena-Lino, Pedro (2020) *De Quase Nada a Quase Rei: Biografia de Sebastião José de Carvalho e Melo, Marquês de Pombal,* Lisboa: Contraponto

About the Earthquake

Kendrick, T.D. (1955) *The Lisbon Earthquake,* New York: Lippincott.
Molesky, Mark (2015) *This Gulf of Fire: The Great Lisbon Earthquake, or Apocalypse in the Age of Science and Reason,* New York: Vintage.

Primary sources I consulted included: eyewitness accounts of the earthquake in letters from survivors which I found in the British Library in London and the National Library of Ireland in Dublin; facsimiles of sermons preached by Father Gabriel Malagrida, stored in the Biblioteca Nacional Library de Portugal in Lisbon; maps of Lisbon in the Biblioteca Nacional de España in Madrid. I greatly appreciate the privilege of having had access to these national libraries, which are such a valuable resource for readers. I offer my sincere thanks to all the staff who helped me to find the exact documents I needed. I have found that carrying out research in these wonderful national institutions is one of the most thrilling and delightful aspects of writing a historical novel.

Researching and writing *Aftershock* was a long-term project. I am indebted to my writing community, my workshop companions and friends who generously read and provided detailed feedback on the manuscript at all stages. Their thoughtful and careful commentaries helped to make *Aftershock* better than it would otherwise have been. To the Troika Writing Group – Anamaría Crowe Serrano, Ross Hattaway and Eamonn Lynskey; to Lisa Harding and Joanne Hayden – I am more grateful than I can say for your perceptive reading, encouragement, unfailing support and friendship.

Finally, I want to express very special appreciation to my editors, Anamaría Crowe Serrano and Doug Kinch for your insightful and meticulous reading, and also for your patience. You were immensely generous with your time and energy in your work on *Aftershock* and you have my heartfelt gratitude.

Liz McSkeane
Dublin, 2025

About the Author

Liz McSkeane was born in Glasgow and has lived in Dublin since 1981. She has a PhD in Education and has worked in Ireland, the UK and Europe as a teacher and educational consultant specialising in teaching methods, curriculum development and assessment. Liz is the author of four poetry collections, one collection of short stories and two novels. In 1999, she was overall winner of the Hennessy/Sunday Tribune New Irish Writer of the Year Award for her poetry. Her short stories and poems have been published in Ireland and the UK and her first novel, *Canticle*, was a winner in the 2016 Irish Writers' Centre/Greenbean Novel Fair.

Follow Liz on:

> X @EMcSkeane
>
> Instagram @lizmcskeane
>
> Facebook @liz.mcskeane

and on her website www.elizabethmcskeane.com